DARE

A ROCK STAR HERO

S.L. SCOTT

S.L. SCOTT

Published in the United States of America
ISBN: 978-1-940071-93-0

Cover Design: RBA Designs
Photographer: Rafa G. Catala
Model: Anselmo Menéndez Arias

Jenny Sims, Editing4Indies
Marion Archer, Making Manuscripts
Marla Esposito, Proofing Style
Kristen Johnson, Proofreader
Team Readers: Lynsey Johnson and Andrea Johnston
Awesome Person I bugged with law school questions: Vi Keeland

ABOUT THE AUTHOR

To keep up to date with her writing and more, her website is www.slscottauthor.com to receive her newsletter with all of her publishing adventures and giveaways, sign up for her newsletter: http://bit.ly/2TheScoop

Instagram: S.L.Scott

To receive a free book now, TEXT "slscott" to 77948

For more information, please visit:
https://www.slscottauthor.com/

For the man that captured my heart the moment we met. My past. My present. My forever.

Flirt.

DARE

PROLOGUE

Dare

BEAUTY ATTRACTS THE EYE, but the soul captures the heart.

That quote was part of a fading mural painted on the side of a laundromat my mom used to take me to on Saturday mornings. Eleven-year-olds don't understand that concept. We take people at face value. After my mom explained what it meant, she took a picture of it and hung it on the fridge right next to the photo of her dream house.

The dropped paint cans clang and roll into the bend of the street as I stand in front of the house eight years later. I take a couple of steps back, trying to find satisfaction in the graffiti. The art doesn't ease an ounce of my grief, but it does remind me of some of the memories I have of her. *Of that time.*

My mom and I drove by this house a million times. She loved the architecture, which she was studying in night school back then. We didn't have much, but driving the streets of Austin to see the eclectic styles of this city was a free form of entertainment. It was our thing.

An ivy-covered brick wall hid many of the details of the 1930s Mediterranean-inspired mansion, but it was always worth the stop on our tour of homes. She once put me on her shoulders so I could take a photo of the house. Right when the camera snapped, a girl, not older than I was, popped her head into the frame. After what felt like five minutes of the Spanish Inquisition, she invited us to tour the grounds.

I followed my mother, and the girl followed me, peppering me with questions.

"Your shirt has a hole near the sleeve. Did you get in a fight?"

I glanced at my sleeve to see I've ruined another shirt. My mom won't be happy. "Yeah, sure."

"How old are you?"

"Eleven. You?"

"Nine last Friday."

"Good for you."

"We should get married one day. I'll be queen of the castle, and you can be my prince."

The girl, a nosy and pesky little thing in pigtails and heart-shaped sunglasses, had her head stuck in fairy tales like they were real. They aren't. At least not for me. Judging by this huge yard and big house, maybe they are for her. "Why not king?"

"Because kings trump queens, and I want to rule. We can take turns if you like. What's your name?"

"Rob."

"Rob is a nice name. Did you know it's short for Robert?"

"Yeah. It's my name."

Not missing a beat, she rambled on. "My dad works with a Bob. I don't like him or the name Bob."

"Good to know." When she tucked her sunglasses into her hair, I looked at her blue eyes that were too big for her head and how wild her hair was despite her efforts to tame it with yellow

ribbons. Something about her had me wanting to warn her to be more careful. "My mom always told me to beware of strangers. You might not want to go on telling everything about yourself, you know."

"You're not a stranger. You're Robert."

"Rob."

She grinned, not letting anything distract her glee.

I shook my head. She'd never make it a day in my neighborhood. I couldn't worry about her safety, though. I just hoped she didn't make this a regular thing, or she'd eventually run into a stranger like my father. He's a taker—escaping virtue and living on vice—and was not a good man.

My mother got the photo she wanted, and then we left. But not before the brown-haired girl, hanging onto the black wrought-iron gate as it reopened, asked, "Don't you want to know my name?"

From all the questions she's asked, I'd already nicknamed her in my head. My mother was already getting into the car, but I stopped just shy of the street and turned back anyway. "Don't talk to strangers, Pepper."

"Pepper?" She raised her chin in the air, a bigger grin than I'd seen so far on her face. "I love Pepper." Her face scrunched. "Why Pepper?"

"Because you ask a lot of questions."

The girl had kind of grown on me by that point because of her friendliness and the way she looked at me like I'd saved her day. I wanted to give her something in return, but my pockets were empty. The laundromat quote was all I'd brought with me. "Beauty attracts the eye, but the soul captures the heart. You have that in spades."

With her hands clasped over her chest, she grinned, showing off the spaces in the front from newly lost teeth. "I'll remember that forever, Robert, but what's spades?"

"I have no idea. The principal said I have spades too, but I was in trouble at the time, so I'm not sure if it's the same spades you've got."

"I hope it's the same." If it had been night, I would have sworn I saw stars in her eyes, soaking in the attention we'd given her. I think it was just the sun that made them watery when we were leaving. The gate closed, but she remained peering through the bars. "We'll have spades together. Okay?"

"Sure," I added through the open car window.

When we started to drive away, she yelled, "See you again someday, Robert."

"See ya, Pepper." I watched her in the side mirror as we drove away. Her arm still waving so hard that she could flag a plane down. "She was weird." I glanced at my mom, who started laughing.

"I thought she was adorable. I know it's hard to believe, but one day, girls won't seem so weird to you, Robert."

"That is hard to believe."

Her laughter picked up, and although she didn't say any more on the matter, she had a smile on her face the whole drive home.

Before the tears have a chance to fall, I look up. I can still hear my mom so clearly in my head. It makes me wonder how long before I forget the sound of her voice.

Exhaling, trying to release some of the grief, I take a picture of the red brick wall where I spray-painted the quote, and leave before I get busted.

When I get home, I print the photo and stick it under a magnet on the fridge next to the pictures my mom once hung—the laundromat, the house, and the photo of that girl.

1

Weatherly

Six years later . . .

It takes my mind a few seconds to figure out what I'm watching and to process what I already know deep down. But to see it in person, to have it confirmed . . . it takes a moment for the pieces to connect—Lloyd weighted over a dark-haired woman, howling like a coyote as he orgasms.

I don't slink away in shame as if I caused this, despite knowing he'll manage to blame me somehow. I'm not even upset, not like I should be for catching my boyfriend having sex with another woman.

A little numb but all around, I'm doing all right. Relief is not the emotion I expected to feel when this day came, but I appreciate it. *When*, not *if*. I knew it was only a matter of time.

I don't love Lloyd Sanders. *There.* I finally admit it,

though only to myself, but that's a start. My shoulders feel lighter as I leave the party, walking down the stairs toward the front door of the house. As soon as my feet touch the sidewalk, I feel a bounce to my step as though my problems are behind me.

Literally. "Goodbye for good," I say to no one in particular. It just feels good to say it out loud.

"Weatherly?" My name is called. When I look back, my friend Stascia is standing on the grand steps of her parents' large white colonial home. "Where are you going?"

"Home." I shrug unapologetically.

"Party pooper." She huffs and crosses her arms over her chest. "Well, if you're leaving me, have you seen April?"

"Not in a while. She told me she was changing into her bathing suit earlier."

"I'll check upstairs. Call me tomorrow?"

"I will." I hurry to my car, running my finger over the spotless silver finish of my Tesla as I move around to the driver's side. The door opens automatically, and I slide inside, pretending I don't hear my name flying from Lloyd's mouth as he comes rushing across the lawn. I'm grateful for a lot of things in life, but a quick getaway is topping the list right now.

He won't follow since he's not wearing anything but his tighty-whities.

The warm night air whips through the car as one of my favorite Crow Brothers songs blares through the rolled down windows as I leave the sleepy neighborhood and head back downtown toward my apartment. The drive isn't far, but I don't want to go home because being alone isn't appealing right now. A mini celebration might be in order since there's no way I'll be able to focus enough to study.

Now no one can say I didn't give this relationship a solid

try, my best effort to make something work that was doomed from the start. The pressure of disappointing others kept me in it, but I'm driving away with my head held high. I can't say I feel great about this victory, but thank God we never had sex. At twenty-three, I was made to feel ashamed for holding onto a part of me that is solely mine to give.

Lloyd Sanders was not exactly the man of my dreams. Maybe I've overthought the whole virginity thing. By how my friends and Lloyd sleep around, it clearly is not a big deal. I should just do it and get it over with. Find some hot guy to lose myself in for a few minutes . . . hours?

In a garage one block off Sixth Street, I park and pay. The sound of music—jazz, rap, hard hitting drums, and what sounds like karaoke—fills my ears before I reach the corner of the lively street. A group of skaters smoke weed at a bus stop, so I walk around, not wanting the contact high. Stopping on the cobbled road, I look both ways, not sure where I want to go.

Through the window of a bar across the street, a band is on stage, and the beat sounds great, so I head that way. "Who's playing tonight?" I ask the bouncer as I pay the cover.

Glancing at his watch, he replies, "The Heroes are on stage headlining. They only have about five minutes left so cover is half price."

"Thanks." I work my way through the crowd and reach the far side of the bar to stand on my tiptoes to see the band.

The bartender leans across the wood bar top, and asks, "What are you drinking?"

I can't see much from back here, so with pursed lips, I scan over the selection of bottles behind him instead. "I don't know. What do you suggest?"

"How about a blow job?" Shock hits me and my mouth

falls open. His hands fly in front of him, and he adds, "No, the drink. The drink! A blow job shot."

A shot? "Oh," I reply, still on edge.

"I just served a group of girls in a bachelorette party. They loved them, and they're easy to make, so it popped into my head."

"I think I'll have a beer. Corona Light if you have it."

He turns and opens the cooler as the music ends. A cold bottle is placed in front of me. "I didn't mean that to sound like it did. This is on me."

"It's okay." I laugh. "And you don't have to give me the beer."

I reach into my purse, but he says, "No, my treat. I was going to ask if you were single before completely blowing it with the blow job suggestion."

He is kind of cute, and now that I know what he meant, it was funny. "I'm sorry—"

"Hey Jake, got a beer back there for me?" A man taps the counter next to me, stealing the bartender's attention. I can't say I'm too upset as the heat from my face drains away.

The bartender laughs, clearly friends with the guy. "I have about five bought and paid for. You have a few fans tonight." Then he looks back at me and gives me a little smile.

The guy next to me says, "Didn't mean to interrupt—*Oh!* It's you." Turning his gaze down, he squeezes his eyes closed and shakes his head. When his eyes reopen, I'm hit with intentions that hold me to the stop, staring deep into questioning caramel eyes.

Jake leans in. "Fuck, I wish you had another song to play." His reply is jovial but direct. "I was just about to get her number."

Swept up in the moment, I forget where I am as something else, a familiarity, takes over. My next breath comes hard, and my heart is pounding in my ears. "It's me?" I whisper.

The rest of the world rushes back into mine, and I look away, breaking the connection tying me to him. His head seems to clear and angles my way. "You should give him your number." He follows that up with a playful wink before taking the beer in front of him and downing a fair amount. But I see something deeper than the lightheartedness he portrays still lingering in his gaze.

He steps back, but his scent—how I imagine the ocean air smells if I was standing on a cliff in Northern California —still lingers, making my knees a little weak.

The distance is welcomed. The quick glances I shared with him have not been enough to take in the full view of this man. Messy dark hair that's been styled with a swipe of his hand tops his broad-shouldered build. He's tall and looks to take life by the horns with calloused hands. Despite smelling amazing and how easy he is on the eyes, he's a little rough around the edges and not afraid to get into some trouble.

There's something so familiar about him that I'm tempted to stare at him a little longer. But that would be rude, so I turn away from his eyes and gaze lower, but I can't resist looking at him. My gaze rises again to find his on me.

Sweat beads at his hairline. Dark stubble dusts a chiseled jaw and around full lips that I believe he licks for my benefit. I can't deny I appreciate the gesture. I do. All the way to my core. Good Lord, he's better than a Greek god carved from marble. His sculpted muscles define the shape of his shirt, making me want to touch that bulging bicep. This time, I resist. *Barely.*

His eyes are the kind of warm that reminds me of being

cozy in front of a fire on an Aspen winter's night. I'm tempted to snuggle against him, but again, I don't. We're strangers. That would make me seem like a crazy person. Though I wonder if it even matters what people think of me anymore. Why do I care?

There are so many preconceived notions and boxes I've been shoved in to fit someone else's expectations. What about what I want and expect? Does anyone care how I want my life to look or how I see my future?

"You have tattoos," I blurt.

Amusement reaches his eyes, and he holds out his arms to show me. "Yeah, a few."

Tattoos wrap around his exposed forearms and trickle onto the top of three of his knuckles. Getting a closer look, I notice how anger infiltrates the black ink, contradicting the grin on his face. Despite the familiarity I feel with him, he's more of a mystery by appearance alone than any man I've ever known.

He's everything Lloyd isn't and will never be. A real man —rugged and confident in a way I know he can back. He is so open to me that my guard falls down. "And why is that?"

"Why is what?"

"You said I should give him my number. So I'm wondering why I should?"

"Ah."

The bartender shakes his head, and mumbles, "Fucking hell, Marquis," before heading to the other end to take a drink order.

Marquis . . . the name doesn't ring a bell specifically, but his face—so handsome that I struggle to look away. "Because good girls like you deserve a good guy to take them out on a proper date. Jake's a good guy," he says.

"What are you?"

"Your daddy's worst nightmare."

"My father's worst nightmare would be me dating someone he considers bad for business. I'm not sure we define bad the same way these days. Are you bad?"

The right side of his mouth lifts. Leaning all the way in, he touches his lips to my ear. His breath against my skin sends a thrill up my spine and goose bumps covering my arms. "Do you want me to be?" *God yes!* "I could be bad for you."

The double entendre awakens the butterflies in my stomach. The bottle slips from my hands, spilling the beer across the wood and startling me back to reality. I jump back from the edge when the liquid pours onto the floor. "Oh, no!"

"It wasn't me, Jake. I promise," Marquis adds.

Though I have a feeling this might be a regular occurrence when Jake tosses the towel at him. "Sure, man. Sure." The bartender throws a towel to his friend who squats down to mop it up.

"The condensation made it slippery." Then I look down as the sexy man wipes the mess at my feet. "Your name is Marquis?"

His gaze is so intense that I can feel it caressing my body when he looks up. *That sexy grin.* "Yes, my name is Marquis."

"He has enough stocked up to cover it." My beer is replaced, and Jake chuckles, but I've missed the inside joke. "Be careful with this one, or you just might find yourself buying drinks for a lead singer who will eventually break your heart."

"Thanks for the advice." I laugh. "But you don't have to worry about me. I won't fall in love anytime soon."

"You sure about that?" Marquis asks.

"Positive."

"Good luck with that," Jake says, then chuckles, glancing at Marquis. "You're going to need it."

The funny thing is I'm not sure if he was wishing Marquis or me luck, but I think I'm going to need it.

2

Weatherly

ANGLING the handsome stranger's way, I ask, "Am I going to need luck?"

"I don't think so." Marquis takes another long pull from his bottle, keeping his eyes on me. "I think luck's always been on your side."

"I could argue that after the night I've had."

Resting his elbow on the bar, he unabashedly looks me over. "What happened?"

Since I don't know him from Adam and will never see him again, I have nothing to hide. "I walked in on my boyfriend having sex with another woman."

"Fuck."

"Still think luck's on my side?"

"I'd say luck; you have a guardian angel watching over you."

"How so?"

"She just saved you a lot of damn time and tears by revealing who your boyfriend really is."

"Sadly, I knew who he was already. I just needed a smack of reality to remind me. Now that I've been hit with that reality, I can't seem to make myself care."

A dangerous for my libido lopsided smirk appears, and he taps his bottle against mine. "We should drink to that."

But maybe I shouldn't.

As much as I'm happy to celebrate that I'm finally free of Lloyd Sanders, my rational side is throwing cautionary cones around this guy and barricading my heart from pounding so loud that he'll hear how he affects me.

Setting my bottle down, I take a deep breath and exhale slowly. I bite my lip while diving into the depth of his captivating brown eyes. He's a one-night stand of a distraction that I can't afford to lose myself in. *Lose myself in . . .* the words from earlier repeat in my head. I'm too busy, too focused on graduating, but I find the thought of sex with this man very appealing.

I should tear myself away for wanting to tear his clothes off, but I stay. Just a minute longer, too captivated to leave. "I should probably get a water."

He turns to the bartender, and when the bartender looks our way, Marquis signals to me. "Water, Jake."

He catches a bottle and twists the top off before handing it to me. "We can't leave a toast hanging without a cheers."

I tap the plastic bottle against his glass. "We will definitely drink to hits of reality." After taking a sip, I ask, "Do you believe in angels?"

The question seems to make him uncomfortable. He rests his forearms on the bar and looks down. "I don't know. Maybe."

Looking to change the subject that has affected his mood, I ask without thinking, "Do you come here often?" I can't believe I just said that. "That is awful. I'm sorry."

"Don't be." His smile returns, and he looks at me. I'm curious as to what's making him stay here and talk to me. "I *am* here often, but I've never seen you here before. I would definitely have remembered you."

"Now that is a little cheesy, but I'll let it slide since you offered me the same courtesy."

Shrugging, he doesn't wear any shame in his expression. "Why are you so pretty?"

This guy could have any girl here, but he's genuinely interested in me. "You think I'm pretty?"

"Of course." His self-deprecating eye roll is endearing. "I'm not exactly original, but I sure like looking at you."

"Thank you."

That makes him laugh, which is deep, speaking to me in a way that hits below the belt in good ways. What am I feeling? Breaking my own rules makes me feel alive. I'm sure it has nothing to do with him or the way he's staring at me as though I just made his night.

After scoping out his left hand for a ring, I ask, "Do you have a girlfriend?"

"No."

"Why not?"

"I haven't met a qualified contender." His voice is smooth with an air of arrogance. "Are you going to drink that beer?"

"No. You can have it." He does too and drinks half. Still stuck on the job opening, I ask, "What are the qualifications?"

He chuckles again. Leaning in, he asks, "Are you applying for the job?"

"I might be interested. Do you offer benefits?" Who am I? I'm flirting like a professional and start giggling like a fool.

After taking another swig from the bottle, he says,

"Depends on what kind of benefits you're looking for. What'd you have in mind?"

I spoke too soon about my flirting prowess. I'm a mess. Put me in a courtroom and I can own it, but put me with a hot guy and I'm so over my head. "I have no witty comeback for that."

"You're too stuck in here." He rubs my temple so gently that it doesn't feel like a point he's trying to make, but an opportunity for something I can't quite place. "Just say what you feel."

And there's my heart thumping against my ribs again. "I feel too much to explain."

"That's okay. When you know, you can tell me."

I wish I knew if this was real or just lines he's used before. Does it matter? He has a way of making me special, which is new and exciting. It also might be my cue to leave before this turns into something I can't handle. Tonight is not the night to lose my virginity, though Marquis has made me consider it. "I should get going."

"We were just getting to know each other."

"This has been unexpected and fun."

"You were unexpected. I'm glad you came out tonight."

"Me too."

Walk away.

Walk away.

Walk—God, how I want to stay. "I definitely have to go now." *I bet he's a great kisser.* My body is getting the better of my thoughts, so I force myself to take another two steps. *And those hands.* Three more steps. I bite my lip again. *Goodness, how I'd love to feel those hands on my skin.* Two more steps. I clamp my hands around the purse hanging at my hip while my eyes trace the tattoos of his arms.

Coming back to him like a damn boomerang, I touch his

forearm, and ask, "What does the skull with the daisy eye represent?"

"One of the angels we spoke about." He touches my skin as though I have a story to tell as well. "You sure you can't stay?"

"Yes. I need to leave."

"That's too bad. You ever want to run into each other again or share a beer, we play here every Thursday."

Before I take another step, I stop. Glancing around the now fairly empty bar, I hadn't noticed how the place had cleared out. "You're in the band?"

A grin crosses his lips. "You didn't catch the show?"

"Just the tail end."

"It got better once you walked in. Come next Thursday."

"Smooth, Marquis. You really want me to come back, or do you say that to all the girls?" He stops with a smirk and tilts his head. Then humor replaces the earnest pause.

"Come back and find out."

Hope bubbles in my chest from anticipation, and my own grin surfaces. "Maybe I will."

"I hope so."

Heat colors my cheeks, a blushing mess from someone so cute wanting to see me again. *Me.* I've been living in a haze, and suddenly, the world is Technicolor. I reach the door, but before I leave, I call back, "See you again someday, Marquis."

"See ya, Pepper." My feet stop just outside the door, and I whip around. Catching his narrowed eyes on me, I see his grin is gone as questions carve into his expression. My heart begins to race along with my mind, searching through old memories that I can't seem to place. "Pepper?"

I take a step toward the door, but the bouncer knocks the kickstand free and puts his arm out. "Closing up. Have a good night." He shuts the door before I have a chance to ask *Marquis* if he knows me.

Marquis.

Marquis.

Marquis.

I can't recall a Marquis, but he was so familiar that I swear there's a level of comfort or security about him even though I can't place his face. I pull up an email that included my parents' invitation list from the huge bash they threw last summer. Not one Marquis—first or last name.

He's not from high school, college, or law school because he would have said so, and how would he have time to play shows if he was? I can barely breathe these days.

I keep landing back on the question that maybe I don't know him, but he knows me. I didn't pay with a credit card. A shot in the dark would hit the mark before landing on Weatherly. But he didn't call me by my name. He called me Pepper, which makes absolutely no sense, yet feels right, good even, for some reason.

Maybe I heard him wrong, but what other word could Pepper be?

See you, *Beggar*. I laugh. I'm pretty sure he didn't call me a leper.

See you, *Stepper*. I am wearing my activity watch. Hrm . . . My gut says it wasn't stepper.

See you, . . . Becker? Pecker? Decker? Maybe he knows my name, and he was having fun with it. Beck. *Becker.* I've heard that mistake before.

Ugh. No. It was definitely see you, *Pepper*. But why would he call me that?

I've never known anyone with tattoos down his arms, and I would definitely remember the sharp edges of that incredible jaw. By the look in his eyes, the innocence of his youth was stolen a long time ago. All the guys I grew up with are still immature and arrogant pricks.

I felt an instant connection, but was the attraction mutual?

At just past three in the morning, my mind is trying to trick me. There's no way I know that guy. Every trail leads to a dead end.

Several days of stubble and messy brown hair, a kind smile that turns into a sexy smirk, and those eyes that seem to see through any lie I never had the chance to tell fill my head.

I don't remember when sleep takes over, but I awake with a headache and eyes that demand to be kept closed. I pull the other pillow over my head. Ugh. "Go to sleep, Weatherly."

How can I sleep when I have those warm brown eyes caressing me like he was undressing me? God, I'm ridiculous and apparently rhyming now. Sweating under the down blanket, I push it off me. But I'm still too unsettled and find myself pacing at five a.m.

Who was he? He's crossed my mind more times than I care to admit, and I'm still no closer to an answer than before I met him.

Tall.

Dark.

Handsome.

He's what fairy tales are made of . . . and sexual fantasies, if I'm being honest.

Lifting the curtain to the side, I open the blinds and stare toward the river. I can just make out the trail in the faint light. I should go for a run, run away every opinion I ever valued more than my own. I've been terrified to defy anyone's wishes, broken down from trying to make everyone else happy at my expense.

Lloyd Sanders wanted to be my boyfriend since we were thirteen and I got boobs. It didn't hurt that our fathers are partners at the same firm we were groomed for our whole lives. His grades were not top-notch despite his daddy handing him entrance to a top university and law school. So he thought he'd get in with the daughter. *Wink. Wink.* But he's never looked at me like that stranger did.

Marquis. He's someone I don't mind spending a few more hours mulling over. I climb back in bed and turn onto my side. Holding a pillow to my chest, I close my eyes with a smile on my face. Here in this apartment, I can be the kind of pretty he called me, living happily in the memory.

Sleeeeep.

Just go to sleep, Weatherly. I silently nag myself to be responsible. I have no business thinking about a man I don't know.

He could be dangerous.

Excitement vibrates in my chest from the thought. Marquis is all I can think about when I should be focusing on more important things, like studying and graduating. Securing a job at the firm. Settling into a place that's all mine. That's what matters, but how can I think about those things when his words race through my veins. "*I could be bad for you.*"

Danger never looked so good. Wonder what he tastes like? Probably sex and cigarettes. I cannot stand the smell of smoke, but on him, I'm willing to lick him clean.

What.

The.

Hell.

Is.

Wrong.

With.

Me?

Tattoos and a good time. That's what. Someone so outside my world that I can't stop my curiosity from being piqued. And he's a musician to boot. Holy heavens. He exudes the whole bad boy vibe.

Why am I falling down this rabbit hole? My mind needs rest, but instead, it begs to return to how he smelled like a trip I've always wanted to take—adventure, excitement—and how my body reacted to the heat that rolled off him in waves, drawing me unconsciously closer.

He's everything I don't need, but I've never wanted someone more, which is crazy. I don't think I've really ever wanted *anyone.* Not really. Lloyd has never been someone I fantasized about, yet every second I see Marquis in my mind, I'm thinking *definitely a good time* while I figure out my next step. A good time? I'm the most uptight person I know. I rarely let myself have a good time. *Could he be just what I need?*

He made his interest known by flirting with me and telling me I deserve someone good and proper, which naturally led me to thinking improperly about him.

What girl wouldn't be flattered by his attention? He's a gorgeous man, and now that I've experienced what that attention is like, I'm tempted to make it a regular Thursday night event.

Taking my phone from the nightstand, I try to recall the name of the band the bouncer mentioned. Since I didn't catch the name of the bar before I walked in, I concentrate on the things I do know: Arms that are large enough not just to hold me but protect me from the world if needed, lips that probably know how to kiss until I'm raw with lust, and that look in his eyes that sees the me I feel inside.

I really need to put these thoughts to bed. If I can just remember the band's name or at least the bar's, I can get some sleep. No matter how hard I concentrate, though, I draw a blank. Too many ethics principles taking up space in my brain.

Throwing my arms up, I bring one down to rest across my head. "What am I doing?" I take a deep breath before putting my sleep mask over my eyes. My body sinks a little deeper into the mattress, and I begin to touch the edges of sleep. One more breath and this time, when I exhale, I drift.

3

Dare

Pepper. She was probably prom queen and every guy's dream in high school. She's now become my fantasy. I don't know anything about the woman I met the other night, but the moment I saw her, I wanted to know everything I could.

Except I didn't ask.

Not her name.

Her age.

Where she's from.

Fuck.

Did I lose the opportunity? That smile, her laugh, the way her nerves got the best of her at times. Her beauty left me tongue-tied. I've never been drawn to a woman more than I was to her.

Standing close had me vowing to change my ways, hearing her voice had me thanking a God I'd lost faith in. But when my eyes met her baby blues, I'm not sure what happened. My heart started racing, fast like it does on stage, but to a different beat—familiar only to her.

Lust.

I remind myself. That's all it was. She was hot in her confidence. Enticing in her shyness, wearing a sundress that left enough room for the imagination and shoes that kept her little enough to tuck under my arm. Not that I did, but she seemed like a good piece to my puzzle.

Sleep begs me to give in, but I'd rather think about the pretty girl from Thursday night. She stood out in that scene. I could tell Shep's wasn't a place she frequented. I yawn again. *A qualified contender.* That makes me laugh. I don't know what the fuck I was talking about, but I like that she went with the flow.

My muscles still ache from lifting weights in the garage this morning, which caused me to play guitar like a lazy shit tonight on stage. I had to get out some pent-up aggression somehow. Next time, it will be on the strings instead because hitting the soundboard to make everyone else louder was a good bandage, but I can't afford to fuck up again. The band needs the gigs because we need the money.

Putting the last three nights behind me has left me lying in the dark with a restless mind. Reaching over, I check my phone for missed messages one last time and then close my eyes.

ONE POUND on my bedroom door rattles it, but not me. After living with these delinquents for four years, I can sleep through anything. Except when the sun shines in blinding me. "Shut the blinds, asshole."

"No. Let's get a run in before it gets too hot."

"Go without me, Lennox." Pulling the pillow over my

head, I try to fall back into the sweet dream I was having about the mystery woman I called Pepper on the fly.

Pepper? *What the fuck?* That made no sense, but it flew out of my mouth before I could think twice about it.

"Nah, man. You told me not to let you coast through this week. We're amping up for summer."

I laugh and then peg him with my pillow. "You sound like a girl working on her summer bod."

Popping up his right bicep and then his other, he tries to snarl. As I said, tries . . . I start laughing, delirious from the shitty sleep. "Look at these bad boys. They aren't building themselves," he says.

"A run's not going to build them either. You need to lift weights for that."

"The run is just the start. Get your ass up. Five minutes and we're heading out."

My shouted, "Fucker," hits the back of his head just before the door closes. I lie on my back, still being blinded by the day breaking, and groan in protest. But then I get up because fuck, I'm awake already. Might as well make the most of it.

I'm grabbing a Powerade before my best friend since childhood has his shoes on. He's not a brother by blood, but by choice. I've known him the longest. Our moms used to laugh about us sharing a twin bed. They left out the part of not being able to afford two, or separate homes, which never much mattered to us. Despite being shacked up in a one bedroom east of downtown, we were rich in other ways. I don't blame our moms because there's no shame in sharing expenses. They both left bad choices to give us a better life.

There isn't a doctor, lawyer, or a white-collar among us in this house our band shares. We're rowdies by circumstance—guys from the wrong side of everything—and gravitate toward the same kind of trouble. Rowdies stick together, loyal to a fault. Too much energy to sit still. Too much ego to take any shit. Too much anger coursing through our veins. Not much money among us.

There was no time to make my mom proud. She went into the hospital for a cough when I was nineteen and died weeks later. I had to watch her suffer needlessly while the hospital tried to ease her physical pain. She was living for me, but I couldn't bear her anguish. I finally told her not to worry about me and let go.

Sometimes my memories get the best of me, but I shake these off, not wanting to carry around the weight today.

Downing half the bottle, I need the electrolytes before burning through more on a run. "You ready to get left in the dust?"

Lennox laughs. "Whatever, punk." He heads out, but I pass him on the front lawn. Four miles in, we reach the east banks of Ladybird Lake. I drop to my knees and try to catch my breath, but when that doesn't work, I lie down while my lungs scream for air.

He sits on his ass and moans. "My legs hurt."

I chuckle. "Mine too."

"That's good, right?"

"Fuck if I know." With my arms spread wide, I ask, "Why do we do this again?"

"Chicks dig muscles."

"Ah, we're doing it for the ladies." Forcing myself up, I stare at the water. Gold flecks reflecting the sun cover the tops of the wind-driven ripples. The interstate is already bumper to bumper during rush hour, and the faint honking of horns is ruining the peaceful morning.

Messing with my laces, I ask, "You say that like you don't

have a crazy ex. You thinking about trying someone on for size for a while again?"

"I think about it, but I'm not there yet." Lying in the grass, Lennox still has his eyes closed. Then he sits up and looks at me. "What about you?"

We don't get deep much these days. Maybe after the heaviness of our childhoods, we prefer to keep things lighter, but it doesn't mean we don't think about stuff. We just don't usually talk about it.

"I don't know. I think about a life that's forked in some ways. One way, I'm settling down. The other, I'm living my dream." I scrub my hand over my face, knocking the sweat from my brow. "I feel older than my twenty-five years."

"You've dealt with a lot in life."

"There are other people out there with worse beginnings. Yours wasn't sunshine, but you don't let that drag you down."

He spins his hat backward while shaking his head. "You either, but I sometimes wonder if that's why I can't seem to find someone sane to date. Like I'm wired for chaos."

Lennox Rey is the quietest guy I know. I'm pretty sure it's something he learned when he was still in diapers. His parents fought worse than mine from the stories we overheard growing up. His dad abided by the same principles mine did—take no shit and take them down first—and it didn't matter if it was a man, woman, or kid. They made sure to get their punches—verbally and physically—in. I stand and start pacing. "We're not like them."

"No," he replies, dusting the grass from his shorts. "But sometimes I wonder if his genes will catch up with me."

"You wouldn't hurt anyone, no dude who didn't deserve it."

He laughs. "When you mention feeling older than your

years, I can relate. We've had some good times, some out-of-control times, and some lows, but we're still here somehow. Guess we're not doing that bad, huh?"

"Nah. Not that bad."

Walking to the edge of the water, he adds, "I'm tempted to jump in the water to cool off."

I know he won't, but it's time to leave the talking behind and get on with our day. I rattle my hand over my hair to shake the sweat loose. "It's hot as fuck. Ready to go?"

Lennox comes back but stops in front of me. "What we've been through, the rough times, no one will understand how two little kids from the east side survived from their mother's determination. We've been brothers a long time, but my mom, you know she's there for you too. Any time. Day or night, we both are."

"I know. Offer stands for you too. If you want my two cents, leave the chaos behind. You deserve better than you've given yourself."

"Are we talking about women?"

"No. You've been dating girls. Step up to the big leagues, brother."

I need to release the pent-up energy stirred inside, something unsettled. I have a feeling it's got something to do big blue eyes and long brown hair. Pink lips that pucker when she's thinking about how to answer and a blush to match when you give her attention.

Pepper.

She's the kind of girl I want to spend more time getting to know. Lennox needs to meet the same. I stop getting ahead of myself about a girl I may never see again and jog instead. The sun is beating down from high in the nine a.m. sky.

"I'm doing the best I can. I'm ready for some calm," he replies.

"Sometimes I wonder if people can change. Like us. Does being good matter?"

"Bad paid off quicker, but when it comes to changing, ultimately, it's up to the rest of the world to decide if someone gets the credit for the effort."

"So basically, it doesn't matter how good we are if someone still sees us as bad? Will we ever outrun our past?"

"Not if I have a say in it." He laughs as he pushes my arm and then takes off running. "Less talking. More running."

"I'm not looking to break any records."

"Suit yourself." When he starts fidgeting with his watch, I know he's setting a stopwatch to time himself.

Despite the restless energy, the heat has zapped me, so I slow my pace. What I don't get is why I'm thinking about this shit anyway.

Lennox is in the shower when I return, so I down some juice and scramble some eggs while I wait my turn. A commotion at the front door sends me rushing to see what the fuck is happening on the front porch. When I open it, I wish I hadn't. Romeo, The Heroes's drummer, is making out with a girl against the wall.

"Warn a guy," I complain, kicking the door closed. I return to the kitchen because the last thing I want to see is one of my friends feeling up a groupie at ten in the morning, or ever.

The doorbell rings a few times before I hear English storm through the living room and yank the front door open. There's a pause, but then he yells, "Lay off the bell and get a fucking room," and slams the door shut, grumbling all the way back to his bedroom.

Romeo finally comes inside and pulls out a barstool to plant himself on. I don't have to see him to know he's most likely eyeing my food. "Just take it."

He's chomping down before a thank you is muttered, but when it is, he at least sounds fucking grateful. While I make the full dozen, since I know everyone is up now, I ask, "Groupie?"

"Yep."

"She here?"

"Nope."

"I'm not going to lecture you on your lays, but have you thought about seeing a chick more than once?"

His head jerks back and confusion wrinkles his brows. "Why would I do something like that?"

I chuckle. "Only asking." Topping another plate with eggs, I set it next to him just as Lennox comes around and gets a fork to dig in. "Thanks, man."

They don't get but a few bites in before English begrudgingly takes the last barstool. "Might as well eat since I'm up."

While the toaster is pushed to its limits with all the bread flying in and out of it to feed four grown men, we have a few minutes of forks against plates, a clanging considered quiet for this rowdy bunch, before English asks, "What was up last night, Dare?"

Turning around to the sound of my name, I shrug. "An off night is all." Distracted by every brunette in the place, I was disappointed that none were her. What do I expect? She's not the groupie type.

English picks up his guitar and strums. "You don't have off nights."

"First time for everything."

"Can't cover you every night," he replies with a snarky grin. Guess he has that right as our lead guitarist.

"So it's not going to be a regular thing?" Romeo asks.

"Consider it one of your hookups," I snap back.

"Very funny." Coming around the bar, he sets his plate in the sink. "I have a job in Dripping Springs. They can use a few extra guys. Cash in hand. Out by five."

English huffs. "I'll go."

Rent was paid, but life doesn't come free. "I'm in," I say. Some physical labor will get my mind off a certain woman and get my head back on straight. It's time to put that fantasy to bed.

After three hours of hauling lumber, my arms feel like gelatin. Not the best for a guitar player with a gig to play later. I look around for the guys, wondering if they're faring any better.

I don't know who's going to live in these mansions we're building, but I already hate them. Does someone really need a house this big? Feeding that ego of theirs with superficial shit won't make their penis grow.

I'd rather have the big dick I got. Seems fair. Though I wouldn't be out here sweating my ass off if I had a stack of cash to rest back on, I still wouldn't trade my dick for a cushy life. I never minded a hard day's work. I mind when it isn't working toward my goals. Extra money goes toward the studio fund so we can finally record our album. So I take another stack of two-by-fours and drop them at the back of the foundation that was just poured.

Five hours after quitting time, I'm on a different stage. Different bar. Different crowd. Same songs. The girl from Thursday isn't here. I know because my eyes have been glued to the audience all night. I catch a few eyes, eyes that top hot little bodies with big tits and tight shirts.

They're not the eyes I want to see, though. I have my whole mood balanced precariously on whether or not she shows up this coming Thursday.

Fuck. What is wrong with me?

4

Weatherly

"WEATHERLY?"

Stascia.

"Weatherly?"

April.

"Get up before we waste the whole day waiting on you."

Definitely April.

Lifting the mask, I open my right eye and then my left. Squinting in the sunlight, I say, "Why are you here so early?"

"Early? It's eleven."

"Eleven?" I bolt upright. "Crap! I'm late." While they sit on the end of my bed, they watch as I run around like a crazy person into my bathroom and straight into my closet where I tug off the T-shirt I slept in and get dressed.

Stascia is lying on my bed when I come back out. My dress is still covering my head, when she asks, "It's Wednesday. We haven't seen you in almost a week. You can't hide from this breakup forever."

"I'm not hiding. I've been busy with classes and studying." I tug it down and adjust it around my hips.

"Do you have to go?" She sticks out her bottom lip, making me laugh.

Hopping, I slip a shoe on one foot and then the other. "I'm so close to graduation that I'm not blowing it now." I hurry into the kitchen and throw my notebooks into my bag before I eye the coffeepot longingly. I don't have time to caffeinate, so I sling my bag onto my shoulder and rush out the door.

I reach the elevator before I realize what I left behind. I run back inside and find my friends still sitting on my bed. I wave them out. "Come on. Let's get a move on."

They groan as they get up and follow me. Stascia loops her arm around mine. "We're going to brunch, and you're coming with us. We miss you."

The elevator door opens, and we move inside together. It's odd that I haven't missed them. Sometimes I wonder how good of friends they are, especially since I had no problem just texting with them all week. "Can't. Have a mimosa for me."

"We'll have three," April replies.

The elevator gods are on my side today. No stops and the doors open in the garage. I untangle myself and run out. "Call you later."

They don't put up much of a fight. I hear Stascia huff, and April says, "Juliette's or Chez Zee?"

So much for missing me.

I pull out of the garage and zip around to head toward the school. When I reach the main road, I give the car some gas and pray I'm not singled out for being so late. My professor loves to challenge budding attorneys. She claims it's to prepare us for working for law firms and in courtrooms.

Thank God she's in a generous mood today and doesn't say a word. I take notes and raise my hand to participate in an experiment, hoping to stay on her good side. I can't screw up again. I'm in the homestretch, so I can't afford to make that mistake twice.

Speaking of mistakes . . .

I see my biggest when I leave the lecture hall to go to my car. Lloyd not only comes at me with a big bouquet of red roses but also with his other hand in front of him in surrender. "Two minutes," he pleads. "That's all I'm asking for, Weatherly."

I keep walking. "That's okay. I'm good."

From behind me, he asks, "What does that mean, you're good?"

"Exactly what it sounds like." I turn around and sigh. "Aren't you ready to move on? To find love with someone?"

His head jerks back. "Find love with someone *else*? What are you talking about? I found love with you."

His confession takes me by surprise. I tilt my head, bewildered by how he thinks what we share is love. "Did you, though?"

"Of course." He shoves the flowers at me. "I know I screwed up, but we'll work through it."

"Hmm, let me guess." I tap my chin, avoiding the flowers. "Like we always do? It's been a week. I thought you'd moved on like I have."

"What the hell are you talking about? Are you not feeling well?"

"I'm feeling great. That's why I thought this," I say, waving between us, "was over."

I can't help but notice how disheveled he looks—usually

perfectly gelled sections of his hair fall over his forehead, the bags under his eyes will require a bellhop to help lug around, and desperation has taken up residence in the lines of his forehead. Quite frankly, it's the best he's looked in years. Real, not perfectly quaffed or put together. Emotions seen in his expression.

I still can't seem to garner any sympathy for him, though. Apparently, *he's* had a rough go of it after being caught cheating.

Me, on the other hand? I've had one of the best weeks of my life. It was so good that I'm struggling to keep the smile from my face. I'll have to get better at suppressing my emotions as an attorney.

Pushing the flowers toward me again, he says, "I've learned my lesson. That's what you want to hear. There! I've said it."

I don't take the flowers. Mass-produced, non-smelling red roses were never my favorite anyway. "Go home, Lloyd."

"We need to talk this out."

"I think you having sex with another woman kind of says it all, don't you think?"

He stomps his foot. "No, actually, I don't think that says it all. It was a mistake, a momentary blip in the scheme of our lives—"

"Yeah. Yeah. She meant nothing." I approach my car but keep talking with him in tow. "I've heard this song and dance. You're repeating your speech from sophomore year in college. The difference this time is that I *saw* you, Lloyd. So I don't want your excuses. I want out. We're done."

"Why are you being so bitchy, Weatherly? Forgiveness is a virtue."

If he was trying to trigger me, he just did it. My arms tighten around my bag to keep from punching him in the face. I've never been the violent type, but he seems to have a knack for bringing out the worst in people. He definitely brings out the worst in me and has for years. With him, I was exactly who he said I was—meek and accommodating. I don't remember dreaming of those traits when I was a girl, but everyone's repeated insults stuck to me like glue, and that's who I became.

With my back to him, I look over my shoulder, and say, "Cheating on me wasn't an offense. It was a gift. Thank you for finally making me deal with what I always knew inside. You're free to fuck whomever you want, but now it won't be at my expense. Goodbye, Lloyd."

I get in my car and lock the doors before setting my bag on the passenger's seat to the sound of him groaning outside. "Come on, Weatherly. Don't be unreasonable."

While I'm reversing, he walks in front of my car, still yapping about how I'm ruining everything, ruining his big plans. "Your father is going to lose his shit when he finds out."

I slam on the brakes, the front of my car just barely pressed to the crease of his overly starched dress pants. *Asshole.* Lloyd always did know how to get to me. Although his face shows the shock from me fighting back, our eyes remain locked in a standoff through the windshield. I have no interest in being with him or playing his petty games, so I shift my car and crack my window. "You're right. He will lose his shit when he finds out you cheated on me. *Again.* So get out of my way or get run over." Although deep down, I wonder whose side he'll choose.

"You wouldn't," he says, glaring with irritation. I saw the same look on his face once when a bug splattered on his windshield and had the nerve to harden before he reached a gas station to clean it.

To him, I'm that bug—nothing but a nuisance in his journey to greatness.

Fuck him. I slam on the horn, causing him to jump and grab his chest. Laughing, I shift the car in reverse and back up to the end of the aisle before righting myself to leave him behind.

He doesn't run after me like he did last night, which means one of two things. He's either plotting his next move, or if I'm lucky, he's accepting our fate. I'm really hoping it's the latter, but my gut tells me it's the former.

A stack of law books waits for me at home, and though I really should be studying, I loop around to Eighth Street and turn down Red River. I search for the scene of the crime on Sixth Street. As I approach the intersection, I recognize the doorway where the gargoyle of a bouncer sat on his stool checking IDs, collecting cover fees, and silently judging everyone who walked through his door.

Since the light is red, I have a moment to lean over my passenger seat and look up at the name of the bar above the awning—Shep's Watering Hole. It's not a place I've been before, but it's a place I intend to return to one day. Maybe even Thursday.

I wonder if the girls would go to a dive like that? I highly doubt it, but it doesn't mean I won't try to work on them. The light turns green, and I start driving again, heading home like I should have in the first place. I can't afford to let my head slip into the stars like I used to. I need to be responsible, but I have a case of Marquis brain. I cannot stop thinking about him. Or smiling when I do.

Curious, I voice command to find a listing for Marquis in Austin, but my car replies, "Calling Marquis."

"No!" I scramble, taking my eyes off the road to find a stop button. "No. No. No. Don't call Marquis."

"Calling Marquis."

"Hello?"

"Oh, fuck."

"Um, hello?"

A voice an octave or two higher than the Marquis I met last night answers. "Thank God. I'm sorry. I have the wrong number."

"No problem."

I end the call with no issue finding the button now when the stress is off. Fuck my life. This is a fool's conquest. I have to get him out of my head. But why does that suddenly feel like an insurmountable task?

I know why.

Iced tea on a hot day brown eyes.

Biceps that the cotton of his shirt couldn't resist clinging to.

My name . . . wait, Pepper is not my name. At that moment, though, when Pepper rolled off his tongue, it was as if he'd said it in another life that tied us together. The problem with studying law is that you are taught to analyze and solve. Surely, that is the real reason I can't get him off my mind.

I also know he's trouble.

He's the sexiest kind of trouble I ever did see, and maybe, just maybe he's the kind of trouble I need to release some steam.

"Call Stascia," I voice command.

"Hello, future Attorney Beck," she answers in a bubbly voice.

I grin and then go in for the kill. "Are you free this Thursday?"

5

Weatherly

To say my anticipation is getting the best of me is an understatement. I'm ready to let loose, but more so, I'm ready to see *Marquis* again. This time, I'm not letting an opportunity slip by me.

It's warm tonight, so I slip on a gauzy, cream-colored mini dress and belt it at the waist before slipping on yellow wedges with ribbons wrapped around my ankles that will get me a few inches closer to the musician's soulful brown eyes.

That is if I convince the girls to hang out at Shep's Watering Hole. It might take some bribing. It will definitely take tequila.

Two hours later, I wave my hand to the waitress. She knows what's up and hurries to the bar. The three of us have been huddled in a corner booth at a downtown eatery for the last hour.

April waves her lipstick in one hand and a small mirror in the other but then stops dramatically. She loves all eyes on her. "So I told him to go fuck himself because he wasn't going to fuck me." Then she applies the lipstick as though she didn't just say something for shock value.

I've been listening, I swear, but suddenly, I feel like I've had my head in the clouds. I've gotten lost along the way of her dating misadventures. "Who are we talking about again?"

"Weatherly." Her fingers snap in my direction. "Keep up. It's a guy I mess around with when opportunity presents itself."

"I thought I was keeping up, but I lost count after the . . . what guy are you on?"

"None. That's the problem. I'm with you whores when I could be with him."

Nothing she says surprises me anymore. I'm sure this sucker is married or has a girlfriend. She'll use him for entertainment and then move on. But my lack of reaction apparently still surprises her because she adds, "Well, you're not a whore in the real way, but my bestie bitch."

"Good grief, April. You didn't have to define the difference. Why does it bother you so much that I've not been pummeled in bed anyway? Isn't Lloyd fucking with my head enough?"

Slender fingers slide through her long black hair, strands falling like a waterfall over her shoulders. "Is he fucking with yours, or are you fucking with his? I wonder if you're playing games with him just to mess with him."

"What are you talking about? I don't play games with his head, his heart, or any other part of that pig of a man."

She's shaking her head and then sighs. "You strung him along forever and then expected him to remain faithful. Are you sure you're not the one in the wrong, Weatherly? And for that matter, don't come crying to me when he moves on. Men like that don't stay single for long."

"One can only hope."

Stascia huffs. "I'm so over the arguing." Whipping her hair over her shoulder, she glares at April. "Who cares if she is a virgin or not?"

The entire restaurant turns our way. Hiding my face behind a shielding hand stuck to my forehead, I whisper, "Okay, this is humiliating."

April is silent, holding Stascia's stare. She finally turns to me, and says, "You reap what you sow."

"You're blaming me for his cheating?"

"If you don't have sex with him, he'll find someone who will. And he did." Her casual shrug pisses me off, but I maintain my composure.

"If it helps you not to worry about me, I haven't regretted one second since leaving him."

"Good for you. We can all move on then." April smacks her lips together, perfectly polished in pink.

The waitress sets the shots down on the table, and I immediately take mine. "Maybe it's time we got a new crew too." I slam down the shot glass, startling them.

April startles. "What is wrong with you? Are you drunk, Weatherly?"

"You know what's wrong with me? This conversation. I'm going out tonight, and I'm not going where our 'crew' hangs out. So you can go out with this," I say, thumbing my chest. "Or you can go out with the others. I don't care anymore."

Standing and putting her hands on her hips, Stascia raises her chin. "Hear. Hear. I'm with you, Weath."

April tries to look pissed, but amusement crosses her face. "Fine. You win. You're also buying dinner."

Wrapping my arm over their shoulders, I say what's on my mind, refusing to hide how I feel any longer. "I know you're used to running this town, but it's time this crew got a new leader."

April throws an arm over my shoulders. "And that's you?"

"For tonight, yes."

"All right." She reaches into my clutch and pulls out a bill to cover our check two times over and tosses it on the table. "Lead the way."

Stascia finishes her shot, then says, "Now this is something I never thought I'd see."

"Us doing shots?" I ask, laughing. "That's every weekend since we were twenty-one."

"Actually, you've been busy for a few years."

"Studying, but it's all going to pay off in a week."

She grabs her bag. "Yes, it will, but I was referring to April relinquishing control."

"Hey," April protests. "I'm not that bad. I can cut loose."

Tugging on her hand, I say, "Guess we'll see."

We take a cab to where I parked the other night, wanting to retrace my steps just in case I was wrong. As they trail behind me, I can see them stepping carefully as they walk.

"This just reminded me why we never come to Dirty Sixth," April says.

Shaking my head, I keep walking. "We're walking on the wild side."

"That's for sure." Stascia jumps, squealing in horror. "Oh my God! That man just flashed me his penis."

I reach the corner and turn back. "How was it?"

At the same time, April asks, "Was it big?" When we make eye contact, we burst out laughing, then April adds, "Basically, the important details," and we keep giggling.

"Ew," Stascia says, raising her voice. "Can we please forget that happened and get to where we're going?"

"Speaking of," April pipes in. "Where *are* we going?"

The band is heard before I spy them playing on the stage. Their backs are to the window, but I see him. *Marquis*. Nice ass in those jeans, but I love his even voice more. "Come on."

I pay the cover charge, and my friends follow me inside. They plug their ears but don't complain. *Thankfully*. We squeeze in at the bar when a group of girls go toward the band.

I'm suddenly nervous to look back, to see him on stage and for him to see me. What if he really didn't mean for me to come back? He'll either be happy, or I'll be humiliated. I have a fifty-fifty shot here, and it's causing my emotions to bounce around.

"I had a feeling you'd be back," the bartender says.

A smile bubbles up as I turn around. "Hi Jake, how's it going?"

"It's been a good week." His palms press to the wood bar top, and his eyes move from me to Marquis and back again. "Do I need to ask what brings you back?"

"That obvious, huh?"

"Not to me. Care to share?" Stascia says.

Jake points toward the stage.

The girls follow, but then confusion follows. Stascia scrunches her face. "I don't get it."

April pulls a cleansing toilette from her purse and rips the package open. "You're into live music all of a sudden?"

"I've always liked live music, but you never did, so I don't get to see many shows."

She wipes her hands with the little wet wipe.

I shake my head. "Can we be cool for one hour, please?"

Offense strikes her . . . I would say face, but her face doesn't move from the injections, so I stick with wide eyes since I'm a pro at reading those. "We are cool. That's why we don't hang out at places like this."

Stascia steps closer. "I kind of like it. It's not pretentious."

"Exactly," I say, smugly. "She gets it. Anyway, this band is great. I heard them last week and thought they were worth seeing again." They both take another look, and this time, Stascia laughs. "See them or hear them? Because I'm seeing them, and it all makes perfect sense why you wanted to *see* them again."

I must turn red as a tomato because my cheeks feel like they're on fire. "I meant hear, but yes, not bad to look at either." Not bad one bit.

She humors me. "They sound great, but I need a drink."

"What can I get you?" Jake asks.

Slapping my hand down, I order, "A round of blow jobs."

"You took my line," Jake jokes.

The creamy concoctions are set before us, and the first thing April says is, "How many calories can they pack into one small shot glass?"

Holding hers up, Stascia licks the rim. "I'm thinking a lot. This tastes amazing."

Jake smiles at her. "Wait until you taste all of it."

With their eyes on each other, she downs it. Their flirting makes me cringe, but they seem to be enjoying it. That's what tonight is about—enjoyment.

The music stops, bringing my attention back to where it should be—on Marquis. He's drinking a beer while talking with one of the guitarists on the left side of the stage. Sexy. Masculine. *A rock star.* The hottest man I've ever seen.

The band gathers in front of the drummer and tune their guitars. A few hits on a drum are followed by the four men dispersing to their own spaces on stage. Stascia elbows me. "How cute are they?"

"Really cute."

"Imagine losing your V-card to a musician. That would be so incredibly sexy."

"It would." That thought has played out in my head many times over in the past week. When they start playing again, I take my shot but am bumped, which causes me to cough.

A shudder runs down my spine because I feel his creepy hand on my shoulder before he says, "That's something I never thought I'd see. Watching you take that shot is hot, Weatherly."

Ugh. I groan, shooting April a deadly glare because I know she's the one who told the guys where we were. I mouth, "Thanks a lot, traitor."

"Maybe he's here to hang out with Stascia and me."

Lloyd leans toward the side of my neck, and says, "Your lips would look so good wrapped around my—"

I elbow his gut, freeing myself from his hold. "Jake, I'm going to need something stronger."

"Coming right up."

Setting a glass down, Jake says, "Whiskey."

"Thank you." I finish the drink under my friends' stares. "A water chaser please." I don't want to get drunk, though I have to admit the alcohol has steadied my nerves. The awkwardness passes, and everyone does what they always do, sink into shallow conversations about money and gossip.

Maybe it's this place, somewhere to let loose without fear of being seen, but April has forgotten to keep up appearances and seems to be genuinely having fun. Stascia falls into her own rhythm, dancing to the music.

I've swayed, even danced to the beat of The Heroes'

songs. Marquis's words are poetry speaking to my heart, his voice caressing my soul with every song he sings. Then April ruins the fun. "Come on. We're going to Bravada."

"I'm staying," I reply, still swaying to the music.

"Why?"

"Because I like the music and the vibe of this place."

After a few rapid eye blinks, she says, "It's been fun to slum, Weatherly, but really? You're choosing to stay?"

"Yes," I snap.

Her head jerks back. "What the hell? Who are you?"

Shrugging, I twist my lips in thought. "Maybe someone you should get to know."

"We've known each other since we were three, so I think I know you well."

"You know the person you want me to be. I'm starting to question if you know the real me at all."

Narrowed eyes and stiff shoulders settle into her disposition. "I don't know what's going on with you. Maybe you've spent too much time with your law books, but welcome back to the real world. I let you lead, but now it's time to fall back in line."

Smacked with her words and her mean girl attitude, I start seeing the side of her I've always excused before. "I won't be 'falling back in line.' I'm staying. If you're leaving, have a good time."

"We're not staying just because you want to."

"That's fine. Have a good night." I walk toward the stage, weaving between people staring at the idols on stage.

I hear her voice, but I have no idea what she's saying. The crowd is too loud, the band even louder. Our friendship has been struggling for years. If she's not in control, then she bites, but she can't control me any longer.

Unfortunately, she can't control Lloyd either. He's had

more than his fair share of shots, and his jackass side is on display. He shoves his way to where I'm standing and yells, "I can get any girl I want, Weatherly! You don't have a say in what happens when you're not around."

"Is that supposed to entice me? Go home, Lloyd."

"Not without you. You're going to take me back, right?" He grabs my wrist, towering over me, and tugs my wrist. "We'll go home together."

"I said no!"

6

Dare

Two songs prior . . .

The strings vibrate under my fingers as I manipulate the steel stretched across the neck of the guitar. My voice reverbs through the speakers when I sing, causing me to grit my teeth right after. Quality has been an issue since we don't have a permanent sound these days. We couldn't hold on to anyone since the pay is shitty and it's a thankless job anyway.

I'll suffer for the dream because nothing is better than playing music and living in the spotlight. My stomach may growl some mornings, but the high I feel on stage every night feeds my ego. The freedom is worth the sacrifice.

The guys play backup as we close out the song. The scruff on my chin scratches across the microphone. Vocally, I travel the bridge before I hit the last chorus. But the words

I wrote years ago and sang a million times suddenly elude me when my new muse appears in front of me.

I blink to make sure my vision isn't playing tricks on me. The woman who flew away last week has come back. *Does that make her mine?*

Stunned, I blink again as if my body has forgotten where I am. My universe spun out of control after she showed up in my life last week. I've been off-kilter ever since. But seeing her now rights all the wrongs, and I hit the notes without effort.

She's an enigma, a dream come to life dancing not twenty feet from the stage. I'd recognize her anywhere, in a crowded bar or if I passed her on the street. I've not had that luck in the past seven days, but here she is, and I start smiling.

Fuck. How is it possible that she's even more beautiful than I remembered? My heart slams against my ribs, keeping it caged from journeying from me to her. The lyrics catch in my throat as I stand there dumbfounded from the mere sight of her.

Lean legs lead to high heels, which make them look even longer. The yellow ribbons wrapped around her ankles show off toned calves. My gaze slides up to a little cream-colored dress with a short skirt that floats around her shapely hips when she spins. Her bare arms are in the air and eyes closed as she dances to the music.

My music.

I'm jabbed in the arm with the head of a guitar, getting my attention, and then bumped aside as English takes over the chorus I'm supposed to be singing. Fucker always did want the spotlight to himself. I know he's just covering for me, so I laugh as we wrap up the song. When I turn back to find my Pepper, I search the area where she was but find her huddled with her friends near the door.

I'm about to jump from the stage to reach her before she goes, but English asks, "What was that about?" The band's lead guitarist may still have his British accent, but I'm sure the queen would be ashamed of the lack of tact he exercises daily. However, that, of course, means he fits right in with the other Heroes of the band.

I wonder where she's from. We definitely don't frequent the same downtown scene because there's no way she would have escaped me. Beauty like hers doesn't hide in the shadows, not even on a dark night.

A face like that—high cheekbones, big blue eyes, sweet cherry lips—is devastating to a guy. I'll never be the same after laying eyes on her.

Guys in ironed pants and polo-type shirts swarm around her. Clean cut. Probably more her type. When one moves in on her, I snap to English, "Nothing," and yank the cable from my guitar. Doesn't matter that I'm coming off a sold-out show or that I do what I love. Those types of guys have always treated me like shit because I refuse to bow at their feet. They're sellouts who are more occupied with how they look and their bank accounts than with the people around them.

"Seems like nothing," English replies sarcastically, returning to his amp to break down the setup.

"I'd call it distracted." Lennox shoulder checks me when he crosses the stage. "Don't make it a habit, Dare."

"You're lucky I like you, Lennox."

"What would you do if you didn't?"

"Fucker." Probably best if I don't take my irritation out on my friends. I pack up my guitar on stage as the other band starts to set up.

"Thought so." He chuckles through his words while clearing the cables.

A commotion in the crowd catches my eyes. Some asshole grabs my blue-eyed baby girl by the wrist. My body stiffens as a growl vibrates through my chest. She doesn't look the type to need saving, but just in case I'm not reading the scene right, I call out to English, "Load my gear."

Nothing about her gives anything less than a pure fuck-off vibe to this guy. No doesn't seem to be an answer he wants. Asshole. I hop off the stage because the fucker should get the message from her body language, but since he doesn't, I don't mind stepping in. Since his momma didn't teach him manners, I will.

"Pepper," I say loud enough to get her attention, but there's a familiarity to the sound of it . . . as if I've said it a million times before.

She turns in the crowd, looking for me. Not only does she find me, but so does the asshole. A flicker of fear flashes in his eyes when he sees me coming through the crowd, and he drops her wrist like he just got burned. His sad attempt at manning up is almost laughable. *Almost.* I keep my eyes fixed on him until he gives her some personal space. Then I shift my focus to the woman at the center of the commotion.

Sapphire eyes with questions filling the irises find me as I emerge from the crowd. The sense of unknown vanishes and reveals a sly smile and a look in her eyes that maybe she's thought about me over the past week as much as I've thought about her.

"Hi," she says with the ease of a friend, a lover. "I've been waiting for you."

Seven days was too long not to see that pretty face. "Feels like forever." Bourbon scents the air between us, and I want to drink her in, taste her, and even though she's right in front of me, I want to skip back to last Thursday and get her name and learn everything about her, not wasting another minute. Her sweet smile causes me to forget the reason I came over, but not for long.

The guy I thought got the message apparently didn't because he says, "Go back to where you belong, dickhead."

I turn to him, my fists tightening from the nerve of this guy. "And where's that?"

As he swishes his arm toward the door, his body gives his fear away. "I don't know. On the other side of the highway."

Eastsiders and Westsiders. It's always been a rivalry in this town, but it's been a while since I was that Eastside kid with a chip on his shoulder. Oh, wait . . . that's a lie. I'm still that guy, and I'm thinking this is the asshole who cheated on her. I punch him.

Landing on his ass, he grabs his cheek with one hand and pushes up with the other. "Motherfuc—"

"Get the fuck out before I call the cops," Jeb, the bouncer, says, pushing his way through the crowd.

"Me?" the douche whines. "He assaulted me."

Jeb crosses his arms. He's an intimidating dude. At six foot six and carrying some major muscle, he's not just a gatekeeper. His size comes in handy sometimes. Not that I was afraid of this asshole, but it's probably best if I don't land another, considering I play guitar for a living.

The asshole eyes me and then Jeb. Pussying out, he tells the douches with him, "Let's get out of here. It's lame in here like the music."

"Oh, that hurts my heart," I reply with a roll of my neck. "Yeah, run along, fucker."

He stops with his back to me and turns around.

Squaring his weak-ass rounded shoulders, he asks, "What did you say?"

Fear is not something I was born with. Dare isn't just a name for me. It's something I defined every day of my school of hard knocks life. Speaking louder for him, I slow it down. "I said. Run. Along. Motherfucker."

In his baggie-ass khakis, he doesn't have the balls to pull a punch against me and definitely not against Jeb. But you always need to keep your eyes on sneaky, snake in the grass fuckers like him. "We're out of here." He grabs my Pepper by the hand and tugs her toward the door.

I shove him in the back, causing him to release her. "You so much as touch her again, and I'll annihilate you."

Her hands land gently on my chest, and when I see her face, her eyes plead before she speaks. "Please don't fight. He's not worth it."

"Not worth it, huh? How about touch me again and I'll sue your ass sideways."

"What the fuck?"

"That came out wrong," he stumbles through his words. Seems his private school education is failing him. "Whatever. Lame." He and his friends leave with what appears to be her friends as well.

I know when to shut up and walk away. At least, these days I do. As for the past, let's just say being the bigger man hasn't always been my strong suit. I don't usually mind a throw down, but after a shitty performance, it's probably best if I don't push my luck. I can't have this place canceling next week's gig because I cause them trouble. The band needs the money.

The brunette beauty presses against me, and asks, "Why did you do that?"

I can't believe I'm having this thought, but hearing the

tone of her voice again as she speaks makes me realize how much I've craved more of her. It's feminine—pretty like a songbird in the morning and confident like a boss who sets her own hours. Damn sexy. "Do what?" I ask. "Fight him?"

With her friends and the trouble gone, she lowers her hands. "Yes." I'm tempted to put them back on me, but there's no way I'm manhandling her like that fuckface did. "Why would you fight him?" she adds.

"Because he's an asshole who had his hands all over you. You didn't seem to like it too much."

"I didn't, but I'm used to it."

"That's bullshit you shouldn't be used to."

"Guys are like that. Well, those guys are like that, whether you want it or not." She sounds pissed, and I like that fire inside her.

"Real men won't treat you like property or control you, babe. You need to ditch the abusers."

Angling toward me, she says, "You're right."

"It's a lesson I learned the hard way, so take my advice and go with your gut. It will never steer you wrong."

"I'm sorry."

"For what?"

"That you've had to learn that lesson."

"Don't be." Shrugging, I say, "That's the good thing about lessons. You learn and move on." Her dress isn't revealing, but damn, I like the heat we create from our proximity.

Little peaks push against the light-colored fabric over her chest and her hips sway to the right, a hand anchored high on the side, drawing my attention to how a little bow pulls it together at the waist. One tug on that bow's end and . . .

"Marquis?"

"What?" I look up to find a genuine smile on her face.

"You were sharing your life lessons with me."

"It's not worth revisiting the past." Shaking my head, I chuckle. "So you don't need to hear shit from me."

"What if I want to?"

"Then stay away from assholes like that, and you'll be a lot happier in life. Why do you keep calling me Marquis?"

Panic filters into her eyes. "That's your name, right?"

"It's my last name."

"It is?" She glances over her shoulder toward the bar at Jake.

Ah. "Jake called me Marquis last week."

"Yes," she replies, looking straight into my eyes—comfort found in her body language. "I've gone over your name a million times, wondering if it was your first or last." I don't even think she realizes how much closer she's gotten to me. I'm not going to tell her because I like that even more.

"You thought about my name since last week?"

Pink colors her cheeks. "Uh, I think I just busted myself."

"You did, but if it makes you feel better, I thought about you and what your name is as well."

"How about Pepper?" A flirty wink is thrown my way.

I catch it because she makes me smile. "I like Pepper." Leaning down, I whisper, "But if I'm being honest, I have no idea where that came from."

I reach my hand out as she tilts her head, her hair silky and running over my fingers like water. "I liked it." Resting her elbows against the bar behind her, she dips her tongue out and wets her lips as she glances at the door. I could watch her do that for hours. "My friends left me."

"Real friends wouldn't have taken his side." Forcing myself to turn away before she thinks it's weird that I'm staring at her, I ask, "Why'd you stay?"

"I wanted to buy you a drink."

"You're not a groupie." The pull to her is too strong. I lean my forearms on the bar and look to the right, looking her over.

"I'm not, but it seemed like a good way to get in your good graces."

"You're already in, babe. Pepper?" I whisper, taking her hand. It's so small and perfect in mine. Soft to my hard. Flawless to my calloused. "What's your name?"

With our hands still clasped, she faces me, the tips of her shoes squeezed between mine. She lifts up, and I let her make any move she wants because, like the first time I laid eyes on her, my world fades away, and I'm lost in hers. She says, "Weatherly."

Her lips press to mine, and the white noise of the world quiets around us, leaving her and me in our own little universe locked in a kiss.

7

Weatherly

"THIS IS NOT how I saw things going."

He looks around as if he knows we have an audience, and then replies, "It's just a kiss."

I rest back on my heels and watch the band that starts to play on stage. "Not to me."

"Hey."

I glance back at him but don't linger long.

Touching my chin, he lifts it just enough to get a full view of my face. Instead of arrogance or some ego put on for the groupies watching his every move, gentleness softens the corners of his eyes. "I don't know why I said that. It wasn't just a kiss to me either." His sweetness is such a contradiction to the leather that wraps around his wrists and the roughness of his touch. "Maybe we should start over. I don't know if Weatherly is your first or last name," he breathes against my mouth. The taste of whiskey and smoky sin lingers on my lips from our first kiss. I take a deep breath and slowly open my eyes.

"First," I reply breathy and desperate sounding, so I clear my throat, but start laughing from my ridiculousness.

"I like your smile, Weatherly," he adds with our bodies still pressed together. My hands wrap over his shoulders and travel down to his biceps because after hearing him say my name, I'm going to need something to hold me up.

He's fit, considering he seems to enjoy the bad boy status. His rock-hard body matches his gravelly voice. I don't know if he parties hard, but I can assume the life of a rock star includes late nights, booze, and groupies. Speaking of groupies, I'm acting like one. "I like your music."

"Thanks. I'm glad you came back tonight."

"Me too." While I'm shamelessly squeezing his arms to get a good feel of him, I receive a quirked grin from him. I have to remind myself not to fall for the bad boy despite how sexy he is. But why am I here? My heart is trying to beat out of my chest, but I have a feeling me standing in front of him has nothing to do with that. Oh God. I think I'm hot for this guy. How is that even possible when I'm a virgin?

Well-built.

Devilish good looks.

Dark brown hair wild from the wind.

Tanned skin from too much time under the sun.

Muscles a T-shirt can't hide command my attention.

I think I just answered my own question.

His body wasn't the only thing on display when he was on stage. His voice captured me in a way that made me feel like the only person there, as if he was singing just for me. His voice is sexy, sultry to match the hot spring night. A vein ridged in his forehead when he sang, and the corners of his eyes stayed soft.

He's rugged and handsome. I know nothing more about

this perfect specimen of a man, but the thought of getting to know him sends a thrill through me.

I can pretend there wasn't a motive that brought me here, but that doesn't make the truth less potent. Yes, I've thought about him *a lot* throughout the week, but something is so incredibly mesmerizing about being in front of a man so . . . virile. So real. *And he seems to be attracted to me. Wild.* But I don't even know his name.

Reading my mind, he says, "My mom would be disappointed in me. I've kissed you but never properly introduced myself." Our hands come together again, but this time, he holds mine like it's a gem—with care and protectiveness. "I'm Dare Marquis."

"Hi. Weatherly Beck. It's nice to meet you."

"Weatherly Beck." He savors it with a dip of his eyes as he sounds it out slowly. "That's a great name." Turning my hand, he kisses the topside.

"Do you do that for all the girls? And more importantly, does it work?" I think I amuse him.

He chuckles. "Every time. Like a charm."

"I have no doubt you know how to charm a girl right into bed."

It's incredibly sexy how he shrugs unapologetically, knowing exactly who he is. He's not phony like Lloyd and the crew. "It's a skill that's come in handy a few times."

"A few times?" I choke on my laughter before turning and raising my hand to get the bartender's attention. From the other end of the wooden bar, his eyes connect with mine, and he acknowledges me with a nod as he comes to take our order.

When he leans over the bar toward me, I order, "Two shots of Jack Daniels and two Shiner Bocks."

"You've got it."

The drinks are set in front of us, and I start to open my purse, but Dare covers my hand. *Dare, his name is Dare*—sexiest name ever. He turns to the bartender. "Throw it on my tab."

He shakes his head. "You ever plan on paying that tab, Marquis?"

"One day."

My heart shifts while I stare into his warm brown eyes. That's the only way I can explain the feelings he evokes. Laws, facts, evidence—those are my forte not this blooming desire inside. Yet this feels right. This is not about logic, but about attraction.

Like taking charge with the girls earlier, I'm forging a new path—new opportunities, new people, new experiences. I try to maintain the cool vibe I've been pawning off as confidence. He makes me nervous, though, so I treat him like a mock trial. One never knows what will be presented in court. I have to be prepared for all scenarios. The only problem is I showed up tonight not actually expecting to talk to him, much less kiss him.

Look at me, flirting on top of that.

"Hey there," Dare says, leaning down until he captures my attention again, bringing me back to the here and now.

"Hey," I whisper in return.

I've been good for so long, doing everything everyone required of me—being an abiding daughter, a good friend, and a loyal girlfriend. Where did that get me? Right here in the middle of Sixth Street at a bar called Shep's. So making the most of the situation, I ask, "Now that you got me here, what do you have planned?"

"So much I could say, but damn." I want to lick the smirk that lifts, the wry grin that makes me weak in the knees. "You're looking for trouble."

"I'm hoping I found it."

"Fuck," he breathes under his breath. "Girl, you definitely found it. I'm up for whatever you want to do."

I'm full of regrets for so many things in my life, like Lloyd, but coming back here tonight will never be one of them. "I think we start with a drink."

"Cheers."

"Cheers." I tap my glass against his, and we drink with our eyes locked on each other. Heat coats my throat as I swallow, and then I take a deep breath to cool it down. I don't need liquor to be courageous, but it's a nice excuse. Since we've taken this relationship to the kissing stage, I steal another, though I'm not sure you can call it theft when the other person is a willing participant.

My body feels looser, my mind freer. "Dare Marquis fits you." It's nice to say it out loud.

"Weatherly."

"Yes?" I like his hands on me, the way he touches me with care—the brush of his knuckles against my arm, the scruff on his jaw against my chin when we kiss, the beat of his shoe tapping to the music against mine.

He cups my cheek, bringing me closer with a possessive pressure that makes me feel treasured instead of like property. "I just wanted to taste it on my tongue again."

My heart beats faster, so I suck in a soft breath before asking, "The whiskey or my name?" My name, I silently pray. *Please say my name.*

"You. All of you. I bet you taste sweeter than whiskey and would leave me drunk for hours after."

My body tilts toward him, moving of its own accord. I'm feeling a little possessive on my own right now, so I loop my arms around his neck. "After? After what?"

"Depends. How does Weatherly Beck like to be loved?"

My body is not my own. I'm all his. Here and now. I'm weak in the knees to his sultry seduction because hearing him talk is the best aphrodisiac. This will probably be my only night with someone like Dare. He's seducing, as I'm sure he's done many times before, and I'm his willing participant tonight. *One night, Weatherly. One night where I step away from propriety and playing by the rules. I deserve this.*

Sexy as it may be, it's still a question I can't answer. "I've never been loved properly."

Leaning forward, he whispers in my ear, "That's a damn shame."

His breath tickles my skin and turns me on. I'm roused by the way he looks at me—ready to devour me—and he has me wanting to love him in ways I've never been with a man. *At least for the night.*

I suck in a breath to steady myself. Good Lord, he has me turned inside out, and my mind stuck in the gutter. The music gets louder as the crowd screams for the next band. We both turn to look as the singer shouts into the mic. Dare turns back to me and opens his mouth, but before he has a chance to speak, I ask, "Do you want to leave?"

"You're reading my mind. Where do you want to go?"

He has my mind spinning and my body begging to be touched. The good girl is gone. He makes me want to be bad. Whiskey at night and coffee in the morning. His whore between the sheets and an angel after we're done? I giggle, not even sure what that means, but I remember Stascia saying that once. "My place?"

"All right, but I need to tell my band. Want to come with me?"

"Sure." Spending more time with him is the only thing I'm certain I want right now.

We only take a few sips of beer before he takes my hand.

His fingers are calloused, and my thoughts deviate to how they would feel scraping across my skin. Compared to the soft skin of my ex, I welcome the roughness and hold on to him tighter.

"Dare?" Between songs and in the middle of the crowd, his name is called. The British accent is easy to pick out above the noise of the bar.

Dare calls to the guy, "What?"

I recognize the other guy from the band, his body lankier but not by much. Still well-built and tall, he gets a lot of attention and seems to revel in it, smiling at the women in the audience as he works his way toward us. His eyes go from me back to Dare. "Coming with us?" he asks.

Dare glances at me, his grip tightening not enough to hurt but to maintain the hold, the connection with me. "I'm good," Dare replies. "Thanks for getting my gear. I'm heading out with Weatherly."

"Weatherly, huh?" The guy checks me out, and then adds, "I'm English, sweetheart. Nice to meet you."

"I picked that up from the accent. So cool."

He laughs. "No, well, yes. I am English, but the guys nicknamed me English."

"Oh. That's fun." God, I sound like my mother. Be cool, Weatherly. "Nice to meet you, too." Although he doesn't treat us like he knows what we're about to do, I feel it. *God, of course, he knows.* This probably happens all the time. Hot musicians. Groupies. Music. And alcohol. It's what stepping out on the wild side dreams are made of.

I catch a silent exchange between the two before English says what's on his mind. "Don't get into too much trouble."

Dare doesn't hide a thing when he looks at me. "Too late."

"I'm not bailing you out," English grumbles.

"You won't have to." Leading me to the exit, Dare adds, "Let's get out of here." No one would know we just met or that we shared our first kiss with a bar full of spectators. No, Dare doesn't hide that he's with me, his hand on my lower back as we reach the sidewalk.

Security is felt in my bones from the closeness. His proximity keeps my tummy wound tight in hopes of more of those kisses and just . . . well, more of everything with him.

I'm nervous and excited about what might happen, and something I've never felt before twists my insides. My fantasy is becoming a reality, so I keep my secret locked tight. Not for fear that he won't have sex with me if he knows I'm a virgin, but that he won't stay after. I'm not sure how I'll feel, but I don't want to feel alone.

I think he might be reading my mind this time because he asks, "We can get to know each other anywhere if you don't want to go home. A bar, restaurant, a coffee shop?"

Reaching the corner, we stop. Before he can speak, I kiss him. And then I kiss him again. But then he kisses me. Stepping apart, I poke his chest. "You are dangerous for me."

"I feel like you're a lot more dangerous for me."

Coming back together, we wrap our arms around each other. "Then we'll be dangerous together." I kiss him and deepen it. Right there on a dirty street corner for everyone to see, I kiss this drop-dead gorgeous man as if I bought the rights to those delectable lips.

When we catch our breath, he leans his forehead against mine. "Where do you want to go?" He scans the street and then turns back to me. "I don't have a car here. I rode in the band's truck. We can catch a cab?"

"I'll get us a rideshare." I pull out my phone and tap the app. "Two minutes."

"Two minutes can fly by when you're playing a song—"

"Or feel like an eternity."

His hand comes around me and pulls me closer by the ass. *Hot. Hot. Hot.* "I was going to add or enough time to kiss you again."

"Just enough time for that." I lift up on my toes and—

"Weather . . . Lee?" comes from the open window of the black SUV.

"That's our ride," I say.

Dare's passion-filled brown eyes sing his emotions straight to my heart. He pushes my hair back away from my face. I recognize the dilemma. I feel it too. But he doesn't keep the driver waiting. "Saved in the nick of time."

"You or me?" I ask.

"Depends how you look at it."

"I'm disappointed. I'd rather be kissing you."

Holding hands, we walk to the car. "I'll make it up to you. I promise."

He opens the back door for me, but I stop and turn back, fidgeting with the hem of his shirt. "Is that a promise or a dare, *Dare*?"

"Don't worry, babe." Stopping me before I slip inside the vehicle, he says, "It'll be everything you want it to be."

I can actually understand the unrestrained desire April has talked about so often. It's as though he has access to every nerve inside me and is playing me perfectly. In sync with my desires. *My needs.* He may be capable of doing that with any woman, but tonight, he's mine. So I remain planted right next to him in this SUV.

Dare's hand comes to rest on my bare knee. When I glance his way, he says, "C'mere, Weatherly." I move closer, drawn by the soulful sound of my name. His arm comes around me, and he says, "Why do I have the feeling that you're going to be the death of me?"

I've lost my damn mind and handed it to my hormones to control for a while. Am I going to have sex tonight? I want to. A thrill races through my body. I need to let go of everyone else's expectations and live for me. I want this. *I want him.* "Don't worry, babe," I reply, using his word. "I feel the same."

8

Dare

We don't travel far, six blocks or so, to the front of newer waterfront condos. I've never bothered catching the name of the high-rise because it fucked up the Austin skyline I loved so much growing up. The city is almost unrecognizable these days with the money and greed that built these towers to the clouds.

Shit. I glance over at her just as the car pulls to the curb. "You live here?"

Weatherly nods as she pops the door and gets out. When I don't jump out after, she leans her head back in. "Are you coming, Dare?"

"Yeah, I'm coming." I slide across the seat and tell the driver, "Thanks, man."

"No worries. Good luck," he says, chuckling.

We're not so sly. It's almost midnight on a Thursday night. Everything about Weatherly and me shouts hookup. Normally, that wouldn't bug me, but she deserves better than to be viewed through that lens.

Standing in front of the building, I look up, my gaze reaching the sky. "Do you live alone?" I realize how creepy that sounds after I say it, so I'm quick to add, "It's a nice building."

"It is, and I do live alone. It's not much. A small one bedroom, but it's home."

Opening the lobby door, we walk into a bright white modern lobby. We pass a twisted-up glass sculpture that's as cold as this building—no heart, no soul. It just exists because someone decided something needed to be here. It's too quiet for this hour. I prefer rowdy talk and energy this time of night, especially after a show.

The guard nods but doesn't say anything as we head to the elevators.

I'm still stuck on the fact that she called it "not much," so I ask, "You own it?"

"My parents own it." The button for the fifteenth floor is pushed, and we lean back in separate corners. I've got my eyes on her. The truth is, I just like to stare at her. An air of dignity mixed with insecurity flickers through her eyes, but then it settles into appreciation of what I think is the look of me too. I don't know why I enjoy that so much. Women always hit on me. I have my mother's dark hair and eyes, which she was always complimented for, and a hard cut to my other features. Chicks dig that.

That Weatherly likes me is different. I saw that other guy. He was soft in a lot of ways, white-collar ways that shield him from working for anything, much less muscle tone. I doubt she would, but if she ended up with someone like me, she'd be saved from those Sunday football parties full of beer bellies and ironing his socks for work the next day.

I love sports, but not at the expense of ignoring this

beauty for hours on end. But maybe that's not the direction her life will take. Fuck, she was given an apartment. "Must be nice." I don't shield her from the sarcasm.

She either didn't catch it or is choosing to ignore it. "It has been."

Sobering silence fills the elevator, but the door slides open. "We're here."

Following her down the hallway, she opens the door at the end and then drops her keys on a table in the entrance.

A "small one bedroom" doesn't fit the apartment I just walked into. "Whoa. That view." A wall of windows greets us ahead, and I go straight for the glass door.

"That's why I wanted it. Plus, as my parents pointed out, it will have great resale."

I slide the door open and step out on the large balcony. It's got to be at least fifteen by seven feet with a lounge chair near and a table for four on the other side. "You could have a party out here."

"I have." She comes out and glances up at me.

The view is great, but Weatherly . . . *Wow*. I lean forward, gripping the railing, and stare at her. She brought me here for a reason. I'm not sure if it's sex, though I hope it is. "Now that you got me here, what are you going to do with me?"

She tilts her head down, smiling under my gaze. "Um . . . I don't know how this works."

The worry that enters her eyes when she looks up isn't a welcome addition. So I caress her face. "How what works?" Though I know what she means, I want her to break through this sudden shyness and say it.

She turns to the city, seeming to mull over her words before speaking. It makes me wonder if she's always this calculated. What happened to the girl from less than an hour ago? Her spark is fading. That just won't do.

I'm about to help her out, but then she says, "I want to kiss you," surprising me again.

I take her arms and bring her to me. Running my hands over her shoulders and higher to caress her face, I say, "Well, since you said it so nicely, I'm all yours."

A smile reappears, bringing with it that confidence that had her kissing me earlier.

Her hands wrap around mine, holding onto me while I embrace her and kiss her under a moon that's close enough to touch from here. Our lips move slower this time, me dragging it out because I like the way she molds to me. When we part, her eyelids flutter open, and she takes a deep breath. "I'm glad you're here."

"Me too."

I've heard people talk about moments they always remember in life, the ones that bring smiles to their faces when recalled. This has that potential. So I hold her by the hips and begin to sway. Questions fill her eyes, but she plays along, wrapping her arms around my neck and dancing with me.

A sky full of stars.

A bright moon reflecting off her hair.

Trust in her eyes.

Yep. This is one of those moments.

I've never danced with a girl without music, but Weatherly feels different. She doesn't feel like a one-night stand, but I can't pinpoint what this is. The dance doesn't last long as we take a breath and step apart. I'd do it again, wanting more of it. *Of her.* Nodding toward the inside, she says, "Let me give you a tour."

I exhale when she goes inside and catch my breath again. I need to get my head on straight. I'm not drunk, but something's got a hold of me. I glance inside, wondering if it's the petite brunette waiting for me. I take another breath and join her because I'm curious where this tour will lead me.

The living room is decorated like something out of a fancy magazine at the checkout stand. Deep blue patterns against white backgrounds. Clean. Dark wood floors warm up the bright space. The kitchen is white with marble counters. Pure money. "It's really nice."

"Thank you. Can I get you something to drink or eat?"

"Sure. Beer if you have it."

Bending down, she grabs two bottles and hands one to me. I twist off the top and then trade her. We sip in silence, looking around the place. I break the ice. "What do you do?"

"I'm in school."

"College?"

"Law school," she replies casually and takes another drink. "Hungry?"

"Really?"

She shrugs. "I'm a little hungry."

I can't help but laugh. "No, I meant you're in law school. That's crazy."

"Technically, I'm graduating." She smiles, bumping past me as she opens the fridge. "I'm on the younger side. Twenty-three. Most of my classmates are twenty-five."

"I'm twenty-five."

She glances at me with a cocked eyebrow as if my face will give my age away. "People are usually surprised to hear my age."

"Your age doesn't surprise me." Chuckling, I add, "I've just never met a lawyer who wasn't assigned to me."

"Well, that doesn't sound good."

"If it matters, you're the hottest lawyer I've ever seen."

That whisks her smile back into place, exactly where it should be. "I'll take the compliment."

"How'd you get so ahead?"

"I already had a two-year degree from the University of Texas when I graduated high school. I was on an advanced placement path."

"And stayed. Impressive."

"I'm a total geek. I skipped a lot of parties to study instead. Do you like peanut butter and honey, or I can make avocado toast on sprouted oat bread? I've been dieting, so I don't have much."

"I don't know what that is, so I'll stick with the PB and H. Studying doesn't make you a geek. It makes you smart. Every reporting period my mom would get a note that I could be someone if I just applied myself. Be someone . . . I always fucking hated that phrase. As if I'm less if I didn't take the path they chose."

Her eyes go wide. "Clearly, they never heard you play or sing. You're amazing."

"Guess bars downtown weren't their scene. Though I ran into my Spanish teacher once at a show my senior year. She was with her friends and drunk off her ass. Kept buying me beers and hitting on me. She was only twenty-two and fresh out of college, but I wasn't going to be the one to ruin her career."

"My science teacher sophomore year offered me private tutoring at his house." Stopping, she stares at the cabinet in front of her. "I had straight A's in the class, sooooo, yeah."

"Fucking creepster." I wash my hands, knowing I don't want to drag the bar into her pristine world, and then lean against the small breakfast bar. "Why are you dieting?"

Her gaze slides my way before she focuses back on the sandwiches. "No reason," she replies quietly.

I learned a long time ago that women will let you know what's on their minds if they want you to know, so I don't push her on the subject. Instead, I stand next to her and grab the honey bear container. "It's been a long time since I've had honey." My mom loved peanut butter and honey sandwiches. I don't think I've had one since she died.

"I was never allowed to have peanut butter sandwiches as a kid, so they've become a favorite for me now that I do the shopping. Do you prefer jelly?"

"Honey is good. I swear all I ate were peanut butter sandwiches." I laugh. "Sometimes, I had butter sandwiches, and if we had extra bills to pay that week, I just had bread."

With a peanut butter-coated knife in her hand, she angles her body my way. "Plain bread?"

Nodding, I say, "You know, I never thought that was weird until now."

"I'm sorry. I wasn't judging you."

"I didn't think you were. I just never remembered about the bread until now."

Looking back down at the sandwiches, she says, "Honey."

"Yeah?"

She starts giggling. "I meant the bread is ready for honey."

"Fuck." I start laughing too. "Yeah, of course." I zigzag honey all over two of the slices. She slaps the sandwiches together and hands me one. "Happy eating." We tap our crusts together and take a bite.

"What is your favorite food?"

"Probably burgers. I'm not a complicated guy. You?"

"Mexican food." She holds her sandwich in front of her and sighs. "I could eat tacos and sandwiches every day, but tortillas and bread go right to my hips."

"You have nice hips."

"Because I don't eat tacos much." She laughs, but it's lacking humor.

"If tacos and sandwiches make you happy, who the fuck cares about a few pounds? You're small as it is."

Like it's Christmas morning, her whole expression lights up. "You think I'm small?"

"Do you think you're big?" I finish my sandwich and dust my hands on my jeans.

"I don't know anymore. I've lost perspective."

I bet that douche messed with her head. Keep her down while he fucks around, hoping she'll stay with him. Fucker. I could beat his fuckface right now for that. I touch her chin and angle her my way. "Listen to me." She looks me right in the eyes, making my throat go dry. As if I didn't think she was beautiful before, her looking at me like I hold the keys to her world is about to do me in. "If I do nothing else tonight, you're going to know how beautiful you are."

She's pretty darn cute with a little honey stuck to the side of her mouth. I'm tempted to tell her, but when she lifts up and kisses me, I steal it instead. It's not the honey that tastes so good. It's her. When she lowers back down, she whispers, "Thank you."

The heat has cooled in the kitchen, but there's still some lingering between us that keeps me glued to her. "Thanks for the sandwich. It was good. When I make them at home for the band, nothing. If I cook a meal, though, I suddenly have three best friends. Not that they aren't already, but yeah, you know what I mean."

"I do. I often eat alone, to be honest. My girlfriends are more into cafes and restaurants, whereas I feel less stressed generally at home since I'm always studying. I cave once a week, though. Figure it's good to get out."

She hasn't finished her food but starts to clean up, so I step in. "Let me."

"It's okay. You're my guest." After rinsing the knife, she drops it in the silverware basket in the dishwasher. I put the other things away from where I saw her retrieve them.

With the kitchen clean again, she heads for the bedroom. "Make yourself at home. I need to get these shoes off. My feet are killing me."

I catch her in the living room before she disappears. "I like the shoes if that makes a difference."

When she turns back, her smile isn't laden with intentions, but relaxed, the comfort of home settling in. "It does."

"Want help?" I lean against the side of the couch, finding the curiosity and allure in her eyes utterly captivating. She comes to me. "Lift," I instruct.

Her shoe rests on my thigh, and I slowly pull the yellow ribbon, unlacing it from around her and letting them flutter free. I hold her ankle and look up. With her gaze fixed on my hand, her breaths seem heavier with each exhale, her lips parting.

Dropping the shoe, I rub her foot, and then work on the other. A peep show of thigh exposed as her skirt balances across her smooth skin. I like her eyes, her trust, and her comfort level with me. I'm not willing to risk losing that by detouring away too long.

For a second, I don't recognize myself. I'm not an asshole to women, but I appreciate them, usually several times over in a night. She turns me the fuck on, but I can't bring myself to rush it with someone so graceful, so delicate.

Delicate—her ankles, her touches, and the sweet glances she thinks she's stealing. The whole situation needs to be handled with care, or we'll end as a wasted opportunity.

Opportunity. I'm not sure what that suggests, but I don't

want to lose it. I take off the other shoe and then look at her standing barefoot before me. Tan legs. Reddish-pink dots her toes. I run my hand over the tops of her thighs before leaning back to take a full assessment of her. "You're a lot shorter than I thought." *Delicate.*

A shrug accompanies a little laugh as she playfully pokes me in the chest. "You're just tall."

"I guess."

"Anyway, I'm not that short. I'm just shorter than you."

"I'll give you that."

She moves in closer. I welcome this kind of invasion of my personal space as she rests against me, looping her arms around my neck and tilting her head to look at me. "What else will you give me?"

The sexual energy between us flares. I'm not embarrassed by what she can already feel I'm willing to give. We're both adults, and I can't hide my body's reaction to her, but these jeans are getting tight. "Whatever you want." Dipping to the side, I kiss her neck. "You just have to tell me."

When I lift up again, her smile returns—confidence shaping it. She kisses me, her body moving against mine. "What do you want, Weatherly?"

"I want you, Dare."

9

Dare

AT SHEP'S, I knew full well she wasn't a one-night fuck. I don't even want it to be quick and duck out. Clearly, I haven't thought this through.

"*I want you, Dare.*" Weatherly's words ring out like music to my ears.

My dick has been hard since we walked in, but damn, it's painful now. As much as I'd like to move this into the bedroom, selfishly, I want more of her first. "Let me see you."

"You're seeing me."

I straighten her hips and watch as the realization of what I want dawns on her face. A little space is put between us; enough for me to take her in from those bare feet to that bottom lip her teeth are troubling. It's the first time I've seen uncertainty reach her features. Shyness, sure, but not uncertainty. "Don't worry, babe. I'm going to have my hands all over you soon enough, but I want to get a good look at you first."

Fidgeting with the bottom of her dress, she tugs at the hem. "What do you see?"

The fabric isn't glued to her, but the material is light against her skin. She's a vision, an angel in the flesh. A woman like this doesn't need her clothes to get attention. She does a damn fine good job all on her own. The dress is fitted at the waist and the hem stops mid-thigh. Her beauty is a thief of the un-redeeming kind, making me feel unworthy in her presence. "You're so fucking beautiful."

I reach down to cup the back of her legs, slowly sliding my hands under her skirt. Getting a good hold of her ass, I pull her to me. "Damn, girl. You feel as good as you look. You have me wondering if you taste just as sweet."

"You tell me," she says, squaring her shoulders. "You've kissed me."

Honey.

She tasted like honey every time I've had the pleasure of kissing her.

I kiss her again, dragging the tip of my tongue over the plushness of her bottom lip. I speak against her parted lips. "I wasn't talking about your mouth."

Her body shivers under my touch, her eyes closing as she presses that sexy mouth to mine and kisses me this time. With a satisfied sigh, she leans back to look at me. She finds my hands and pulls me toward the bedroom. One of those perfectly polished eyebrows goes up, and that grin I'm sure gets her whatever she wants on the regular is aimed at me. "Let's find out," she replies.

I'm grabbed by the front of my shirt and tugged through the doorway. Our mouths crush together, our bodies grinding against each other. I'm not just tall but hard for her. I give her all six foot three of my solid muscle when I spin us around. Anchoring my hands above her head, I pin her with my hips and my lips.

The back of my shirt is invaded as her hands hold me to her. Our lips part, and I cup her face, tilting to the side to kiss every inch of her swanlike neck. "Dare," she breathes into my ear, "I want you."

"I want you, too. God, so much." She's the reward I don't deserve but will savor for every second I have her. I bend down and lift her into my arms, but when I turn around, I don't make a move.

Plush bed, lots of pillows, jewelry hanging from a little stand on a dresser that resembles a tree. Clean and pretty. *Expensive.* Just like Weatherly.

While I have to share a run-down house with the band, she's over here living in luxury. These west side girls sure know how to live the high life. *We're miles apart, physically and in stature. Why does she want me?*

I'm too dirty for this space, too dirty for her. Dried sweat from the show sticks to me as I stand in a room unlike any other girl's room I've been in. I don't want to mess it up. I set her down carefully, but I hate that I've put doubt in her eyes, or that she has to ask, "What's wrong?"

This isn't a world I'm used to, making me feel out of place.

I'm not good enough.

I'm not rich enough.

I'm not worthy.

That shit from my childhood still hangs around the recesses of my brain. "I'm dirty." I reveal only a small fraction of my confession. "I'm afraid to touch anything." I look at her light-colored dress, the fabric so thin that if it got wet it would be see-through. "Including you." I hold her hips and then push to put space between us. "I need to shower."

"I like you touching me. I like dirty," she says, rubbing against me. "We can be dirty together." She's trying so hard that it's difficult to justify why I feel she's out of my league.

I don't want to disappoint her, so I kiss her, giving her what she wants, giving myself what I crave. Her back is against the wall, and my hand finds its way under her dress. Sliding my hand between her thighs makes her purr and her body writhes.

Wet.

She's so wet that I stop taking my time and find her sweet promise land. The tips of my fingers are under the lace, and I'm met with soft curls. Her mouth is open as I kiss her breaths away. Nails dig into my shoulders when I pause. "Don't stop, Dare."

I'm not going to leave her hanging, but as much as I want her, to go deeper, I stop when I see how the moonlight floods in, highlighting her beauty. Everything about this woman is angelic, and here I'm taking her like I'm the devil incarnate. "I played a show at a bar that I wouldn't take you to if you were mine much less spread the germs all over that white bed."

"I like that bar, and the sheets are fine." One of her hands is against my chest, keeping the connection. "You can take a shower if you'd like, but you don't have to for me."

"I want to for you."

Pulling that lip under her teeth, she looks me over, and then says, "We can shower together?"

Where did this goddess come from? She'll have me sinning before I realize what crime I committed. I said I was her daddy's worst nightmare, but with her, I wonder if I don't have to be.

I walk across the room, needing the distance to clear my

head and to be out from under her enticing floral scent. It's pretty like her. She's too easy on the eyes. I need space to think, so I start pacing. "What are we doing?"

She smiles. *So fucking innocent.* "I thought we were going to make love."

"Make love?" My eyes practically bug out. "Love doesn't factor in with the physical."

"Okay," she says, her gaze heading toward the opposite side of the room. Lowering her voice, she asks, "What do you call it? Sex?"

"Fucking. You can say it, Weatherly." We can keep this lighter despite the heaviness of the connection between us. This is just another night. She's just another girl. I repeat it, trying to feel the meaning, but the words don't sink in, so I fight them instead. I crack my neck, my shoulders tensing, feeling these walls closing in on me. "Call it what it is because if you're wanting something from me, it won't be love. I don't make love, babe. I fuck. Let's not pretend it's anything else by hiding behind sweeter words."

My words knock the wind out of her sails. It's best this way. Girls like her don't date guys like me. I'm a fun distraction from her aspirations. Scoring an M.R.S. from some country club fuck like that douche earlier tonight has probably been drilled into her head since she was a little girl.

Her chest deflates as she stares at me. I'm taken aback momentarily by the icy glare before she thaws and the smile that reached her eyes earlier disappears. She stands, keeping me in her sights as she moves toward the bathroom, but she doesn't leave. "I thought we'd have a good time and . . ." She shrugs. "I don't know. I'm not good at this."

"Good at this? What's this, Weatherly? Sex with a stranger, revenge for catching your boyfriend fucking some other girl, bragging rights for bagging a singer? What do you want from me?"

Anger flickers through her eyes, but she steadies her emotions. Must be the lawyer in her.

I take a breath to calm down, and then say, "I get it. This was good under the guise of dimmed lights and a busy bar."

"But changed since we came here? I'm confused. I don't want anything from you." A furrowed brow, closed eyes, and the way she pinches the bridge of her nose reveal the war inside her head. Exhaustion replaces the other emotions. "I thought we were having fun, that you were feeling the same thing I was, but clearly you're not." She moves through the living room into the kitchen where she dropped her purse on the counter. "I'll call a car to take you home."

What the fuck am I doing? My ego doesn't get bruised easily, but damn does this place intimidate me. But she's done nothing wrong. Everything she's done is right, so right. "I don't want to leave."

"Then what do you want?" Our eyes stay fixed on each other, softening the tension. She cocks an eyebrow in challenge, causing me to smile.

"You're going to make a good lawyer."

That elicits a grin of her own. Setting her phone down, she rests against the counter. "I think we came here full of fire and . . ." She blushes. "Did the flames burn out?"

"God, no. I've never wanted anyone more." I just wanted more from her than anyone else before. Running my hands through my hair, I move to the sliding door again. With my fingers woven together at the back of my head, I stare out into the night, but then catch her reflection in the glass. When I see sadness take hold of her, my arms fall to my sides, and I turn around. "I'm not used to doing sweet and gentle, but for you, I want that."

I go to her and caress her cheek. "I should have gotten you off, but if you want to call it a night, I'd be happy just to see you again."

"You would?" she asks with a shake to her voice as she stares at my chest.

"Sure, I would." I lift her chin. She's been dancing between sweet and sexy all night, and it's genuine, not an act. It's been a long time since I met anyone not tainted by life, but here she is, standing before me like it's possible to wrangle the sunrise and share the hope that a new day brings. "Any guy would be lucky to take you out on a date."

"Under all that bravado, you say some pretty nice things."

Thinking about her apartment, the way she's dressed . . . for fuck's sake, she's going to be a lawyer. She's welcomed me into her private world so freely. Gave me her trust without asking anything in return. That's not something I'm ever given without conditions, but she just did. I kiss her cheek and then her lips because she's hard to resist, but also because she deserves the beautiful life she's living. "You deserve nice things."

"Look around you, Dare. I have *nice* things, but they don't define me. I'd like to see you again. We can take things slow if you want. I promise I'm not clingy. If you want to leave tonight or stay until morning, it's up to you."

"That simple, huh?" I reply.

"That simple. No strings attached."

"A plan laid out like a business deal." I chuckle while shaking my head. "You don't understand," I say, grinning. "I want to stay, but I want to get to know you before we head back into that bedroom again." I stop stressing about how I didn't shower before the show or that my clothes haven't been washed since last week. I slide my hands down to hold her by the waist. "Let me take you out on a date, Weatherly?"

I'm rewarded with one of her smiles that feels more like a prize. "I didn't take you for the charming type."

"Don't confuse me for those guys you're used to. I don't hide behind titles, résumés, or lies. I'm not the charming kind. I just tell the truth. But so you know, parents don't usually approve of me, and girls who usually hang around only want one thing from me. I'm not saying this to scare you off. Quite the opposite. I want you to know what you're getting into."

"If you were that bad, we'd still be in that bedroom."

I shrug. "What can I say? You caught me at a weak moment. I don't want screw this up."

Lifting up on her toes, she cups my face. "You're doing everything right." Holding me to her, she kisses me. When she lowers back down, she adds, "You want to take me on a date?"

"I do. Would you like to go out with me?"

She nods. "When?"

"How about Sunday or Monday? I have a show on Sunday night, so it would have to be late. I'm free all Monday, though."

"Monday works better for me. I have my exam on Monday, so I'll be studying all weekend before then."

"It's a date." Three words I never expected to come out of my mouth, but it's what she deserves. She's not a fuck and run. Her genuine sweetness, her enticing sexiness, her hidden passion—I want it all, but I won't rush it. It's as though something is causing me to press pause, knowing it will be worth it. And somehow, pressing pause never felt so right. So good. Maybe she's the fresh start I've been searching for.

It's a date.

10

Weatherly

I WAS ready to give him the whole kit and caboodle. My V-card on a silver platter. Dare Marquis didn't want that . . . *just that*, I should say. He set a ground rule, which still makes me swoon. He wants to get to know me before we make love —*fuck*—whatever it is we're calling it.

A date is an unexpected turn of events.

A plot twist I never saw coming.

Can he be dreamier?

He just proved he can't.

As much as I thought I was ready to take the next big step, and I'm not referring to earning my law degree, I'm not. At least not on a one-night stand. As for a two-night stand . . . that's a different story altogether. If he so much as kisses me like he did tonight, I'm afraid I'll pounce.

What he called dirty, I call sexy as all get-out. I wanted to lick that sweat right off his body, ab by hard ab. I may not have seen those muscles of steel, but I felt them a few times, and he let me. For someone who seems to enjoy my hands on him, I'm not sure how he restrained himself. I was practically feeling him up.

Dare Marquis is an anomaly.

I thought for sure he would be all into de-virginizing me. Unvirginizing? *Hmm.* I'm not sure what the proper term would be, but fucking works, too. Yet *he* put the brakes on. I guess I should have asked what it was that made him want to get to know me better when everything was heading toward action in the bedroom. Or so I thought.

Checking my phone for messages, I find I don't have any. I guess the girls are mad at me. I'm not up for playing by their rules these days.

I take my phone out to the balcony, rest on the railing, and smile seeing his number programmed in. Seems silly, but I love that we exchanged numbers and set a date. I call him.

"Hi," he says, his husky voice making me want to cradle the phone to body parts other than my ear just to experience what this man's voice can do.

"Hi. Maybe I am clingy." I laugh out loud nervously, waiting to hear how he reacts.

"Nah. It doesn't make you clingy if I'm glad to hear from you."

Looking at the cars on the street below, I hold the phone a little tighter and smile. "You are?"

"Yes, babe."

"I'm glad to hear your voice, too."

I also hear a slow and heavy breath come through as if he's relaxing in the car he caught home. His friend came to pick him up since it seems we don't live too far away from each other. "I'm regretting leaving," he says with a low chuckle.

"I am too. Do you want to come back?" Hope rings in my ears so I know he can hear it as well.

"As much as I'm tempted, you need to get some sleep so you can study this weekend. I'm going home to get some sleep because I'm no good to anyone right now."

I don't let my disappointment be heard so easily. "I know you're right."

"But it feels wrong."

"Yeah," I reply, keeping my voice lower, our conversation more intimate. "It does."

"Is that why you called?"

After so many highs tonight, a taste of what's to come, I say, "I don't want to be alone."

There's a brief pause, and then he says, "I can come back."

"How far away are you?" Sounding too eager, I confirm that I have no game.

"Almost home."

Toeing the glass wall below the railing, I say, "I'm sure it's a hassle."

"None at all." I love that he doesn't pause to mull it over at all. He adds, "I'll be there in twenty minutes."

Twenty is too long. I should have never let him leave. "Twenty? I thought you were close?"

He chuckles. "I am, but I want to make a stop first."

"I'll leave your name at the front desk."

"See you soon, babe."

"See you soon."

I'd taken off my belt earlier, so the wind whips around my legs, causing my dress to balloon. Despite the warm night, I decide to take a bath. My calves ache from the wedges I wore, and I want to get clean. Nothing's going to happen, but it will feel good to be clean just in case.

After unlocking the door, I start the water for the bath and then pour a glass of white wine. I return to the bathroom, twist my hair up, and check the water temperature. While it continues to fill, I dig out a T-shirt and a pair of boy short underwear, setting them on the bathroom counter. I don't think the small booty shorts will be a problem. He felt the curve of my ass, but the shirt will cover it anyway.

I pour my favorite bubble bath into the tub and then step in. My muscles ease under the warm water as the scent fills the air. I slink down a little farther and rest my head back. Heated kisses and Dare's hands on me fill my memories and tighten my tummy. I would have had sex with him tonight.

Will I still? He has me so wound up that I may not be able to keep my hands off him.

I slip my hand under the water, knowing what I need—to get off. He had me so close just from a simple touch. *God, so close . . .*

Fifteen minutes means I need to be quick. As the memories of Dare's hands on me come flooding back, I anchor my feet against the curve of the tub and use the resistance to work myself into a tight coil.

Panting breaths.

Dare—pressure for my pleasure while stroking me.

Quickened hands.

Dare—fingertips slipping under the fabric and into my wet lips.

Frenzied little ministrations pull a moan from my core.

Dare—the roughness of his skin mixed with a tender look in his eyes as he explores my entrance.

"Ah," I let out, my heart beating fast and my breaths coming hard as my body shivers underwater. I exhale long and slow and then take the wineglass by the stem, relaxing back. I sip at first and then quench my thirst by finishing it. It's good to release some of the pent-up tension Dare's inspired in me. Especially since he's returning.

"Hi."

The glass spins loose in my fingers, but I manage to hold on to it despite jumping a mile high. I look back toward the door and see Dare leaning against the frame—all glorious ten feet of him. At least he is to me. "Hey," I reply, sitting up with the bubbles covering me.

He thumbs behind him. "You didn't answer, and the door was unlocked. Hope you don't mind me letting myself in."

"No. I left it open for you." Pushing off, he comes to the side of the tub. His swagger is backed by how his confidence, or maybe even cockiness fills his strides. His hair is wet, and he's wearing different clothes. "You changed."

"I showered."

Fluffing bubbles in my hands, I blow some at him. "I guess you don't want to join me then?"

A smile creases his cheeks. "If I get in there, it will get dirty real fast."

"But you showered?" One second passes before I catch his drift. "Oh. Yes, you're probably right."

Taking my glass, he finishes the wine. *Why is that so sexy?* "Want me to clean your back?"

"Do I want your hands on me again? Yes, and please." I move through the water slowly as the bubbles start to dissipate. With my legs bent, I wrap my arms around my thighs and rest my chin on my knees.

He sits on the marble side and takes a bottle of shower gel. Holding it to his nose first, he says, "Smells good."

"It's my favorite. Lavender." I close my eyes when his hands flatten against my back and rub, massaging my shoulders and down my spine. "Mmm. You're spoiling me, Marquis."

"I'm okay with that."

His hands are slick with soap and water, sliding against my skin. The tips of his fingers are so close to the sides of my breasts that I'm tempted to open up to let him have access. Having him bathe me feels so good, erotic even.

Taking it slow with him might be my hardest challenge yet. After he rinses me, he leans down and kisses the top of my head. My cheek comes to rest on my knees so I can get a look at him. "Why'd you come back?"

"Because you invited me."

"Then why did you leave in the first place?"

"Because I needed the space to think."

"And you got that space?"

He grabs the towel from the shelf and holds it wide open. "Too much when it comes to you. It's late. Let's get you to bed."

Even though he's facing me, he holds the towel far enough in front that when I stand with my back to him, my backside is covered. I wrap the towel around me and turn around. "And what are you going to do?"

"I'm coming to bed with you." He offers me his hand. When I take it, he adds, "To sleep."

I step out, but he doesn't make a move, so I land in his arms, which he wraps around my waist. Kissing my forehead, he then closes his eyes and takes a deep breath. "You smell amazing."

Since I'm positioned at his neck, I've been taking inhales of him as well. "You do too."

He exhales and moves to the door, leaving me dripping wet on the rug. "I'll wait out here and let you do your thing."

I nod just as the door closes. From the sight of him to his

scent, I practically become a puddle of my own right here on the bathroom floor. Good Lord, he makes me want to do crazy things.

Pushing down the crazy thoughts I'm having about ravaging him and feeding him while we lounge around naked, I brush my teeth and then get dressed. New messages light up my phone screen on the counter, catching my eye. They must be heading home and just noticed I never met up with them again. They didn't care earlier, so I don't mind leaving them waiting until tomorrow.

When I open the door, Dare's not in the bedroom, but a pale pink rose with beautiful fluttery petals is in my hello gorgeous mug on my nightstand.

Smiling to myself, I pick up the rose and hold it to my nose, letting the fragrance fill me. The scent matches my favorite perfume, which is the one my grandmother used to wear. I stick the stem back in the water and then find him on the balcony lying on the chaise.

"Come here," he says, eyeing me from my face to my bare legs.

Even without a lot of room on the chair, it's easy to snuggle against his large frame, resting my head on his chest and one of my legs on his. After his arm comes around me, I whisper, "Thank you for the flower. It's one of my favorites."

"I'm glad."

"When I was a girl, my grandmother had this huge rose garden next to the cottage where she lived on our property. You could smell them twenty yards from the house. She loved the old-fashioned doubles best. Like the one you brought me. I love their complications. All those petals blooming to be seen." I tilt my head up. "Where did you get it?"

"My roommate. Romeo has a small garden on the side of the house. He grew up on a farm in Marble Falls."

"I bet it's beautiful in Marble Falls."

"I've only been out there once, and that was in winter. They had winter crops but not the colorful stuff. His parents helped him set up the garden, and he inherited their green thumb." His breath is warm like his body when it hits the top of my head. "I think he grows flowers to save money when he wants to give them to a girl."

Giggling, I look back above the city, tracking a plane as it crosses the sky. "I must admit it does feel special. I've actually never received anything other than the no smell store-bought roses." His arms tighten just enough for me to cozy in again. "Thank you for making the effort."

"I've never done this with a girl."

"Held someone in a lounge chair?"

"Made an effort."

I close my eyes, listening to his heartbeat. "I'm the first?"

"Yeah, you are, Pepper."

I'm his first. I probably shouldn't like that idea as much as I do. But I realize that perhaps we were meant to be each other's firsts but in different ways.

11

Dare

EVEN IN THE DARK, my eyes have adjusted enough to see her smile in the moonlight as she hovers over me with her hands pressed to my chest. "We can sleep together." Falling back down in laughter, she adds, "Actual sleep."

"Just sleep," I repeat. I don't know why. Maybe for me. Maybe for her.

She pushes off to get up but then holds her hands out for me. "Come on."

In the bedroom, she climbs under the covers on the side of the bed where I left the rose on the nightstand. I come around the far side of the bed where she's left room for me. Before I start undressing, I ask, "You sure?"

"I'm sure."

I tug my T-shirt off over my head and toss it on the bench at the foot of the bed. Her eyes move over me, and I see her bite gently on her bottom lip. My shoes are toed off and my jeans come down. Wearing only boxer briefs, I lie down next to her.

The contrast of her hair against the white sheets makes it easy to see the outline of the strands fanned across the pillow. Her shoulders rest above the blanket while covering her from the collarbone down. She about killed me when she walked out in a T-shirt with the collar cut out. The gray shirt hung off one shoulder with smooth legs underneath.

Temptress.

I didn't bother to hide what I know she could feel beneath her when she laid down. The woman turns me on and lying here in a bed with her two inches away isn't helping my cause. I can be good. We can get to know each other. We should take it slow. How slow? "How slow do you want to take this?" I ask.

She bursts out laughing. "I'm so glad you said it. I've been wondering the same thing." Rolling onto her stomach, she props herself up on her elbows next to me. "I mean kissing can't hurt anything, right?"

"If there were rules, kissing wouldn't be breaking them."

Inching up higher, she says, "Definitely not breaking rules."

"It's like first base." Stopping close enough for me to roll over and kiss her, she smirks. *Seductress.* So I do as we shift to get more comfortable, which lands her half on top of me. I'm not complaining. Not one bit.

Our mouths are too busy to complain anyway, but my hands. Damn. I want to touch her all over, but I'm a good boy . . . for now. By how she's kissing me, our lips parting, our tongues caressing, little moans rumbling from deep inside her, she's eliciting my bad side.

My hand dips into the dramatic curve from her cotton-covered hips to the soft skin of her waist. I want to go higher, but I don't. I'll let her guide me, show me what she likes and what she wants. First base, I remind myself despite wanting to steal second.

Her knee presses between my legs, and our bodies start a dance of seduction. The softness of her legs tangling with the roughness of mine—hard and soft mingling.

This is foreign. I'm used to instant gratification, not building anticipation. Making out is not something I usually do, but with her, it feels good. I want to learn every ebb and flow of her body, her likes and dislikes, and to make her feel better than she's ever felt before.

Don't get me wrong. I always get my partner off, but it's going to be so much sweeter with Weatherly. Another one of her little moans encourages me to maneuver on top, kissing her harder, pressing my body to hers, and wanting to swallow every last sound, groan, and kiss she'll give me.

God, I could survive off the air she shares, her lips the way they mold to mine, and her hands hold me to her—pulling me closer as if that was possible. I come up for air and look into those big blue eyes to find the sky buried inside.

She relaxes beneath me, happiness shaping her face. I push wild strands of hair away from her face and continue to stare at her beauty. She mimics me by pushing my hair away from my eyes. "I told you I came back because you invited me, but that wasn't the only reason."

"Why did you come back?" she asks, staring into my eyes.

"I couldn't stay away." I could claim my confession was a way to woo her, but it's also the truth. I'm drawn to this woman. Deep down, my soul twisted the moment I walked out the door. I held the phone in my hand the entire way home, willing it to buzz in my hand. So when it did, I already knew I would return.

I have no regrets that I'm the one she's tangled up in instead of the sheets.

"Dare?" she whispers, "if those are the kind of lies you tell, I'll take them any day."

Emotions run heavy, our sexual tension running hot. I kiss her just because I miss her lips on mine. I miss that little moan and the way her hands feel possessive as she starts to knead my back like a kitten. *Fuck me.* I'm doing the one thing I said I wouldn't with her—*falling under her spell.*

"If we can't break the rules, then let's bend them." A hand slinks under the covers, and she gets a good grab of my ass. I return the favor. And when her knees butterfly open for me . . . it's more than a spell I'm feeling. I want her. So badly. "I always did hate rules."

My hips are moving of their own accord, my dick hard and wanting to bust through those little cotton underpants she's wearing. "Fuck." I push up and roll to my back annoyed as fuck at myself and cursing this damn taking things slow pact we made.

"What's wrong?"

"I'm not used to this."

Surprise reaches her features. "Making out?"

"Hanging out in a girl's bed, in this sense, is fairly new for me."

"So you've never had a girlfriend or stayed with a woman overnight?"

Lowering my arm, I drop it to the bed. "I have, but—"

"But?"

"I was going to say, but this is different."

Smugness creeps onto her face, but I'm happy to let her revel in the compliment. "How so?"

"I want to be here. I want to stay the night."

Reaching over, she caresses my face with such care as she runs the tips of her fingers from my forehead to my chin. "I'd like that."

We lie in silence, our gazes locked together as our fingers weave to become one hand. Bonded. Intensity fills the room, leaving no voids between us. She looks away first, and says, "I need water. I'll be right back."

While she walks away, I'm given a great view of that peach of an ass. *Goddess.*

As soon as she's gone, I swing my feet to the floor and dig my phone from my jeans. I have three text messages: two from chicks wanting to hook up and a third from English telling me to hit it and get back at a decent hour. A spot at the recording studio opened up tomorrow night, so we have to spend the day rehearsing.

She's not back yet, so I skip the chicks to reply to him.

Me: *What time for rehearsal?*

English: *Ten.*

Me: *I'll be there.*

Weatherly returns with two bottles in her hands. "Sorry about that. My friends had texted, wondering where I was. Since I didn't reply earlier, they kept texting. They're relentless. The only way to get peace was to reply." She hands me one of the waters.

Wrapping my hand around hers, she grins as her eyes go from the bottle to my eyes. "What'd you tell them?"

I catch her hesitation before she looks away to return to her side of the bed . . . because apparently, we're already that couple who has sides of the bed. The funny thing is it doesn't bother me. Do I want to be that couple with her? Do I want to be part of a couple at all?

"That I'm home. Safe and sound."

"What makes you think you're so safe?"

When I lie down, she cuddles against me, and I wrap my arm around her. Her head rests on my chest, palm over my racing heart, and with conviction, she replies, "Because I'm with you."

"And here I thought I was one of the bad guys."

"Never."

I hold her a little tighter, liking how her body fits to mine. Liking her so much.

I WAKE up to the sun reflecting off the lake. Grabbing my phone from the nightstand, I check the time. "Shit," I grumble. Why am I awake at eight a.m.? And why is the sun so fucking bright at this hour? I roll away from the window, dragging the pillow out from under me to cover my head.

Then I see the rose on the other nightstand and bolt upright. Holy shit. I'm at Weatherly's. But where is she?

I toss the covers off and look toward the bathroom for the sound of life inside. The lights are out in there, so I walk out of the bedroom, but my heart stops as fast as my feet when I do find her.

The T-shirt she wore last night hangs off one shoulder down to her elbow. Her hair is twisted in a messy knot on top of her head. Dark-brown rimmed glasses rest on her nose and a coffee cup in her hand. She sips as she rests her arms on the railing, lost in her thoughts.

The whole world can see her legs and that delicate skin of her shoulder. I'm tempted to cover her up, to bring her inside and make her get dressed, but the vision of her stuns me, rendering me speechless.

She takes another sip before catching me in her periphery. Fucking hell. Her smile beats any sunrise inspiring a new song.

I join her on the balcony, spinning her around so I'm pressed against the railing instead of the whole world getting a front-row view of her fine ass.

"Coffee?" she asks, relaxed in my arms.

"Definitely. I haven't seen this hour of day in a while."

"Lucky you. I didn't want to wake you, but I need to take a shower and get to school."

"Yeah, I have to get home. We're rehearsing today and have a studio booked tonight."

She takes my hand and we go inside. I watch as she pours me a cup of coffee. "Sugar? Creamer?"

"It's fine without."

After squeezing between me and the bar, she wraps her arms around my middle. Face-to-face, I kiss her. Weatherly tastes like the best morning I've ever had.

She has to go.

I have to go.

I set the mug down on the counter behind her and cup her face. "I wish we could stay."

Disappointment seeps into her eyes. "I do too."

"When will I see you again?" *Please say tonight.*

"I think we're back to Monday."

Nodding, I bring her into my arms and hug her. "I guess so."

With her head resting on my shoulder, she says, "If you want to come over after you leave the studio, you can."

"I'll be there until three in the morning."

"That's okay. Tomorrow's Saturday. We can sleep in."

And just like that, we made a plan.

"I'll be here."

Sharing coffee in the morning with a beautiful woman I

haven't fucked. Never had that. Yet she wants me here. I actually slept with a woman. *Slept.* It's a lot to think about before my brain is fully functioning, though, but I won't take the words back.

I'll be here.

12

Weatherly

Dare is hot!

Like really hot.

I'm burning up, but don't want to move a muscle. If he keeps sleeping over, I'm going to have to reconsider this down comforter. Although it's a lighter one, since I live in Texas, it's too much when I have him to keep me warm.

Two nights in a row have me feeling downright lucky to have this man in my bed. The way we've fallen into this habit so easily feels dreamy, feels right.

Should I be concerned that I'm already thinking of *we* instead of *me*? Probably, considering Lloyd and I dated, and I use the word dated loosely, for years, and I put him off sexually the entire time.

Things happen for a reason. I saw the signs, but I lost track of the destination. Under pressure to be perfect in school, my appearance, and to stand quietly by my man, I realize now that it wasn't the destination I lost track of. It was me.

Confidence feels great, just as Dare does. Better than Lloyd ever did.

Looking at the nightstand, I see my phone was blown up overnight with messages. Is it bad that I've been avoiding my best friends?

"Are you always this restless on Saturday mornings?" The husky morning voice coats my neck.

I giggle and turn in his arms. "I'd be lying if I said no. I have so much to do before I graduate that I don't get to sleep in much these days."

With rough fingers, he pushes away the hair that's fallen in my face. I don't have a lick of makeup on, but he looks at me like I'm a beauty queen, which feels liberating. *He likes me as I am.* I run my fingers over the stubble of his cheek and watch as he licks his lips. "So much is going on in that beautiful brain of yours. What's on your mind, Pepper?"

"My friends are mad at me."

"For what?"

"They say I ditched them."

Cozy morning coffee eyes look surprised. "You didn't ditch them. From what I remember, they left with that asshole and his friends."

"I know, but they already seem bothered by me trying new things."

He smirks. "New things like me."

With my hands tucked under my cheek, I smile. "I don't think they like this side of me. I've always been Switzerland between them and the peacemaker. It was so easy to let April have her way when I had bigger issues to worry about than where to brunch on Sundays."

"If it makes a difference, I like this side of you very much."

Touching his cheek, I say, "Thank you."

"Your friends will come around. Maybe they just need to get used to the idea that you have someone else taking up your nights lately."

"Is that what you're doing?"

"I can't give you much, but time is something I will happily spend with you."

I wish I could slip into sleep again just to make this moment last a little longer. Everything with him seems to be going a different speed. We talk about going slow, but I know it won't last. My emotions are attaching to him in ways I've never experienced before. I don't want casual when being open and feeling free, which he allows me, is who I've always wanted to be.

Is it insane to feel this strong of a connection with someone I barely know? Logically—*yes*. Emotionally—*no*. Emotions involve the unspoken, a vibe, a reaction that causes a physical change to occur. That's Dare. When I took the time to look into his eyes, I felt my insides rearranging in recognition, my heart saying I know you.

It makes no sense, but it's how I feel when I'm with him. This is new and so good that I now regret wasting time on a man who never made me feel alive like Dare does. "No one has ever slept over." I make my confession and close my eyes quickly, not sure how he'll react.

"But he was your boyfriend." Not a question but a realization.

"I think he was a boy who was a friend, who was not really what a friend should be, much less more than that."

He blows out a long breath. "I don't know why I said anything. I don't want to talk about him, especially when we're like this."

I promised him we could sleep in, and since he's only been here for five hours, he needs the rest. Despite needing to start my day, I like his arms around me too much to change a thing. "Everything else can wait. Get some rest."

He closes his eyes, and I start mentally ticking through my to-do list for the day. Number one—appreciate the fact that this man holds me like I'm his personal teddy bear. The thought makes me grin.

This is such a contrast to the pride he carries around when he's on stage. Even here, he doesn't share much or fill the silence with small talk. He says what he needs and seems to enjoy listening to me. I realize I have a voice in our relationship. Equals. That's something I'm not used to, but enjoy so much.

I THOUGHT he was fantastic in the evening and nighttime hours, but they hold nothing to seeing him in the morning light. Two hours later, he makes his way into the living room where I finally escaped after another hour of lying with him.

He looks tired, but his eyes still hold the warmth befitting the morning sunshine. I say, "You're very good looking."

He chuckles. "Thanks. Fortunately, I look more like my mom's side of the family than my dad's."

"Why fortunately?"

His eyes momentarily close, and he appears to want more sleep by how he rambles to the glass door. There's no peace in his movements. "That's heavy for this hour. Coffee?" He starts for the kitchen before I can get up from the table where I was reviewing my exam notes.

"Breakfast?" I ask, leaning against the opposite counter from where he's pouring his coffee.

He looks back at me, leisurely scanning my body. "Your

tits look fantastic in that white tank." He forgets the coffee and comes to me. Running his fingers under the top of the rolled down boxer shorts I'm wearing. A strip of my stomach is revealed, and he says, "You're sexy without even trying."

I'm trying, all right, because his attention is utterly intoxicating. I wrap my arms around his neck and peer up at him. "How was the studio session last night?"

"Not as productive as we'd like, but the album's coming along."

"Small progress is still progress."

"True." He kisses my temple. "I'm starved." I feel his craving against my leg. "You said something about breakfast?"

Ah. "Yes. Food. The thing *isssssss*, I didn't buy much yesterday. But Austin Java is around the corner, and I could really go for some blueberry pancakes."

His hand slides over my shoulder as if he just can't stop himself from touching me. I have the same struggle around him and run my hand over his abs. "You want pancakes. You get pancakes."

My phone buzzes on the counter behind me. Looking over my shoulder, he says, "If you have other plans today—"

"I don't. You're my plan today." Glancing over my shoulder, I see more messages from April and Stascia. "I should probably send a quick message, though."

"I'll leave you to it." He goes to the balcony and walks the length.

Picking up my phone, I read my messages.

April: *Meet for brunch?*

Stascia: *We miss you.*

They both betrayed me the other night when they chose to join Lloyd and his crew over hanging out with me. But it feels good to be missed, and at least Stascia isn't sweeping it under the rug like nothing happened.

Me: *Can't today, but we can meet this week and do some shopping for the party.*

Stascia: *I'm in. Just let me know when and where?*

Three dots wave on the screen for April and then disappear, causing me a little anxiety. What is she going to say? They appear again and then her message follows.

April: *It's good to hear you're alive. I've already had my dress designed and have a fitting this week. You can shop without me, but I'll plan a meal and tell you where and when.*

Sadly, it's been the opposite, which speaks volumes. It's clear she doesn't care what I've been up to but just wants to control our interactions. It's always been on her terms or nothing. She has to have the last word.

April: *I bet you've been bored out of your mind without us.*

I sneakily watch Dare return to the bedroom and gather his clothes in nothing but sexy boxer briefs. The muscles in his arms flexing together and that ass . . . I bite my lip as I watch him bend over. I could watch him all day and have plenty of material for lonely nights. So it's easy to let her dig slide right on by because one thing he is not is boring.

Me: *I'll text you after the exam. Have fun today.*

We get dressed and though I'm tempted to put on makeup, I don't. And Dare doesn't say a word other than, "You look beautiful."

I could melt onto the wood floor of my apartment, but I'm hungry, so we leave holding hands. Let me repeat —*HOLDING HANDS.*

I'm so choked up by the sweet gesture that I struggle to speak for most of the walk. The girl behind the counter turns around with a coffee cup in her hand. When she sees Dare, her face lights up. "Hi."

My hand is abandoned as he shoves his in the front pockets of his jeans. "Hey," he replies quietly.

I'd love to say I move to the side to look in the pastry case, but I can't take my eyes off this awkward exchange. I'm not saying I'm forgotten. I'm not at all. Dare is acutely aware of me standing there, but he seems to be at a loss of what to do. His gaze hits me and then the floor tiles when the other woman says, "I haven't seen you around in a while."

He replies, "I didn't know you worked here."

The light of excitement fades from her eyes when she looks my way. Going into work mode, she asks him, "Breakfast for two?"

"Yes," he says, "This is Weatherly." His eyes meet mine, and he takes my hand again. "This is Kayla."

"It's nice to meet you," I say, my etiquette kicking in despite the growing weirdness.

Dare references the chalkboard menu. "The pancakes, right?"

"Blueberry."

He leans against the counter casually as he reads the menu. "Two pancake platters. She'll take blueberry, and I'll have the buttermilk. A side of crispy bacon. Black coffee." He glances at me. "How do you like your coffee?"

She starts coughing, but it sounds like it grew from a scoff. God, I want out of here. "Café mocha, please."

He rubs my back and then pulls his wallet out. "I got this."

"Thank you." I turn toward the door. "I'll be outside."

My feet are heavy; the reality of being with a popular musician has caused the lightness of our walk here to evaporate. Dare Marquis is a "ladies' man" as my mom would call him.

I pick a table closer to the restaurant against the

windows. If I look in, I can see them locked in conversation. Since I left, they no longer keep up pretenses. With a sigh, I turn my attention to the street, watching Austin wake up for a new day.

Jogger.

Cyclist.

Delivery driver.

A mom and two kids.

There are plenty of people to watch, but I can't keep from looking back. Dare pushes through the door and sets a coffee cup in front of me. "Listen, Weatherly." He takes the chair to my right at the little square table. "I'm going to be upfront with you because that was uncomfortable for you and me."

"Who was she?"

"She's someone I saw a few times. It didn't go anywhere—"

"Clearly, she wanted it to."

"I didn't."

"Why? She's pretty. Seems nice."

Rubbing his chin, he looks down the street one way and then the other. "Nice enough, but we didn't have chemistry." The sun strikes his eyes, the brown bright and clear.

"Did you sleep together?"

His hand covers mine. "Not like we have."

"We literally slept."

"We have time for the other kind." I twist my wrist around so our fingers can fold together. "This looks bad, and I know it does, but I want you to understand the difference—"

"Between her and me? I'd like to know as well." I sip my coffee, liking the comfort of the heat.

"I can't erase my past, and I don't feel shame for it. We

didn't date. We hooked up. I'm not sure if it changes your opinion of me, but I hope it doesn't."

I set the cup down and spin it around. "Does it make it better or easier to swallow the truth if she was the one pursuing you? Because I was the one who came back to Shep's to see you. What does that make me?"

"Not the same thing."

"But why?"

"I went home with her because I knew what she wanted from me. A quick fuck. Nothing else. Nothing serious."

Is that what he thinks I want? Do I? Did I when I went back to Shep's on Thursday? I look away from him as I mull this over.

"Hey." He touches my chin. "I don't know what we're doing or what this is between us, but I like it. There's a connection I feel with you that I haven't felt in a long time. I thought about you all week, Weatherly, hoping you'd come back."

The door opens, and Kayla is carrying two plates. "I'll be right back," she says after she sets them down.

Hot pancakes are always a great distraction, but I'm losing my appetite sitting here waiting for her to return and leave again so we can continue this conversation.

She shows up with utensils, syrup, and the plate of bacon. "Can I get you guys anything else?"

"We're good," he replies, not quick to get her to go, but grateful. "Thanks."

She dashes in like she couldn't get out of here fast enough.

We're alone again, so I look at Dare. "It looked like you were arguing inside."

"I never made her any promises." Pouring syrup over the

pancakes, he keeps it flowing until it runs over the side of the stack.

"You make it sound so simple. She's upset, though, so she didn't get the no promises thing."

"She did. She wants to travel down memory lane, but it's a dead end."

There's a lump in my throat. "For everyone?"

"I'm here with you. I won't disrespect you by engaging in her fantasy to avoid hurting her feelings. If I do, I hurt yours, but I also have no intention of seeing her again, so I won't pretend."

He exhales. "I haven't seen her in three months or longer." Sinking the side of his fork into the stack of pancakes, he stops and looks at me. "I'm in a band that plays at least five days a week. It's easy to find me if you're looking." He shoves a bite in his mouth.

"She wasn't looking?"

"She just broke up with some asshole from San Antonio. She's looking for another hookup. That's all."

I find relief in his words. "So what you're saying is she's not heartbroken?"

"She's heartbroken. I'm a real catch." He laughs.

"Is that why she's upset?"

He's about to take another bite when he leans over our platters and kisses me. The sweetness of the maple syrup and his lips mixing together cause me to stay and savor him a second longer. He leans his forehead against mine when our mouths part, and whispers, "She's upset because I never had breakfast with her."

13

Dare

WE CRASHED after the heavy breakfast. *Or I did.* Squinting my eyes open hours later, I discover Weatherly's no longer in bed.

I sit up and look around, but she's not next to me. I find her in the other room studying at the table. Her head is propped on her hand, and she has her glasses on. It's an unexpected sight and so quiet that I almost feel like I'm invading a private moment. Much like I did when I saw her in the bathtub. I'll never forget how incredible it was watching her get off.

"Do you know how sexy you look in those glasses?"

Her smile shines before she turns my way. Waggling the temples behind her ears, she asks, "You think?"

Silly girl. "I know." Crossing the room, I see an open notebook and a thick book spread out before her next to a stack of various other books.

"Is that a fantasy of yours? The librarian or hot for the teacher?"

I rub her shoulders and kiss her head. "It wasn't before, but it sure the fuck is now." I come around and sit next to her. "What's this?" I ask, tapping the stack.

"Law books."

"I thought everything was online at this point."

"It is. My eyes get tired staring at a screen, so I like to read both online and on paper. How'd you sleep?"

"I don't know what that bed is made of, but it's like sleeping on a cloud."

Laughing, she sits back. "I'm glad you like it. I like it better with you in it." Closing her book, she stands to stretch her hands toward the ceiling.

My mom had the biggest heart of anyone I know. Even though her kindness was abused, she never stopped loving or living life. Weatherly reminds me of her in how open, how accepting she is, holding her heart in her hands to be stomped on. But I won't be that guy. I'm not my father.

"I like everything about you." That's not something I say lightly, but I say what I feel, opening myself up to her . . . to be hurt.

"I thought for sure I'd find some things about you that would be utterly intolerable." She comes to sit on my lap. Flipping my hair to the other side, she continues. "Your hair or that unshaven, scratchy face. The way you wear your sleeves rolled up in a way that insinuates cocky bastard."

My face sours, but my arms hold her right where she is. "I'm not sure I want to hear more."

"Your jeans are ripped, and I can tell that's not how they were bought. But you know what I thought would really send me running?"

"My face?" I joke. "You haven't knocked that yet."

"That's just it. Nothing about you is intolerable at all. You're quite the opposite. So damn—"

"Tolerable?"

"I was going to say sexy."

With a nod, I add, "I can handle sexy." I take her hand and turn it over to kiss her palm before rubbing it with the pad of my thumb. Skin as soft as her amazing bed, but strong when she holds me.

"You sure can," she replies, pressing her lips to mine and kissing me. "Thank you for having breakfast with me."

"Don't do that."

"What?"

"I told you that I didn't have breakfast with Kayla, and now you're thanking me for having it with you? No. Don't do that. If I'm here or having breakfast with you or anything else, it's for purely selfish reasons. So you don't owe me anything, Pepper. You got that? If I'm with you, it's because I want to be. So let's not twist this around like you're the lucky one. You're not." I kiss her palm once more. "I am."

Her expression softens. "You think you're the lucky one?"

"Brains and beauty. The full package." I set her on her feet. "But you need to study, so I'm going to get out of your hair."

"I like you in my hair."

I grin, feeling as high as this apartment is in the sky. Standing up, I lift her chin to take in her gorgeous face. "Where'd you go to high school?"

Her head tilts to the side, her eyes bright from the daylight that floods this place. "Where did that come from?"

"Curious." I shrug. *Truthfully, I want to know everything about her.*

"I want to know everything about you."

Running her hand over my chest, she pats it over my heart. "Catalyst Prep. Where'd you go?"

"Thompson East. Our worlds couldn't be more different, but somehow, we collided in this universe." I kiss her, knowing it might be the only time I get to for the rest of the day. Our tongues mingle, and our hands roam.

When we get a quick breath, she whispers, "Stellar collision," and then kisses me.

"That's what we are." Touching her face leads to her shoulders and then lower. I can't help it. I want her so fucking much. When she rubs against me, I slide my hands under her shirt, my dick aching from being this close. "You turn me on, babe."

"I don't want you to leave."

I pull away, our fingers the last to part. "That's why I need to. You need to study for your exam, and I need to get some stuff done before the show tonight."

She follows me to the bar where I dumped my keys and wallet last night when I tried not to wake her. I scoop them up and stuff them in my pockets.

We hold hands to the door because I'm not as ready to leave as I sounded before. Looking at her—an angel ready to sin—her body, her eyes, her lips draw me to her like no other ever has. *How can someone be so addictive?* I take a risk and make a move. "Instead of us making a habit of asking when we'll see each other next, why don't we just see each other?"

"See each other around?" she asks. "Or see each other every day?"

"I'm liking the sound of every day and tonight."

There's that pretty smile. She moves her hair over one shoulder and angles her hips toward me. "Tonight sounds good."

"Then it's a plan. I'll come over after the show."

"I'll leave your name on the guest list and the door unlocked."

Chuckling, I say, "That's my line." I wiggle her by the hips. "If you ever want to come to a show, you can. Just tell them your name, and you'll get in."

"I'll be on your guest list?"

"Every time."

There are no more words. She just moves into my arms, wrapping hers around me, and we stand there in an embrace. It's been a long time since I've felt safe in someone's arms, but I do in hers and hope she feels the same. I kiss her forehead and back away. Facing her the entire way to the elevator, our eyes stay on each other. She's definitely someone I want to wake up to for more than two days. "If I don't go now, I'm not going. Study. Make me proud on that exam, Pepper."

"I will."

As soon as I turn to punch the button, I hear her say, "Hey, hero?"

"Yeah?" I ask, laughing.

"Make me proud on that stage. Okay?"

I smile. That's something my mom used to say to me when I went to school. *Make me proud, Robert.* No one has said that to me in years, and I want it. I want to make her proud.

"You got it, babe."

SWEAT RUNS DOWN MY NECK, trekking beneath my shirt and down my spine. I finish out the song and yank the cord from my guitar. Passing English, I say, "It's hot as fuck in here." Fuck it. I set my guitar on the stand and hop off the stage.

Cutting across the bar to the back, I signal to the bartender where I'm heading.

Because the other band canceled at the last minute, we were asked to play two sets tonight. The money isn't bad, though the crowd is lackluster. I'm glad it's a flat fee and not based on the cover charge.

Dirt at my feet. Oaks overhead. There are worse places I've played. Standing outside isn't much cooler, but at least I get an occasional breeze.

Romeo comes outside, twirling his sticks in his hands, and parks himself on a bench I wouldn't deem safe to sit on. He doesn't seem bothered, so I'm not. "It's hot in there. We get it. We're all fucking hot, but it's good money, Dare."

"So what you're saying is that I can't have a fucking minute to myself?"

"You can gripe all the fuck you want, but we've played this shithole a dozen times, and you got through it. What gives tonight?"

I lean against the trunk of a tree. "Do you ever get tired of this?"

"What's this, Dare?"

"The struggle and not going anywhere."

"Isn't that why we're here? To get somewhere. To show the audience who we are, to play our music for a living? Weren't we recording until three in the morning last night to get somewhere? Since when was playing our music not getting anywhere?"

Resting my head back, I know what the issue is, and it's not the Texas heat even though that does fucking suck. It's Weatherly.

Thinking about her pristine place, high style in a high-rise I couldn't afford in my wildest dreams. Even when her hair is a mess, she fits right in there.

But do I?

She acts like I'm something special, but she'll find out soon enough that I'm nothing more than an asshole who can't take her out like she deserves, like she's used to. "Fuck!" I push off and walk a few feet away. "Why am I being such a pussy over this?"

Romeo looks confused but is smart enough to let me work it out on my own. Lennox comes outside followed by English, and they're both drinking beer. After handing us each a bottle, English says, "It's fuggin' hot as Hades." Just when I think I'm used to his accent, he starts drinking, and it gets thicker than ever.

Lennox drags a chair over and sits. "What's with the mood?"

Romeo laughs. "He's having an argument with himself. Probably best if we leave him to it." He stands to leave but pats me on the shoulder before he goes inside again. "Good luck. Clearly, you need it." His laughter fades as he sidles up to a group of pretty girls drinking wine nearby.

"Very funny." I call to the group, "Never trust a guy named Romeo." That gets a fluttering of laughs, the ladies liking the attention.

English lights up, watching us from a few feet away. He usually isn't one to get involved in petty shit, but sometimes, he just can't help himself. He exhales a smoke circle above his head, and asks, "What are you going on about?"

Lennox snaps, "When Dare's in a bad mood, we're the ones who suffer."

I glance at Lennox, surprised by his irritation. "You coming to get your digs in?"

A hard glare hits me, and he narrows his eyes. "We've all got problems, man. Some of us are just better at controlling our reactions. I'm not in the mood to cater to your attitude.

It's boiling tonight. So fucking what?" He turns to leave but stops when he gets to the doorway leading back inside. "Remember when it didn't matter how hot it was? When we weren't so self-involved that just playing your guitar was enough?"

When I don't reply, he looks back at me. "You've got to find the drive inside. It's the only way to survive."

I'm not even sure we're talking about the same thing at this point.

English stubs his cigarette into the dirt. "If this is about that west side chick, I'm gonna be pissed."

"Why would it be about her?"

"Because I'm not blind. I saw how you looked at that high and tight body of hers, willing to fight her battle." He crosses his arms over his chest. "I'm not saying you wouldn't help a damsel in distress. I'm just saying she didn't need your help, but you were right there in her business. What gives, Marquis?" I don't answer fast enough for his majesty, so he fills in the rest while shaking his head. "Fuck. Tell me you're not getting attached to this chick. Now is not the time. We're almost finished with the album. Tonight gets us over the halfway point. Don't get distracted by great tits and ass."

"What if they're really great? Can I then?" I start laughing.

He doesn't . . . at first, but then he does. I knew he'd come around. After a heavy sigh, he says, "We're so fucked. How much time have you spent with her?"

"Not enough."

"Well, that 'not enough' is more than we can spare. Set it aside for a few hours and get back in there." He starts laughing. "You sucked on the repeat. Hope you aren't that bad with your girl."

"Fuck you." I flip him off but laugh alongside him as we return. It's hard to stay mad when they make so much sense.

Lennox and Romeo return to their spots on stage and are ready by the time I'm plugged back in.

When I step up, I adjust the mic stand and turn back. "Sorry—"

"Oh God, he's going soft on us," English groans, bringing the humor. "Shut the fuck up and play like we know you can. That's apology enough."

We've said our mantra since our first gig, so I'm not going to stop now. "Are we men, or are we heroes?"

"Heroes," they say loud enough to catch a few sideways glances from backstage.

"Fuck yeah, we are. Let's show 'em." Stepping up to the mic, I count in, "One. Two. Three. Four."

14

Dare

My hands move on instinct. Despite the lights shining in my eyes, I step up and start singing. For three minutes, I become someone else. In three-minute increments, I'm who I'm meant to be.

The Heroes have a ticket to the top. Our band has paid their dues ten times over, and we own every venue we play. With our name on the marquee, the place has filled up for the second set. It's not only a sea of girls here to watch the hottest band in town, but everyone gets down to our sound, losing themselves in the music and dancing to the rhythm.

Closing my eyes, I let my mind escape to last night as I sing the melody I wrote years ago. The words have morphed, mean more, and carry a weight of what's growing between Weatherly and me. The lyrics coat my throat, and I let the words carry the intensity. When I open my eyes, they fix on baby blues that see right through this armor I use.

I lean in and sing to her. It's not the first time, but it's the only time she was standing in the audience knowing it. She smiles with the power of the sun on the brightest day. Her heat reaches me and digs deep inside, setting my soul on fire. I'll burn for her just as I have since I first saw her talking to Jake.

We spend song after song locked in each other. She could be standing alone for all I know because I can't take my eyes off her. She's a vision too strong to ignore. I couldn't anyway. I became the musician I am because of a muse I never knew until two weeks ago. *Weatherly.*

She consumes my thoughts, besetting my soul with the desire to know her better. Through touch, kisses, and whispered words, I've started to open up to the possibility that I've met someone I could care about. She's caressed her way into a crack of my heart.

There's no way for the good to shine in if it's never been broken.

Broken. My mom and I were broken when we left my dad, but we survived. We left the fear behind. And even when things were tough financially, she always found the silver lining. Weatherly's light is just the first to shine inside me since my mom died.

As I hit the final chorus, my arm flies into the air and my head tilts back. The world comes crashing back into reality as applause and wolf whistles fill the venue. "Fuck. Yeah." I soak in the glory I'm long overdue.

When I look into the sea of people again, my girl is so easy to find—beauty like hers can't hide in the dim lights. Her hand is on her chest, and a sweet pink is creeping up her neck. The prettiest rose would falter from the sight of my blushing beauty.

I'm off stage as fast I can, ready to see her. A tray of beers greets us, and English has polished off half a pint before loading his guitar into the case.

"Great show," he says.

Lennox laughs, his good mood getting the best of him. "It was a killer set."

Romeo adds, "Dare's cat scratch fever from that sweet kitty in the audience is working for him."

A, "Fuck you," accompanies my middle finger.

English wraps cables and knows all the right buttons to push to irritate me. "The ladies are not going to be happy if he's off the market."

"Let's not get ahead of ourselves." I don't even know why I say that. I've got my side in her bed already. I need to take my own advice.

English says, "What's up? The infamous Dare Marquis doesn't stick around any one girl for long."

He's right when it's come to others, but is he wrong when it comes to Weatherly? "Get off my dick all right already."

"No one cares about your dick, Dare." Lennox leans against the wall and looks out into the bar. "Speaking of dicks. Dick James was here again. I don't see him now, though."

"I saw him out there with a shit-eating grin like he can make or break us with a mention. Fuck him," English replies.

I've been long over the hope of the famous Austin DJ singing our praises on his radio show. I pack my guitar, and say, "Why do we care if he was here or not? He comes to the shows and then never says a fucking word on air the next day."

Lennox grabs an amp and his gear bag. He heads for the back door where we parked, but says, "We're his guilty pleasure."

Romeo says, "Fuck him. We do fine without his pimpin'." He snaps his mouth closed and looks away.

It's not like him not to fill the empty space, so I look up and find we have company—the topic of conversation himself—Dick James.

"I knew you had it in you," he says.

I cross my arms over my chest defensively. "We've always had it in us. You just didn't appreciate it."

"You weren't ready before. I've waited." He crosses his arms, resting them on a belly that wants to bust at least three buttons.

"Same songs, man. What's so different tonight?"

Lennox passes behind me with an elbow nudge to the back. The band eyes me having a conversation they'd like to be having. It doesn't take four of us to sell ourselves to someone who came to us. I can handle it, so I nod to Romeo when he carries his bass drum off the stage.

"You. That's what's different." Leaning in, he says, "I'm not trying to be an asshole, but guitarists and drummers are a dime a dozen in this town. Even singers. But what sets musicians apart is the way they manipulate their instrument. You've got a good voice—rough around the edges, like you. Grittier than other bands that have come out of Austin in the past few years. I dig your sound, but what I dig more is the way you captivate your audience. There's not a set of eyes not on you when you stand behind that mic."

"I didn't notice. I was too busy playing our music." I don't tell him it's because once my girl showed up, no one else mattered.

He reaches in front of him and squeezes his hand. Grinning, he adds, "Tonight, you took 'em by the throat and didn't let them land until the last note. You can use that line if you want."

My throat is raw from singing, so I nod with a garbled chuckle. "I think I'm good on lyrics." I've been more than inspired lately.

"You good on money, too? That's what the music biz all comes down to."

"What are you saying?"

He looks behind him and then leans in as if he's holding all the secrets. Rubbing his chin, he says, "What do you want, Dare? To be a band working gig to gig, a solo career, or a star?"

"We're The Heroes, not the Dare Marquis band, but the last part doesn't sound so bad."

"You keep playing like you guys did tonight, and I can get a deal on the table." Taking a step back, a girl who looks like she could be his daughter comes up beside him. Dick wraps an arm around her, and adds, "I'll mention the band on air . . . soon. You guys deserve some recognition."

"Thanks. We appreciate it."

Just past Romeo, Dick stops again and turns back. "Think about my offer."

I don't feel the need to say anything. I already made myself clear.

English has his guitar in hand and gear in the other but stops on the way to the van. "So what'd he say?"

"He's going to mention us."

English hollers a yes as he heads outside. Romeo follows him out, shouting his own excitement. Lennox turns around and eyes me. "He was hinting at a solo deal. You're not interested in branching out?"

"Only interested in what's best for the band, Len."

His gaze darts to a shadow that reaches my feet. "Is loyalty worth a deal?"

"Yes. You wouldn't take a solo deal either."

"I don't have your talent."

Weatherly rounds the corner and raises her hand just enough to wave. "Hi."

Lennox takes my case, and adds, "Another time." When he passes, he smiles and gives her a nod. "Hey."

"Hi," she replies shyly. "Great show."

"Thanks. See ya, Dare."

"See ya, man," I say, keeping my eyes on her. When we're alone, I feel the tension soften from my shoulders and give her a grin.

With just a few feet between us, I could reach out and pull her to me, kiss her hard like I've wanted to do since we parted ways earlier today. Ah, fuck it. I'm a man on a mission. Closing the gap, I cup her face. Before words are exchanged or the rest of our problems invade the space, I kiss her. I kiss her so she won't remember the music or the world that vividly surrounds us. I kiss her so she'll only remember me.

With us in need of air, we back away, but I can't keep my hands off her. Our lips clash together again not caring who sees us or where we are. But I force myself off her and grab her hand. "I don't want to take it slow with you."

"Me either."

Thank. *Fuck.*

15

Dare

WEATHERLY'S HANDS push against the marble, her strength and the back of her head pressed to the unyielding tile. An edge of tension splinters from the corners of her eyes.

I kiss her cheek and then the other. Rubbing her temples gently, I ease the creases formed and kiss her forehead. "Open your eyes."

When she does, I change speeds and slow this down by dragging my nose along hers and capturing her lips to kiss her gently. I remove the clip from her hair and watch as the strands fall, the water making them stick like glue to her skin. I set it on the ledge and take her face between my hands again, the frenzy from ten minutes prior still rushing through my veins.

Our lips were locked. Hands everywhere. Clothes tugged. Heat rivaling the dead of August. The apartment door was opened, and she had me pinned to the back of it before I came up for air.

My shirt was yanked open, and her hands were rubbing over

my abs to the sound of buttons bouncing across the wood floor. Her shirt came off next, but I was nice enough to leave it in one piece. "I could fuck you right here, and it wouldn't be soon enough."

Her mouth left my chest, and she licked her lips. "Salty."

"To your sweet."

Shower. "Come with me." I take her by the hand and pull her into the bathroom.

Fast forward to the now . . .

Fighting the sound of the shower raining down around us, I ask, "Why are you tense? You still good with this, with us?"

Her hands move through my hair, her nails making my scalp tingle from her touch. "You're all I've thought about. Weeks of *what-ifs* became *what can be*, but I worry—"

Her eyes are bluer against the white marble and brighter with desire, but worry weighs on her shoulders. "What do you worry about, Pepper?"

"I saw the look in your eyes, the recognition you couldn't hide, when you said it's you."

"I don't know why I felt it, but I know you feel it too."

"I thought you came over because of Lloyd—"

Swift to press a finger to her lips, I warn, "Don't say his name. No more when we're like this."

I flatten my hand on her chest and spread my fingers, letting water pool and then roll over them. Moving it across her skin, I keep my eyes on the wake my hand leaves as I slide it back and forth through the soap, keeping her slick.

Breathtaking.

I caress her neck, the tips of my fingers weaving into her hair. Leaning my head against hers, I whisper, "I don't want the world to ruin us."

Goose bumps ripple over her skin until she's covered.

Her arms loop under mine, and her hands press to my back where she was washing me with care minutes before. I hold her to me but tilt my head to see her eyes.

"No one but you and me between these walls. Salty and sweet," she says.

"Yes. No one but you and me."

I kiss her again, drinking the droplets from her lips. Our tongues mingle as I run my hands down the sides of her body. I lean back enough to watch her nipples tighten as her back arches. I have no fucking chance of lasting twenty seconds with this heavenly creature. "Fuck, you're beautiful," I say, but it mixes with the fall of the water. So I look at her eyes—a brighter blue like spilled paint on a white canvas.

"Kiss me, Dare."

"With pleasure." I start on her neck, the water making it so smooth and easy to glide lower. The top of her shoulder entices me to leave a mark, stake claims, and take her in ways I've never wanted with another woman. Something about her speaks to something deep inside me. I've never let my emotions sidetrack me, which is a skill that has served me well.

Until now.

Until now seems to be a running theme when it comes to Weatherly Beck.

Moving lower, I take her tits in my hands, caressing them as I leave my mark on the top of her right shoulder.

She moans, feeling that pleasure I promised. What she doesn't know is there is so much more to come, including her.

Wrapping my mouth around a pert nipple, I feel her body shift against me. The taste of soap, water, and every wet dream is savored on my tongue. I squeeze a handful of one breast while sliding my other hand over her stomach and lower until I reach her soft peach.

The sound of her harsh breath has me watching her like a hawk, not wanting to miss a second of her release. But she teases with those lips parted for me. *Fuck me.* It's impossible not to want to push against her leg, needing relief.

Her body moves so perfectly that the tip of my middle finger slips into her sweet nectar. "Dare," is murmured in my ear when she leans her head against mine.

I can't stop touching her. I want my hands on every inch of this stunning creature, to have those damn pink lips speak into my dick. I run my thumb over her bottom lip one time, putting pressure to see if she's into it.

Her lips close around me, and she begins to suck.

I want to fuck her so badly, but Jesus, I'm not going to survive watching this, so I lower my attention. Circling her entrance, I finally dip inside and watch her reaction. Her lips release me as her tits straddle my arm. Sinking onto my finger, she whispers, "I want you so much, Dare." My name a kitten purr of a sexy whisper.

I thrust against her side as my finger pushes inside her body. Turning her so we're under the pouring water, I take the back of her hair and pull it gently down until all she sees is me above her. "I'm going to come so hard for you, babe. You want that? You want me to fall apart for you?"

"I do," she says under a heavy breath. "I do, Dare."

"The way you say my name . . ." My eyes drop closed, and I add another finger, swallowing every Dare that follows and swimming in the heat of her as she consumes me—mentally and physically.

Her.

God, yes.

My blue-eyed beauty.

Weatherly holds me tight as her breath comes on a mewling moan. Her thighs clamp around my hand, and she begins to shiver, sending my orgasm spiraling through my body. I keep thrusting against her and finger fucking her until I'm overcome—"Jesus, fuck." My eyes seal closed while my body comes hard and fast against her hip.

When my breathing returns, I catch her as her body comes to rely on me. With red cheeks and a sparkle to her eyes, she tickles my neck with her laughter when she looks up at me. Her weight rests in my arms, and she grins with lidded eyes. "I get it now."

"What?"

"What it feels like to be free."

Taking her head in my hands, I kiss the top, understanding what she means. "There's freedom in falling, for leaving this world even if only for a few seconds. The weightlessness, the ease of burden . . ." I push my emotions down and try to refocus on the physical instead, but when I look at her and see the way her spirit shines in her eyes, knowing I put that look in her eyes, sex aside, I start to fall, just a little . . . *or a lot.*

When I release her, she rests against the shower wall. "I'm so hot."

"You are." Taking a handful of soap, I caress her shoulders and start cleaning her body. "So hot."

She giggles and fans herself. "I mean, heated. I'm burning up. The water is hot."

The water's been cooling slowly since we got in the shower. So I take her current situation as a compliment. "Let's get out." We finish up and turn off the water.

Her smile lasts while drying off and then longer until she brushes her teeth, making me curious. I saw her get off the other night, but seeing her reaction now has me wanting more than sex with her. I want to know her on a deeper level. "Tell me something that no one else knows about you."

Her back is to me, her head dropped forward. Rubbing her temple, she replies, "I used to think all guys were assholes."

"What changed your mind?"

"I met you." She brushes her teeth.

"I'm an asshole too. You just haven't given me enough time to prove it."

Laughing with a mouth full of toothpaste, she spits in the sink, and then says, "Let's hope you don't. I like the notion of one perfect guy."

"I'll do my best not to shatter the image." With my ego fed, I brush my teeth.

Wrapped in a towel, she leans against the counter next to me, waiting for me to finish before pouncing into my arms. "So," she starts, "what should we do next?"

I can't hide my smile as I look at her. Grabbing her ass isn't half bad either. "And by next, what do you suggest? It's two in the morning."

Kissing me, she stops and squeezes her legs that are wrapped around me. "I have a few ideas." She smirks.

So fucking hot for this woman. "Does it include the bed?" *Please, God, say yes.*

"God, I hope so." *Finally.* Praise the Lord.

I carry her into the bedroom. "Now that we're clean, we should definitely get dirty again."

"That was so cheesy." She's too busy laughing to feel the way my heart beats against my chest or the way I gulp a little too hard around her. Being smooth is not something that comes easy when she's near. I set her down, and she tucks her legs under the covers.

"Can't always live up to the lyrics, babe." I push the covers aside and crawl over her, kissing her along the way to my side of the bed. Relaxing back, I feel the mattress shape to my body, but I want to shape to hers, so I move on top of her and settle my legs between hers.

Holding me to her, the laughter has died down, and she says, "I've never felt like this with anyone before."

The word *anyone* bounces around my head. I'm not letting others invade our space. Happiness sings in her kiss when our lips reunite. When she opens her mouth to speak, I kiss her, ending the conversation. We have time for that tomorrow. Tonight is only about this. *Us.*

16

Dare

I KISS her neck and then lick her earlobe before taking it between my teeth, tempted to skip the foreplay. I'm ravenous—skin-to-skin, heat-to-heat, thrust-for-fucking thrust—for her. Abiding by my own rules, I ensure the lady always comes first. Every time.

The memory of watching her come made me come. Getting her off got me off in the shower. It's going to feel so fucking amazing to be inside her. I might not last long, but I know it's going to be worth the wait to feel her body squeezing around mine.

My lips return to the creamy skin of her shoulder, kissing her until a small red mark begins to bloom. Her chest is rising and falling, her mouth open, as I appreciate her body with mine. My mouth is on her. My hands run over her hips. My lyrics are sung to a symphony of soft moans. She whispers, "We can have sex, Dare."

There's no confusion this time. She doesn't bring up the notion of creating or making love. My chest constricts. *Love.*

I need to keep my head in the game. Love has nothing to do with sex. They live miles apart, so there's no use deliberating the issue.

Except we're different. Not just from a few days ago, but inside as if my insides have rearranged to make room for something new.

For love?

For her?

For both?

I've always believed it's impossible to love someone you just met. But when I rise from kissing between her breasts, I see more than lust in her eyes. I don't think Weatherly could hide her true emotions if she tried. Yet, I've become a master of disguise.

I can appreciate her body and listen to her as she speaks of her goals. That's what I do to try to show her the emotions I hide. But now I wonder what it would be like to drop my guard, or to talk about the changes she created inside.

"Dare?"

I regain my focus on the woman in front of me. "Yeah?"

Stroking her fingers through my hair, she asks, "Are you okay?" Her voice is so quiet I'm worried I've made her feel less. The way she studies me, I almost expect her to have a pen and pad in hand.

"More than okay, babe." Hide. It's what I do best. "How are you?"

"I'm good," she replies unsteadily with her heart on her sleeve.

Closing my eyes, when I kiss her chest, I'm greeted by a strong beat. Looking up once more, I catch a glimpse of the smile on her face. I savor the feeling, the emotions she doesn't voice but shares through her touches.

My skin comes alive every time she grazes the tips of her fingers across the plains of my back. I lean forward and kiss her stomach as I go lower. I want my mouth on her. I want to taste her on my lips, to have her call my name like a sin that she's possessed.

"I'm nervous," she whispers just as my hand reaches between her legs.

"Why are you nervous?"

I hate when she looks away from me. Her gaze is trapped on the ceiling and she shrugs. "I just am."

"What are you feeling?"

She looks at me and nods. "This matters."

"It matters to me too." Then I swallow the pride that protects me, and add, "You matter to me, Weatherly."

I'm given a smile that feeds my soul, making me feel more than liked . . . "You matter to me too, Dare."

"Do you want to stop?"

"No, I want to be with you." She lies back, inhales a long breath and then exhales. "Okay, we can continue."

I don't know why that makes me laugh, but it does. "All right. I'll be down here if you need me."

That makes her giggle. Then another nod is given as her shoulders relax against the mattress. I stop wasting time because there will never be enough time to spend with her.

Lifting her knees, I situate my shoulders under them and kiss between her legs like I kiss her mouth. Gently, I take my time to get acquainted, then deepen to satisfy the hunger I feel inside.

The first taste has me pressing my erection into the mattress. The second reminds me of the peach I called her, the nectar juicy and summer sweet. The tip of my tongue teases her clit, and then I suck until she can't restrain her hips.

So I do, holding her steady and intensifying the sensation.

My hair is tugged, but she's stubborn, not giving into me just yet. Her heat has me fucking this mattress like I want to fuck her. When my hair is yanked, I look up with my mouth still on her. The blue of her eyes is overcome by the pupils as she watches me.

Regulated breaths turn ragged, and her back arches. "Oh God, Dare." A murmur that builds like her orgasm. And then I win.

My name rolls off her tongue like a swear word that's done her wrong. I ground my dick into the bed until her body releases and then stills.

I lick the glistening sweat that's formed across her chest and higher until I'm firmly planted on her lips. Her dark hair is a mess, and her eyes wild with a lusty fire. Lips red from bee stung kisses and teeth that dug in. As much as I want to fuck fast and fuck hard, I savor her—the way she looks, the moment we're sharing. *Her*. It comes down to her, making sure she's satisfied and that she's happy.

Am I worthy of this woman?

I fucking hope so because she's become the answer to every question that pops into my head. That's got to be a sign of things to come.

Not minutes, hours, or days. I need more than tonight to explore Weatherly Beck's body. If I kiss her just below the collarbone, she giggles. If I gently bite her earlobe, she moans. When I pull her down the bed by her hips, she sits up, wide-eyed.

Kissing her neck is one of my favorites, though. She smiles with her eyes closed, and goose bumps cover her arms. Seeing the bliss on her lips makes my heart beat faster and puts my soul at ease. I think it's called happiness, but I don't let myself delve into that too deeply. I can overanalyze that another day.

As she comes down from her orgasm, her gaze finds me in the light filtering in from the bathroom, and then kisses me with her craving getting the better of her. I recognize the hunger.

Positioned between her legs, I scatter kisses across her shoulder, ready, so ready to push in. *Oh shit.* I stop. Opening my eyes, I sit up. "I don't have a condom. It was in my gear."

"I have condoms."

"Thank God." I don't even try to hide my relief. Making out and getting off has been fun, but my body is high on her —her taste, the feel of her, those little moans she gives.

My body is heavy as I lie still, resting my arm on my forehead while she stretches toward the nightstand. "I should have been prepared." I haven't been thinking straight since I met her.

"I got us covered." She laughs through her words. "Literally."

"Funny girl." Eyeing her backside, I check her out. She's got a fine ass—round hips, fullness to her backside. I give it a good squeeze because fuck it, that's my girl's, which means it's mine.

She turns back to me, a satisfied grin sitting squarely on her cheeks. "Like that, hero?"

"I do. A lot."

Her smile grows, but the smugness is gone. A rosy glow colors her cheeks against the white sheets. It's a sight I could get used to. Maybe I can clean up—not just my appearance but also my life—for her. Maybe Weatherly is the one who will inspire that change like she's inspiring my music.

She snaps with one hand, and a foil packet appears in her other. I chuckle. "Nice magic trick."

"Don't get too excited. It's all the tricks I have."

Taking the condom from her, I rip it open. "It's the only one I need. At least for now." While I slip my hands under the covers, she runs her fingers into my hair.

The lightness from a moment ago has slipped from her expression out through the open curtain where the moonlight sneaks in. When I'm covered, I shift back over, resituating myself. Reaching between us, her pussy is still wet and ready for me. I kiss her forehead before kissing her sexy mouth.

Holding me by the back of the head, she sinks back into the pillow, our eyes latched on to each other's. Her grip is strong, the muscles in her arms tense.

"Don't be nervous," I whisper, "I'm going to make you feel so good." She nods, but she doesn't relax. I wait until her gaze settles back on mine. "I'll go slow. Nothing to worry about, babe."

"I'm not worried."

When we kiss again, her body opens for me, and I start to sink into the heat, but stop . . . or should I say, I'm stopped. Finding her eyes again, I kiss her cheek. "You all right?"

"I'm good." She clears her throat. "Fine. Just fine."

"Wow, you seem fine. Just fine." My sarcasm slips out, but I follow it with a grin to lighten the mood. Unlike any woman I've been with—elegant, wholesome, yet sure of herself in every other way—she's throwing me off this time. "You're tense. You sure you want to do this?"

Exhaling, she closes her eyes. When they reopen, she touches my cheek. "I want this. I want to be with you like this."

This girl is a goddess. *How is she . . . unsure?* She said that she hadn't been loved properly, so it's my job, my fucking privilege to do just that. "We'll make love slowly. I promise." The words were said before I could stop them, my damn emotions joining in.

I lean into her caressing hand when she smiles. *Busted.* No use hiding the slip. I get back to business and reach between us to dive into her heat again until her hips start moving.

Now she's ready.

Pushing forward, I replace my hand with my cock as her warmth welcomes me. An exhale coats my neck, and she butterflies open so I can go deeper. Her pussy embraces me, and my breath gets choked in my chest. "Fuck, you're tight."

"Too much?" she asks, her eyes fluttering open, the nerves returning by how her hands hold me.

"God, no. You feel incredible." So right. Overwhelmed, my eyes beg to close. "I want to stay like this forever." The mattress is firm enough to rest my forearms while I start a slow glide until I'm engulfed inside her. "Fuck." I drop my head down, needing to take this in. "So good, babe."

Her body relaxes, the tension escaping. Rubbing my back, she coaxes me up again, and a gentle smile urges me on. "So good."

God, she's got me so wound around her finger already. This can't be normal. It's not for me. Is it healthy to feel this . . . what's the word, optimistic, about someone you're fucking? That can only mean one thing. *Trouble.*

"Are you going to move, Dare?" she whispers in my ear.

"Huh?"

"Less up here," she says, rubbing my temples. "And more down there."

I like that she's loosened and having a good time. Can tease and smile. As it should be. "You're cute. You know that?"

She waggles her eyebrows. "No, but I like that you think I am." Squirming beneath me, she adds, "Now about that down there part—"

"Yeah. I got you covered." I pull almost all the way back and then push back in. Not fast, but taking my time and watching her face, making sure she feels as good as I do.

From her eyes to how she holds a smile or lets it slide away, I take every clue and hint to what she likes and give her more of it.

We kiss.

Thrust.

Moan.

Move together.

I'm so close. *So close too fast. It's not fair to make demands, but fuck* . . . "Come for me, babe."

"I want you to come. Come for me," she replies, wiggling her hips and thrusting right back. Her eyes close as her nails begin to dig into my arms, our bodies slick with desire. Her breaths stagger, and then her body tremors; little earthquakes embrace me, and I fall into her sweet abyss.

My head lands beside hers, and my body settles sated with my weight balanced on top. Not for long. The desire to see her is too strong. I toss the condom and push up so I'm above her to see that glow has deepened. *Fucking gorgeous.*

I need her to feed this fix, a yearning that's growing to be a bigger part of her life. I take instead, kissing her because she's become my weakness. "How are you?"

"Good," she responds, sweeping my hair away from my eyes. "And tired, but in a good way."

"Yeah. Me too." I maneuver to the side, and my eyelids dip closed. I don't like the distance or that we're not touching.

Reaching between us, I take her hand in mine and bring

it to my lips to kiss. Being with her is more than good, it's . . . That four-letter word keeps coming to mind, but it stops in my throat before reaching my lips. Thank fuck. Feeling an inkling of connection like that is normal, I convince myself, but saying it is a whole other animal.

My eyes fly open, and my regulating heartbeat speeds up again. I clamp my mouth closed and try to settle back into the bliss. I can't, though.

I look at her again. It's when I lay eyes on this angel that I realize it's not just me she has wrapped around her finger, but my heart that's in trouble.

17

Weatherly

THE OUTLINE of Dare's face can be traced in the faint moonlight of the room, his upper body revealed after the sheets slipped down. As my eyes adjust, I can make out the details from the tattoos that cover his arms and part of his chest to the stubble that must be at least three days' growth.

I love how manly he is—thick muscles, hair on his chest, a man who uses his hands for more than tipping a caddy. I don't just feel wanted around him. I feel needed as though I'm a positive addition to his life instead of a responsibility.

Seeing Dare Marquis in my bed is unexpectedly satisfying. Or maybe this is how sex makes you feel. A new version of my old self. Have I changed? The molecules of my makeup rearranged? Is this a new start to my old life? Can sex give me a fresh start? I'm not sure. I hope so.

Muscles I've never used have come to life. It's all so new I'm not sure what to think except that he's a good man. He could have had sex and walked away days ago, but he stayed to get to know me first. We don't have our full histories detailed out or even a lot of how we spend our days. We have what we've built inside these walls, what's become ours alone. I find so much comfort in his presence and peace lying in his arms that this night could never be a regret.

I scoot off him and check the sheets, just in case, but it's not like I don't have a toy I use to get off. Of course, it's all clear. But honestly, there's nothing like the real thing. I feel incredible. *God, I'm so glad I waited for Dare, though. The pleasure . . .* I blush thinking about him inside me.

He's sleeping as if it's his own bed—deep with contentment on his face. I try to see beyond looks with people. I've been judged my whole life. My pretty face is a nice distraction to my "heavier hips" as my ex referred to them.

I'm "pear-shaped" according to April and criticized for how I look, but with Dare, I like me. I like the way he sees me and treats me as though I'm just as pretty as I'm supposed to be when you're a part of high society. Growing up in this world exposed me to the trappings, but I see through their money and jewels. I see their greed and the backstabbing.

My friends tend to focus on more shallow things to keep up appearances. Even knowing this, April's comments still sting. For the most part, I'm treated like a frenemy.

Dare is a breath of fresh Austin air.

I smile looking at him. There's a bump on the bridge of his nose that I'm tempted to touch. It's not big, but I like the imperfection. He's real. Everything about him, he owns without apology.

Peeking open his eyes like the sun's too bright, he catches me staring. It's not the sun shining inside his eyes. Moonbeams flicker like fire. Before he says anything, he strokes his hand down my hair and caresses my cheek. "Hey there."

"Hi."

"Can't sleep?"

"Can't sleep." I could blame the hour, but I know it's not. It's Dare and the way I feel the same inside but somehow different as if my heart has reorganized its priorities. I take a chance and tell him what I'm really feeling. "I can't sleep knowing you'll be gone soon. I'm not ready to say goodbye."

He grabs his phone from the nightstand. "It's only four in the morning. Am I being kicked out of bed?"

"Tell me this isn't a one-night stand."

The large palm of his hand rests on my hip. "This is the third night I've slept here. A one-night stand usually includes one night, max, and then a mutual goodbye." His thumb rubs my skin, comforting me. "You're not a late-night call. You're my girlfriend."

"I am?"

He sucks in a breath as if he needs the reassurance. While his hand moves up my arm and over my shoulders, he exhales, and I receive the warmest of smiles. "I'm not good at the whole boyfriend thing, but if you want to try this out with me, we can."

Yes. Yes. Yes. But then I pause to process what he said. "Why aren't you good at the boyfriend thing?" Memories of catching Lloyd in bed with someone else come to mind.

"I've never really done it," he says. "Like at the restaurant. I hurt someone unknowingly."

"You said you weren't dating."

"No commitments were ever made, but it doesn't matter that she misconstrued what we were. I hurt her. I don't want to be a source of pain for you." Such sincerity is heard in the softer parts of his confession. When his eyes seek mine, he chuckles. "Also, I know when to lock down a good deal."

I laugh. "Am I a good deal, Dare?"

His expression turns serious, and vulnerability sneaks in. "The best, Pepper. Don't ever let anyone treat you otherwise."

My heart squeezes, making me feel special every time he calls me that. Then my logical side barges in to ruin it. "We barely know each other."

"That's a lie." He starts kissing my neck, his hand resting on my chest, and then whispers in my ear, "You feel that, babe?"

My beats are strong, giving me away, so I nod.

He says, "Feel how connected we are beyond the physical. This is bigger than us."

Pretty words wrapped in an erotic tone lure my body closer, back into his arms. He's convincing, but I already know what he means. "I feel it. It's chemical." Changing us forever. I don't give a voice to the last words, but I feel it just like he does. "So you're my boyfriend?"

"If you'll have me."

I kiss his chest. "Every chance I get."

When we make love again, we share more than our bodies. Whispered words of affection and some laughs. We fall into each other, having fun in a new way. Between pillow talk and smiles, I discover how he likes when I'm on top but then likes to finish on top of me.

My body aches but still begs for his, my throat dry as I call out his name. As I lie in his arms after, my swallows become harsh as my emotions get in the way. I made a deal before I realized what was on the line. Not just his heart, but mine.

This is how I've been hurt before. I trusted without

thinking. But nothing is similar between Lloyd and the man who not only is hogging the bed but also claiming my heart. My mind revels in the thought of Dare being my man. I'm for sure going to call him that too. My man. Tingles spin up my spine, and I smile like a loon in the middle of the night.

"You're wide-awake, aren't you?" he asks.

Giggles come bursting out. "I am, my man."

"My man?" He catches on before I have to explain. "Ah. I get it. My woman." His chuckle bounces my head off his chest, but he soon calms again.

"I'd love to know the rules of this relationship."

"We make up our own as we go along."

Resting my chin on him, I look at his face. Such a great face. "No matter what the hour, if I get lonely I can call you?"

"You can call me when you get lonely."

"Dare?"

"Yeah?"

"I'm lonely."

That makes him grin and hold me tighter. "I think you've gone drunk with power. What am I going to do with you?"

Cocooned in his arms is the only place I want to be. Just like this. Safe. Cherished. Love—*liked*. "Stay just like this." I tuck my head down and curl into him as much as I can. His skin is heated from sleep, his heart beating heavily against his chest. I listen to the fire inside, willing to be burned if I can stay this happy until morning.

He kisses the top of my head. We're quiet except for our real thoughts that I worry can be heard through the weight of the silence. I never want this to end, but the lie I've held inside is starting to eat me alive. "I have a confession."

"So do I." His tone is balanced precariously between

worry and a harsh truth. Leaning back, he says, "Look at me, Weatherly."

I do, not just for him but also for me, the fantasy never better than this reality under any circumstance.

He says, "I'm not a fancy guy. Your place is nice. You're nice. Your world is so fucking nice. If I could give this to you, I would." His head is shaking as shame saddens his features. "I can't. I need to be upfront with you. My money goes to bills and the band, and there's not much left over after that."

"Then why did you pay for breakfast? I didn't expect that, and you didn't have to do it."

"I wanted to buy you breakfast. I just thought you should know that money's not frivolous for me." I notice how his eyes look around. He's kind enough not to say anything regarding the apartment.

"It's not to me either." I sigh. "I know I'm fortunate, but I want to stand on my own feet, which means I have to start looking for a job soon."

"Will you stay in Austin?"

It's the first time I hear a hint of worry in his tone. "I have a job secured. It's always been understood that I'll work for my father's firm after I take the bar exam."

"That's the exam this week?"

"Part of it. This is the ethics portion of the exam. I finished the cumulative tests the past two weeks."

"Doesn't sound like you have anything to worry about then."

Sitting up, I'm careful because he doesn't need to hear about my problems, but I've had revelations recently that keep playing on a loop that I want to share with him. "I'm not sure I want to work there anymore. I'll give up my dreams if I do."

"What do you dream of?"

"Being valued." I almost shock myself by my quick answer. I hadn't pinpointed it before, but that just came to mind.

The grin that lifts his cheeks reveals a sense of pride he's feeling. "You should be valued. If they don't, it's not the place for you. Don't compromise your values for a paycheck."

"That's what I keep thinking. Why would anyone in that office respect me when the only reason I'm there is because my last name is Beck?"

He sits up. "You are more than your last name, Weatherly. Don't be afraid to show them who you really are."

Slipping out of bed, I grab my robe from the closet to put on. "I sound childish, but I'm afraid to tell my dad."

He's up and pulling on boxers. Coming over to me, he runs his hands over my arms. "Why would he want anything less than happiness for his daughter?"

"You haven't met my father. Happiness isn't a factor when he makes decisions. Money. Repercussions. Connections. Those are his main concerns."

We walk into the kitchen together. I grab two bottles of water, but he opens them, and says, "What a sad way to live." His words strike me, and I stare at him. His brow furrows. "What?"

I've had so many thoughts about my future and have been burrowing my worries inside, but I'm so glad I shared them with him. "You're right."

"So if you agree, what's the issue?"

Wow, I'm beginning to feel emotional. "If I would have told anyone else, they would have told me I'm wrong." I wrap my arms around his middle, resting my head on his chest. "But you didn't do that. You told me to pursue happiness."

His engulfing arms surround me, and he kisses my head. "The money will come because we always excel at things that make us happy. So always choose happiness over money."

"There's no better person I could have talked to. You pursue your dreams every day."

His chuckle vibrates through his chest. "I'm ready for the money part, though."

"Yeah," I say with a laugh. "I get that. But will you ever regret what you're doing?"

"No. Neither will you. Take the risk and you just might find that the bigger risk was not doing anything at all."

He's taking on my stress, sharing the burden with me, and allowing me to see the light, the opportunity ahead. I didn't have to ask. I didn't beg for him to listen. He's here, present in the conversation unlike anyone else. It's never been more clear that Lloyd and I were never meant to be.

Dare's actions speak as loudly as his words. If not more so. He's here for me, to protect my dreams, and wants to see me succeed. This is what I've never had. Dare is amazing. I smile and kiss his chest. *He's my man.*

I say, "Thank you."

"For what?"

"For being my boyfriend."

I like when he laughs, and this one is hearty. "You're enjoying the titles, aren't you?"

As I feel the stress melt away, at least for the night after sharing my concerns, my voice pitches from giddiness. "I am."

"So am I." A giggle slips out, and I shiver with excitement. He's here, handsome and so awesome.

"You're not going back to sleep, are you?"

I shake my head with a ridiculous grin on my face. "Not a chance."

"It's not even five in the morning, but whatever you want to do, I want to do. So what are you up to?"

"Ice cream?"

"Mm. I could ice cream with you."

"Did you just make a verb out of a noun?" I ask, leaning against the counter.

"I did."

"I approve of this." Why do I bother resisting him? I'm attached again and kissing him. His scruff scrapes my lips for the billionth time, but I don't care. Every kiss from him is worth it. Dare isn't just any guy. He's my guy.

Ten minutes later, while eating a bowl of rainbow sherbet, I sit on one counter while stretching my feet to reach the opposite. It's a small enough space, even for me to reach.

"Does sherbet even count as ice cream?" he asks, sitting across from me.

"Of course, it does," I reply righteously and then take another bite.

He sets his empty bowl down. "I don't know. It's called sherbet for a reason."

"You didn't seem to mind it."

"I could go for some mint chocolate chip."

"So what you're saying is, if I'm sherbet and you're mint chocolate chip, you'd kick me out of bed?"

Hopping down, he wedges my knees apart, settling between them. After I feed him a bite of my sherbet, he says, "I could never kick you out of bed, babe. You feel too good."

"Ah," I say, laughing and throw in an eye roll. "One time and it's all about the sex now."

"If I'm remembering correctly, it was actually one time in the shower and twice in bed. That makes three times. My math might be questionable sometimes, but my sex never is. Anyway, tonight is just the beginning." His chilly ice cream lips kiss mine.

I set my bowl down and rest my arms on his broad shoulders. "If that was the beginning, how does it end?"

Our lips meet in the middle again, and our tongues embrace. Lifting me up by my ass, I wrap my legs around him, and we head back to the bedroom. "Guess we'll find out."

18

Weatherly

We slipped into sleep so easily in each other's arms that I didn't know I had fallen until it was too late. That rings true for more than sleep.

The light of day makes its way across the room until it's too bright to pretend it's still night. I should be tired, but I can't seem to do more than catnap with Dare here. I don't want to miss a moment of this. *Why dream when I have the real thing?*

And even though part of me thinks I shouldn't think he is the real thing this soon, no one ever sat and ate ice cream with me, or asked me what I dreamed of.

Lloyd never seemed to want me for me. And I don't think the cheating really had anything to do with me not putting out. That's certainly one thing that's been made clear by Dare's slower approach to us. I could think that I wasn't enough for Lloyd, but now I don't think he even considered staying faithful a necessity. *Did he ever really want to be with me?*

Do I care? Looking at Dare, at his peaceful face, I can confidently say no.

I stroke his hair from his forehead, something that feels as natural as breathing. That should probably scare me, but I find it exhilarating instead.

He stirs, slowly waking and looking over at me. A slow smile makes an appearance while he lies back. Rubbing his eyes, he asks, "Do you ever sleep?"

"Yes, but I have too much to stay awake for these days."

His hand is big, encasing mine. "For someone with a major test coming up, you seem calmer than you should be."

"There's no use in stressing. I have all day today to study. Give me another hour to enjoy this."

"One hour, babe. I'm not going to be blamed for your downfall."

"Too late," I joke. Kind of. "Can I ask you something?"

Settling his hands behind his head, he's wide-awake now. "Shoot."

"Do you call all the girls babe? If I go to one of your shows, will they all respond the same?" I've wrapped this question in a teasing bow, but I really do want to know. The real question is if he sees right through me.

A side-glance reaches me before I can start backtracking. "Are you looking for reassurance, *babe*?"

"I just—"

"No. The answer is no. I don't call other girls that. You may not like to hear this, but most I never call back either."

"Would it bad of me to admit I like hearing that?"

"Yes, but I like bad girls." Rolling over, he pins me down.

I'm more than a willing victim and spread my legs to give him full access. "I like being bad with you."

"Good." He kisses me while his hands slide up my arms

until my wrists are above my head. He looks down at my body with his intentions shining in his eyes. "You ready to go again?"

The words are kind of crude, but I find it so hot that he says what's on his mind. I hate beating around the bush. Anyway, another round makes my confession ancient history. "I thought you'd never ask."

I MISS HIM.

This is so dumb.

How can I possibly miss a man who just left a few hours ago?

Focus, Weatherly. Focus.

Ethics.

Principles.

Exam.

I tap the book and refer to my laptop for the notes I took. I blink a few times before I realize I'm done. I can't do this.

Pushing my laptop away from me, I close the book and sit back. Months, years have led to tomorrow. If I've learned nothing else, the last couple of days with Dare have taught me that I've spent more time studying than living.

I'm ready for the next stage, ready for what life has in store, to achieve my goals. I was directed down this path, but it's one that I'm interested in, so I'm excited about practicing law.

Dare is right. If they don't value me, then they don't deserve me. I feel lucky for even knowing such a kind and talented man. But you know what? He's a lucky guy because I'm also a catch, dammit.

After slipping on socks and sneakers, I twist my hair up

into a messy bun. I can't make this an all-day thing, so I stay in yoga pants and a baggie T-shirt. I do swipe on some mascara before I head out, though. Dare likes to stare into my eyes, and I can't say I mind. I'm sitting in my car like I have no place to go. I do. I just don't have an address.

He's my boyfriend, so I should know where he lives. I say, "Call Dare."

This time, my car gets it right. Thank goodness. "Hi," he answers, and from his tone alone, I know he's smiling.

"I'm lonely."

"On my way."

"No!"

"No?"

"I like your enthusiasm." Calmer, I reply, "But I'd like to come over to your place. I want to see where you live and see your room, roll around on your bed, and maybe do more."

"Maybe?"

Laughing, I add, "I definitely want to do more."

"Texting the address."

The message pops up on the screen. "On my way." Looking at the map before I pull out of the garage, I say, "You only live ten minutes from me."

"Yeah, seven or eight if you get all greens. Hey, I'll see you when you get here. I need to do a fast cleanup."

"Okay. See you soon." It makes me feel weird that he lives so close, but I never knew. He's been right here all along. I pull down a street and look around. All those years, I was warned about the east side, and now that I'm cruising to hang out there, I notice there's nothing to worry about. It's a quaint neighborhood for the most part.

When I find Dare's house, I pull to the curb and smile when I see the ranch-style home. The trim could use a fresh coat of paint, and the yard needs mowing, but it's nice. Nicer than most on the street and more than I expected from how tight he told me his money is.

Coming out on the porch, he leans against the railing. "To what do I owe the pleasure?"

He's showered and in different clothes than when he left my place, so sexy. I walk up the driveway, my insides flipping from the smile I'm given, the one that I evoked. "So this is where the magic happens?"

That handsome grin rounds as his jaw drops and eyes widen. "You really want to talk about hookups with others?"

Horror hits. "Oh, God no! I meant the music. The songs. This is where you write songs."

"Ah." He greets me at the bottom of the steps, laughing. Wrapping his arms around me, he says, "I could really get used to you."

I'm not sure what he means, but from what I understand about his reputation, I think it means a lot. Tucking my head against his chest, I could live in this man, and I still don't think I'd be close enough. Plus, he smells so good. "I hope so."

"Come on." Taking my hand, he leads me to the door. "I'll show you around."

There's not a grand entrance, but a small foyer with a table littered with unopened mail, an open can of Coke, and various keys in a bowl. My mind is going wild thinking about the parties they must have. "What's with the keys?" I ask as he shuts the door.

"Keys left behind that we found after parties." He stops and stares at the bowl a second, then starts laughing. Glancing at me, he adds, "It's not what you're thinking. We're not into the swinging scene."

I shrug with a laugh. "I wasn't judging."

He angles toward me, and the humor is gone. "I'm not really one for sharing the things I care about."

"What do you care about?" So I goad him. Sue me.

Big hands clasp around my waist and he leans down to kiss me, but then detours to my ear. "Music, my family, and my band." I close my eyes when his lips touch the shell of my ear. He whispers, "And you."

My knees go weak, so I steady myself the best I can by holding onto him. Never once has anyone looked at me or treasured me the way Dare did just now. Until now, I had no idea how incredible it felt to be wanted so much. "We're a whirlwind romance."

"No, babe. We're a hurricane in the making."

I suck in a staggering breath and lean into the kisses he's placing on my neck. We are a hurricane in the making. I just hope we aren't destroyed in the process. Maybe because I'm coming down from the high we've been living on, but that's the first time I've had the thought. We can live in our bubble, the four walls of our houses protecting us, but eventually, we'll be exposed to the outside world, his and mine. I'm not sure how they'll come together, but I'm building my armor. Because being in his arms, no matter where we are, beats the life I was living without him.

Hurricane in the making.

"Let me show you beyond the bowl of keys."

My heart was starting to feel heavy. I needed the levity. "Speaking of swinging. Did you ever see the live-action version of *The Grinch*?"

His nose scrunches. "Were we really talking about swinging?"

"Kind of. I learned you're not into it."

Shock hits his face. "Are you?"

"No. God no. I'd be too jealous for that, and I don't want someone else's hands on me."

"Just mine?" I hear the smug tone before I see the waggle of his brow.

"Yes, Romeo. Just yours?"

"Just my what?" a guy—brown hair, tall, attractive, but different from Dare—comes from the kitchen and asks. I can see he'd get his fair share of attention. These guys have a running theme of the band it seems and own their sexy rock star-ness. "I once dated a chick who was into that." He leans against the back of the couch and pops a cherry in his mouth. I recognize him as the drummer. "I didn't realize it until I was being offered this guy's wife in exchange for my girl." He stands up and drags his hand down the front of his jeans before holding his hand out. "You're Weatherly, right?"

Dare rolls his eyes in annoyance. "Well, thank fuck, Romeo, or I'd be in a lot of trouble right now."

"Romeo?" I start laughing, shaking his hand. "I was calling Dare Romeo, but I see what happened there."

Romeo shrugs. "It's a name everyone knows, but I don't think people expect to meet one. Good to meet ya."

"You too," I reply, stepping back again.

"Don't leave us hanging. What happened with the guy's wife?" Dare asks.

"She was hot. Great tits." His eyes dart to mine. "Sorry. She was ready for action, but she was married. I'm more than happy to fulfill a fantasy, but I want no part of breaking up a marriage. Fuck that. When I get married, it's forever."

Nodding me toward the hall, Dare asks him, "So you're getting it out of your system now?"

Romeo laughs and then pops another cherry into his mouth. "Like I said, I don't mind fulfilling a fantasy. I'm a fucking rock star, baby. On stage and in bed."

"Okay," Dare groans, his hand tightening around mine. "I think we've had enough of this conversation."

"I'm curious, though." Before I'm pulled away, Romeo asks, "What were you saying about *The Grinch*?"

I laugh, suddenly embarrassed that I'm talking about swingers. "There's a scene that no one ever talks about where he sees them dropping their keys into a bowl at a Christmas party. I never caught it until I saw it last year. Are they dropping their keys in the bowl so they don't drink and drive, or are they swingers?"

Both of them stare me with their lowered brows, but then Romeo starts laughing. "I never noticed it, but I'm gonna look for that scene next time it's on."

"Can we please end this conversation?" Dare tugs me toward the hall.

This time, I shrug in amusement. "Guess we'll never know," I muse. We're moving quickly, but I note the couch doesn't match the loveseat or the chair that's crammed on the side. The large screen TV isn't mounted on the wall, but sits on the hearth with all seating angled in that direction. Interesting design. Manly. Rugged. Not a care in the world. So much Dare.

I envy his freedom. "At fourteen, I asked for a teal papasan chair. My mom said it belonged in a home with a futon and that would not be our home."

"We used to have a futon until Lennox's mom bought us the couch." He asks, "Do you want anything to drink? Water? Soda? Powerade?"

"Water is great."

Romeo has settled on the couch and flicked on the TV. With his feet perched on the coffee table and a cup of water in front of him, he looks content.

Dare says, "The kitchen. We're a messy bunch."

"It's clean." I run the tips of my fingers along the laminate bar top as I pass three mismatched barstools until I feel something sticky and wipe my hand on my pants. This is not how I envisioned his place. Although when I think about it, I didn't know what I imagined. I can still see him fitting into my space so well that I never gave his place much thought.

"We try." Catching what I did, he adds, "Sometimes we fail. Helen—"

"Who's Helen?"

"Lennox's mom. She pops by and straightens for us sometimes. Does some light cleaning, and nags us, but it's all good coming from her."

"That's nice of her."

He hands me a glass of water. "She's like a second mom to us . . . to me."

The way he tacks that last part on has me wanting to know so much more. "How so?"

"She was always there for me just as my mom was there for Lennox growing up."

"That's so nice." I continue following him. "I like the house."

"It's small, but it works." We walk toward the back of the house again. He says, "Living room. Bathroom. My room." Opening the door on the left, he guides me inside first.

The door is closed, and I stand there, looking around. It's not big, but I love seeing his life surrounding me. A guitar on the bed with a notepad and pencil next to it. A basket of laundry that I can't tell whether it's clean or dirty. The blinds are bent in places, but they let in good light. "It smells like you."

"Is that a good thing or a bad thing?"

"Good. Definitely good." I set my glass down on the

nightstand and then sit on the end of the queen-sized bed. "Did I interrupt you when I called?"

"I was tinkering with a few riffs and lyrics, but you're a nice distraction."

Running my hands over the comforter, I smooth the creases. "How many girls have been on this bed?"

An eyebrow rises. "I don't bring girls back here," he says.

Taking a second look, a deeper look into this room, and then at him, I ask, "Why not?"

"It's where I sleep. This is where I find peace when the world out there is being a dick. This is the place I clear my head and write music. It's weird, but I can't really explain it."

I stand. "I'm sorry. We can—"

"No. That excludes you."

My heart thumps in my chest as my soul opens its arms to embrace everything about this opportunity. "It does?"

"I like that you wanted to see the house, and I really like seeing you on my bed."

Sitting back down, I rest back on my elbows, making myself at home, and poke his jeans with the toe of my sneaker. "What are you going to do with me now that you have me in here?"

"The goddamn death of me," is muttered under his breath before he says, "I have a few ideas to pass the time."

He climbs on top of me and dips to the side to kiss my neck. It's amazing how I went from a virgin to Hero whore. Though I can't say I'm upset. Quite the opposite actually. "I am one hundred percent onboard with passing the time with you if it involves this bed."

"Depends."

"On?"

"My plans most definitely include this bed. So tell me: missionary or bent over the edge to take you from behind?"

My teeth dig into my lip. "Decisions. Decisions."

He whispers, "Let me help you out. Either way, you're going to come."

"Then it's a win-win for me." I kick off my shoes. "I'll take one of each please."

The right side of his cheek rises into a mischievous smirk, and his eyes hide the devil inside. "You got it, babe."

19

Weatherly

THE COLORS and designs inked across his skin could keep me occupied for hours. There's such an intimacy to them as if I'm a voyeur to another life he's led. "You have a lot of tattoos."

"I do."

Sitting next to him with a borrowed baggy T-shirt hanging around me, I want to know so much more about him. Even though I came over to get a break from studying, I think it was also to learn more about him.

Dare is so unique. His drive, his passion, his talent, his . . . innate kindness, and this afternoon has been incredible. Talking. Kissing. Making out. And then talking some more. It has been cathartic stepping out of my own life for a few hours and lying around in his. Revitalizing.

And truth be told, if I don't know the work inside and out by now, I'm not ready for the exam anyway. I know I'm ready. So this time is for me.

I trace the tattoos on his chest, inventing stories in my

head. "How did you ever choose one piece of art to display forever on your skin? I imagine this fiery sun on your forearm was a sign of victory after battling Helios in the Greek heavens. The black skull with a daisy for an eye adorning your bicep—was for your siren's honor you fought to defend against a pirate at sea."

He rubs over my crisscrossed legs. "I like your versions better. Lots of battling going on."

Shrugging, I say, "What can I say? You fighting was a turn-on. You fascinate me. A date. Your last name. Fire. So many tattoos blend into each other and work so beautifully together. Do they have meaning?"

"Don't all tattoos? They should."

"A friend of mine got a coffee cup because she loves coffee." A faded bluebonnet on the underside of his arm is almost hidden in the lines of a maze that creeps through the other designs. "It's on her ass so her parents would never find out. She forgot about it though and wore a thong at her pool once. She still hears about it."

"I don't have money to burn that way. I had to save or trade for every one of these."

"I was never brave enough to get one. I was threatened with the loss of my trust fund if I did."

Resting his head on his hands, he looks me over. "I've never known anyone who had a trust fund. Isn't that the kind of thing you should keep on the down low, so unsavory types don't come snooping around?"

"Everyone I know has one so I never thought it was worth hiding."

"I don't."

I stop to collect my thoughts. Pushing the virginity lie through omission aside, I say, "I didn't know I needed to hide anything from you."

"You don't, Weatherly. I'm not after your money."

"What are you after?"

He lies there staring at me. When his gaze dips down, he runs his hand over one of his biceps. He sits up and kisses me. "You."

"You may be my dad's worst nightmare, but you are proving to be a dream come true to me."

"With enough room and time, I'm sure I'll screw this up somehow. Anyway, maybe your dad won't hate me."

Rubbing my fingers over the sun on my forearm, I laugh. "He says tattoos are the sign of devil worship."

He chuckles. "Can't wait to meet him." Seeming to catch himself too late, he backtracks. "Forget I said that. Dumb joke."

The notion never crossed my mind that he wouldn't meet my dad or my mom. Dare is someone I'm dating. Images of worlds colliding flash through my head and I pause. He's a part of my life, but I haven't been thinking about anyone else when we spend time together. He fits in my world, but I'm not sure how everyone else will treat him. I hope with the respect he deserves.

"It wasn't dumb. Of course, you'll meet my family. But maybe we should hold off until we have an actual first date before we get that far." I kiss his shoulder. "Since an interrogation is standard protocol at the Beck dining table, we'll have more to say, to share with them other than sex and lots of sleeping together." I let the conversation go to save us both from having to justify anything we're not ready to.

He connects freckles on my thigh, seemingly fascinated by them. "Are we still on for tomorrow night?"

"I didn't mention it to pressure you into taking—"

"No pressure. I want to take you out."

"But money's tight."

"I didn't tell you so you'd pay for things. I told you because I can't pay for everything you deserve. I can afford to take you out tomorrow night. Whatever you want to do."

"Are you sure?"

"I'm sure." His gaze extends to the nightstand, and he reaches over to grab his phone. "I have a show tonight."

"I want to come."

He winks. "You did. Twice. As promised." Patting his chest, I laugh, loving that we can talk so openly. It's freeing. Moving next to me, he puts his feet on the floor. "Your test is tomorrow, so I can crash here. I don't want to wake you."

"Wake me. I want you to come over."

"And I want you to study and get some rest. Tomorrow is a big day."

I'm tempted to argue, but I feel it might be wasted energy. Also, this was supposed to be a break that turned into three hours in bed, so I can't complain. "Yeah, I probably should get back." It's just past five, so I climb out of bed and eye the notepad on the floor while I get dressed. "You're working on a new song?"

"Always."

Tugging my shirt over my head, I ask, "What inspires you?"

"Life." He stands and stretches. "You."

I sit on the edge of the bed to put my sneakers on but look up. Keeping my voice quiet, just between us, I ask, "What about me inspires you?"

"What doesn't inspire me about you?" An answer comes out so naturally that he doesn't have to think about it. He sits next to me and rests his hand on my thigh. "That birthmark on your left shoulder blade, the way your hair tapers to the shape of the top part of a heart at the nape of your neck. There's a freckle where your thigh meets your leg that reminds me of an acorn. The twenty different blues that make up your eyes, the valley of your hip to waist that reminds me of riding my bike as a kid with no hands. The color of your bare lips after being kissed. Strawberry juice that remains after enjoying the sweetest summer treat. Your incredible mind and the way you face life. You are tenacious and funny, brave, and so smart."

My throat is thick, the simple act of swallowing suddenly difficult. "I don't know what to say. That is the most beautiful thing I've ever heard. I think you know more about me than I know about myself."

"No. I've just been fortunate enough to see you."

Simple. To see me. He sees me.

His words are like a salve to my soul. I move onto his lap. "Thank you for taking the time."

"You're immortalized in lyrics, but there's nothing like the real thing." He kisses me and then stands, setting me on my feet. "I need to shower. You need to study."

"Will I get to hear this song inspired by me?"

"Definitely. I'm hoping it's one of the songs we put on the new album. That's if I finish it. I'm going to work on it a bit more before we hit the recording studio to record another song this evening. A slot at seven opened up, and our friend who works there called."

"I should leave you to it." I put my shoes on. A few minutes later, he's walking me out. His roommates are loud, even boisterous, talking about a game on TV when we pass back through the living room until they see me, and everyone goes quiet. Except Dare. He asks, "What?"

"Nothing," they reply and pretend to look busy—drinking or fidgeting with the remote. Obviously putting on a bad act.

When the front door closes, I say, "That was awkward."

"Ignore them."

"Kind of hard. What was that about?"

We cut across the grass to the curb. "Like I said, I don't bring girls home."

"But you let me invade it." Feeling incredible, I twirl in front of the car and right into his arms. "Thank you."

"I'll take this kind of invasion any day, babe." He chuckles, catching me. When my car door opens, grabbing our attention, we don't get a chance to get lost in each other again. We both know it's time to go. He shakes his head. "I will never get used to how tech-insane this car is. Wild what money can buy."

I don't want to talk about the car, and luckily, he doesn't want to either. I'm pulled into a soul-searing kiss and melted to the street under his heat. Right when we part for air, he says, "Kick ass on the exam and I'll see you tomorrow night, babe."

I think I'm still running my fingers over my sensually scorched lips when I park in the garage. Dare's kisses should come with a warning label: devour at own risk. The side effects are long lasting.

THE AUDITORIUM IS QUIET, the soft rustle of papers the only sound heard except for the occasional cough or frustrated sigh. Though I struggled to get a good night's sleep without Dare in my bed, I'm happy to finally be here.

Principles of conduct.

Legal ethics.

Everything is covered, and I feel solid with my answers.

I walk out knowing I did everything to the best of my skills. It's now a waiting game for results, and eventually the rest of the bar exam. I walk outside and breathe, just breathe in the sunshine, the relief, and my future.

Turning my phone back on, I check for messages and find three from Stascia.

Stascia: *Own the exam. You've got this.*

Stascia: *We have to go out and celebrate. Text me.*

Stascia: *How did it go? Are we on for tonight?*

I stop and readjust my bag on my shoulder, then text her back.

Me: *Thank you! It's over. Thankfully.*

When I reach the parking lot, I'm about to finish typing to send the text, but I'm greeted with long legs, broad shoulders, and a roguish grin that make me stumble or maybe that was my heart shifting back to align with his axis.

"Hey, Pepper?"

Dare is leaning against the side of an old beat-up truck with a bouquet of wildflowers in his hands. Unlike Lloyd, who was thrusting his non-smelling mass-produced roses at me in an apology, Dare stands in contrast with yellow and white daisies tied with a yellow ribbon.

As if he couldn't get better after those kisses, and orgasms, he manages to do it. He pushes off the truck and meets me more than halfway when I start walking to him. With the flowers in one hand, he wraps his arm around me and kisses me in a slight dip.

My eyes close, and I savor every second I have with his lips on mine. Righted and trying to catch my breath, I ask, "What are you doing here?"

"Came to support my girlfriend." *Thud.* I'm dead. Right here on the sidewalk. "How'd it go in there?"

"In where?"

"The test you just took inside that building."

He makes me lose my mind in the most wonderful of

ways, if that's a thing. I grin, feeling my hot cheeks with my hands. "It went well. But you're here."

"I am," he chuckles his reply. "I picked these for you. Hope you don't mind wildflowers."

"No." I take the bouquet, and the ribbon trails over my skin. It's probably just coming down from the adrenaline of taking the exam that has me feeling extra emotional. "They're so pretty. It's the most thoughtful gift I've ever received. Thank you."

"You're welcome." Stepping back when other test takers start filing down the sidewalk, he shoves his hands in his pockets. He looks back at the truck, and to me again. "I thought... You know what? I'm here because I fucking hated not being with you last night. I know I said seven, but how about . . ." He checks the time on his phone. "How about two thirteen instead?"

It was then that I knew I wasn't in over my head, but I was falling for this man and didn't want to be saved. My heart had been circling the depth of my growing feelings like prey, but him showing up just for me, to see me, to be with me, to support me, has changed the course of everything.

Acting indifferent as if this isn't the highlight of my life isn't even an option. I throw my arms around him and embrace him like a cat above water. I pepper his face with kisses, and the best part is he lets me. Dare doesn't care about propriety or PDA. He holds me by my ass and captures my lips in a red-hot kiss.

He's holding me so high that when our lips separate, I'm looking down at him. "What'd you have in mind, hero?"

An hour later, we're standing at the edge of a river with rapids to our right and a swimming hole in front of us. "It's beautiful here," I say, slipping off the flip-flops I stole from my car before we left the law school parking lot.

I twisted my hair on top of my head, shed the blouse for a Heroes tee he was wearing, and rolled down the truck windows to let the wind blow through the cab this beautiful May day. I texted Stascia that I'll need a rain check when we stopped to get gas in some dive stop that had bars on the windows. I stayed in the cab.

A catcall for my man from another woman at the station got me out of the truck and staking my claim by kissing him right there with a gas pump in hand. I didn't blame her. Since I stole his shirt, his abs were on full display for everyone to admire, so I get it. I just don't want to share.

While he laughed his ass off at my jealousy, I licked his chest for good measure. I didn't even give a damn.

In just his underwear, Dare climbs to the edge of the overhang and jumps in without a second thought. The water is so clear that I can see him before he comes up for air. When he surfaces, he asks, "You jumping in from the rock or swinging on that tree rope over there?"

Glancing at the knotted rope, I don't even know how that works. "What should I do? I've never done either."

"Damn, girl."

I turn to scan the area. "There could be snakes or wild animals, waiting to attack."

He floats in the water so effortlessly. "I'll protect you."

"I'm not sure this is safe? And aren't we trespassing?"

"Everything's owned in this world. Remember how we bent the rules together? Jump in like you did then."

"Bent? We full-on broke our own rules." I eye my skirt hanging on a tree.

"Then break them again with me. Come on. The water feels amazing."

I debate putting it back on, but startle when he says, "Weatherly! Get. In. The. Water."

This time, I decide that I should push my boundaries and experience new things. Stepping outside of my comfort zone, I pull the shirt over my head before draping them on a low hanging tree branch.

Live in the moment, Weatherly.

"C'mon on, beautiful. Do it. All you have to do is jump."

"All I have to do is jump," I say to myself as I tiptoe through the water on the rocks to where he jumped in. He's wading in place in the water below watching me, but I can tell he'll be there in a heartbeat if I slip or worse. I gulp at the thought of falling.

This time, I'm the one who gets catcalled. It's so unexpected and takes me out of my reeling brain. Laughter breaks through the fear, and I begin to live in this moment right here. Shaking my ass, I give him a little show in my bra and panties to earn every note of that catcall.

He calls up to me, "There's my girl."

When I reach the same spot where he was, I stand there staring. "It looks a lot farther from up here."

"It's an illusion. It's only seven or eight feet, babe."

"But you're a rebel." There's a wobble to my knees I've never felt before. "I'm scared, Dare."

"Don't worry, I'll be right here. All you have to do is jump away from the rocks and in front of me. You'll be okay, and then you'll be a rebel, too."

A rebel is something I never thought I'd be, but like so many other aspects of my life, he brings out the best of me. So I suck in a breath and take the plunge.

My heart races as I fly through the air with my eyes squeezed tight. My body tenses when I hit the cold water and soar under. I'm only under for a few seconds, but in those seconds, I open my eyes and see him under the water with me.

Freedom. Safe. Secured in his arms, I pop up for air and squeal in delight. "Oh my God, Dare. I did it. I did it." I look back at the rocks and point. "I jumped off that cliff."

"You did it. You conquered your fear and went for it." Anyone else would have corrected from a cliff to a rock but not Dare. His smile is so genuine with pride.

His hands are still around my ribs as we tread water together. I move closer, wrapping my legs around his middle and my arms around his neck, and kiss him.

I did conquer my fear and went for it, just as I went for him. And not only that, he came after me. He was the one who couldn't wait until seven to see me. He was the one who picked flowers himself and surprised me with such a beautiful gesture as wanting to see me sooner. I don't think I've ever felt as valued as I do right now. Valued. My soul vibrates from the relief of completing my exams and with the joy this man instills in me.

An addictive combination, and one I very much want more of.

Because I'm brave.

Because he's mine.

Then we kiss again because under the sunshine in the middle of a hidden emerald pool, there's never been a more perfect moment than this.

20

Weatherly

DARE HARDENS UNDER ME.

My body is quick to respond—ready, blooming—just for him. Peering around the secret emerald pool, I begin a steady but slow gyrate. "I want you," I say.

He looks over my shoulder and then with a sly grin, his eyes shine bringing out the gold of the centers. "Right here? Who's the rebel now?"

With him holding me afloat, I dip my head back into the water, close my eyes, and soak in—him, the sun, completing the exam—this perfect day. I lift back up. "It's a good day to try new things."

"Do you know how beautiful you are?"

"No," I answer honestly.

We may have only met recently, but I feel like he reads me better than anyone because he says, "I'm going to change that. If I do nothing else for you, one day you're going to realize how beautiful you are."

The water glistens off his lips, and I kiss him, my hold

tightening, never wanting to let him go. Leaning his head against mine, he closes his eyes. The man who seems to always have everything under control appears to lose a little. "I . . ." He looks at me. "I don't want to hide how I feel about you."

"Don't hide," I whisper, "and I won't."

It's the first time I've seen him nervous. His Adam's apple dips as he takes a deep breath. "I care about you very much, Weatherly. It's strange to admit something like that this soon after meeting you, but it's true. I feel connected to you in a way I've never felt before."

"Connected as if we've known each other our whole lives."

"Yeah," he says with a short nod. "It's hard to explain. I don't know what it is that underlies this between us."

"Beauty attracts the eye, but the soul captures the heart."

I'm released, and he pushes back through the water. With a few feet between us, his eyes narrow, locked on mine as if he's seeing a ghost. "Why'd you say that?"

This perfect day crashes around me. "What?"

"What you just said." His tone is harsh, demanding. "Why did you say that? How do you know that quote?"

Flailing my arms in place underwater, my heart is racing, a fear sinking in. "It just . . . when you said there's something between us it popped in my head."

"Why?"

"I don't know, Dare." My arms are tiring, so I start swimming to the side.

Swimming next to me, he asks, "Are you okay?"

"I'm fine." I reach the side and step carefully on the rocky waterbed, stumbling, but catching myself before I fall.

"Don't get out."

I shoot a look back at him. "What just happened?"

He comes to stand near but keeps distance between us. Like his mood, his expression is hard to decipher, so I don't bother. I'm not in the mood for a guessing game.

"I'm sorry. I've never heard anyone else repeat that phrase."

"And?" I reach the edge of the trail and tug my clothes from the tree branch.

"How do you know it?"

The quote rattles across my lips again as a memory flashes—the fortress wall as I always called it as a kid and the spray paint. "I saw it on a wall." The shirt falls over my head and down my shoulders, and then I wrangle out of my wet bra. "Why are you angry?"

"I'm not. I'm . . ." He climbs out of the water and stares up at tall treetops shading us. "That quote means something to me. It's important. I didn't expect to hear you say it." His back is turned to me, and I don't know if I'm being kept from his emotions, or if he needs a minute.

I take another plunge and touch his shoulder. "You can talk to me. Anything you say will always stay between us."

When I see his eyes again, he says, "I don't need reassurance. I trust you, Weatherly."

"Then what just happened? Why are you upset?"

The tension eases in his expression. "My mom used to say that quote."

"Really?"

"It's sacred to me."

I find myself gravitating closer to him. "I didn't say it to disrespect you—"

"I know. You spoke from the heart like she always did. I was just caught off guard. Anything to do with her . . . I don't take my memories with her lightly."

"It just popped in my head. I haven't thought of that

quote in years." Then his words replay in my head, so I ask, "What do you mean memories with her? Memories from when you were little? Or—"

He walks to where he dropped his shoes and jeans. Pulling off his wet underwear, he tugs on his jeans, not caring if the whole world sees. "My mom died."

I had started pulling on my skirt but stop. "Dare?"

"What?"

"Why didn't you tell me?"

"Why would I bring that up?"

While he continues getting his shoes on, I zip the flowy skirt on the side and button it at the waist as I tug down my wet panties and slip on my flip-flops. "Because we're dating. A short time, but still. I want to know you."

Dropping his head back, he pinches the bridge of his nose and then settles his gaze back on me. "You do know me." When he returns to my side, he rubs my hip. "I should have told you sooner, but this isn't an easy subject for me to talk about. So I wouldn't just throw it out there."

I catch a glimpse of the mom tattoo and date. Running my finger over it gently, I ask, "What is this date?"

He looks down at it as if he's seeing an old friend and holds his hand over mine. "That's the day she left my dad. A new beginning. A fresh start. She escaped so we could live again. That's our re-birthday. Our survival day."

My heart clenches as I listen to the pain morph into hope in the turn of his words. When he lifts his hand, I lean forward and kiss his tattoo. "Your mom sounds like an amazing woman."

"She was." He looks down between us and scratches the back of his neck.

When he laughs, I ask, "What is it?"

"Hearing you say that quote . . ." There's nothing but

reverie in his tone. He looks out over the water and then up toward the cloudless blue skies. I'm brought in for a hug. "It means a lot to hear it again. Thank you."

The emotions pour from this man, a purported bad boy and a rock star. I don't know what to say, so I don't. I just embrace every part of him that fits in my arms and appreciate him the best I can.

A smile finally settles on his lips. "I've never wished that my mom could meet anyone . . ." Shyness lights his eyes. "Until now. Until you, babe."

Caressing his face, I hold him in my hands. "I wish I could meet her as well. I'm sorry I can't. I'm sorry for your loss."

"She's a loss to so many, but I still feel the space in my heart, the hole she left behind."

"I feel helpless."

"This is not your burden, Weatherly. She told me to live a good life. To be happy. I feel like I've been doing both since I met you."

Three words keep tickling my tongue, but I clamp my mouth shut, well aware it's too soon for that declaration. Which makes me laugh since I never said it to my ex at all. I didn't even have the desire. That kind of says it all about my life before Dare. Maybe the day I met him is my re-birthday as well. "I feel the same about you."

We start back for the car, not in the same hurry as when we arrived. "You once told me that your mom would be disappointed you had kissed me, but not properly introduced yourself. I didn't pick up on that then."

"It wasn't a big statement, just something I said."

"Maybe, but she would be proud of you. Kissing aside, you're an amazing man. Talented and kind. You would make any parent proud."

Under a giant oak tree, he stops us and kisses me. "Thank you. I'm not a lawyer or anything." He taps my nose. "But I like to think she would love hearing me play. She gave me my first guitar."

"I know she would." He catches me batting my eyelashes, but I don't make apologies. I do love watching him play and hearing him sing, his passion pouring from all the broken pieces he's put back together.

We toss our wet undergarments in the bed of the truck and get inside. He starts it to get the air blowing while I fasten my seat belt. As soon as it clicks into place, he reaches over and tugs. "Secure," he says, speaking to himself. He did this on the way here too. Another way he shows me he cares. I'm spoiled rotten with his affections.

When he's settled in, I admire him—his profile, his hair, his kind heart. "Your hair looks good like that."

"A mess?" he asks, roughly running his hand over it.

"Yes. It's very sexy."

I get a wink. "Thanks. You're sexy. It was almost impossible not to make love to you back there."

Again, I could say something about how he chooses to use making love versus fucking, but it's just another way for him to show me how he feels. I don't want to ruin anything by pointing it out. I'll just enjoy it instead.

When he starts driving, I pull my lipstick from my purse and flip down the visor to use the mirror. I gasp from the sight of me.

"What?" he asks.

"I look like a horror show or a whore show. Either is fitting."

"What are you talking about?"

My surprise heads his way. "What do you mean, what I am talking about? I look like a raccoon from my mascara running down my face. It's obviously not waterproof. My concealer and foundation are completely gone. Look at the little rosacea spots on my cheeks and these freckles."

"I have been. I like them. I don't know why you hide behind all that gunk. You don't need it."

Pointing under my eyes, I ask, "And the raccoon eyes? How is this sexy?"

He shrugs. "It is to me. Not that it's running under your eyes, but that anytime I get to look at you is good. You're just naturally pretty. You don't even have to try."

My hand is pressed to my chest from feeling sappy inside. "I'm never prepared when you hit me with your best lines."

His grin softens, and he says, "They're not lines, babe. You act like I'm the biggest player out there." Leaning back, he controls the steering wheel with one hand while the other reaches over to rest on my thigh. "I've slept around, but everyone does. It was always safe sex if that worries you."

Everyone does . . . *not technically*, but that's neither here nor there now. "I trust you."

"Since I have your trust, I have a confession to make." I brace myself from the turn this conversation just took. He says, "Your bra and panties are see-through when they're wet. I didn't tell you because you looked fucking amazing. So I'm blaming your body for ignoring any signs of raccoon eyes."

"As my boyfriend . . ." I try for serious but can't keep a straight face. "You owe me the truth about that and my makeup. What if someone saw me?"

"Someone did. The only person who matters, Pepper."

"Let me guess," I reply sarcastically, and then punch him

in the arm. "You?" Since he's too busy laughing to say anything right away, I roll my eyes.

"Yes, me," he *finally* replies. "I promise to let you know next time. Boyfriend's honor."

"Saying such sweet sentiments will get you laid every time."

"That's the plan."

"You're ridiculous."

"You love it, though." He squeezes my leg gently.

I love it . . . and you. "I do." I play it off with laughter.

Just as we reach downtown, he asks, "About that date tonight . . . ?"

21

Dare

I KICK the fridge door shut and dump the sandwich makings on the counter. Pulling bread from the bag, I slap it down on a paper plate.

English comes around the corner and opens the fridge again, scratching his chest and letting the cold air out. "I'm not going to say I'm jealous, mate, but I'm fucking jealous. She is bangin'."

"Get some fucking manners," I snap.

"I thought getting laid on the regular was supposed to relax you," he laughs through his words. "Maybe you're doing it wrong."

English may be the shit stirrer of the four of us, but I'd be hard-core teasing him if the roles were reversed. "You're not fucking funny, so drop it." I was already over the conversation before it started. I have no intention of keeping my relationship with Weatherly on the down low, but I'm not in a mood to talk about her with them today. I'll never hear the end of it even though I might not this way either.

The silence causes me to turn around. His mouth is hanging open with an unopened beer in his hand. "What?"

"What do you mean what?"

I roll my eyes. "You're being annoying."

"Me?" He shakes his head. "Must have been good pussy."

"Fuck off."

"Damn, dude. Got your girly feelings in a twist?"

I need to rein it in, whatever *it* is—feelings, impatience, stuff I don't want to think about right now. "Get off my dick. I'm tired."

The spritz of the can opening sounds as he walks past me. He elbows me in the back but is smart enough not to say anything. His laughter is still annoying as fuck. I toss the deli meat bag at his back, landing it solidly against his neck. I find that funnier than it should be and start laughing.

He's quick enough to catch it before it hits the ground, stealing it. "Turkey. My favorite."

"Fucker." My pride has me slapping lettuce on the bread between two slices of American cheese before dousing the other piece with mustard. "I don't need turkey anyway," I mumble.

Lennox comes in and sets his mug in the sink. "What's going on? Where have you been all day?"

"Everyone wants to ride my jock today. You guys really need to get a new pastime."

"Talking isn't the same thing as riding your jock, man. You don't want to talk, fine with me." He grabs bread from the bag and drops them into a toaster. "Why are you so defensive?"

Talk. Talk. Talk. Talk.

He'd never betray our friendship or the family creed our mothers ingrained in us—*you're never alone, and we're brothers till the end*. His opinion matters, so I need his acceptance of Weatherly no matter what side of Austin she comes from.

So he's right. I am defensive. Protective. The whole fucking range when your heart is on the line. This is new for me, but I get the feeling it's new for her despite having an ex. "She's not like the others."

Lennox has a wild side he lets loose sometimes, but he's also the peacemaker of the group. "That's a good thing if you didn't know. So why are you in a bad mood?"

"It feels weird to talk about her. Fuck me. Maybe I am full of girly feelings." I shake my head at myself. "I don't want talk about her that—"

"That disrespects her?"

"Yeah. Pretty much."

"We don't normally. Groupies are groupies. They want the attention. They get it sometimes. Girlfriends are off-limits. We know the rules." He stops and turns to look at me. "Is she your girlfriend?"

"Yes." I don't need Lennox's approval. I don't need anyone's, but that doesn't stop me from wanting it for some dumb reason. These guys aren't just like brothers to me. They are my brothers. We've been to hell and back together and survived. They can read me like no other. Beyond reading me like a book, it must be a vibe I'm putting out that tipped them off. Though I'm pretty sure it might be this stupid grin I can't wipe from my face.

"Cool." Biting into his dry toast, he walks out as if it's no big deal that I have a girlfriend. Is it?

Glancing at the time, I have an hour before I need to leave, and the doorbell rings just in time. We may have fucked, made love, and everything else in between, but I still want everything to be perfect tonight.

"Hello?" Helen calls as she walks through the front door.

"Mom?" Lennox leaves the kitchen. "What are you doing here?"

I walk out to greet her and to free her hands, but she smacks mine instead. "I could have brought the stuff in."

She waves me off as she hugs her son. "Peesh. It's not heavy." Looking at Lennox, she asks, "How are you doing?"

"Good. In the neighborhood?"

"I'm here for Robert, but it's always good to see my son."

Since my mom died, he's never once complained about seeing his mom or her talking to him like he's a baby. As annoying as that can be, I'll never have that again. It makes me miss my mom even more, but I'm lucky to have Helen.

When she spots the toast in his hand, she adds, "Let me make you something to eat. I brought lasagna over for you boys. It's your night off, right?"

Lennox takes the cooler bag into the kitchen. Helen hugs me. "Len, that's Rob's bag. You can just leave it on the counter for him." She leans back and smiles at me. "She must be special."

"She is."

Helen takes my face in her hands and then pinches my cheeks. "Such wonderful news."

She says stuff like that all the time, stuff my mom would have said. They were best friends, so it makes sense, but it also makes my heart clench. "Thanks." I nod toward the bag. "Thanks for helping me out."

"You know I'm happy to anytime I can. Anyway, you made it easy by having the menu planned out. I just put it together. You want to impress her, huh?"

I smile, and now I feel fucking stupid, but just thinking about Weatherly gives me the grins. "The best I can."

"Be you, and that's good enough." I follow her to the kitchen, and she unzips the top of the bag. We peek inside, and she explains what's in each dish. "Bring the dishes and bag back when you have a chance." Over her shoulder, she says, "Lennox, fetch the lasagna from the back. That thing weighs a ton."

English comes in. "Good to see you, Mum."

"You too. You hungry?"

He rubs his stomach. "Always."

"Good. I'm going to heat up a homemade lasagna."

"You're too good to us," he says.

"I have a feeling it's the only real meal you'll have this week."

"Taco Bell makes a mighty fine taco."

I start laughing, but he gets a glare in return for that. Helen turns back to me and lowers her voice. "How are you, Robert?"

"I'm good. This weekend is on my mind."

She zips the bag closed and leans against the counter. "I've been thinking about Sunday."

"Me too."

"Are we sticking to tradition? Visit her and then go back to mine for an early dinner."

I nod and feel my chest grow heavy. "Sounds good."

"If you have a show—"

"We don't. I kept the schedule clear, so I'll be there."

Lennox sets the humongous dish down on the counter. "This will feed us for a week."

"Good," she replies. English comes in with a grocery bag and places it on the counter. "I brought salad and dressing. Can you help me make the garlic bread?" she asks.

English is on it. "Yeah. I can do it."

Lennox comes around, catching a glimpse of me and seeing more than I wanted to reveal. "What are we talking about?"

Might as well let him in on it. "Sunday," I reply. "You coming?"

"I wouldn't miss it."

Clapping his back, I say, "Hitting the shower." I hug Helen. "I sent the money to your account. Thanks again for doing this."

"My pleasure. Have fun tonight."

"I will."

"I hope to meet her. Maybe on Sunday?"

I stop just as I reach the living room. What Weatherly and I have and are to each other is still new. We may be jumping ahead in some ways, but I worry about laying too much at her feet. What if I'm in deeper than she is? "I'll think about it."

As I walk down the hall, I hear her tell Lennox, "He's got a girlfriend. Have you met anyone?"

She makes me smile, but Lennox makes me laugh when he replies, "No one you'd approve of."

"Try me."

"All right. She's in my bed."

"What?" Helen's voice pitches.

He chuckles. "I'm kidding, Mom."

"Peesh. You boys are going to give me a heart attack."

I start the shower, thinking it will be quick, but my dick has other plans. Apparently so does my mind as memories of her in that tub come back.

Delicate. She's even delicate when she masturbates—little circles, quick fingers with pauses built in to enjoy the sensation. A vision I've added to my sexual arsenal file already.

I step under the hot water and let it pour over me. It feels so good on my shoulders, loosening the tension I've been feeling since I left her earlier. I run the soap over my body and then give my cock a little extra attention—a firm grip and slow start, moving to find the rhythm that will help me to chase down an orgasm.

Her face—mouth open, eyes closed, head pushed back displaying that delectable neck.

Her moan—wanton, tensed, lower as if she'll be overheard.

Her body—perky tits glistening from the water covering them, bubbles clinging to her knees.

The memory of her is perfection and gives me all the material I need to get off. My hand slams against the wall, and my head drops lower. I succumb to the darkness, sinking until reality resurfaces.

Exhaling all the excess energy, I push off the wall, ready to see her again. This time I hope to get through the meal without wanting to attack her. She deserves romance, and I'm the guy who's going to give it to her.

ARRIVING EARLY, I pass the time by working on a song I started the other night. But the cab of this truck isn't big enough for me to play my guitar properly, so I get out and release the tailgate. Sitting on the end, I strum and try to remember the beginning.

My fingers find their way, and the melody starts coming together. The right place. The right time. My creativity has been flowing lately, and I give Weatherly all the credit.

"Hey, hero, what are you doing out here?"

Seeing Weatherly takes my breath away. Her hair flows free, a pair of jeans hugs her hips, and her voice matches the melody I just sang. She's become my muse. Maybe she's the one I've always been singing to.

She stands between my legs, pressed to the guitar, and kisses me as though she's missed me. The way she moves, her lips pressing to mine, her hands on me. She's sex on fire. When she lands back on her heels, I say, "You keep kissing me like that, and I'm not sure we'll make it out of this parking spot."

Her happiness beams through her smile. "That threat sounds more like an invitation since I don't think I'd have a problem with that."

I hop down, shaking my head. "Death of me. This girl," I mumble, putting my guitar back in the case. I shove it behind the bench in the cab and come around to help her in. "I was going to come to your door."

"Stan, the doorman, called to tell me that I might be interested to know there's a man playing a guitar in the parking garage."

I laugh. "Oh, yeah? What did you say?"

"Nope, no interest here. Not one bit. Then I grabbed my purse and got here as fast as I could."

"Gotta be careful these days about those rogue guitar players."

"For sure. I hear they're making women weak in the knees everywhere they go."

"Like a hit and run."

She leans against the side of the truck, staring up at me. "With swoons and great music. They've been known to kiss well too."

"Really?" She licks the corner of my mouth, practically panting.

"Mm-hmm."

Resting my hand on the top edge of the truck, I lean down so I'm closer to eye level with her. "Sounds dangerous."

"For my body," she says, very convincingly. Grabbing my shirt, she pulls me closer. "You should protect me."

"I'm the bad guy, remember?" I whisper.

"Then why do you feel so good?"

"Bad things always feel better than they should. But you know what?"

Her breaths come heavy. "What?"

"Bad things taste even better than they feel."

"Is that so?"

"It's so." I kiss her.

My hair is tugged before her hands slide down and wrap around my biceps. Kisses become frenzied, but then she breaks for a breath. "You're right. You taste incredible, like sherbet in the middle of the night." She pokes my stomach.

Chuckling, she has a point. "I'll give you sherbet because I know how much you like it. So if that's what I taste like to you, I'll take it, babe. You ready to start this date?"

"I sure am."

I pop the door open and help her in. "You look pretty."

Looking down at her lap, she plucks the top. "It's just a shirt and jeans. No big deal."

"Big deal or not, you still look pretty to me."

Her cheeks pink as she sits. "Thank you."

"You're welcome." I'm about to shut the door, but I kiss her again instead. She's my girlfriend, and like a bolt of lightning strikes, I realize how amazing that is. Since she's still waiting on me, I hurry around to the driver's side and get in.

We leave downtown, and I cut across Bee Caves Road to 360 and go south. It's a great night to be out. She's still high on finishing law school and can't seem to keep her hands off me. "I want to celebrate."

"That's what I've planned." With the wind blowing

through the cab of the truck and my girl by my side. Life is good. *Very good.*

I park. When we get out, I pull my guitar and a blanket from behind my seat, and then reach into the back to grab the padded cooler bag.

"What's all this?" she asks.

"I thought I'd treat you to the third best view in town."

Excitement flashes in her eyes. "The 360 Bridge and water. It's beautiful here." We walk across the large flat grassy land. "Iconic Austin."

While we spread the blanket out on the ground, she asks, "If the bridge is the third best view. What are the first two?"

"Your apartment's view of the city is second."

"And the first?"

"Isn't it obvious?" I pause, taking in all of her. "You."

22

Dare

"THE CICADAS ARE SINGING WITH YOU," Weatherly says, lying on her back. With her hand on her stomach, she stares up at the stars. I continue strumming an instrumental version of one of The Heroes' more popular songs. I'm just messing around, but she smiles. "I like that." She peers back at me. "What is it?"

"Don't fuck around when I'm out of town." I start laughing, setting my guitar down. "It's a line from a song that English wrote after his girlfriend cheated on him."

She sits back up and laughs. "And here I thought it sounded romantic."

"I slowed the tempo."

"I didn't know he had a girlfriend."

"He doesn't," I say, "because she fucked around when we were out of town." The line still makes me chuckle, and I've sung it a million times.

Over a blanket of empty containers that hold the

remains of pasta salad, various fruit, and cupcakes, her laughter rings around us and keeps me smiling. Watching a boat cruise by, she says, "I love being near the water."

I wrap my arms around my bent knees. "I'd like to have a house out on the lake one day, some property to let my kids run free without worrying, and to be able to have the whole place wired and amped without any neighbors close enough to complain. It's a big dream."

"You'll have that one day. I know you will. You're on a path to success."

I return my gaze back to her and smirk. "Says the lawyer."

"It's not my dream, but it was a goal. I proved to everyone I could do it."

"You sure did. What's next?"

"The bar exam in July." She gets up and moves to sit in my lap. With her tucked inside my arms, she adds, "And, well. We happened so fast, so I don't know if you'll be into this or anything, but I've been meaning to ask you if you'd like to come to my graduation party?"

Hearing her stumble over the invite has me tightening my hold on her, but I'm surprised by the invite. We said no hiding and here she is taking a big step for me. "I know it feels like we're not on steady ground with so much still to learn about each other, but I appreciate you asking me."

"It means meeting my dad, mom, and everyone at my house." She twists to look me in the eyes. "We've joked about it, but as we also said, I don't want to hide us. You're a part of my life, and I want you there. Only if you want to be there, though."

"I want to be there for you." Pushing that long east side versus west side down, I'll do this for her. "When is it?"

"This coming Saturday. Are you booked?"

"Oh. Um. Yeah. Let me see what time we go on." I pull out my phone and hit the date. "What time is the party?"

"It starts at six."

I kiss her cheek. Knowing how she's putting herself out there for me has me feeling on top of the world. "I'll be there. We don't go on until eleven. I can cut out around nine to meet up with the band."

"Thank you. You know, I've been thinking. I don't know them well, but maybe the band would like to come? I'd love to have them there and get to know them better."

"Are you sure? They can be rowdy."

"It's only for a few hours. No one is getting wasted or anything. There will be my dad's associates and friends. This feels more like for my parents than for me anyway. But the band will make it more fun. What do you think?"

"I'll ask them." Rubbing my hand over my head. "It's nice of you to offer. Will your friends be there?"

"Yes. They've rsvp'd."

"Have you heard from them today?"

"I heard from Stascia. She texted."

"That's good."

"Yeah." When she looks out the window, I ask, "Are you okay?"

She smiles and leans her head to the side. "You don't have to worry about me. I love being here with you."

"Good."

A siren sounds behind us, and we look back to where I parked. "Ah, shit." We stand and watch as a cop walks toward us. I mutter, "What the fuck? "

The flashlight shines in my eyes causing me to squint. When he directs it in Weatherly's, I'm ready to take this fucker down. "How can I help you, Officer?"

Waving the flashlight on the ground around us, he says,

"This is actually private property." His eyes check out the picnic. "You don't have alcohol out here do you?"

"No."

His eyes have stayed on me for the most part, but there's something about the way he looks at Weatherly that stirs anger inside. "You okay, ma'am?"

Surprised by the question, her head jerks. "Yes. I'm fine. Having dinner with my boyfriend."

His gaze slides back to me. "Boyfriend, huh?" There's a long pause, and then he nods. "Someone called it in." Angling the flashlight toward the nearby offices, he adds, "Like we have nothing better to do than break up lovebirds having dinner. Sorry about this, but I'll need to ask you to pack up and leave."

"No problem." We bend down and start packing up the empty containers.

Weatherly is on her knees, helping. She looks up at me and says, "It was a lovely meal. Thank you."

Well, damn. Can I get any luckier? I steal a kiss. "It was lovely because of the company."

The cop whistles and starts walking back with us. Small talk is not something I want to make with this guy, but when we reach the truck, I set my guitar down and hold open the door for Weatherly. "Have a good night, Officer."

"Have a good one." He gets in his car and sits while we load in.

When I put the cooler bag into the back, she says, "Might want to put that up here. We wouldn't want it to blow out like our underwear."

I chuckle while shoving it behind my seat and put my guitar case on top of it. "You think someone on that dusty old back road has found them?"

"I hope not. I'm still mortified."

Climbing into the cab, I shut the door and start the truck. "Don't stress about the small stuff. I'm fairly sure no one wants our underwear."

"You're right. They weren't my sexiest anyway since I was dressed for my law exam."

"Legal briefs."

She giggles over my bad joke. Reaching over, I squeeze her knee, making her laugh even harder. "That tickles."

The siren flashes. Eyeing the cop behind us, I shift into drive. "Guess we should get moving."

"Do you want to come over to mine?" she asks.

"You don't want me to take you out? Go somewhere and have a drink to celebrate you finishing law school?"

"We can do that at mine. I have a bottle of champagne I've been saving for this occasion."

"I've never had champagne."

"You haven't?"

Shrugging, I reply, "Guess I haven't had an occasion for it."

"One day, you will."

I keep one hand on the steering wheel and one hand on her leg. "And what occasion will it be? My wedding?"

"When you sign a record deal."

Her certainty takes me by surprise. "You think?"

"I know. You're amazing. The music is amazing. The Heroes are going to be huge one day."

"I appreciate that, babe."

"I only speak the truth." I turn to go downtown when she says, "You've mentioned kids and a wedding. So that's in your plans?"

I hadn't thought about it but said what I thought. I guess

she brings it out in me. "The grand plan. Not something I think about—"

"Sounds like you have a little."

I grin, not sure if she can see me or not in the dark of this cab. "A little." I glance at her. "Very little."

"Okay. Okay. I get it." I can practically hear an eye roll in her response. "You don't want to talk about it."

"The basics are that I do see myself with a family one day. I want the life I didn't have, and I can create that. What about you?"

"I would like to be married. I also want to start my career, but I can see being a wife and mother. I think it would be amazing to have a family of my own."

I slip my hand to the base of her neck and rub. "Seems we're on the same wavelength."

"Better to know now than down the road when it's too late."

"True." I turn on the radio.

She starts laughing. "Okay, I got the hint. How about we talk about the next week? That's less intimidating than a lifetime. What days do you play?"

I pull into her parking garage and find a guest spot on the second floor. "I have to check the schedule, but I think we're booked every night but Wednesday."

She hops out of the truck and comes around. "What can I carry?"

"I'm only taking my guitar with me." I lock up and hold her hand while we head to the elevator. She lets Stan, the doorman, know I'm parked in the garage, and we go upstairs.

Setting my case down just inside the door, I turn and lock up as she heads to the bedroom. "I'm going to change clothes. The champagne is in the wine cooler if you want to pop the cork."

"Glasses?"

"Left cabinet. Top shelf."

I pull the bottle out of the little fridge and study the label. I took Spanish, so I don't know what this says in French. I bet it's expensive. I've just popped the cork when Weatherly strolls back out dressed in those booty shorts I like so much on her and a tank top that could pass as a second skin. I approve. She clearly has no idea how incredible her body is.

I'm so used to women trying to impress me with their tits and ass hanging out of some skimpy lace that Weatherly being herself is more of a turn-on than the others ever were. Graceful and natural. *Gorgeous goddess.*

"You ready to celebrate, hero?" She picks up one of the glasses and holds it between us.

I pick up the other. "Here's to you, babe. I may not have taken this journey with you, but I'm so proud that I have the honor of being here now." I tap my glass against hers. "Here's to you. Congratulations."

We drink with our eyes locked. It's fizzy and tastes all right, but I prefer beer.

"Aw, thank you," she says and takes another drink, finishing half that fills the fancy glass.

I top it off, and then we go out on the balcony. She lies down on the lounger while I lean against the railing facing her. "What are your dreams?"

"To be a lawyer."

"Really? That's what you dreamed of as a kid?"

She takes another sip and looks past me at the stars. "What I dreamed of could have never come true." Her eyes find mine. "So does it matter anymore?"

"Yes. It matters."

"Then tell me yours. Did you want to be a musician?"

"Music wasn't a part of my childhood. Silence. Complete silence was." I finish the champagne in my glass and set it down on the table. "It must be the fucking bubbles making me stupid." Standing there staring at the lights of the city, I guess it's just time to open up. "My dad hated noise. He never wanted a kid. He didn't want a wife either." I laugh, but it's humorless. Just a nervous habit I can't seem to break when I talk about my childhood. "He wanted someone to wait on him without them having a say. My mother and I were neither. She was too strong, and I was too much of a kid—loud and boisterous—both of which she adored and encouraged once we were gone."

"Dare?"

"You don't have to feel sorry for me or anything. As I said before, she left him. She took me and nothing else." It took me years to get the sight of her bloody and beaten out of my mind. Sometimes, it was so horrible in my dreams that I swore it couldn't have been real. *But she had scars, internal and external, to prove that it was true.* I can't help but wonder if that aided her eventual downfall. Bruised her inside where no one knew until it was too late. She shouldn't have died so young . . .

Her hand rests on my back as she moves to my side. "What happened to him?"

"I don't know, and I don't care. Fuck him."

The heat she brings when she leans her cheek on my back is welcomed. I close my eyes and savor the feel of her. "You and your mom deserved better."

"We did, but we won in the end. He didn't realize the force she became. She was studying architecture when she got sick. She loved to drive around and study the unique buildings and houses of Austin."

She comes around and rests her forearms on the railing next to me. "What was her favorite style?"

"I forgot the name. Vintage Mediterranean isn't right, but it was something like that."

"Like old Hollywood homes. She'd probably love my parents' house. It's an old Mediterranean. You'll get to see it Saturday."

"We probably drove by it one time or another. As for my dreams, we don't make a lot of money now, but the potential is there. So anything is a possibility."

"When you get a record deal."

I smile at her and rub her back. "Yes, when we get a record deal."

"Do you mind me asking how your mom died?"

"She had pneumonia. She had a cough for a while, and then she just couldn't get out of bed to go to work. It was so quick. That was the worst part of it. No time to process her sickness or the finality of her being cut from my life. She deserved to live a long life, ya know?"

"I can't imagine how hard that would have been. You must have felt so alone."

"Yeah, I did. But I had Lennox and Helen."

"She sounds amazing."

"She has been there for me . . ." I feel my heart thrumming, and add, "She helped me with the picnic."

"That was nice. I hope to meet her one day."

Wrapping my arm around her, I pull to me. "I want you to meet her." I lean my head against the top of hers. What I've learned about Weatherly is that she is kind. Selfless. Thoughtful. *Loving.* She just invited me to join her and her family and friends to celebrate her graduation. I want her to be a part of my tradition. "So Sunday is this thing we do each year. Helen is going to make dinner after. Maybe you'd like to go?"

Her arms wrap around me, holding me so tight that she makes an *oomph* sound. "I'd love to. What's the occasion?"

"My mom's birthday."

23

Dare

DAYS DRAG because I've been living for the nights.

Nighttime is Weatherly time.

My senses are heightened around her, my emotions mixed up. She acts bigger than her small frame exposes, making me feel protective over her, though I haven't earned that right. Or the job as her boyfriend, technically.

I don't know if we make sense or not, but she feels right. So I'll take the job title and fulfill the requirements as long as she lets me.

Her diamond earrings catch the passing headlights, sparkling on her ears. She wears the tiniest gold band around her middle finger. There's no doubt that the jewelry is made of the real stuff. Precious metals and stones I can't afford.

Yet.

This car, though . . . Fuck me, it's nice, though it still pales compared to her. Her skin is softer than the leather seats of this expensive car, reminding me that she'll bruise easily if I'm not careful—physically, emotionally. Her eyes tell more of a story of what's going on in her head than the fancy screen on the dashboard can ever map out.

Tesla's are expensive, but Weatherly is exquisite.

I don't think I've ever once used that word. But here I am, using fancy as fuck words to describe the feelings I have for this woman.

I'm fucked. Shaking my head, I stare out the car window to distract me from the crazy going on inside my head. "Not to be nosy, but since I've been inside you, I figure I have a right to ask a few personal questions."

"That's so crude, Dare." She glances at me, that fire lit inside her baby blues. Then she laughs, and her gaze returns to the road. "And so hot for some reason." I think she has a few crazy ideas going on inside her head too. Maybe I bring it out in her. Now that's hot. "Ask away."

"How does a twenty-three-year-old afford a car like this?"

She tightens her grip on the steering wheel, which has her hands perched at nine and three, just how we're taught as kids. My girl is so responsible.

She might find my crudeness hot, but for some reason, I find her good girl image so fucking sexy. I don't know if I want to defend her from the world or taint her so no one looks at her the same way I do. Right now, I'm leaning toward the latter.

"I'm sure you won't be surprised that my parents gave me the car for Christmas."

"That's quite a gift. Santa's generous at your house."

"Yes. Very generous," she adds quickly.

I scoff. "I got a bottle of whiskey under my tree. It was a tree made of beer cans, so maybe it was fitting."

Her gaze latches onto mine briefly before returning to the road ahead. "I'm sorry."

"Don't be. There's nothing I hate more than people feeling sorry for me. I shouldn't have said anything." I turn to look outside the window, though I'd rather be still staring at her. This is not healthy. I'm not sure we are either, but I'm taking the risk without regret.

"I didn't mean—"

"I know what you meant," I snap, my twisted emotions getting the better of me. "Don't worry about it."

She goes quiet, and I feel like shit for snapping at her. "Fuck." She didn't do anything wrong. I need to set my ego aside and fix it. "I'm sorry. I didn't mean to say it like that. I'm okay with a beer can Christmas tree. Gifts don't mean anything to me," I lie. "I don't need shit given to me. I'm fine earning my way."

What am I doing? Why *am* I upset? Whatever I'm burnin' up about, she didn't cause it. I reach over, sliding my hand under her hair at the nape of her neck. "I'm tired. That's all. I have a lot on my mind, and with my mom's birthday coming up, I tend to be a little more live-wired with negative energy."

"It's okay." Even in the dark of the car, I see a pink color her cheeks. It reminds me of the roses growing on the side of the house—soft, delicate, intoxicating. "Do you visit your mom's grave much?"

Her tentative tone leaves me feeling worse for snapping at her. "We can talk about anything. Nothing is off-limits to you. I don't talk about my mom much, but I'll talk about her with you." I exhale the anxiety I've been feeling as the date nears, and then add, "She has a plaque. We had her cremated. I was nineteen, and we had no money so a grave and a coffin . . . funerals are expensive."

She keeps her eyes on the road as I ramble, "She wanted to be cremated. Hated the thought of taking up perfectly good space in nature. She was big into recycling and saving the planet. Earth Day was a real holiday to her."

"You must have so many wonderful memories."

"Yeah," I say, still grinning. "We once went to the beach to save the turtles. It was the only vacation we ever took, but I'll never forget catching her staring at me with so much pride, her frame couldn't hide it. She called it 'deliriously happy.' I thought she was nuts. I was only saving a few turtles."

"You saved turtles?" She mulls through the worlds thoughtfully. "That's the sweetest thing I think I've ever heard."

"I was just doing what I was told."

"Did you enjoy it?"

I take a second to remember how good I felt that weekend. "I did."

"That's beautiful." She's ripe with heartwarming emotions taking over—long and low exhales, her hand on her chest, her eyes glued to the outside—but I feel it, too. We're losing ourselves in each other, in each other's lives. The past and future. If we're not careful, we may miss the only opportunity we'll have to swim before sinking.

I'm hoping it's too late for her. It is for me. I don't want to be saved if I get to fall with her in my arms.

The mystery that she is to me makes me want to unravel her slowly, yellow ribbon by yellow ribbon . . . I whip my gaze to her again while visions of pigtails and yellow ribbons pop into my head. "Weird."

"What?" she asks.

I shake my head. "Just a memory."

"Care to share?"

"It's nothing. Not a memory I recognize."

The blinker flashes as she slows down to turn left. Turning off the winding road, she replies, "What was it? Maybe we can work our way back?"

"Doesn't make any sense. I just saw a girl with ribbons in her hair." I touch the top of my head like an idiot. She's not even looking.

"Hrm. Cousin?"

"No. I feel like my father targeted my mom because she was parentless when they met. And then he did a great job of isolating her from extended family."

"That's awful."

"Doesn't matter now."

We both sit quietly as she drives a little farther before she pulls off to the side and parks. "What color were the ribbons?"

"Yellow."

"I love yellow. It's my favorite color."

"Like your shoes." She's looking at me like I just grew a third eye, so I add, "The night I took you home. You had yellow ribbons wrapped around your ankles."

"I did," she whispers. "You remember that?"

I laugh lightly, but I remember every detail of our first night together, of her. I shrug. "It wasn't that long ago."

"I know, but . . ." she says, fidgeting with the hem of the cutoffs she slipped on before we left. "You did. I didn't think guys paid attention to that kind of stuff."

"I don't." Reaching over, I take her hand. "Normally. But everything about you is worth remembering." I kiss her.

Our lips part and she whispers, "Thank you."

We get out of the car and meet in the middle, our

shadows stretching out before us from the headlights. We went on a late-night excursion after my gig on a whim. Since I took her to one of my favorite places, she wanted to bring me to one of hers. I ask, "This is your favorite place?"

"It's not as cool as trespassing at a secluded swimming hole, but I love Mt. Bonnell. You can see forever."

"I haven't been here in years."

She's staring up into the inky night sky, her lashes long and her hair flowing like a waterfall over her shoulders. "You can see a million stars even though we're not far from the city."

I only see her, and that's enough for me.

When she catches me looking her way, a smile spreads, and she reaches for me. I take her hand and then rest my other on her lower back. "Dance with me."

Her laughter is music to my ears, and we start to sway. So willing to give me so much of herself without question. It's addicting. *She's* addicting. "There's no music, but you still like to dance," she says. "Why is that?"

I rest my cheek against her temple and keep dancing, hearing every note of our hearts beating together. "When I'm with you, I don't need to hear the music. I feel the rhythm." I spin her around and pull her back in. With my lips to her ear, I whisper, "Do you feel it?"

The gentle breeze is a chorus to her breathy whisper. "I do."

Under the crunch of gravel beneath our feet, I close my eyes, quieting my mind so I can tune in to listen to every pulse of her soul. But my heart pounds too loud, so I pull back despite the weight of our connection holding me there. Her gaze lifts, and for the first time in my life, I'm scared. "I feel . . . a lot for you, Weatherly." Despite some foreign desire brewing inside me, I fight it, running my hands through my hair and walking away.

I don't get ten feet before I have to turn back to the woman who blindsided me weeks prior. I never saw her coming, but now that our lives have collided, there's no recovering. "Why is it like this between us?" I ask.

"I don't know," she says, a slight plead to her tone as confusion wrangles her brows. "I don't understand it either. I don't know why I feel like this with you. I'm not irrational or spontaneous, but you make me want to throw caution to the wind."

"I'm the asshole who told you I don't make love since there's no love to be found inside me. But then I made *love* to you. I fucking made love. We made love together. This isn't normal. At least not for me. I know it's not for you either. So what do we do?" I turn around and stare off the cliff into the distance. If it were day, we could see for miles. At night, it's dots of lights across the hills. Otherwise, it's too dark to get lost in a view.

When I turn back, I notice she hasn't moved an inch from where I left her.

The lights illuminate her silhouette, and I stare like she's the devil herself or an angel in white. Is she? Can she save me? I try to reason through the insanity I feel rambling around my gut. "That makes two of us." I look at the stars, hoping to find the answers I need.

I hear the gravel as she moves closer, cautious with every step as if she'll scare me off. She can't scare me more than I am about what we are already. "I feel a lot for you, too, Dare."

She makes me feel weak, and I struggle under the range of emotions pumping through my veins. *Too much?* She makes me want to share the stuff I don't share with anyone. "You make me feel crazy."

Her feet wedge between mine as she settles against my chest. Our arms go wide while our hands stay clasped. *Perfect puzzle piece.* "No crazier than I am."

I swear I see the stars in her eyes. "So damn addicting." I lean down and kiss those delectable lips, wanting her to feel everything I do.

When she kisses me back, I realize she already does. But when feelings are stirred inside, I know we'll find ourselves in each other. And that not only makes me feel fucking justified in how protective I am over this woman but possessive. I won't own her like she already owns me.

She needs to soar, and I need grounding. Whether we work or not with others, we work together. That four-letter word starts bouncing around my heart, causing it to swell.

I'm so screwed.

I need to cool things down before kissing turns into me wanting more right here on the side of this cliff. "C'mon. Let's go for a walk."

With our legs dangling off the side of a cliff, I pull her back from the edge every time she leans forward. "Damn, woman. Be careful."

"Are you afraid I'll fall?" She laughs and then runs her hand up the back of my neck and into my hair. With her lovey-dovey eyes on me, she sighs happily. "Too late, hero."

I give her a light elbow nudge and wink. She rests her back on me, laying her trust in my hands. I wrap my arms around her, secretly giving her the same. "You worry about me?" she asks.

"Yes. Why haven't you heard from your friends?"

"I've been texting with April and Stascia, but I haven't been in the mood to go out."

"Why not?"

Leaning forward, she twists to look at me. "Because I like my time with you, and even though I'm not hiding our relationship, I'm enjoying this time alone with you."

"I'm enjoying it too."

She laughs to herself. "If I told them about you, we wouldn't have any peace. Trust me. They'd be there all the time."

"I can't complain about our alone time. I like it. A lot. But what about your family?"

"I stopped by their house today. My mom wanted to share the party plans. She told me she's proud of me for graduating."

"And your dad?" I watch her carefully. There's turmoil brewing where her family is concerned.

"My dad wasn't there. I'll see him at the party."

"You'd tell me if I was causing you problems, right, Weatherly?"

She turns back to face the city. "You're not." She glances back with a smile on her face. "You make me happy." Resting back again, she stares ahead into the vast darkness with her head on my shoulder. "Can we go to your place tonight?" She teasingly pushes out her bottom lip.

I kiss that lip and then bite it just enough to make her squeal. "Come on. Let's get you to bed."

As we walk back, she stops when we near the car. Looking me right in the eyes, she pats my chest. "You make me feel like the most beautiful woman in the world."

"You are beautiful." Cupping her cheeks, I add, "Don't let anyone ever tell you otherwise."

Her happiness is slipping away, some reality other than ours taking up space. "And if they do?"

"Tell them to come see me."

The joy seen in her eyes is enough to comfort me. "I think you're very dangerous for me, Dare Marquis."

"Not any more than you are to me, Weatherly Beck." There's no saving us now. We're too far gone. A lost cause to love. My mom told me to never close off my heart, and if this is what love feels like, I'm okay with it.

24

Weatherly

DARE IS COMPLICATED.

His emotions run deep and silent while he carries a lot of pain with him. I wish I could ease it, but that gorge is going to take time to fill. As strongly as I care for him and he cares for me, I'm hoping we have that time together. He's everything I always hoped to meet and never thought I would find.

I tiptoe into his house, but he doesn't bother to hide that he's home. "The guys sleep like bears. We won't wake them," he says.

"Good. I feel sticky from the humidity. Do you mind if I take a shower then?"

"Not at all."

"You going to join me?"

"I took a shower before we met up. I'm clean, babe."

"Who said you'd stay that way, hero?" I shoot him a wink.

He rolls his eyes and laughs. But he also starts

undressing so win for me. His shirt flies off, and he works on his jeans. He's naked before I have a comeback.

Resting my arms on the bathroom counter behind me, I snort. "That didn't take much convincing."

"What can I say? I'm a sucker for a woman who's wet for me." His hands take hold of the waist of my underwear.

"Do those lines work on all the women?"

"You say things like that as if the answer will change. It won't, Pepper. I don't use lines. I let my heart speak to you."

"What speaks to the others?"

"My dick."

Shoving him back, I laugh. "So crude."

"And hot. You know you love it."

My heart squeezes, and I answer honestly, "I do love . . . it." I almost forgot to tack that last part on.

I suck in a deep breath just as he swoops in, his lips covering mine, and we kiss. As I wrap my arms around him, our lips part, but our eyes stay on each other. "What goes on inside that beautiful head?" he asks.

Sometimes, I worry he'll lose interest, but I'm starting to realize we're not just about sex. "When someone cheats on you, trust is broken, and a protective wall is built. But you came into my life before construction had time to begin. So I worry about getting hurt. Are you going to break my heart, Dare?"

"No."

Simple.

Honest.

Direct.

"I'd never break your heart, babe." He reaches behind the curtain. "C'mon, the water's warm."

We step in, and after I rinse my body, he steps under and drops his head back. "Feels good."

"See?" I can't revel in my righteousness because he's breathtaking. With slicked back hair, wet from the water, his eyes are intense, studying me, peering into the soul he knows he already owns. It's the first time I've seen him bite his bottom lip, and it is not disappointing at all. I run my fingers through the hair above his ears. "It's always better sharing."

He laughs. "Okay, you win this round, but once I saw you naked, I wouldn't have been able to stay away." He winks, and yes, I swoon. He really is dreamy.

He's such a charmer when he wants to be, and it seems he wants to be with me. I'm happy to be spoiled, though I'm not used to it. Cars. The apartment. School. Superficially, I've been given every advantage in life. Emotionally, I try to believe my parents did their best, but I feel cheated.

Tightening my hand around him, I admire his body. Almost as if it's a habit, he reaches to muss his hair up. His face is tan, his eyes lighter when not hidden behind the dark strands of his hair. His jaw looks sharper, his lips fuller, his brow stronger when his face is fully exposed for the world to see. Dare's striking features make me weak in the knees.

It's not a toothy grin, but his smile is kind, almost shy from the compliment. Holding me by the waist, he says, "A lawyer, huh?"

For someone who is used to performing in front of crowds and stands at the forefront of the band, he doesn't seem to like attention as much as I would've suspected. So I play along, following his lead to a different topic. "Yep."

"Damn. Sexy, gorgeous, and smart." Tilting his head back, he stares into the heaven above. "Thank you, God."

Through a giggle, I say, "I didn't take you for the religious kind."

"I wasn't, but you've made me a believer."

If I'm not swooning from his sweet-sexiness, I'm smiling. "I don't even remember laughing before meeting you. You make me happy. It feels good."

Dare turns us around so I'm under the water. "You looked cold."

"I'm not. I'm good with you." I return to touching him.

"Why don't you laugh much?" he asks.

"Huh?"

"You said you don't remember laughing before we met."

"Oh, um. I don't know. I think I'm just too busy to enjoy life most days."

"Too busy is no way to live." One of his hands dips between my legs, and he rubs gently. "How are you feeling?"

"Better than I have in years." Keeping my eyes steady on his, I move my hand through the water and keep rubbing him, though not as gentle as he's treating me. "How are you feeling?"

A finger slips between my lower lips, eliciting a heavy breath from my chest. I struggle to keep my eyes open when the sexual sensations start taking over, but I do.

"Stop thinking so much. Just feel, Weatherly." His voice is muffled against my neck as he tilts and starts kissing me. I could die happy listening to how he says my name, his tone deep and warm. Another finger is slipped inside me as my mind rolls like a wave, toppling over itself to reach the shore, the release better than the adventure.

I lean my head back. "Tell me you're good for me."

"I'm a bad seed, babe." He picks up speed—not too fast and not enough to send me over. The most blissful torture.

"That feels so good. *You* feel too good to be bad for me."

Meeting my gaze, he says, "I'm just what you need, but you know what?"

"What?" Breathy. Wanton. Full of need. With his hands all over me, I can't think clearly.

"You're the woman I've been waiting for."

Needing to settle my unsteady thoughts, I step out of his reach and hold on to the wall. As the water bounces off his shoulders, I tread carefully back to him. My head is swimming—in this night, this conversation, *in him.*

"Does that scare you?" he asks.

"No."

He presses me when I'm at my weakest. "How do you feel about me?"

"I don't know, Dare. You're not something I can put into words quite yet. You're a feeling instead."

"How do I feel?"

It's too soon to dive into the deep end of our emotions, but I can't lie when it comes to this, my feelings about him. "You don't scare me. Feeling so much does. I was living so safely, kept in a small box, and you lifted the lid. You brought daylight. I'm still getting used to being my own person."

"How is that possible? You're a lawyer."

"That's books, studies, school. All the safe places I ventured. It was my comfort zone. But there you were, opening my eyes to so many incredible things, to life and living for myself instead of everyone else. I've traveled to Europe, New York, LA, Florida, so many places. So confined to what I was shown—great works of art, symphonies, big concerts, charity balls—but I'd never seen someone with raw talent like yours. It's you. Just like you said to me the first night. Everything I've done led me to that moment in time, that bar, that night, to you."

Our bodies reveal the change in the water's temperature. My nipples harden as goose bumps cover my skin and his.

He shuts off the faucet and grabs a towel from the rack. Wrapping it around me, he says, "Your life led you to me, but I was there waiting. You weren't a girl at the bar. You were the woman I was meant to meet but somehow already knew."

"Life is full of mysteries, and I can only assume that our paths crossed in another life."

"Another life that feels so much like this one." He grabs another towel, covering his lower half. Blowing out a long breath, he looks at the ceiling for a second, and then says, "It's late. I'm talking nonsense."

"It is late, but you make perfect sense to me." He makes more sense than only in this conversation.

He carries our clothes as we leave a wet trail across the ceramic-tiled hall to his bedroom. It's not messy, just as it wasn't the other day. I have a feeling he's a bit of a neat freak. When I think about him at my place, he's always helping straighten up and the first one to start cleaning any mess in the kitchen. He's so different from anything I expect. Full of wonderful surprises.

I'm handed clean boxers and a tee while he slips on briefs before we climb into bed. Lying on our backs, our bodies aren't touching, and I wonder how I ended up here. Not in this bed, but with him. I know the circumstantial evidence directs me right to the answer, but did the universe have a hand in us meeting? I feel we're more than luck or chance.

That doesn't change the facts of what was going on in my head the night I went back to the bar. I blurt, "I returned to Shep's because I wanted to sleep with you."

It's dark, and when I look to my left, I can barely make out the grin. "I know." His voice is low and gravelly. Smug. So sexy.

"What do you mean you know?"

I feel his shrug move the mattress, and then his laughter shakes it. "You don't think I recognize that googly starstruck look in a girl's eyes? I've seen it a million times, babe."

I pop him in the arm, but that doesn't hinder his laughter. "I was not looking at you with googly starstruck eyes. I simply found you utterly irresistible. There's a difference."

"And what might that difference be?"

"You called me Pepper."

The laughter stops, and I hear him take a breath, his eyes reflecting his inner thoughts. "Yeah."

We both look at the other once more, my eyes adjusting to see his unreadable expression. He says, "I shouldn't have brought you here. The sheets aren't clean and—"

"I wanted to come. I wanted to be in your space." I can smell him on the sheets and roll to my side and close my eyes. I love that he wishes he could make things perfect. He doesn't realize it's already perfect to me because it's him. "I like it here. It's comforting."

He strokes the back of his fingers across my cheek. "You deserve better."

"Dirty sheets, Dare? It's you. You told me no girl has been here, but I'm here, so I'll take you all night long. If you are referring to you, who's to say you're not the better I deserve?" The back of my hand bumps into his under the covers. When my pinky wraps around his little finger, I say, "I think you're amazing."

"Amazing, huh?" A crooked smirk works onto his face. "What's so amazing about a broke rock star?"

"That you pursued your dreams in the first place. You don't owe anyone anything. You live free."

"I'm damned proud of the name the band built around town, but I still live paycheck to paycheck. Gig to gig."

Sitting up, he leans against the wall. "I'm doing what I set out to do—"

"And what is that?"

"Play by my own fucking rules, but a soft place to land in an apartment decorated to the nines wouldn't be a bad place to crash sometimes." He winks. "Hint. Hint."

"My parents own the apartment. I don't own anything but clothes."

"There's freedom found in that. You can pick up and go anywhere at any time."

"I'm not that brave."

"You're braver than you know." He kisses my head, but it's not enough. I feel so connected to him emotionally that I connect us physically.

Moving onto his lap, I straddle him and hold my hands to his chest.

"Do you know how much I want you? Do you feel how hard you make me? You're the perfect wet dream of sweet and sexy."

Before I can speak, he sits up and grips my jaw, kissing me hard, kissing me like we won't get another chance. He engulfs a little moan and then reaches under my ass to flip me flat on my back before hovering over me. "How about we take these off?" he whispers, lifting my legs. The boxers are dragged down my legs, but not wasting any time, he sits up and removes his, bringing us skin to skin. *God, how I love his heat.*

Maneuvering between my legs, he presses against me, and says, "I want to fuck you so badly."

Not thinking, *feeling*, I say, "Do it."

"Fuck." His face is tense, all the pain warped into his closed eyes and forehead. It takes a moment, but he seems to regain control right when I had lost mine. "We shouldn't fuck without protection."

He's right. I was caught up in the moment, throwing that caution to the wind like I mentioned on Mt. Bonnell. But this isn't something we should leave to chance, even if I'm on the pill. "Do you have a condom?"

"Yeah." He pops out of bed and goes to the dresser. Pulling out a few, he tosses them on the bed before climbing back in. "You ready, babe?"

This . . .

Connection.

Sex.

Us.

Whatever we are, I want more of it.

"So ready."

25

Dare

Beautiful to look at but dangerous for my heart.

The lyric rolls around my mind as my beauty sleeps in my arms. I want to write it down, but deep down, I know I won't forget. *Like her.* She's already embedded herself right into the soul I vowed to protect. Somehow, Weatherly Beck has weaseled her way into a fortress I built years earlier.

Quick like the hours.

Sly like the wind.

Love came whispering where the pain pours in.

I've never been more drawn to someone before. Weatherly has blossomed in front of me. *For me.* "You were timid when we first met and now so bold," I whisper.

Her eyelids flutter open, the tips of her dark lashes tapping her skin. I didn't mean to wake her, but I'm not upset about it either. I like seeing her eyes with safe harbors surrounded by deep blue oceans. Angling her head back to give us space, she yawns, but then says, "I wasn't timid. I was nervous."

"Of what?"

"That you'd say no."

"I knew it." I chuckle lightly.

She pokes my ribs, and I laugh harder. "You're ticklish."

When she jabs me again, I can't stop the laughter that follows. "No. No. No. Stop. Stop." I grab her hand and bring it to my lips and kiss. "Please."

Giggling, she says, "Don't think I'm going to forget that you're ticklish." She singsongs the end, teasing me. "I'm going to tickle you silly when you least expect it."

"Ah, babe. The key is sneaking up on me. That's the real challenge."

"I'm not worried. I now know your Achilles' heel, and I'm not afraid to use it."

I'm at a loss. She plays dirty, and I have a whole lot of respect for that. "What's that?"

"Me."

She's got me all figured out. I kiss her hand to distract her. "Why were you nervous?"

"The way my heart beat hard in my chest when I first saw you and then quickened in the next. I've never felt anything like it."

"Love at first sight." I cringe the second after I say that. *Fuck.* What am I doing? *Retreat. Retreat. Retreat.* "Maybe . . . If that kind of thing exists."

The tips of her nails draw lines on my chest, and I can't help but hope they remain long after I leave this bed. "I like to think it does."

Moving up next to me, she brings my head to the crook of her neck and rubs lightly through my hair, her nails making my scalp tingle. I close my eyes to remember this, us like this, and how good this feels.

The sheet is pushed to the side, and she climbs on top of me. Straddling me, she's a temptress, no longer timid or nervous, but owning who she is, who she's always been before she was allowed to bloom.

With her bare breasts and slick pussy, it's so hard to remember that she might need time to recover when all I want is to bury myself deep inside her again.

She lifts my chin with her finger. "The next time I watch you on that stage, you're going to call me babe for everyone to hear."

As if I could get harder, that does it.

Fucking hard as a rock under her and all she did was sit on top of me and declare she wants me to call her babe in public. "You're mine, and I'll tell the whole fucking world."

With daylight spanning across the room and nowhere else for our true feelings to hide, she kisses me. As much as I have the urge to be inside her again, I kiss her back, sharing my past through each caress, sharing an intimacy with her that I've never shared before.

Our lips part, and we both take a breath while opening our eyes. Time has slipped out from under our thumbs. "The day's starting," I say. "Do you want to sleep?"

She looks toward the window. When she turns back, she says, "No. I want to have sex again."

We kiss, trying to keep this night to ourselves and live inside our bubble a little longer before we let others in. The beauty that she brings into this world should be cherished, so I do, kissing her collarbone. "Why do you taste so good?"

There's no verbal answer, but her body tells me everything I need to know. Nipples firm and press against me, head tilts back, and hips rock. She leans forward, putting her lips to my ear. "Dare?"

"Yeah?" I struggle to reply, wanting to be inside her again.

"Make love to me."

When I reach toward the nightstand, she stops me. "I want to feel all of you. I'm not tired, and I'm thinking clearly. You don't have girls over, and you said you don't have unprotected sex—"

"I don't." I pull back and look at her face, her eyes, trying to read her mind. She lifts up on her knees and takes my erection in her hand. "You're on the pill?"

"I am." She sinks down.

"Fucking hell. So—"

"Amazing."

Grabbing her hips, I release everything that isn't her. Weatherly. Pepper. My girlfriend. "You feel so good, so good, babe."

I start moving faster because my body demands it. Feeling good is an understatement to how she makes me feel. Powerful. Invincible. Loved.

This time, I don't let that last emotion stop me. I embrace it like I embrace her. "Tell me how you feel."

Planting her hands on my shoulders, I give her all the control, letting her own every thrust along with owning me. "Deep. Dare. So good. Mm. God." She leans back on her hands shortly after, her mouth falling open, and her eyes closing. "Oh, God." She heaves every breath uncontrollably. "Dare. Dare. Dare . . ."

Moving my fingers, I find her clit and focus on her. That spot behind her ear that makes her purr. The taste of salt against her dewy skin. My soap lingering on her body from the shower last night.

Her mouth closes, and she tilts down. "I want you to come, Dare. Come for—" She gasps again, her body trembling on top of mine as her orgasm grips her. "Yes. God, yes."

So close to trailing after, so I pull her off me and come. "Fuck."

We stay like this—my body covered—for minutes. When I can finally breathe normally again, I search for her eyes. That's when I realize how all-consuming she's become to me. I look away, my chest squeezing in ways that feel too much after what we just did. Overwhelmed, I twist like a tornado inside.

Her swallow is heard in the quiet room. "Why did you do that?"

My words catch in my throat because I'm about to tell her the truth, and not only does it kill me from the thought of not having her here, but I don't want to hurt her. "You don't need me or anything else holding you back in life."

"You aren't holding me back." Panic is felt in her fingertips as she presses them to my shoulder and looks over me. It's seen in her eyes. "You've shown me there's more to it than the life I was leading."

"That's why I pulled out. I won't be to blame for taking that away."

"Nothing is being taken away." She lies next to me, staring up at the ceiling. "I'm not arguing with you about it. I'm not ready to have kids either, so I get it."

"But that doesn't mean I don't want to be with you."

Her hand caresses my cheek. "I overthink everything, but us, I won't. I'll take what you're saying at face value."

"Good." I grin. "Can you grab me a washrag?"

She gets up and goes to the dresser, but stops when she sees the small metal frame. Leaning in, she says, "You do look like your mom."

When she turns back as if to confirm the resemblance, I

say, “Can we have this conversation when I don’t have cum all over me?”

With a laugh, she says, “I guess there’s a better time to have it. Bathroom?”

“Yep.”

She slips on the tee she had on earlier and slips out the door to the bathroom across the hall. Quick, she returns and tosses me the washrag. I get up and wipe myself while she disappears again. I catch her before she climbs back in bed because I see her rub her temples, I ask, “You okay?”

“I have a headache, and I’m a little sore.”

“I hurt you?”

“No. You didn’t. It felt amazing. I’m just not used to it.”

“Sex?”

“That . . .” Her eyes drop to my dick. “And you.”

“Nothing I can do about my size, babe. But I can get you some ibuprofen.”

She laughs, climbing in bed. “Ibuprofen, water, and rest. I think I can use all three.”

“Coming right up.” I pull on basketball shorts and go to the kitchen. After refilling our glasses from earlier, I get a few pain relievers and return. I don’t want to only tell her how much I care about her. I’m determined to show her.

Despite being fairly fast, she’s asleep when I come back in. I sit beside her, moving the hair away from her face. Hope has a conniving way of sneaking into the room and implanting itself in my heart.

Fuck.

I’m so screwed.

I get back in bed and snuggle around her, careful not to wake her. We both need rest, and it’s easy to find sleep with her here when I close my eyes.

We’ve not been asleep long enough when she kisses me

on the head. When I open my eyes, she says, "I'm going. I have to do a few things today, but I'll see you tonight. Okay?"

"Okay," I reply groggily. "Call me later."

She stops at the door and turns back. "Not text you?"

"I want to hear your voice."

Even though I'm tired as all get-out, I peek up at her fast enough to catch that smile I love so much. "I'll *call* you later then," she says.

"Hey, babe?"

"Yes?"

"Have a great day."

"You too. I'll see you tonight at the show."

I try to fall asleep again, but shortly after she leaves, Lennox barges in. "He did it!"

"Get the fuck out, Len." I pull the pillow over my head.

It's ripped away, and I sit up like an idiot trying to reclaim it. "Give it back. I'm tired."

"Dare! Listen to what I'm saying."

"What are you saying, fucker?"

"Dick James just mentioned The Heroes on the radio."

It's too early to decipher his words. "What?"

"Dick. Fucking. James, Dare. He just recommended the band on the radio before he played one of our songs."

Jumping up, I grab the pillow and throw it back on the bed. "Dick did?"

"Yes, motherfucker. Dick James just pimped us out."

"Holy fuck." We run out of the room where English and Romeo are celebrating. Romeo grabs English, and they shove each other and then hug it out. "Dick James!" Romeo yells. "Final-fucking-ly!"

We yell a few more times and then all jump in the pool because what else are we supposed to do at ten in the morning to celebrate our lives changing forever? Hopefully . . .

We rode the high of the radio promo, and just as promised, my girl was in the audience when we took the stage. That was our best show ever and when I called her "babe," she turned bright red. Sure enough, I saw those stars in her eyes again.

26

Weatherly

"So you'd never get one?" The rough pad of Dare's finger scrapes over my hip bone.

"I didn't say I believed the same as my father," I reply with us sprawled across my bed.

"A tattoo on you would look incredible." He kisses the soft, pale skin of my lower belly where the sun never reaches. "Right about here."

"No one would see it there."

Peering up at me, he waggles his eyebrows. "I would."

If blissfully happy is a thing, I have it. I muss up his hair. He'd do it anyway, hating when it's too "neat" as he calls it, so I let the slight wave waterfall across my hand. The brown of Dare's eyes is lighter compared to the dark that surrounds us. I roll my fingertips over the muscle of that amazing V that leads to all good things and then higher, stopping just beneath an abstract heart tattooed on his chest. "This is my favorite."

His hand covers mine, and he says, "I got that one right

after I heard our song, 'Abstract Heart,' on the radio. One of the biggest highs of my life."

"I didn't know you had a song on the radio before?"

"Years ago. An old DJ friend got it put into circulation for a few weeks. The thing about having dreams come true is sometimes they crash and burn right after. Nothing came of it."

"That sucks, but you had a song on the radio. Something most bands will never have."

"I remember seeing an interview with some band from the 80s like A-Ha or Kajagoogoo—"

"Who?"

"Doesn't matter. My point is they were asked how it felt to be a one-hit wonder."

"What did they say?"

"Better to hit once than never." His gaze hits mine. "That just always stuck with me."

Thinking about the meaning, I nod. "It's true." I still don't know what a lot of the tattoos mean to him, but I'm enjoying the slow burn of learning about each one in due time. "More to come?"

"Tattoos and in music."

We've packed months of adventures into the last week. From hidden swimming holes to late-night shows to kisses in the a.m. and jogs along the river at sunset, we're building a life together as if we've known each other longer. We kiss, the plushness of his full lips embracing mine, keeping me cocooned in our little bubble. This kiss isn't about the sex to come. It's about the strings that already connect my heart to his. "I trust you, Dare." *With my heart and happiness.*

His gaze moves up to mine as he lies next to me again. "I trust you, too." Turning, he brings me closer by a gentle pinch of my chin. "Wholeheartedly." I'm kissed again, slowly and steady—*wholeheartedly*.

I love that we have the big talks between the sheets. Maybe we're unique in that way, but here, our guards are down and our hearts are open. There's no judgment by him or me. We can say what we feel and do what we please.

Freedom.

Anyway, with his job taking place at night, our nights become our days. So I'll take him at midnight or two a.m. I'll take him whenever I can get him.

He has a lot on his mind by the layer of fog that's set in his eyes. "How do you pay for things when you don't have a job?"

That question might offend some people. April would be. Lloyd would be. As for me, I understand where he's coming from. "My parents said they'd pay my way through the bar exam. I take that in July, so I have a little time."

"And that's what you've been doing? Moving from studying the other exams to the bar?"

"Yes."

He climbs out of bed and starts pacing. Watching him scratch the back of his neck, I realize it's the first time I've seen him awkward. It's kind of charming with his lopsided twist to his lips and the curve that curiosity carves into his eyebrows. "Your father . . . What's he like?"

"Judgmental," I deadpan.

Stopping at the window, he moves the curtain to the side as if he's scoping the area out for security purposes. "That doesn't help."

"I didn't know you got nervous."

"I do when it comes to parents. I haven't met many over the years, but this is important to you, so I want to make a good impression."

I climb out of bed, not feeling the need to wrap the sheet around me or run into the bathroom to grab my robe before his eyes land on my bare body. No, I walk right up to his naked body and lift up to kiss him. His hand stretches across my backside and holds me there as we share another.

As if I do this all the time, I leisurely glide my hand over his hard abs and our kiss deepens. I never knew how much I craved seduction until my lips met his. He tastes like heaven mixed with an added hint of honey. *Delicious.*

An unbridled passion is felt in the way his fingers finagle their way over my skin, making sure he's touched every part of me. I revel in his hands, the way he looks at me, and how we fit together.

We fit—body, soul . . . *forever?*

Could he be the one for me? Are soul mates a real thing?

I'm an evidence-based girl, and nothing around me would support this theory. Thirty years ago, both families benefitted from my parents' match. Do they love each other? Sure. I'll give them that. Are they soul mates? I don't think their well runs that deep.

April . . . who knows what goes on in her head. It's strange to even think of her right now when we haven't talked in days. Considering how hard she can be on me, I don't believe she cares that much about me. I could show her how happy I am with Dare, and she'd insert her negativity. I worry about him coming to the party. He can handle that crowd, but can I?

There's no way I'm backing out now. I refuse to give in to them or their opinions anymore. As for April, she's just a miserable hag. She would never admit that she gloats in other people's misery. That is a sign of weakness she would rather ignore than amend.

As for Stascia, her heart is usually in the right place, but sometimes, popularity goes to her head. The only expectation of her growing up was to be pretty, and she has it down. I wish her family could see how funny and clever she can be when given the opportunity.

Watching my real-life version of the statue of *David* has my thoughts returning to the future. Dare Marquis makes it so tempting to jump five steps ahead and live wild and free. He asked me to move in with him. Temporarily, but still. I'm thinking he's just as invested in us as I am.

I say, "I won't sugarcoat it because that would be doing you a disservice. There's no winning my father over. He has to win at all costs, so your best bet is to play into his hand, humor him, and always agree with him. If he gets even a whiff of blood in the water, he'll attack."

"Not helping, Pepper. Not at all."

"Play his game, and he'll leave you intact." I get a glare for that one, causing me to giggle. "Okay. Okay. For real, just steer clear of him except when I introduce you. I'll make it short and sweet, and then we'll get the hell out of there."

"The party? Are you coming to the show? We go on late."

"No, his office. He'll be holed up in there reigning from his throne. I'm going to try to make the show."

The muscles in his shoulders ease. A little. "Good. How about your friends? We didn't exactly get off on the right foot."

"Focus on Stascia. April will get jealous and try to win you over just to get the attention."

"She sounds charming."

I laugh, but it's sort of a snort-scoff.

Dare shakes his head. "You're really no help."

"You only have to be you. I adore you, so they will." I do adore him, so much. Everyone will compare him to Lloyd, but once they meet him and see how he treats me, there's no way they won't love him like I do . . . I freeze to the spot . . . love him like I do . . . Only my eyes move to see him out of the corners. That's what this feeling is, the one that overwhelms me and has me thinking about him all the time.

I didn't feel this with Lloyd. He was like a cousin that was fun sometimes and awful others. That Dare cares so much to be nervous shows how much he cares about me. This is a big event in my honor, and he's the first one to want to celebrate and support me.

Where have my friends been?

My family?

A few texts here and there and a quick visit are all I've gotten. The funny thing is that time has flown, and I haven't felt like anything was missing. Dare is doing more than all of them combined. His love speaks to me through every one of his actions.

Suddenly, the phrase *love him like I do* doesn't scare me. It comforts me.

Reassured, Dare gets back in bed, taking me with him. His hands are behind his head, and he lies back on propped up pillows. "One last question."

I cuddle right into this tattooed god's arms. "Hit me."

"What do I wear?"

"Do you have a tie?"

THE HISS of the door hinges rubbing together wakes me. When I open my eyes, the room is still dark, but there's enough light pressing against the curtains to know it's daytime. Dare closes the door behind him and comes to the side of the bed. "Sorry. I tried to be quiet," he says.

"It's okay. I've slept long enough."

"I brought you coffee and some donut holes. I didn't know what you'd like."

I rest against the headboard and pick up the cup of coffee from the nightstand. "I love both. Thank you." I take a sip, and then ask, "What time is it?"

"You could use the rest, so I let you sleep."

A sinking feeling fills my gut, sloshing around with the coffee. "What time is it, Dare?"

I glance at the clock at the same time he answers, "Just past eleven thirty."

"What?" I don't mean to shout, but panic takes over. I push off the bed and set the cup on the dresser. "How is that possible?" Pointing toward the curtains, I say, "I've become a night owl. It's screwing with my days."

"What's wrong?"

"I'm late." I run into the bathroom and start the shower. Twisting my hair up, I catch Dare's reflection as he leans against the doorframe.

"What are you late for?"

"I'm supposed to meet my mom and dad for lunch at the house."

"That's good, right?"

"Yes. It's a recap, so to speak, of the exams and what's next."

Moving to the tub, he sits on the ledge. When I walk to the shower, his eyes follow the curves of my body. I stand a little straighter and walk a little slower. I open the glass door and step inside, but still hear him ask, "What's next? After the exam?"

While I wash my hair, I reply, "A job."

"At your father's firm?"

Thinking about what I want, I rinse and finger conditioner through my hair quickly. I've spent years trying to figure out what I want. I wasn't brave enough to even consider other possibilities. That's not who I am anymore. "I'd like to hear his offer."

"So you might turn it down?"

"I don't know. He may not even give me an offer."

"Why wouldn't he?" He opens the fogged-up glass door.

I lift my head from under the spray to find the kindest smile on his face. He says, "Hi."

"Hi." I wash my body, but I'm tempted to drag him in with me. Screw it. I reach for him.

"You're late, remember?"

"I don't care."

"You will later." He shuts the door. "We have all night, babe."

Like always, he's right. I finish up and turn off the shower. He never leaves the bathroom until I do. Once I'm dressed, I grab my Louis Vuitton and slip on my Tory Burch shoes. My mom likes designer, so I wear her gifts since I know she'll approve.

I apply my lipstick and then turn toward Dare who's sitting on the bench at the foot of my bed.

"Wow. You look like a movie star."

"Is the dress too much?" I look down fanning out the pale pink dress with the black velvet belt.

"No. You're just so pretty."

I'm so late, but I take a minute to sit on his lap. With my arm around his shoulders, I say, "Thank you. What are you going to do while I'm gone?"

"Music. Write and play a little."

"Are you coming back to my place tonight?"

Standing, he sets me on my feet, and then takes my hand to lead me to the door. "I'm wherever you are, babe."

I'm about to race out the door, but I stop, and go to my

junk drawer in the kitchen. Digging through the mess, I find what I'm looking for. I return to my handsome boyfriend and give him a key. "You can stay all day if you want, but if you leave, you know you can return."

Holding the key up, he says, "This is a big step."

"Look at me, being all brave."

A quirked smirk strikes his face. "Look at you, indeed."

"I'll see you later at the show." I lift up and kiss him. "Wish me luck."

"I wish you everything you ever dreamed of, Pepper. Go show them who they're dealing with." He kisses me.

"Break a leg, hero."

27

Weatherly

THE IVY-COVERED RED BRICK WALL, *aka* the fortress as I called it as a kid, leads to the grand wrought-iron entrance. I click the remote and drive onto the west Austin estate. The expansive property is a rarity in the city limits, but enough money can buy anything. I'm not ungrateful. It's a beautiful home. I'm just so unsure where I stand with my parents and their expectations these days, so my nerves have kicked in.

I haven't heard a peep about breaking up with Lloyd, which speaks volumes. I'm not sure how to break the news to them that we aren't meant to be, but I'm hoping when I do, they'll be happy for me because I'm happy.

I reach the back parking near Gram's cottage and grab my purse. Before rushing in, even though I'm an hour late, I look around. As an only child, I used to have great adventures here, living in my own make-believe world. I was a pirate one day and a princess the next. It was the only way I could stave off the loneliness.

When did the magic disappear? *I know.*

On my thirteenth birthday, I sat across the desk from my dad who told me exactly how my life would be. Then I was dismissed to attend my party. Today feels eerily similar. *Be brave.*

I hurry to the house, cutting across the lawn. Barging into the kitchen, I say hi to the staff but rush down the hall without running. Standing outside his closed doors, I tug on my skirt and then knock.

"Come in," my mother calls from the other side of the solid wood doors. I take a deep breath, and on the exhale, I slide the doors open.

The wood paneling and the tall bookcases that line the wall give an aura of seriousness. The books aren't classics, but law and research books, and encyclopedias and reference material. There are a few collectors' editions on the top shelf, but I've never been able to reach them. I tried standing on his chair once. I was five feet too short.

This isn't a place for laughter and good times. It was designed for business and intimidation. The heaviness of the room makes it dark even in the middle of the day. Leave it to my mother to have the table moved by the window.

She smiles as if she's seeing the person she always wanted me to be, but then she glances down and does a once-over. "Burch and Vuitton together? That's quite a statement, Weatherly."

"They're designers who aren't lunching with us. They won't know I mixed and matched."

"Matched is a bit of an overstatement." She scrunches her nose. "Doesn't matter now, I suppose. We're glad you could join us since you're the woman of the hour. "

Originally from east Texas, she has a Southern drawl that befits how she sees her role in life—wife, mother, junior leaguer, and perfect hostess.

My father is twenty years older than she is, and she had me by my age. So sitting here at twenty-three, they both see different paths for me. She wonders about marriage and kids, and he's worried about my career. It's never dull when it comes to expectations around here.

No matter what I do, it will never change the fact that I'm not the mini Bonnie she did her best to mold. Her rules were too confining for my wild spirit as a child. Now they're too submissive for who I want to be as an adult. I can respect her decision to support the man in her life in any way that helps him succeed, but I prefer a partner where I'm an equal and decisions are made together.

My grin is tight, but I still remember my manners. "My sincerest apologies for being late. I've been studying late into the night." I greet my father and kiss him on the cheek and then my mother before sitting down.

They both take their napkins from the table and fan them out before setting it across their laps. When I sit and do the same, he says, "We're quite proud of your accomplishments. You're a year older than I was, but that shouldn't hurt your opportunities." His compliments usually come with a side of dig.

He's a brilliant man—calculated and ambitious—which has served him well in life. He took a small fortune he inherited and multiplied it ten times over by the time he was forty. Now in his late sixties, he's grown it a hundred times.

"I'm also two years younger than most of my classmates." I fail at keeping the snark out of my tone.

My mom smiles pleasantly as she picks up her fork. "Delightful, dear. The party is going to be beautiful. Have you found a dress?"

Yes, let's move on from unsavory topics. *Blech.* I laugh inwardly at my joke. "Nothing that has wowed me."

"It's too late to have something custom made. Now you'll be shopping off the rack."

I roll my eyes. "It will be okay." Picking up my fork, I stab a strawberry.

She goes on . . . "And if it has to be altered, I can put in a call but this is very last minute. You have thighs from your father's side of the family. Not any dress will work."

"I'll find something. You don't have to worry. I'm meeting Stascia after lunch to go shopping."

"How is she?" she whispers as if the paneling will tell her secrets. "I heard she has no prospects."

"Boyfriends, marriage, prospects for what?"

Ticking off her fingers, she says, "Any. The poor girl doesn't have a job either. What will happen to her?"

"She's twenty-three, Mom."

"That's my point. I was consoling Kathy the other night at bridge. She's distraught over her daughter."

"The dramatics must run high over card games. Stascia is fine. She doesn't work because she doesn't have to."

My father says, "Neither do you, but look what you've accomplished."

"You say that like I had a choice."

His heavy brows lower as he looks at me. "You didn't?"

"Not if I wanted your approval."

"My approval was never a factor. You did what you believed you should, and you will reap the rewards for that. You'll thank me one day for setting you on the right path."

He says it like I ever knew there were other options. There's no use arguing with an attorney. My mother claps her hands once. "We haven't even eaten the first course. What about April?" my mom asks so genuinely. She loves gossip. "I heard she was considering moving to New York to model but decided to stay in Austin. She's always been such a pretty girl."

All of this is news to me. "I have no idea. We haven't spoken recently."

"Have you fallen out?"

"Yes, to put it bluntly."

"That's too bad. You've been friends since you were little girls. Hopefully, your relationship will be mended by the party this weekend."

My father has been eating quietly but looks up from his bowl of fruit and then rests his hands on the table. "I've pulled strings. We'd like you to join the firm on the junior partner track. Same as Lloyd. He's been a good worker for two years now. There will be a lot to prove as a Beck."

"I can imagine." I'm about to take a bite.

"There will be no special treatment."

"I didn't expect any."

"Long hours."

"I understand."

"Do you, Weatherly?"

I set my fork down, and my stomach growls from being teased with this same damn strawberry. "I do."

"You'll be reporting to Lloyd—"

"What? Why? That has to be a conflict of interest since we dated."

He starts to take another bite but drops his fork and steeples his fingers, seemingly frustrated. "He said you'd complain."

"Complain? I'm asking a question."

"You don't ask me questions. I'm the boss of this household and at the firm. You'll do as you're told. Period."

"No special treatment. *Got it.* I'm supposed to accept your word as final."

My mom covers my hand with hers. A look of concern is written on her smooth face. "We've been worried about you, but you seemed to need time, so we gave that to you. Lloyd told us that you've broken up. He said it's temporary, a little bump on the way to the altar."

"It's not a bump, Mom. It's a boulder."

"He told us you were acting beneath the Beck standard and spending time with a hoodlum."

My eyes go wide. "Acting beneath the Beck standard? A hoodlum?" I burst out laughing, though I know this is a new low and not funny in the least.

"Stop answering everything with a question, Weatherly," Mom says.

Shooting her a look I know will irritate her, I reply, "Only doing what you taught me. Make the other person feel important by asking questions."

Her offense sends her hand to her chest. "What has gotten into you?"

"A hoodlum." *In more ways than you'd ever imagine, Mother dear.* I stand and toss my napkin down. "I came here with the expectation to hear how I've disappointed you. You've managed to meet that low."

My father stands. "Sit down. You're being disrespectful."

"You know what's disrespectful? Walking in on your boyfriend fucking someone at your best friend's house. Not that the location matters. It was just a new day and opportunity for Lloyd Sanders. Or did he not tell you that part?"

Still sitting, my mom tosses in the napkin. "A dalliance isn't worth ruining your entire future."

A dalliance? I could stand here all day arguing, but they aren't going to see it from my perspective. Tears don't threaten because Dare is right. I'm not that same sugary sweet, timid girl anymore. I'm bold like pepper. *His Pepper.*

"I may have walked in here with a chip on my shoulder, but I still hoped for the best. I refuse to accept anything less than what I deserve. Lloyd is less than I deserve. Me working under him at the firm is less than I am worth. If you don't see that, then I'll find work elsewhere." I take a step back, surprised everything blew up so quickly. With my temper flaring, I need to clear my head. "I should go."

My father sits down. By his posture, he's ready to continue lunch on his terms. "This is not an open-ended invitation, Weatherly. I thought we'd agree and put this conversation to bed. The party is the perfect opportunity to announce your decision. A positive decision, of course."

I stare at him, his age starting to show for the first time. Maybe it's not about him aging but about me growing up. I'm standing on an even playing field for the first time with this man who I've idolized my entire life. I see him for who he really is. "You didn't hear me at all." I shake my head and sigh because he refuses to see me for who I am.

"I won't be embarrassed by your erratic behavior, Weatherly. You're a Beck, first and foremost. It's time for you to follow through with our plan."

"Your plan. I never had a say."

"I'm giving you one now. I just hope you agree with me. There's no choice when it comes to Lloyd."

"I can say the same thing."

My mother huffs. "End this. We were supposed to have a nice lunch and discuss your future." Her eyes are on me. "We were under the impression you wanted to work at Beck & Sanders. What has changed?"

"Me."

"You've always wanted this," he says.

"Before I realized I didn't have to." I look at my shoes and the designer emblem emblazoned on top. I actually like the shoes, but they feel dirty to me now and not in the not-clean sense.

The tapping of my dad's fingers reveals his impatience. It means time is running out to talk in a reasonable manner. "If you need a vacation, take one, but don't make the mistake of thinking a job will be waiting for you when you return."

"I don't need a vacation. I need a life. One of my own and not yours." I swallow, and then say, "I'm seeing someone I care about, and I've invited him and his friends, my new friends, to the party."

My mom finally stands. "Well, lunch is ruined. I'm hoping the party won't be." When she comes to me, she adds, "I don't want our family fighting. You've come so far. Don't detour from your potential."

"You're not going to say anything about me dating someone else? Or the fact that Lloyd was cheating on me?" Her shoulders rise as she takes in a deep breath and gently falls as she exhales . . .

"I look forward to meeting this young gentleman." *And ignores me completely once again. It's no wonder I've never felt heard . . . until Dare.* At least he graduated to gentleman.

"Dad?"

He moves to his desk and settles into the leather wingback chair. His eyes harden on me. "You have until the party to give me a final answer, Weatherly. Don't disappoint me."

"Or what?"

My mom's arm comes around me, and says, "We've taken enough of your father's time." I'm swept out of the room like dirty secrets are swept under the rug. Once the doors are closed, we walk to the sitting room. She stands in front of the windows that give the illusion we own the world—

perfectly mowed grass, a sparkling turquoise pool, blooming flowers, and trees giving us complete privacy.

When she turns to me, she says, "I'm wearing ivory. You always look so pretty in blue." With that said, she leaves the room, and I roll my eyes.

28

Weatherly

THE SALESLADY HANDS me a glass of champagne. "Thank you," I say just as Stascia rushes in the front door of the boutique.

"Sorry. Sorry." She eyes the glass in my hands. "God, I could use a drink."

I hand her mine. "Take it. I haven't even had a sip yet."

"Thanks." She downs half, which is so unlike her, and then looks at me. "I've missed you."

Hugging each other, I close my eyes, present in this genuine moment. "I've missed you too."

Another glass is brought over, and then we're directed to the back salon where the high design is kept. "I have dresses in from Paris that I think you'll die for," the saleslady says, dragging her fingers across the fine fabrics. "Pull what you like, and I'll start a dressing room. I'm Chantal if you need anything."

When we're alone, we riffle through the racks. Chantal is in and out, taking what we pull. The conversation is stilted, and I hate it. I hate feeling this disconnected from her. So I stop this madness. "I miss you, but I haven't missed April. That may make me a terrible person, but I can't turn my back to her without feeling like I'm going to be stabbed."

Stascia's hair is pulled back on top, but her blond locks fall in soft waves over her shoulders. That's when I notice she's wearing less makeup than usual and no lipstick at all. Jeans and a sleeveless silk tank cover her body and simple red flats are on her feet. She normally dresses like she's going to meet an enemy.

Breathing a sigh of relief, she says, "I've been feeling so alone without you, Weath. Other than drinks last week, I've been avoiding everyone, especially April." She drops onto the puffy ottoman centering the room. "I just don't know what's going on. I feel lost."

I sit next to her. She says, "My parents are worried. My mom thinks I'm joining a cult because I wore yoga pants when I wasn't going to yoga."

"She told my mom that she was worried about you."

We laugh lightly. "She's nuts. Can I be honest with you?"

"Always."

"I think seeing you graduate has made me question what I'm doing with my life. Then I realize I was supposed to think about that before I graduated college. What can I do with an art history degree?"

"What do you want to do?"

"I don't know. I just thought I'd be married by now and raising a family, but I feel weirdly insane for thinking like that in this day and age."

"It's okay to want to do a million things, but you need to figure out what will make you happy."

Lying back with a hand full of dresses draped across her,

she says, "You're seeing someone." She studies me. "Someone who makes you happy."

I won't hide Dare. "I am."

When she sits up again, she asks, "That's why you pulled away, isn't it?"

"I pulled away because I was lost, and I rediscovered who I am. April is toxic to my well-being." I lower my voice, but I'm not afraid to speak my mind. "You were toxic for me. You were mean to me over stuff that doesn't make up the whole of who I am." Or any part of me anymore.

The hangers rattle around her lap. "I'm sorry. I owe you so many apologies I don't know where to begin." Her sincerity has settled into her pretty features, her heart speaking for her. "I was scared to be April's next victim. I didn't want to feel her wrath. I'm so sorry, Weatherly."

All these years she's been cruel and condescending . . . Part of me wants to hate her for that, but in some ways, in showing her true colors, I can see where the hatred should lie. *April.* Stascia feared April's scorn . . . just as I did.

"She treated us terribly. I wish you would have trusted me enough to confide in me. We could have managed things together. I always felt like an outcast from you two."

"Maybe we can start over, begin again?" I roll my head to the side, and she looks my way.

"It's not like we didn't have good times. I wouldn't have stuck around if it was all bad."

She takes my hand, and we hold them together. "It wasn't all bad. We've had so much fun over the years. But I'm truly sorry for the bad there was."

"Me too," I say. *She's already been a victim of April's cruelty. I won't make her a victim of mine.* "I'm not happier without you. I know who you really are on the inside. That's the friend I need."

"I'll be that friend if you give me another chance. I'm hoping we can start again."

"I'd like that." I hug her because I not only missed her, but I also missed sharing all the good things happening with someone who knows me. Though I'm thinking Dare knows me better than I could have thought, considering the short time we've been in each other's lives. "Friends again?"

"Friends forever. Now about this someone who puts that glow on your face. Do I know him?"

"You saw him, but I can't wait for you to meet him properly."

"I can't wait either. Is he coming to the party?"

"He is."

"This should be fun."

This party is going to be amazing or go up in flames. Only time will tell. "Fun indeed. Hey, are you busy tonight?"

"Completely free," she replies, standing up.

"Want to see a band with me?"

"Absolutely."

THE NEXT DAY . . .

TENSION HAS BEEN HANGING in the air all day.

I've broached the topic of the party several times, but Dare acts like everything's fine. It's not. He's paced the apartment like he's on patrol for the past hour. His nerves are making me anxious.

I hold the garment bag in one hand and my shoes in the other. "I'm leaving for the house soon. My mom set it up. Stascia will be there. We're having our hair and makeup done before the party."

"I'm glad you've made up with her."

"Me too. Are you getting ready here or at home?" I hate that I call the other place his home when this place feels so much like our home these days.

"Yeah." He nods and leaves the bedroom. I hear his heavy steps across the floor and follow him. Setting my stuff down on the back of the couch, I ask, "What's wrong?"

His tall build and broad shoulders rest on the metal frame of the balcony door. "Nothing's wrong, Weatherly. Just wondering if it will ever be like this again."

"Like what?"

"Just you and me." He glances back at me. "My house is full of guys. There's not much privacy. I like the peace of being here with you."

My heart roars to life, and I go to him, swooning like the googly-eyed starstruck girl I am when it comes to him. "We have that, so why are you worried?"

His arm comes around me and embraces me. "Whatever happens after we leave here, remember we said whole-heartedly."

"We're not going into battle, Dare."

"Aren't we? This is our first night with your family and friends. We need to wear our armor because if you don't think they're going to attack, you're wrong. I've dealt with those types of people my whole life looking down on me."

Slinking out from under his arm, I give us some space to air our dirty laundry. "I'm one of those types of people."

"No, you're not. You were saved in time."

"My hero," I reply sarcastically, staring at the busy city street below.

"You didn't need me. You just needed to be reminded of you."

"You've done a good job." Giving him the credit, I glance over at him.

Sliding his hand along the railing, he stops when he's against me again. "You did that for me as well. I was so distant to who I used to be that I was becoming numb. You changed that. You brought my world back to life, and I don't want to lose you."

"You won't. Remember? Wherever you are, I'll be right there next to you. I promise."

"Famous—"

"First words. This is just the beginning, babe." My gut tells me he's not looking for me to reassure him, but my heart demands I do. "Wholeheartedly. I won't forget."

The slightest of nods is given in return before a kiss turns deep and intoxicating. Like him.

Catching sight of the time, I enter the apartment with him following me inside. He sits on the couch, and asks, "What are going to do about the job?"

"It's not an offer I'll consider."

"Maybe you should."

"And work under Lloyd? No."

Rubbing his closed eyelids, he shakes his head. When he looks at me again, he says, "I agree, but I worry about the damage this will cause with your family."

"Working under those conditions will cause damage." I sit next to him. "It will be okay. I will be okay. You don't have to worry about me."

"That's what boyfriends do. They worry about their girlfriends."

"You don't have to this time."

"No timid to be found. So bold."

"I'm like you."

"How's that?"

"I won't compromise my values for a paycheck."

His arm swings around me, and he brings me against his side. With a kiss to my head, he says, "Bold. Just as you should be."

I get up to finish packing my things, but look up when I don't hear him.

Resting back with his eyes on a to-go coffee cup, he tugs at the flap of the lid. He's a guitar player, but he doesn't tend to fidget with things. Taking a breath, I sit next to him. "I'm sorry for rushing off."

"It's okay. You don't owe me a damn thing, babe." The casualness of his tone and the distant look in his eyes unsettle me. I can see the imaginary walls rising around him. I just hope it's in preparation for tonight versus for me.

"I know, but what if I wanted to owe you a damn thing," I say, using his words against him.

Setting the cup on the table, he takes me by the legs, and drags me onto his lap. I love our size difference. While his hands roam the skin under my shirt, he kisses me. "If you need anything, call me."

"I will. Just remember it's a party. Parties are supposed to be fun." Laughing, I add, "Don't be nervous." Admiring him in the sunshine that streams in, he's never looked more handsome. "I wish I had more time."

"We do. Remember? We have all the time in the world."

Poking his side, I tease, "Now you're the optimist."

"Just facts. You'll be cat-scratching around me again soon enough."

Although I roll my eyes, his arrogance is sexy. "You know me too well." The feel of his hands comforting me brings peace to my mind and my heart. "Today will be fun."

"Yeah." He nods unconvincingly. "Fun."

At least he's trying. I tilt up and kiss his chin before I need to dash. "I'll text you later."

He escorts me to the door. "Need help carrying all this?"

"I have it." I lift up and kiss him once more before heading down the hall.

Dare remains standing in the doorway of my apartment until I load onto the elevator. The door closes, and my heart sinks. As much as I want to keep this good feeling in my heart alive, dread sets in as I think about the day ahead.

WHAT WILL I tell my friends?

Stascia knows, met, and loves Dare, though she seemed partial to Romeo if I'm being honest. Hell, I'm not blind. I'm surprised they didn't hook up. She's been quiet today, though. Knowing we're going to face April again has us both tangled up in our thoughts.

All she cares about is my virginity, so maybe I just get it out of the way at the very beginning. Do I climb to the top of the house and shout it from the rooftop? "I'm no longer a virgin."

Or do I casually say, "Pass the canapés and, by the way, my cherry has been popped."

"My vote is for the latter," Stascia says.

My face heats. "Oh my God. I thought I was talking to myself."

Coming to stand behind me, I look up from the vanity and into her eyes reflected in the mirror. With her hands on my shoulders, she smiles. "It will be okay. Dare's amazing, and you can see how much he cares about you. Everyone will see it and adore him too. Except maybe Lloyd. But he's an asshole, so there's that."

I start laughing. "He is and thank you."

"You don't have to thank me. Friends support each other through thick and thin. If anyone gives you trouble, send them to me to handle."

I'm still giggling. She the least confrontational person I know, so that's how I know she means what she says. "Your bravery is shining through."

"What was it you told me last night? Own your dreams? Part of owning mine is helping others achieve theirs."

There's nothing I can say better than how she said it, so I lighten the mood. "I think I'll mention the loss of my virginity on a need-to-know basis. I won't shove it in their faces. I mean, really? I haven't lost all sense of decorum."

"I'd love it if you did, though." She slips on her shoes, and then says, "I'll see you out there."

Looking in the mirror, I try to read my own eyes. There's something locked in there that is keeping me from being totally free. Although this isn't it, I do think I should tell Dare. I don't want to keep any secrets—big or small.

He won't care, but it's important to me that he knows that I gave him more than my trust. I guess that's why it matters. Once it's given, it can't be re-gifted. It ties me to him forever in a way I think he would like. I've never once regretted it and am in awe that I will always share this with him. I hope this speaks to his heart as much as it does mine.

I text him, not able to hold in my excitement.

Me: *I can't wait to see you again.*

Dare: *It's three hours.*

Me: *Three hours too long if you ask me.*

Dare: *I'm always asking you. I can't wait to see you either. We're leaving in thirty. If you don't recognize me, I'll be the one with the googly starstruck eyes.*

Laughing, I type: *I've seen that look a million times, babe.*

Dare: *LOL. I'll be the one in black then.*

Me: *Sounds sexy.*

Dare: *I'll show you sexy after the party.*

Me: *Like I said, I can't wait.*

With that, I feel ready to start this party. I head downstairs and go straight to the bar. April finds me fast. "Where have you been hiding the past couple of weeks?"

"I've been spending a lot of time in bed."

Dare's hands all over me.

Tongue scraping across my chest.

Mouth between my legs and on my lips.

His humongous—Two fingers snap in my face. "Earth to Weatherly."

"I'm right here." Physically, but my mind is still thinking about how he's going to show me sexy after the party.

We both pick up a glass of white wine, and she scopes the grounds. "Nice party. Congrats on graduation."

"Thank you."

Her eyes dart around my face, investigating every freckle and mark I have as if it's been years since she's seen me. I feel so different from a month ago, so I understand her reaction. And then I don't when she says, "I thought you'd be different after you graduated law school, but I see some things never change."

I nod, looking her directly in the eyes. "You're right. Some things never do."

My mom joins us, kissing me on each cheek. "So proud of you, honey."

April takes the opportunity to leave, and I let her. "Thanks, Mom. For everything," I say, waving a hand toward the event. The sun hasn't set, but the house keeps us shaded. "It's beautiful. I love the lanterns and lights."

"It turned out perfect." Her eyes light up. "Ooh. The Yorkes are here." She dashes off to greet the guests.

I look around. The party is mostly their friends and my dad's business associates. Stascia grabs my arm, and says, "Come on. Let's do this together."

We walk around to the other side of the pool to the crew as they've always been called—Lloyd's friends and mine—but with every step, I can feel how the dynamic has changed. I'll be polite, but I don't intend to spend much time with them.

Everyone is laughing when we approach the bar. April and Lloyd are off to the side together in a heated conversation. "Hi," I say, curious to what they're talking about.

April looks miserable as if I interrupted more than a casual conversation. Lloyd's an ass, so I don't care about him. She stares at me with an unreadable emotion. Is it hate? Anger? Sorrow? Pain?

"What's wrong?"

Lloyd snaps, "Nothing. Where have you been?"

"None of your business," I reply, amused by his annoyance.

"You haven't been taking my calls."

I nod. "That's what broken up means."

He huffs in anger, looking up at the sky. "You're acting erratic just as I told your dad."

Shock engulfs me. "Erratic? It's called happy, Lloyd. It's hard to recognize, I know, but it's what I am. Happier than I've ever been."

I start laughing, but when April's eyebrows rise, I follow her gaze behind me.

She asks, "Who is that?"

With happiness read in her eyes, Stascia says, "Oh my!"

When I look behind me and I see why they're gawking. "Tattooed god."

Dressed in head to toe black, he's not only looking dapper in a tie and dress pants, but holy hell, he's hot. The man in black casually strolling across the lawn puts Johnny Cash to shame. Not to discount the rest of the band because not only do their personalities shine through, but they just injected a whole new level of energy into this stuffy party.

English is wearing a pink polo with the collar popped, tucked into plaid golf pants. Lennox looks great in black pants, a white shirt, and skinny tie. It fits his personality that I've seen—subdued, but cool.

Leave it to somebody named Romeo to pull off a royal blue suit and white shirt in a sea of gray. All are wearing sunglasses, and I think every woman here is staring . . . the men too. Especially Lloyd.

April asks, "Your dad hired a band?"

In the next breath, Lloyds asks, "Who the fuck is that?"

They are a sight to behold, and my smile grows as a shiver of giddiness runs through me. "That's my boyfriend."

29

Dare

Fifteen minutes prior . . .

Romeo is texting in the back seat next to me, while upfront, English gives Lennox a hard time about his clean car. I whack him on the arm and add my two cents. "Since when did we start complaining about Lennox's cleaning habits? Keep it up and you're going to be scrubbing the toilet."

English pats Len's shoulder. "Dare's right. Thanks, man. Don't stop cleaning the toilet. We good?"

Lennox laughs. "We're good."

Finally noticing we're in a different part of Austin, Romeo says, "Nice neighborhood."

Instantly recognizing these streets from all the times my mom and I drove them, I reply, "The west side."

English turns back to me. "This is where your girl grew up?"

"Yeah. Her parents still live here."

Lennox slows down so we can get a proper look at the neighborhood. "The map says it's here, but there's only a wall."

"Keep going," I say, my heart sinking to the pit of my stomach. "The entrance is ahead."

"How do you know?" he asks, his eyes hitting mine in the rearview mirror.

"I've been here."

English asks, "You've met the parents?"

"No." My mouth goes dry as I look at that red brick wall, the same wall I once graffitied, the same that barricades the house my mother loved most.

The guys keep talking, but I sit staring as we cruise along the wall. When Len approaches the wrought-iron gate, a vision of yellow ribbons, gapped teeth, and being peppered with a million questions comes to mind. *Pepper.*

Holy shit. "Stop the car."

Slamming on the breaks, Lennox turns back. English and Romeo are staring at me as well. Lennox asks, "What's wrong?"

I pop open the door, rushing around the back of the car, and crossing the lawn. "What the fuck are you doing, Marquis?" English yells through the window.

Memories flood my mind as I look around. A little girl in pigtails swinging on the wrought-iron gate, hearing her last words said that day, "See you again someday," and the house I've seen on a picture that hung on my fridge for years. "I've been here before. This is her house. Pepper."

Romeo stands next to me. "Who's Pepper?"

"Weatherly."

"I'm confused."

Glancing at him, I say, "You and me both." In the

distance, a valet is directing the car to the back of the house. English calls to me, "Come on."

I look at the house once more before Romeo and I return to the car. My heart is racing from the memories rushing through me. How is it possible? Can Weatherly really be the same little girl? Is Weatherly Pepper?

That name slid so easily off my tongue the night we met at Shep's. It didn't make sense then, but it does now. The car stops, and we get out again. Lennox tosses the keys to the valet, who says, "I've seen you guys play. You're kick-ass."

"Thanks," Len replies.

English pops his pink collar. "How do I look?"

"Like a pussy," Romeo replies, making us laugh.

We can see the party décor and guests before we're seen. It gives me a quick second to scope it out, but when I find what I'm looking for—blue dress, long brown hair, beautiful—we make our entrance.

Make no mistake that we're well aware we stand out like sore thumbs. We've spent our lives defending the honor of the east side only to walk into a west side party like we own this place.

Jaws drop. Annoyance read on the faces of several dick-heads, but counteracted by the gawking of women. We head straight to the bar where my girlfriend is standing with her friends. When we near, the girl with black hair says, "Your dad hired a band?"

Weatherly ignores her and runs into my arms.

I hold her in my arms, inhaling everything about her into my lungs, her words as a girl still echoing in my head. I dip her because if we're going to make a show of this, might as well make it memorable. I kiss her so fucking hard that her weight is rested in my hands. When our lips part, I still hold her. "See you again someday," I whisper in her ear, repeating the words she once said to me.

"What?" She pulls back to see my eyes. When she doesn't, she lifts my sunglasses onto my head. "What do you mean? You're leaving?"

"No." I search her eyes for the connection to be made, but all I see is curiosity. "Just heard that once."

She smiles and grabs my hands. "Are you ready to meet my family?"

"No, but we have to do it, so there's no point in delaying the inevitable."

"Good attitude."

We don't get far before her ex is in my face. "What are you doing here?"

Guess this is how it's going to be played. Good to know. I ignore him and turn back to my girl. "Who are we meeting first?"

"My mom."

But douche doesn't seem to get the message, probably due to all that inbreeding in the family tree. He adds, "Leave it to Weatherly to mess around with the help. Was filet mignon not to your liking? You had to go choose the chuck beef?"

"Stop it, Lloyd," Weatherly snaps.

Lloyd digs that fucking hole deeper. "Unless you're serving hors d'oeuvres, employees don't mingle with invited guests."

Enough. "Listen, *Lloyd*. I'm not here to cause problems—"

"Then leave," he says.

I'm about to punch his fucking lights out, but pause when I see the look of horror on Weatherly's face. Then I realize the expression isn't aimed at me. It's aimed at him. So is her arm just before she swings.

This is not what I want her taking away from being with me. I catch her fist and bring it to my mouth to kiss. "You have soul and feistiness in spades, Pepper."

Her blue eyes widen like morning skies as she stares into mine, flickers of recognition coming back.

As predicted, once we left our little world of two, some would try to destroy us. That's how the east side and west side work. My friends and I don't belong here, and seeing the large man filling the doorway, the same man who her ex has darted to lap at his feet, reminds me that everything I do is a reflection of her. She's worked too hard for me to ruin her future.

I try to recall her previous words. "This is a party. It's supposed to be fun."

"How can you—"

"Wholeheartedly." One word is all we need to get us back to who we are, who we'll always be together.

She takes a deep breath and nods. "Let's go find my mom." Dragging me away, she wraps her arm around mine. "I'm sorry for—"

"No, you don't have any reason to be, but he should be."

"Yes, he should."

A waiter holds a tray out for us. Weatherly laughs, and says, "You should try the canapés." I don't know why she finds that so amusing, but I'm digging this little shrimp pastry thing.

We round the pool deck, and her hold on me tightens. "Mom, I'd like you to meet someone."

Weatherly looks so much like the petite brunette. Her mom's smile wavers for a millisecond before it returns. "Hello, I'm Bonnie Beck. And whom might you be?" When she speaks, she sounds like she's from another time and place.

"This is Dare," Weatherly says. "Dare Marquis."

"It's nice to meet you, ma'am."

"You as well." Glancing at her daughter, she says, "Where have you been hiding this handsome man?" We shake hands as she eyes me with a smile. The Southern charm is laid on thick with Bonnie Beck.

"In my apartment," Weatherly replies, matching her mother's grin.

Apparently, Pepper has a sarcastic side when it comes to her parents. I approve.

"Ah, I see your humorous streak is still intact." Bonnie laughs and turns back to me with her hands clasped in front of her. "Dare is an unusual name."

"My mom was very unique. She once told me she cursed me when she chose it because that name brought out my wilder side in spades."

I catch Weatherly's eyes with a smile hidden inside, but then it registers because she asks, "Spades, huh?"

"One time when I was sent to the principal's office, he told me I had personality in spades."

Bonnie keeps a look of fake interest plastered on her face, but my girl is staring at me like her heart recognizes mine—full of love and that connection we've always felt to one another. Her smile has faded, but hope lives in the softness of her expression.

Oblivious to what's really happening, Bonnie says, "Your mother sounds like a charming lady."

"She was." My gaze turns to her. "She passed away some years back."

Bonnie's grin falls, and she rubs my arm. "I'm so sorry to hear that. My condolences."

"Thank you. I was fortunate to be left with a lot of amazing memories."

"That's wonderful." Looking past me, Bonnie adds, "I should say hi to the Johnstons. If you'll—"

"She had a saying that always stuck with me." When I have their complete attention, I continue, "Beauty attracts the eye, but the soul captures the heart."

"You have that in spades," Weatherly whispers right after. She sucks in a shaky breath while she remains staring at me. "Dare?"

"Yes?"

Bonnie asks, "What are we talking about again?" When we don't answer, she adds, "Weatherly's name can be traced back to England, like her lineage. Our family was not on the *Mayflower*, but they came shortly after."

I look at Bonnie, wondering how she can miss what's right under her nose. Her daughter's silence should be the first hint, but Weatherly isn't what they care about. Image is. So as much as I can appreciate the history lesson, I hear the underlying message loud and clear. I'm not welcome here.

A man comes to stand behind Bonnie. This is not a man to be messed with. His hardened eyes stare at me, but soon turn to his left. He says, "Weatherly, I'd like to speak with you in private."

"Dad," she says, her tone subtle but clipped as if to hide the discord between them and failing. "I'd like you to meet—"

"We can meet later. My office. Now."

Adding please doesn't soften the blow. His glare leaves me when he walks toward the house. I won't take his bullshit or let him belittle her. "I'm Dare Marquis."

Her father stops and turns around. "Dare Marquis." He

doesn't offer his hand. Just says my name and then leaves again.

Fuck him.

Weatherly says, "I'm so sorry, Dare."

"He treats you terribly." Her mother slipped away when I didn't notice. "Are you going?"

"I have to."

"You don't have to do anything. You're choosing to."

"You're right. I'm choosing this meeting because I've worried about my future my whole life, and now it's my turn to have my say."

"So you've decided what you're going to do?" Looking around, she seems to have so much on her mind, and I don't want to add to her pressures. I say, "You take the meeting, and I'll be here when you return."

"I don't want to leave you."

"I'll be fine. I'll be with the guys."

"If you're sure?"

I suck in a deep breath and let my heart reply, "Wholeheartedly. Now go get 'em."

A smile graces those lips I want to kiss again, but I refrain. Weatherly nods and then walks toward the house. When she looks back, sadness has staked its place in those beautiful eyes. I'd love to take away her pain, but as I look around, I understand what she meant by feeling free with me. I don't fit in this world, but more than anything, I don't think Weatherly does either.

30

Weatherly

I'M NOT SCARED to face my father despite how heavy my feet feel as I tread down the hall.

"*Weathhherrrleeee.*" The slur of my name cautions me when I round the corner. Bob Sanders, of Sanders & Beck, my dad's partner and Lloyd's dad, throws his arms open for me. Scotch sloshes in the crystal highball, causing him to look down at the pristine wood floors he's ruining. "It's good to see you again."

I've known him my whole life, but history doesn't make me fonder of him. I try to avoid him, walking around him, but the hall is only so wide. "I'm here to speak with my dad."

"No hug for your dear old friend?"

"He's waiting."

"He'll understand." I'm grabbed and pulled tight into his arms. My shoulder jabs his chest, but I wish it were my knee to his groin. "You've grown up." His putrid breath hits my nostrils, and I pull away, but not in time to avoid his hand cupping my ass. Pushing off, I say, "Don't touch me like that."

His head jerks back. "A hug. Fine." His hands go up in surrender. "Girls these days are—"

"Like father, like son. Assholes these days—"

He grabs my arm and yanks me closer. Anger takes hold of his mood. "Listen, little girl—"

"Everything okay?" Stascia asks, coming out of the bathroom.

I pull back, stunned by his behavior as my arm screams through the pain he caused.

Bob backs away. "Fine. Just fine." Then his sleazy side comes out again. "It's been a long time, Stascia."

"Not long enough." She eyes him as I walk toward her.

Wrapping my arm around hers, I whisper, "What just happened?"

She looks back over his shoulder and rubs my arm. "He's gone. You all right?"

"He just . . ." When we stop, I stare back down the hall. "He grabbed me."

"I saw. He's such a creep. He managed to cop a feel of side boob in front of my parents at our Christmas party, and they were completely oblivious."

Standing in front of my dad's office, I say, "He's sneaky and disgusting like his son."

She nods and then notices where we are. "Going in?"

"Yeah." I glance at her. "Wish me luck."

"You don't need it." Her smile is confident.

"You sound like Dare."

"He's a good guy."

"He is."

She takes a few steps toward the backyard, but stops and turns back. "Do you want me to wait?"

"I'll be fine."

"I'll keep an eye on Bob." She winks. Before she disappears around the corner, she adds, "I'll also have a drink ready for you."

"You're the best." I don't need to gain strength by taking deep breaths or building myself up inside. I'm already strong. Bold. I knock but don't wait for him to allow me in. I open the doors. All the lights are off except for the green banker's lamp on his desk. I glance at the books at the top of the bookcase out of habit, and then say, "Hello."

"Sit down." My father doesn't look away from the computer screen. I sit on the edge of the chair and wait for the acknowledgment I deserve. The building silence brings tension along with it or maybe I brought that defensiveness inside with me.

He finally looks up, and when he does, I don't see my dad. I see a man who's ready to cross-examine me. All business. No kindness is found in his eyes or body language.

It saddens me that this is how it's going to be, but I can play his game.

"Did you think about the position at the firm?" he asks.

"I didn't need to. I won't work under Lloyd."

Disappointment comes in a frustrated sigh. "This is about your boyfriend being jealous of Lloyd. Making you turn away from the biggest opportunity of your life for his gain. Don't be blind, Weatherly. That guy is using you." Rubbing his fingers together, he adds, "It all comes down to money and getting a hold of your trust fund."

"You don't know him to judge him. You didn't have the manners to shake his hand, so you have no right to talk about him."

Rubbing his temples, he then slaps his hands down on

the desk. "This is exactly what I didn't want for you. A man is controlling you—"

"So it's okay if you do it, but not anyone else?" I realize what I said too late. "Dare does not control me like you and Lloyd do. He loves me for me. He wants me to do what makes me happy."

"He's an intruder to our lives. What kind of name is Dare Marquis anyway?"

"He sings in a band." Why would I say that like it's not true, like it's a stage name?

"A band? I didn't think it could get worse. What are you doing, Weatherly? Having a bout of insanity?"

I sit there taken aback by his accusation. Lowering my voice, I say, "I won't defend my relationship or my sanity."

"Because you can't. Dump the loser and take the job. You start on Monday."

"No. I don't. I won't compromise my values for a paycheck." Standing, I'm about to go off on him, but even I know not to argue with someone who will never truly listen. It's a losing battle with him. I walk to the door, but before I open it, and with my back to him, I say, "I'll find work elsewhere."

"You'll find a place as well." I whip my attention back to him. "That apartment is corporate housing. It was loosely justifiable when you were interning and then spent the last year preparing for the exams so you could work for Sanders & Beck. It's not anymore. You just kissed everything goodbye and for what?"

I finally realize that this was never about me. This is about someone doing his dirty deeds, his bidding, and not saying a word. He can have Lloyd, but he won't have me. Lifting my chin, I reply, "Love."

"Love will leave you pregnant and alone while he travels the road and sleeps with groupies."

"That's Lloyd you're describing. He fucked around on me for seven years, and I looked the other way. Dare wouldn't hurt me. He'd end it first."

"So that makes him noble?"

"No. It makes him human." I leave because the pain I feel inside is starting to pulse through my veins.

My father's voice travels down the hall behind me. "You have until Saturday to be out of that apartment."

He doesn't have to worry. I'm already gone.

31

Dare

A WAITER PASSES BY, and I say, "You should try the canapés."

Lennox orders a beer and then asks, "What's a canapé?"

Sipping whiskey, English still has his sunglasses on, though the house shadows us from the sunset. He pats Lennox on the back, and says, "A canapé is a bite-sized appetizer, mate."

Romeo circles round. It's hard to keep us rowdies apart. "Why don't they just call it an appetizer then?"

English shrugs. "The French have fancy words for everything."

"Yeah, the whole fucking language is fancy," Len strikes back with a laugh.

"Valid point," English laughs through the words. "Can we talk about Dare's badass girlfriend? I'd say it was a fair match even without the punch."

Picking lint off his blue suit, Romeo says, "The dude is like six foot to her five two, five three."

Stascia says, "Lloyd's a pussy, so Weatherly definitely could have taken him."

We're all laughing as they move closer together.

"Oh fuck," Romeo says, laughing. "She's right on." If she's hot, he'll talk. "I was saying the same thing." Romeo smirks, and Stascia is already falling under his spell.

I see Weatherly's other friend and her ex nearby. Checking my phone, we don't have much time before we need to go. I look at the house, but there's no sign of her yet.

English and Lennox finish their drinks while Romeo finally scores Stascia's phone number. This girl is so out of his league, but I don't butt in. I do make the mistake of making eye contact with the Queen Bitch herself. She's been snubbing her nose to us since we showed up.

But she's on a mission. Flipping her hair behind her shoulders while squaring them, she comes over. "It's Dare? As in truth or dare?"

From the first impression I got of her at Shep's and from how she treats Weatherly, I knew it was only a matter of time until she inserted herself where she doesn't belong—Weatherly's and my relationship.

"Yep."

"You know Weatherly is one of my best friends, yet she never mentioned you."

Stascia moves in front of her. "Stop, April. Don't make a scene."

"Me? I think we're well aware of who's making the scene here." She pushes around her and comes at me. "You show up calling our friend your girlfriend and acting like that holds some power with our crew. It doesn't."

I check my pockets and then hold up empty hands. "Lookie there. I'm all out of fucks to give."

English taps me on the shoulder. "Let's go. We have a show, and this bullshit is messing with my vibe."

"No fucking joke." I should probably come up with some great comeback, but she's not worth my time. Weatherly needs to watch her back. I left mine unprotected, and she fires her first real shot, "Save us the trouble, Dare, and leave Weatherly alone. You got what you wanted, so move along to another victim."

When I stop, Lennox speaks under his breath, "Let it go, man."

Unfortunately, I can't when it comes to my girl. I turn around and cross my arms over my chest. I shouldn't indulge this bitch princess, but I need to know what she's talking about. "What is it I got exactly?"

"Her virginity."

Weatherly's?

Thinking back on our first time, I start to wonder if I treated her right. Did I hurt her? Did I take it slow or fuck her? *Fuuuck!* I pinch the bridge of my nose.

"Fucking hell!" Lloyd throws his glass into the grass and stomps it into the pieces.

April whips her attention to him. "Shut up, Lloyd!"

"I've waited fucking years, and he gets her in two weeks? It's not fucking fair."

I'm tempted to correct him to one week, but my ego doesn't need the glory, and the woman standing in the nearest doorway distracts me.

Weatherly.

April pounces like she's cornered her prey. "You didn't know?" Cackling like a badly-voiced Disney villain, she adds, "Someone had to do it, but I expected someone with a little more class." She slow claps. "Well done. Bravo. You bagged a Beck." The snark is gone and anger surfaces. "Now run along, back to the east side, and leave my friend alone."

Stascia yells, "That's enough, April. Why are you doing this? Why are you hurting Weatherly on purpose? She's not even here to defend herself or him."

Still feeling sick that I might have failed her, I glance over her shoulder to see my girlfriend has been listening to everything.

"Why would I care about them?" April asks. "They're not like us, Stascia." She sets her eyes on Romeo. "Or are you wanting to slum it with him now?" April's been so careful to keep her voice down, to be the innocent among the mostly older guests. Lloyd, on the other hand, storms inside.

Coming to stand between Romeo and me, Stascia says, "I'll choose them any day over being associated with you."

April points at a group of people on the other side of the pool. "Well, maybe your parents would like to hear how you blew their financial advisor last year."

Romeo steps in. "If they were consenting adults, we have no right to judge." He gives Stascia a wink.

"Fucking hell, Romeo." I turn to the source of contention, and say, "Look April, you can throw all the trash talk you want my way, but why are you hurting the two women you call best friends?"

"They don't have my back. They don't care about me or what's going on in my life." She finally breaks, her voice rising. "It's always about them. Always."

Stascia sighs and goes to her. "We do care. You've just always been so closed off."

She pushes her away, and screams, "You don't, or you would have noticed that I've been in love with Lloyd for years."

A gasp draws their attention to the woman who needed

to hear how they truly feel about her. With a trembling voice, Weatherly asks, "That's why you slept with him?" April spins around to see Weatherly standing there, defeated. "That was you at the party . . . under him, wasn't it?"

There's a tilt up of her chin and righteousness to her tone as if she's owed a debt. "So what? You weren't satisfying his needs."

"Satisfying his needs . . ." Her lips purse like she just tasted a lemon, and then the pain returns. "It wasn't the first time either." I'm tempted to step in, but something tells me she'll need me more after than now. She needs to hear this chick and the betrayal. The truth is hard to hear, but it will give her something solid to move forward on.

"You don't care about him like I do."

"I don't care about him at all."

April walks toward her with tentative steps. "I tried to tell you a million times, but—"

"But you didn't. Instead, you stabbed me in the back." Her expression softens when she sees me. Her steps sure. That's my girl right there. Bold.

"You can't be serious," April says, raising her voice. "You're choosing them over me?"

"No. You made that choice when you screwed me over."

Exasperated, April throws her arms out. "I've defended your fat ass for years, but you're willing to throw me away on a dive bar, second-rate singer."

Weatherly startles and stills with her back to that hateful bitch. What the fuck? Who says that about their best friend? *April.*

I step in. "With friends like you, who needs enemies, you backstabbing—"

"It's time to go, Dare." Lennox grabs my arm.

Security runs from the house, waving their batons. "You need to leave this property immediately."

With balls of fucking steel, April carries on, "Everything you've worked so hard for will be gone. Are your parents and friends going to take my side or his? You know the answer. Are you willing to walk away from everything and everyone in your life for that guy?" Through my anger, I stare at the house behind them while her insults shoot right through me. "He's a loser . . . Are you going to support him . . . Poor . . . east side . . ."

I walked these grounds with my mom and remember thinking it was the closest to a castle I'd ever seen. The people who lived here must be so happy, just as it made my mom happy to see the architecture. But the people here are evil. However, they're from Weatherly's world, and even though I can see how different she is to them, what if I do drag her down? She's become bold and strong and can clearly hold her own with these people, but why should she have to? Is that what I bring to her table? Conflict with her friends and family? *Fuck.*

I thought only two things triggered my anger. Talk about my mom and the band in a bad light. But it's now three. Insulting Weatherly.

I need to walk away to preserve my mom's memory. I need to walk away and allow Weatherly to stand on her own . . . something she *can* do. She deserves the world—not through a fat bank account but through connections and the life she's earned. And I'm not sure I can give her that.

"Dare?" Weatherly calls after me and then runs to my side as I head for the car. I don't look at her or say a word. I can't. "Why are you leaving?" She clings onto my arm. "Please don't go."

I'm struggling to leave this woman. I want her, but I want

no part of these people. "I won't be their prey or token entertainment."

"You're not. To me, you're not."

I detour to the side of the house and search for Lennox's car parked on the long driveway but don't see it. She catches up to me again with tears welled in her eyes. "Please stay, or better yet, I'll come with you."

"That's how it's always going to be. Don't you see, Weatherly?"

"Pepper. Call me Pepper or babe."

"Don't you get it?" I hate raising my voice to her, but nothing else is getting through that beautiful brain of hers. "This is beneath you. *I* am beneath you."

"You're not. Not at all."

"Fuck," I shout, my anger getting the best of me. I reach the front lawn, and the car is still nowhere to be seen. Whipping around, I yell, "Go back to your party, Weatherly."

She sucks in a harsh breath, holding it as my words. Her bold turns timid as the words seep into her soul. Her lips part and tears well. She's so fucking beautiful in her anguish. We stare at each other, but this is the one time I can't give in.

April is right. Her mom. Everyone. She deserves better than what I can give her. "Love doesn't pay the bills, Weatherly. It's only been a few weeks. Are you willing to sacrifice your whole life for a . . ." I hate myself for doing this, for even thinking it. It's a lie through and through, but I push her away, hoping it's in her best interest. "We've had fun—"

"Fun?" She backs away, anger turning her pretty blues from sky to fire. "What are you saying? That I didn't mean anything to you?"

"Weeks, Weatherly."

"I don't need years to know what I feel." The tears don't

fall, but she's fighting every emotion running through her head. Her eyes are wild with worry. I hate it. It's never something I wanted to cause her, but it beats the pain and disappointment she'll feel if she stays with me. It's only a whisper, but she says, "You told me we had all the time in the world. And you called me an optimist."

"I lied. I was cynical back then."

"This morning?" she questions.

"Whatever."

"Don't play this off. You're not the cynical type."

"Maybe you don't know me as well as you think you do."

"I could say the same to you, but I'm still here fighting for us."

Rubbing my temples, I close my eyes. When I open them, the frustrating beauty has personality in spades on display—hands on her hips, toe tapping, trying her best to portray impatience. I see through her. "I know you better than anybody at that party."

I'm rewarded with a smile. "It's true. You let me be exactly who I am. No pretenses or walls. Just me. That's why I'm here, Dare. I believe in us. We have all the time in the world to be together. I promise we do."

"Think of your future, of the life you're trying to build. It's not fair for me to step in at the end. You need to take that job and own it. Show those fuckers who you really are."

"You're giving up on us and think that's fair?" She stands her ground with her arms crossed. "You're telling me what to do, thinking you know what's best for me. That makes you no different than my father or Lloyd. This breakup isn't about me. It's about you."

I can't say her words don't sting. The accusation that I'm anything like the men who dismiss her is a shot to the heart, but that anger will work in her favor when I'm gone. It's the strength she needs to move on. She deserves to be happy, but it will be on the back of hating me first. Is this what being selfless means? It fucking hurts if it does. "You can believe what you want, Weatherly. I'm done. With this scene. With this argument—"

"With me."

"I'm leaving," I say.

"If you walk away . . ." I don't hear her behind me this time. Her jagged breaths fade in the growing distance between. "Please don't walk away."

I stop once more, my soul tied to hers, holding me there. I will never forgive myself for this. Never, but if I learned nothing else from my mother, I once learned that destiny exists. Good and bad. It's all part of some master plan. She left something bad to find a life she loved. I'm leaving my heart behind hoping Weatherly finds someone better than me, someone who fits her society.

I walk away.

32

Dare

"HOW DARE YOU USE ME!" she yells before I'm shoved in the back.

I turn around and grab Weatherly's hand in the air before she has a chance to land it across my face. "I didn't use you. You know I didn't." *Fuck! Why can't she just walk away?* "Why didn't you tell me you were a virgin?"

She reacts as if I hit her, blinking and then her anger returns. "I didn't owe you that information."

"You're right. We didn't owe each other a lot of things, but we shared anyway."

I admire her profile—the delicate slope of her nose and her chin. Long lashes that fan across her cheekbones and pursed lips in pink. When her blue eyes meet my eyes, she says, "I wanted to tell you. I almost did before we . . . had sex, but I didn't want to ruin it."

"The moment? The night? What didn't you want to ruin because from my perspective there was no possibility of it being anything but one of the best fucking nights of my life?"

"I thought you would see me differently and treat me like . . . Ugh. I don't know. I wanted it to be like it is every other time for you. I wanted to be good, good enough to where you didn't notice the difference."

"For fuck's sake," I yell, my tone deep as exasperation sets in. "You deserved better than you got. I don't know. Wining. Dining. Romance. We can always fuck, but we'll never have that first time again."

"I didn't want any of that. I didn't need it. Our first time, *my* first time was perfect to me."

My ego has to put that chip back on its shoulder. "For the record, I noticed. I just thought you weren't active in that sense." Satisfaction isn't found in my pride. Not with her. I'm struggling to push her away, though I know it's for her own good. "Whether you are or were doesn't matter anymore. You can't see it now, but when I'm gone, you'll see I'm right. You might even thank me one day."

"Gone? Like nothing we felt or experienced matters? I guess I'm not as strong as you because I will never thank you for breaking my heart." She comes closer and shakes her head, contempt written in her expression. "You said you'd never be a source of pain, and here you are hurting me more than they ever could, and you know why?"

I shift out of her reach. "Why?"

"Because I cared about you more than anyone else before."

"I understand—"

"You understand nothing about me," she yells and then looks at the sky where the clouds have rolled in.

"I understand enough to know you need to be

surrounded by someone who cares about you. Really cares about your well-being."

"And that's not you?"

Stascia comes around the house, but when she sees us, she leaves us alone again. Backing up, I need to make the break and get away. "It can't be, but promise me it won't be Lloyd."

"If you walk away, you have no say in who I spend time with."

"He'll never love you like. . ." The words "I do" stay locked inside my heart. I add, "Like you deserve to be."

She finally lands a hard stare, leveling me to the spot. "I'm deserving of other people's love. Just not yours? You know what? Leave." She spits her hate. "Leave because I hate you anyway. I hate you with all my being, Dare Marquis."

My goal has been achieved. I take one last look at the woman I know I've fallen head over fucking heels in love with but need to release so she can soar. Her hands are balled into fists at her sides, and her anger burns in her eyes. Good. "Anytime you think of me, remember this moment right here. Okay, babe?"

This time, I don't get an argument. I get her back as she walks away. I used to be untouchable, hardened from the abuse of my father and the loss of my mother. But my chest aches in new ways, a vacancy growing with every step I take. I keep walking to spite these hateful people as if somehow I'll win by leaving my heart behind. It will find a rightful home. That just can't be with Weatherly and me.

The sky cracks open, and when the rain pours down, there aren't trees to protect me. *Or from the pain.* So I lower my head, shove my hands in my pockets, and pass the expensive parked cars without a second glance.

If this is what a life of luxury means, then I want no part of it. I pull my phone out and text Lennox.

Me: *Where are you?*

Lennox: *The valet parked my piece of shit down the street. He was busy, so I left to get it. I'll be there in a minute. I finally found it.*

Rushing across the lawn, I duck under a tree to avoid getting any more wet than I already am, but there's no use. I'm already soaked. Staring at the front of the house, it was from this angle that my mom took the picture that hung on our fridge forever. I blink away the memory of her standing with her camera. Pepper pestering me with her head in the clouds crazy ideas. She never said she wanted to be a lawyer.

That's what this world did to her. Instead of celebrating who she was, they aligned her with their goals. Well fucking done.

I'd rather live in poverty than have my dreams taken away from me. Guess they never knew that dreams came free.

Checking my phone again for a message from Lennox, I see minutes have passed without her, but time is still moving too slow. I need to get out of here before I change my mind. I look at this house that now haunts me and take a breath. This is for the best, I remind myself. This is best for her.

The rain works its way through the branches and leaves to find the top of my head, so I tilt down and close my eyes. My heart will heal . . . will it? Doesn't feel like it.

Fucking hell, get here already.

"Dare?"

The pain in her voice rings through my hollowed chest. Me hurting is one thing. Her, *a whole other.* That's not something I can live with even if I'm living without her. I look up and see her standing in the rain that's grown heavier, not twenty feet in front of me.

The emotions that still connect us are reflected in her eyes. Tentative steps bring her closer, a delicate approach in uncertainty. She says, "I didn't mean it. I don't hate you."

I can't manage the right words. I know shame lives in the lies I told. Telling them in good faith, for her greater good, doesn't change the pain I feel inside.

The horn of Lennox's car is muffled, but it causes her to look that way. I confess, "I know you don't. Just like you know how I feel about you."

"I have a favor to ask. One before you go."

There's no way of me denying her anything I have the ability of giving her. "What is it?"

Her arms lift just away from her body and her head tilts back, closed eyes accepting the tears of heaven raining down on her. When her eyes return to mine, she taps above her heart. "There's no music, but our song is always playing inside here. Dance with me, Dare."

I push my own pain away and go to her. With one hand on her hip and the other holding her hand, we begin to sway. It may not last long, but while we dance, my cheek against the top of her head, I feel whole again.

A hiccup in her breathing and the stiffness to her frame gets my attention. I pull back just enough to get a good look at her, thinking it's the last I'll get.

But something's wrong. Her lipstick smudged and her makeup not clean from rain, but smeared from tears. The more I stare at her, the more my heart quickens from seeing the damage done.

Mascara swiped to the sides.

The pink that was bright on her lips earlier beyond the borders.

A flaming red handprint across her face.

Grabbing her close, I hug her, then step back to see the rest of her as my blood boils from the realization that someone hurt her, hurt my girl.

The anger those heartless bastards caused earlier was tempered, but seeing her touched, mishandled in ways that would cause her pain has me ready to kill whoever dared to touch her. Careful, but firm, I caress her face and search her eyes. "Who did this to you?"

The tear gates open, and her body releases the flood of strength she's held inside. "He said it wasn't fair."

"Who?" I ask, but I already know because I witnessed his tantrum out back. I'm running before she has a chance to confirm. Taking the steps by two, I barge in the front door and run down the hall. Stopping just inside the living room, I find Lloyd laughing with his buddies. They toast with fucking shots before they see me, giving me enough time to spot red scratches just above his collar and the same color of Weatherly's lipstick on his shirtsleeve. "Motherfucker."

I tackle him sideways like an animal attacking him. I land two solid punches to his face before I hear Weatherly scream. "Don't do this, Dare. Please."

Lloyd kicks me, but Weatherly is right there in the mix when I swing, so I yell, "Get back."

She yells, "Don't hurt him, Lloyd," and then kicks him in the shins as hard as she can.

Yelping, Lloyd gives me an opening, and I take it, shoving him into a side table. A crystal lamp wobbles and then tumbles down, barely missing me, but hitting him on the chest before shattering to the ground.

English and Romeo pull me off before I get in another hit.

Held back by his friends, Lloyd tries to kick his legs as if that pussy move will do anything. "You're a dead man, Marquis."

"Fuck you! You can come after me, but you better fucking stay away from Weatherly."

He wipes his hand under his nose, dragging blood across his skin. "I'm bleeding! You hit me. That is so lame." He snaps his fingers. "Call my dad."

"If you ever touch her again, I'll kill you."

"Hear that?" He's lifted to his feet. "Did everyone hear that threat?"

Dragging me backward, English says, "Get your ass outside, Dare. These are not the jack-holes you want to threaten."

"Fuck them." I struggle to gain my footing on the slick floors. When I'm finally righted, they remain holding each of my arms and force me out the front door. I'm tugged onto the lawn across the driveway where they throw me down in the grass. "Fucking hell, it's wet," I complain.

"So are you, fucker," English spits. "Cool the fuck off and get in the car. We're leaving."

When I get up, I'm covered in grass and debris. *Fuck.* These were new clothes. I can't care too long because I'm missing Weatherly. I look toward the door as Lennox rounds the circular drive in front of me, but she's not there.

The back car door flies open, and Lennox says, "Get in, Dare, before you get arrested."

Romeo throws his hat in the ring, pissing me off, and adds, "Or worse, we get arrested because of that stupid stunt."

The keystone cops security comes racing down the steps, yelling for me to stop, so I get in the car, and Lennox takes off. The guys are boisterous—laughter, hoots, and hollers not only fill the car, but the outside as they shout into the fifty-mile-an-hour wind.

I want to tell them to shut the fuck up because I left my heart behind with a girl who didn't come after me. Not even to check on me. *Why should she?* I showed her exactly who I am deep down, played that hateful part until she hated me. But did she really tend to Lloyd? *Shit.* Did she choose the guy who hurt her . . . over me?

A sinking feeling has me slinking in the seat away from Romeo and pressed to the door. My head is out the window just enough to close my eyes and let the wind whip past me.

He hurt her physically.

I hurt her emotionally.

I knew the damage I was doing, and no matter how that bow is tied, it won't make a prettier package. The ugly truth shines through, and I'll never see her again.

"It's what she needs," I repeat, hoping to believe that can outweigh the damage I've done. It's too hard to get past the fact that I don't know what's best for me, much less her. Did I fall for the bullshit those people fed like a canapé, served up on a silver tray? "Fuck!" I slam the bottom of my fist against the door.

Everyone goes quiet, causing me to look around. I see Stascia on the other side of Romeo. "What?" Nothing makes sense tonight. I turn to look out the back windshield as if we're still there, but we're long gone, Weatherly abandoned. "Why are you here, Stascia?"

Romeo snarls and wraps his arm around her. "She's with me."

"I didn't mean it like that. I meant why aren't you with Weatherly? She needs someone on her side."

Stascia looks at me nervously as though I'm the bad guy. Not Lloyd, but me. Some of the first words I ever spoke to Weatherly come back to haunt me—*I'm your father's worst nightmare.* I wasn't. The people he surrounds her with are.

I think those words rang true when I said them but were quickly rendered meaningless because I never expected to fall for her like I did.

Does anyone see love coming?

Weatherly Beck blindsided me, but to know that we have a history deepens our connection in a way that I couldn't predict. How is it possible that she's the same little girl I called Pepper?

I yank my phone from my pocket and call her. Despite everything I said to her, I needed to get out of there, but I can't have her thinking I left her by choice. The phone rings . . .

Ring.

Ring.

Ring.

Voicemail.

Leaning forward, I say, "Stascia, call her. *Please.*" Even I can hear the desperation in my voice.

She's calling before I finish my sentence. Holding the phone to her ear, she glances at me, but then stares at her lap where Romeo is resting his hand.

Of course, he fucking does. He's picking up chicks when I'm losing my soul.

She hangs up and then her fingers are flying over the screen. "No answer."

"Is that like her?"

"We text more, but if we call, we usually answer. I just sent her a message."

"Thanks." I do the same, hoping she'll read it.

Me: *I'm sorry. Please tell me you're all right.*

I stare at the screen, willing those three dots to appear. Please. Please. Nothing. Like how I feel.

Stascia says, "You're right. She wanted me to go, but what am I doing?" When she starts crying, Romeo says, "I'll take you back."

Lennox pulls into the driveway. "No way. We have ten minutes before we need to leave. Get your shit loaded because we have to go. We are not missing this gig."

"I'm calling a rideshare," she says, standing at the back of the car. "Where am I?" Romeo stays with her as we file toward the door.

Before we go in, I ask Lennox, "Do you mind loading my gear? I want to take a quick shower. I need to clear my head and get this dirt off me."

"No problem." Just inside the house, he turns back. "The right thing isn't always the easiest."

"It was wrong. I made the wrong decision. I should have stood by her, not abandoned her."

He stares at me, recognition seen in his eyes, but an unfamiliarity circling. "You love her."

Not an accusation, but a revelation. I nod, the words clogged in my throat.

He nods in return, then grins. "It was bound to happen some time. Even the mighty eventually fall."

"In love?"

"In all things worth fighting for."

I'm left standing on the front porch with his insight, amazed by how true his words are.

Unfortunately, time is running short, and I can't let them down. We need the money, so I go inside to get ready, knowing I don't have the time to make things right. But as soon as the set is over, I'm finding Weatherly. I need to know she's okay. I need her to know that I love her.

33

Dare

I MISSED a pickup on the second song. The audience didn't notice, but I did. So did Jake manning the bar and Jeb. The bouncer poked his head inside to see what the problem was. Just me fucking up.

It doesn't matter because the crowd doesn't care. We're selling out a Saturday night at Shep's more than a busy Thursday. That means our price tag just went up.

So I start singing as though my life depends on it. Six songs in and my voice is strained as I take all the night's aggression out on my guitar and this mic. I hit the low notes and then lean back, strumming the alternate version of the popular song. My fingers slide against the metal of the strings and then beat down on them once, and it goes silent.

"Abstract Heart" is a crowd favorite, and they fill in, singing the chorus until they reach the end. I stomp on the pedal, the drums and all three of our guitars kicking in again, riling the fans into a frenzy as we close out the song.

Sweat springs from my forehead when I bend to get

another shot that's been lined up on the side of the stage. I flip it over and tank it down, then pick up another to finish before the set is over. Romeo says, "Slow down, man."

"Hit the kit and mind your own fucking business."

He stands, his sticks in one hand. "You want a fucking fight? Make sure it's worth defending because I'll fucking throw down, but don't take your shit night out on me."

English reaches for a shot, and then says, "Gentlemen. Gentlemen, what seems to be the problem?"

Romeo has his eyes glued to me just as mine are to him. "Nothing."

"Then let's play some rock 'n' fucking roll."

I turn back, and it's as if I can see where Weatherly once stood—a vision with long brown hair and eyes that shied away when admired. She was so out of place there was no way she could blend in.

Going through the motions of the next two songs are easy when I pretend to see my girl waiting for me. A commotion at the door brings me back from memory lane. I keep singing despite seeing that asshole Lloyd barge his way in; I keep playing as if he didn't bring four cops with him.

Nope. I don't break the beat because the show must go on, and if I'm going down, I'm going down giving the best damn performance of my life.

English's steel-toed Doc Marten's land at the back of my heel to get my attention, but he still plays. I pull back while Lennox takes center stage, and English says, "We got your back."

The cops are waiting—arms crossed, staring at me—for the music to stop. I exhale, knowing what's about to happen. I take one last shot, and this time, Romeo gives me a nod. "We're not just heroes." He slams into a drum solo and then ends the song. "We're brothers."

The cops push past Jeb and Jake, who appeared to be doing their damned best to talk them out of it. While we start playing the next song, Stascia rushes in and runs straight to Lloyd. A finger in his face. Anger in her face. We may not hear what she's saying, but it's obvious it's not nice. When he knocks her hand away, he's fucking lucky Romeo can't see him or he'd be on the floor already.

I sing my fucking soul out, but the cops aren't appeased. We start into the chorus as the cops push through, barging through the entertained crowd to jeers and moans. When they reach the edge of the stage, one leans forward, and says, "Get down."

I keep singing.

Beneath me, he tugs at the ankles to my jeans. "Now."

I keep strumming like nothing's wrong.

"You resisting?" he shouts, the purple and blue lights from outside hitting his badge. Someone knocks into him, and a fight starts off in the corner, distracting the other two cops.

The beat isn't broken when one of them climbs on stage and grabs my arm. I'll sing until I'm pulled away. I'll play until my wrists are cuffed. My cord is yanked from the bottom of my guitar, and English jabs the cop with the head of his guitar. When the cop focuses on him, he shrugs. "Oops. Sorry about that, wanker."

"You want to come with us too?" the cop shouts in his face.

"Damn, dude." English waves a hand between them. "Ever heard of a Tic Tac?"

Bumping him sideways, he breathes all over him. "What did you say to me?"

English looks down and closes his eyes briefly. When he runs his hand over his hair, making sure it's back in place, I know that will only lead to bad news. He's preparing. Yep. He straightens his shoulders and spits, "I said your wife likes to suck my dick."

"Fuck you, you fucking loser. Hands behind your back."

He raises them into the air instead, soaking in the glory of the cheering crowd. English laughs, then tells the cop, "Take a bow, man. You're on stage with the greatest fucking band of all time."

"Never heard of you."

"You want to be charged with resisting arrest?" The other cop is back at me, pulling my arm off the guitar. I finally relent before he breaks both. The crowd below moves in upset tidal waves, pushing and pulling, causing the other two cops to struggle to reach the stage. Napkins have been tossed, and a few beer cans have kissed the air.

Romeo and Lennox storm over. Lennox is never one to start trouble, but he's finished plenty. "What's the charge?"

The cop doesn't reply as he yanks my arms.

"If you can't tell by the guitar around my neck, I need my arms." Fucker gets rougher.

Lennox shoves the neck of his bass between me and the cop. "You can't just arrest him. What are the charges, or I'll have this place rioting?"

From this vantage point, front and center stage, it already is. Lloyd is pushed, and the last cop down there can't get to the stage from the barricade of people.

The guy behind me yells, "Cuff him."

Lennox unplugs and stage dives into the crowd, but a cop tugs him down. Neither is seen until enough people clear to see Lennox face down with a knee to his back. "Fuck." Helen is going to kill me.

The strap around me is released, and my guitar hits the edge of the stage, and then crashes to the ground. My heart sinks as I drop to my knees, too late to save it. "Goddammit!" As if being arrested wasn't bad enough, first I lose Weatherly and now my guitar. "Fucking hell."

Romeo shouts, "Motherfuckers." He's nabbed as soon as he jumps off the stage to try to pick up the pieces of my guitar. Jake dives in to help out.

One by one, we're shoved to the door and pushed against the wall while the police catch their breath and radio for backup. Not two feet from me, Jeb is in a serious discussion with one of them, trying to get us released by pleading our case. Standing in front of me, Jake says, "Sorry, man. They had a warrant."

"Not your fault. Will you get our gear? We can't afford to buy new stuff." The thought of my guitar being broken still pains me. Assholes.

Jake glances at the stage. "We'll lock it up in the office."

Lloyd walks by proud as a fucking peacock. Stopping in front of me, he says, "I kept my promise, Marquis. Good luck bailing out."

Since I'm going to jail anyway . . . I knee him in the balls.

He goes down.

And then I do, the cop pulling me from the lineup, dragging me outside, and shoving my face to the trunk of the car. "Are you stupid? Do you know who that guy is?"

"Yeah, an asshole who hits women when they say no."

"Is that what this is about? You cheating with his girlfriend?"

"He thinks his money can buy anything, including my girlfriend. She wasn't having it."

"So he hit her?" The cop is gruff, but I see a hint of empathy in his eyes. "Sorry, man. She needs to file a report. C'mon." I'm loaded in the back of a cop car with Lennox, who is smiling.

Not expecting a shit-eating grin, I ask, "What are you so happy about?"

"Feels like old times."

Laughing, I kick his shoe with mine. "Your mom is going to kick our asses."

"Not once she sees the video."

"What video?"

"Almost everybody in that bar had a phone aimed at us. How much you want to bet that video goes viral?"

"Two bucks?"

That makes him laugh. "If nothing else, we just left a major impression on the Austin music scene."

"You always find the silver lining, man."

SIX HOURS LATER, we're still sitting on a bench lined up against the wall in a drunk tank. We've witnessed two guys piss in the corner, four asleep on the concrete, and another that they quickly removed when they realized he was picked up for beating the guy who sold him a piñata because it was empty. Good thing too. He had crazy eyes. High as a fucking kite.

Yeah, it's a motley crew in here.

I'm so tired I want to go to bed, but we made a pact that none of us will sleep. You never know what kind of trouble you'll find in jail if you dare to rest your eyes.

Seven hours.

Romeo is led back into the cell. "They're charging me with threatening an officer with a weapon."

"What weapon?" I stand to stretch my legs.

"My sticks."

"That's not right." English produces a toothpick that

somehow got by when he was booked in. It's been hanging out the side of his mouth, and I have to give him props. It does make him look tougher.

But no toothpick can counterbalance those plaid pants. I ask, "Why didn't you change clothes?"

"What's wrong with my outfit?"

Lennox deadpans, "That you called it an outfit is what's wrong."

We fist bump because that was funny as fuck.

English rolls his eyes. "Whatever. You guys just don't get fashion."

The four of us are standing, and though Lennox is pacing, he stops to say, "We'll get the charges dropped, Romeo."

"Guess we'll see. I have a rap sheet like you guys. Petty shit, but we're not minors anymore. I'm a little worried."

He's right. We might need to be worried this time.

"Robert Marquis."

I turn toward the door. "Your lawyer's here."

"I don't have a lawyer."

He shakes his head in annoyance. "You want to talk to him or not?"

"I'll talk to him." *Whoever he is.*

I'm led down the hall to the visitation room and seated with my hands cuffed behind me. The door squeals open, and as soon as I see him, I groan. "Fuck me."

"I pulled strings to speak to you one on one." I stare at him—big build, condescending expression on his face, gray and black hair, and shockingly light blue eyes. I don't see my girl in him at all besides the eyes. "I'm Broderick Beck, Weatherly's father." He holds his hand out.

Fucker.

I wasn't worth his time at the party. I can only imagine

why I'm worth it now. I remain quiet, but I damn well hope he doesn't hear my heart beating out of my chest. I rattle my hands, making the chains of the cuffs jingle. "I'd shake your hand, but I'm a little tied up right now."

Although I laugh humorlessly, he doesn't even crack a smile. He says, "I'm paid very well for my time, so wasting it here on you is not in my or my family's best interest. So let's get down to business, shall we?"

I don't owe him anything.

He says, "I don't want you to see my daughter again."

I lied. I definitely have something to say about this. "Is that your right to decide?" It's interesting he has no idea we're already done.

"Everything to do with Weatherly is mine to decide. I need you to listen carefully. You will not see my daughter again, nor contact her in any way. She has a future I'm trying to protect and you will not ruin everything I've done to get her to this point."

"Seems she did the hard work—"

"While I pulled the strings."

"It's time to let her go and find—"

He slams his fist down. "Don't tell me how to raise my daughter!"

"She's not a child. Know how I know?" I quirk an eyebrow just to piss him off. "She doesn't slam her fist down in a tantrum."

The chair flies out from behind him and tips over. Leaning over the table, he shoves his finger in my face. "You're a fucking little maggot on the bottom of my shoe, Marquis. A no-good loser with a shit father and a dead mother."

Red.

The room goes red as I burst from my chair and lunge

forward. "You're a fuck, you fucking manipulator!" That lands me flat on my chest with hands trapped behind.

"Down, Marquis." The guard shouts at me like I'm a dog and then pulls me by my arms to the floor. I land on my ass, the cuffs stabbing into my back. *Shit.* Tears strike my eyes as my anger turns to pain.

Beck comes around to stand over me, my arm pinched under his shoe. "Stay away from her. That's your last warning."

The guard rolls me and starts lifting me as another runs into the room to get me up. When I'm standing, I look her father dead in the eyes. "And if I don't?"

"Then I'll make sure you'll spend the next ten to twenty years in jail. You think I don't have connections, that every judge in this city doesn't want their cut on the side? I have them all in my pocket. Fuck with me, and I'll fuck with you. Why do you think these guards are still standing here?" He stabs his finger into his chest. "Because I haven't dismissed them."

I have a chip on my shoulder, but this man has Mt. Everest on his. I push my emotions aside. "What happens to Weatherly's wishes? Doesn't she get to decide how she lives her life?"

"No. Her future is none of your concern."

"Let me guess. She'll be given to Lloyd to produce some babies and carry on whatever the fuck his last name is." Hellfire burns inside me. How can he want her with that guy? I use the only ammo I have left. "He attacked her. That's what landed me here. I tried to defend your daughter, to get revenge on her behalf."

"That's not how I heard the story."

"That man you think is so great struck her across the face. Check out the scratches on his neck and then tell me whose story you believe. But it doesn't matter what they say. Weatherly knows the truth. She'll never choose him, and she'll hate you." I'm yanked back. But stubborn like I've always been, I add, "It's your move, Daddy Beck." *Fucking asshole.*

"Take him away."

The guards pull me to the door, but I go willingly. I'm back in the cell with the guys again.

For the next three hours, I contemplate how much my life has changed in such a short time. One month is generous. Weeks. Weatherly came into my life and twisted me inside out. Everything about her, about us, was amazing. *One amazing moment in time.*

Love found me when I least expected it. I don't hide from the label. I now know that's what I felt . . . what I still feel.

I had it all.

I had Weatherly.

We deserved more time.

Now I'm sitting behind bars realizing I've lost it all—my girl, my freedom, my guitar. My heart.

We're exhausted, angry, and all humor has been lost. Then we're finally released. Upon booking us out, I ask the guard, "Who bailed us out?"

A finger drags across the screen. "Bail was posted at seven a.m. Just took a while to get the paperwork wrapped up."

"But who did it?"

He pauses while squinting at the old monitor. "Weatherly Beck."

34

Dare

I HAVEN'T FORGOTTEN what day it is.

I'll never forget.

My phone's dead when we catch a cab home, along with everyone else's. So I don't know if Weatherly called or if Helen's been trying to get a hold of us.

I get an answer when we pull up to the curb. Helen's car is in the driveway, and she comes out of the house, waiting on the porch. We drag our sorry asses up the sidewalk, but I can't look at her, not because of anything she did but because of the disappointment I've caused her. She says, "I waited at the park."

Lennox shakes his head. "We ran into some trouble last night."

"So I hear."

Gathering courage, I look up and am met with her brown eyes that are so like my mom's, considering there's no relation. What would my mom say about this mess? I hate to think about it.

Helen asks, "What happened, Lennox?"

"We were arrested. Long story. Can we do this inside?"

"Are we going later?" English yawns. "I need to go to bed."

"Yeah. Later works." I let him off the hook. We're dead tired, so I can't ask more of them than they already did. Fuck, they spent the night in jail basically on my behalf.

In the living room, Stascia stands, dragging her hands down the front of her pants. "I hope it's okay if I'm here. I was worried."

Hope momentarily blooms because if Stascia is here, then maybe Weatherly is too. But Stascia's somber expression is enough for me to read what she doesn't want to say, a slight shake of her head just before Romeo moves around the couch and greets her. Finding my eyes, she says, "I didn't know what to tell her." When she glances at Helen, my hopes dash.

Weatherly isn't here.

Romeo signals down the hall, and they go to his room.

Helen stands outside the kitchen. "Is someone going to talk to me, or do I have to listen to the police scanner to get the details?"

I chuckle, and then I remember why she used to listen. Her ex was a dispatcher. She could sleep when he was working. Any other time, the not knowing where he was caused her too much stress.

A knock on the door stops us in our tracks. My heart leaps like a fool's, and I rush to answer it. Some guy in a red hat, who looks shady as fun, shoves an envelope at me. When I take it, he says, "You've been served."

"Fuck." The guy's dashing across the lawn like a deer running from a hunter. Yeah, run, fucker. "What a shitty job."

He shrugs as he gets into his car. "It pays, dude. Today, it paid well." He hightails it down the street.

I go inside and open it. Helen stands beside me reading it. "Protection order?" Her voice pitches. "Who's Weatherly Beck?"

"No fucking way," Lennox says, joining my other side to read it.

I'm too numb to voice an opinion.

Lennox says, "You know she didn't file this, Dare. You know that, right?"

My throat is thick, closing in on me. My chest hurts in a similar way when I found out my mom was sick.

I hand the papers to Helen and walk to the sliding glass door, staring out at the blue skies that don't match my mood. "*I hate you with all my being, Dare Marquis.*" Yet she came back . . . "*There's no music, but our song is always playing inside here. Dance with me, Dare.*" I'd wanted to dance with her all night, to hold her in my arms forever.

Now there's a legal reason for me to stay away, not just emotional.

Helen says, "Fifty feet, Robert."

"What?" I turn around with my arms crossed over my chest.

"You can't be within fifty feet of her for six weeks and then the case will be reevaluated."

Lennox flips out. "That's ridiculous. He didn't do anything to her."

"I hurt her, and they hold all the power."

"If you hurt her so badly, why'd she bail us out?"

Rubbing my temples, I tense my lips. "I don't know, man." I want to be upset, but for some reason, none of this surprises me. This is how the rich win. "It's not going to look good to have this against me in court."

Helen comes and hugs me. "We'll figure it out. Let's take things one step at a time. Why were you arrested?"

Lennox starts talking, knowing I need the break. They sit on the big couch, so I kick back on the smaller one, putting my feet on the table. He explains my side and then what happened at Shep's, and I let him. I feel too messed up in my head to reason through any of this, especially Weatherly.

Add the restraining order and there are a whole lot of what the fucks filling my brain. I plug my phone into the charger on the side table and rest my head back. Long stories are long and short stories are long when it comes to Lennox and Helen Rey. It's something I've always appreciated and hated. Today, I appreciate it.

Despite the frustration and anger built up in my bones from the past twenty-four hours, my body betrays me by my eyelids growing heavy. Soon their voices begin to fade.

The squeal of front door hinges and exchanged whispers between Romeo and Stascia wake me. I sit up slowly, my body aching in revolt. If I wasn't stiff, I'd be impressed that I didn't even manage to actually lie down on the couch. Just fell asleep how I sat.

I'm still dead tired, but the day is passing, and I haven't had a moment to myself to think, or do anything else. Grabbing my phone, I see two hours have passed, and there are no messages other than from Helen early this morning while we were in jail. "Whatever," I say as if it makes up for not hearing from Weatherly.

But then I remember the restraining order. "Eh, fuck."

The aroma of freshly brewed coffee fills the air. I don't normally drink coffee at five at night, but since I'm basically starting my day, I indulge. Like Lennox who's just made himself a cup. He stirs his coffee and looks up when I ramble in. "We should probably leave soon. Bathroom's open."

Seeing him reminds me of Helen and disappointment tugs my shoulders down some. "How's your mom?"

"I talked to her. She's not happy about the situation. Not upset at us, but on our behalf. She left to take her anger out on some pasta. You know how cooking is like therapy for her."

After getting a mug, I take the coffee carafe and fill it. "A healthier way to burn through anger than getting arrested, that's for sure. I'll take a shower before everyone else is fighting for it."

"They're ready." He sets the spoon in the sink and looks up at me. "Today is important to all of us. We just figured you could use the extra sleep."

I pause for a second, letting their gesture, their support sink in. "Thanks."

I'm glad to have this family. We may not be perfect, but after what I've witnessed from the rich and famous across town, I'd pick them any day. Not that I'll tell them that. They have egos and shit, and I'm in no mood for that. Just past the bar, I add, "For the coffee, too."

"Yep."

I head for the shower to clean off jail, not going to sugar-coat where I spent the night. Thirty minutes later, we're out the door. We cruise through downtown to pick up the truck, and I jump out to stop into Shep's. The bar is open, but the crowd is sparse.

"Bad night," Jake says, rolling a keg toward the bar. I help him, and we carry it over instead.

"I've had better."

Chuckling, he says, "I bet. I have your equipment."

I follow him to the back room. "If you pull the truck around to the alley, you can load it out the back door."

"Thanks." After texting the guys, I step into the room and seek out my broken guitar.

Jake hangs around. "What was the arrest about?"

"Assholes running the world."

"Yeah." I hear him kicking his heel against the cement floor. "He hung around and asked for a drink." Just as I find the case, I look up at him. He says, "I told him we don't serve his kind."

"What kind is that?"

"Dickheads. There's even a sign posted at the entrance by Jeb."

We laugh, and although the night and today are hanging in my heart, it feels good to release some of the heaviness. "He's a lawyer, so that probably didn't go over well."

"Let him sue me. When he tries to ruin my business by having the band arrested mid-set, I don't give much of a fuck if he needs a drink. I had other shit to deal with."

I return to shake his hand. "Thanks for being a friend over these years. The band appreciates all you've done for us."

"You filled my bar every Thursday for the last year, and any other time I booked you, like last night. Thank you. But when you make it big, don't forget the small guys. I want one performance on that stage out there, and we'll call it even."

"That's a deal. Speaking of deals, I was wondering if we can get paid today?"

"Well shit, Dare, you guys didn't finish your set."

"Not for lack of trying."

Hitting my arm before he turns to leave, he says, "I'm kidding. Best show in town last night. I'll even pay you the full wage. I can't have you missing Thursday because you have a broken guitar." He pulls an envelope from his back pocket. "I had a feeling you'd stop by."

I tuck the money into my back pocket and shake his hand again. "I appreciate that."

Walking away, he calls back, "You still have an unpaid tab."

I laugh. "How many drinks do I have bought and paid for back there?"

"Five last night."

"Maybe we should call it even as well."

"Probably the only way it'll ever get paid, so I guess we'll call even."

I'm still laughing when I lift the latches to my case. It wasn't an expensive guitar, but it was the first I ever bought. Guess I'm feeling a little sentimental.

She served me well, but with a broken neck and a crack to the body, she's played her last show. Running my hand over the strings one last time, I give her a squeeze and then return it to the case.

They honk the horn out back, and English and Romeo walk in the propped open door. "How's the guitar?" Romeo asks.

"Busted. Jake paid full wage. I'm not trying to bust you upside the head with this, but I need a plan if we're not missing another gig."

"What is it?" English asks.

"Can I borrow a little extra to buy another one?"

Romeo grabs two of his drum cases by the handles. "I don't have a problem with that. We got paid in full, and your girl bailed us out, so I can't complain."

I'm not sure how I feel about those words coming so easy. Bail and my girl. I'm at a loss for both. As much as I want to see her, to hear her voice again, I need a minute to clear my head from the muddied waters of last night. There's only one place that can help, and we're heading there right after we get this damn truck loaded.

English stacks two amps and carries them to the door. "No problem here."

Lennox won't mind, but when I tell him, he agrees without a second thought. I pat his arm before going back in to finish loading up. "Thanks, Len."

Before we pull away, Jake comes up to my side of the truck. "Hey." He holds up a business card. I crank down the window, and he adds, "This guy was here last night. Saw the whole thing go down and asked me to give this to you." I take the card. "You should call him. I've already checked him out. He's legit."

"Thanks." I flip it around to read it.

After pumping the gas and using his magic on this beat-up jalopy, Lennox asks, "Who's the card from?"

"Some guy named Tommy from Outlaw Records."

"Outlaw?" He slams on the brakes and stares at me. "Outlaw Records? That's Johnny Outlaw's record company."

"Oh, yeah. You're right."

"Wonder what they want?"

"Guess we'll find out." I put the card in the tray between us on the floor. "To the park."

"Yeah."

After a quick stop by the store, we arrive at a small park near an art installation of an abstract heart sculpture.

Helen greets us and gives me a big hug. "I miss her everyday."

"Me too."

She takes a look at me, doting on me like I'm one of her own. My hair is pushed away from my eyes, the knot of my tie I put on in the truck straightened, and a kind smile is given as she takes a good long look at me. "She was a beautiful woman inside and out."

"Beauty attracts the eye, but the soul captures the heart." No one embodied those words more than my mom did. Until I met Weatherly.

Kneeling, I touch the brass plaque that's aged to greens and rusty, a muted shine still fights to catch the evening light. I run my fingers over each letter of her name—Laura Grace Marquis.

My mom's remains have long been scattered among the places she loved most—the beach where the turtles come ashore, the brick wall that surrounds Weatherly's house, and here where her name remains a symbol that she walked this earth. She was an angel among us but still resides inside me in a million memories.

To have her name added to the marble wall at the base of this sculpture would have tickled her. She forever lives as a part of the art she adored.

I miss her. I miss her voice, her laughter, her unconditional love. I just miss her so much.

But with all that's happened over the past few weeks, the mere thought of Weatherly's house has me dedicating more time to the other woman in my life. I still haven't had a minute to process the fact that we met when we were so young. My mom would have told me destiny brought us together fourteen years ago, but that's not a belief I ever subscribed to. Do I now? Did fate play her hand when it comes to me?

If it did, then it was cruel to rip it away so quickly.

Weatherly has turned me into a believer, but we have a big mess to clean up, if it even can be. She fell just as hard as I did, and we landed at each other's feet.

I made a mistake by pushing her away. I knew it then,

but I fell for all the bullshit being spewed about her life being better without me. If my gut is right, her life is better *with* me, just as mine is with her.

Wanting a second chance is one thing, but how do I get around the legal proceedings? How do I overcome a restraining order to even talk to her?

The answer is right behind me.

Fifty feet to be exact.

35

Dare

WEATHERLY.

Pepper.

Babe.

Girlfriend.

She's gone by a lot of names, but today, she's here without a defining name. Maybe friend fits. I'm not sure. She makes me unsteady in my normally straightforward life. I don't know what that means, or anything else these days. My world is so turned around that it's inside out. A lot like my heart.

She stands as close as she can, and I take that to mean she had no part in the fuckery in her life that pushed this order through. I know fucked-up situations all too well. I survived them. I'm used to being betrayed by the system. My mom went to the police, social services, and anyone else she could beg for help. No one came through for us.

I was too young to be in the know about the details, but when we left my dad, he was too self-centered to know it was for good and smart enough to stay away. As the sun heads toward seven o'clock, it's still broad daylight and easy to see the tear streaks staining Weatherly's cheeks, confirming the injustice of the life she's currently trapped in the middle of.

Helen rubs my back. "Do you want me to talk to her?"

"Yes." She starts walking, but I ask, "What are you going to talk about?"

Smiling, she says, "I'm sure there's plenty to say."

Romeo, English, and Lennox stand nearby—my brothers, my band, my best friends—the quietest they've ever been in contrast to their usual rowdiness. "Should I be worried?" I ask.

English laughs. "Can't get worse."

We stand around watching the conversation from fifty feet away. Weatherly breaks down, her face hidden in her hands as sobs wrack her small frame. Helen wraps her arms around her and embraces her. I know the feeling of those arms holding you when you feel your loneliest, the most pained.

From this distance, I can see Helen wipes the tears from Weatherly's face and then give her that reassuring smile that everything will be okay.

Will it? I like to believe we will, but I don't know. With fifty feet dividing us, it's feeling damn near impossible. This is something love can't fix. I'll end up in jail if I cross that line.

When Helen returns, she says, "Are you ready to go?"

I glance at Weatherly as she looks back one last time before getting in her car and leaving. "What did she say?"

"What do you believe?"

"I don't know what you mean."

"Okay," Helen says, tapping her chin. "What about . . . Do you love her?"

"Uh." I shift back, not expecting that, but the discomfort of the situation follows me. Distraction is the best remedy. I need to distract myself from facing the truth or having to say it out loud. I run my fingers along the edge of the sleek sculpture. "Um."

Tugging at the collar of my shirt, I try to let some air in. The heat has finally hit me, and I'm starting to sweat. She fills in the answer for me. "So that would be a yes. She loves you, too."

Surprise rips through me, and I whip around. "Did she say that?"

"She didn't have to. She's here because you invited her. She showed up for you. It's time to show up for her."

"She filed a restraining order against me."

Rolling her eyes, she laughs. "You know she didn't."

"I don't know shit except what that piece of paper I was served says."

"Don't be stubborn, Rob. I know things appear insurmountable right now, but love finds a way."

"If I don't find myself in jail first."

"She wanted me to tell you she's sorry. She's working to get the charges and the order dropped, but these things take time and a certain finesse."

Fucking great. Another reason for her to have to deal with that asshole who had us arrested. He should have the restraining order against him. He's the one who struck my girl. *Fuck. She shouldn't have to do this.*

"She's a very clever young woman. I'm sure she'll figure a way out." Helen walks to the plaque, and says, "Happy Birthday, Laura." The tips of her fingers linger as she closes her eyes and whispers something I can't hear.

When she walks away, she goes to her son and hugs him. Lennox holds his mom and then hangs back while she, Romeo, and English head to the car. Stepping closer to the marble base, he kisses his hand before placing it on the brass name. "Happy Birthday, Laura. Miss you."

He leaves, giving me a few moments of solitude with her. I visit. Not as often as I should, but there's something about this day that makes me feel grateful for the blessings I've been given. Even though she was taken away too soon.

I sit in front of the sculpture. It takes me a minute to warm up to the marble and talk about things.

My hand lingers on the plaque. "Happy Birthday, Mom."

I've always felt she was experiencing my life with me, so maybe she already knows. "I love her, Mom. There's nothing rational about us and nothing that makes sense about our lives coming together, except one. Love. But is it the right time? Maybe we weren't meant to meet yet. The band is doing well, so should I put all my energy into that dream, my heart be damned? Tell me. That seems like the only true impossibility. I walked away, but I don't think I can forever. Let me know if I'm fucking up by harboring feelings when the world is conspiring against us."

I have a feeling it's worse to deny my feelings than to live with the consequences of fighting for someone you love. I stand, knowing I have already been given an answer. My mom was looking out for me fourteen years ago when she insisted on taking that picture.

"Maybe the question isn't if it's a good time, but accepting that love arrived right on time. Right when I needed it most." I grin and touch the plaque once more. "Thanks, Mom. You always did know best."

When I get in the truck, Lennox asks, "You ready?"

"I am."

I THOUGHT it would be a quiet dinner. With so much on our minds, hanging over our heads, and the unknown ahead, dinner at Helen's is still entertaining. I'm glad. Mom would have liked this—the jokes, the laughter, Helen's famous piña colada cake.

We have to clean before that cake is served, though, so the band gets busy in the kitchen. I finish clearing the table and start drying a pot when Helen says, "Robert?" and then nods toward the hall when I look her way.

I go to her, wondering why she needs privacy since we're usually fairly open as a family. Taking hold of my arms, she rubs them, and says, "Forget about the past twenty-four hours. Don't let that get in your head."

"I'm trying, but I have a feeling that this could end up being something I can't get out of this time."

"Things will work out. I'll help you however I can."

Hugging her, I say, "Thanks, Helen."

"You're more than welcome." She tucks her hair behind her ears, and asks, "While I have you here, do you mind getting a box on my bed?"

"Yeah, no problem."

We go in opposite directions; her back to the kitchen and me to her bedroom. When I open the door, the box is on her bed just as she said, but Weatherly is stealing my attention. In shock, the doorknob remains in my hand.

She stands, her hands fidgeting, looking awkward. I'm not sure if she wants to run to me or away by the wide-eyed look of her eyes. As soon as I close the door, she throws herself into my arms, and I hold her, my soul returned.

It's been less than twenty-four hours since I held her, but

it feels like an eternity. I kiss the top her head, and not wasting another second, I say, "I love you."

"I love you so much."

With our arms still wrapped around each other, our eyes find each other. Tears stream down her face, and she adds, "I'm so sorry. I'm so sorry, Dare. Please forgive me."

"You didn't do this."

"I didn't know they would go to this extreme because I said no."

We release each other, and I walk to the window, peeking out through the sheers. "You told your father no?"

"I did. He gave me no choice."

I return to her and cup her face, just happy to be seeing her again. "Bold and brave. But you didn't toe the family line, so that left them no other choice than to hurt you by trying to hurt me."

"He kicked me out of my apartment as well. I found out it's a corporate apartment."

"Where are you going to live?"

"I have savings and credit cards. Even my trust fund. They can't take that away. I'll be fine staying at a hotel until I figure out what to do next. My bigger concern is you. I feel terrible. I'm so sorry for what's happened to you."

"So am I." I release her and sit down. "I'm charged with assault and battery, my guitar is broken, and then I was hit with this restraining order."

Sitting next to me, she says, "I'll fix this. I promise I will."

"I don't know how you can. They don't listen to you. Don't you see? You were good for them when they could control you, but that's not who you are. So they have to blackmail you into submission."

"They can't. You've made me see that my complacency

has allowed them to walk all over me, as if I'm trapped in winter, and suddenly, it's spring. A new season of rebirth."

"There's freedom in that."

"For the first time in forever, I'm taking charge. They can put a mountain in our way, and I'll move. They can sanction orders and enact laws to keep us apart, but I'll fight every step of the way to get to you." She cups my face. "I love you, Robert Marquis."

It's momentarily jolting to hear my first name come from her lips. "I remember. I remember everything from that day."

"You do?"

"I do." She asks, "Did you know you once told me your name was Rob?"

"Yes, and you told me it was short for Robert."

"I was a know-it-all back then, dying to talk to anyone who would listen. You listened."

"You talked a lot."

"I've changed some since then." She takes a deep breath, a weight lifting. "You told me not to talk to strangers. But strangers were better than the monsters surrounding me."

I hold her to me again. "I wish I knew then."

"Dare?"

"Hmm?"

"Your mom was a beautiful human."

My body wrenches around her from the realization, and tears flood my eyes. Squeezing them closed, I try not to let them fall, but as soon as I catch Weatherly's blues on me, they do. "You met her."

"I did."

How did I forget that? *She met my mom.* Something about that brings a small wave of peace to my heart. She kisses the bottom of my chin and lifts up to rest her cheek against mine. Holding my head to her, she whispers, "She was so sweet to me. Asking me about my favorite things when I was bugging you."

"What'd you tell her?"

"Peanut butter sandwiches."

A laugh bursts from my chest. "Peanut butter sandwiches? You told me they were your favorite because you never got them as a kid."

She shrugs. "I didn't. That's why I love them so much now. They feel like a treat. But back then, I wanted your mom to like me. And to my nine-year-old brain, peanut butter seemed like an in."

"It was. She loved peanut butter sandwiches, but you know what she loved more?"

"Honey," we say in unison and then laugh.

"That was your mom's secret," she adds.

"Adding honey?"

"Yes, because it makes life so much sweeter."

I've been choked up all day, but seeing how life loops around in mysterious ways gives me hope. "That's what you made for me the first night I stayed with you."

"Imagine how boring those sandwiches would have been if I'd never met your mom."

"Imagine how boring my life would be if I'd never met you?"

She smiles, the light filling in the cracks of my heart. I kiss her because it's been too long since I've had my lips on hers. She says, "You know what else she did?"

"What?" I ask.

"She tied the yellow ribbons in my hair into bows, held my cheeks in her palms like you do, and told me I was as pretty as a daisy. We were always meant to find each other again."

"It was only a matter of time. And the first night we met, I untied yellow ribbons from your ankles."

"Some call that kismet."

"I call it meant to be."

"I like your version better."

Kissing her forehead, I say, "Me too. Now about you being here . . . that could get me arrested."

She steps back and says, "I'm going to get the charges dropped. I swear to you, Dare. I've been sick to my stomach since the moment you left the party."

"You didn't come after me."

"I was locked in the office until you were gone."

"Why would they do that?" I know the answer, but I still can't believe the lengths they'll go. "You should press charges for that and for Lloyd's attack."

"I can't because I'm trying to get them to drop yours."

"Fuck mine. I'll work it out. You need to be free from those monsters."

She's shaking her head. "I'll be fine, but I swear I will get every last one of yours dropped before the hearing." Sadness invades our happy space, and her expression falls. "I need to sneak back out before I'm caught."

I hold her so tightly to me, and then we kiss hard like I like it and soft like she does. It's perfect. *Like us.*

I return to the kitchen table and set the box down. Lennox says, "About time."

When I see they've finished the kitchen, I return to the bedroom. The window is open, and the curtains are blowing. I shut it and lock it down. Standing in the doorway, Helen asks, "How'd it go, Rob?"

"Great. I'm not sure where we go from here, but wherever it is, we decided it will be together." As it should have always been.

"I'm glad. She's a lovely young woman."

"She is. Thank you, Helen. Thanks for never giving up on me."

"Not a chance, kid. I would never give up on you."

In the living room, English's face scrunches. "Is that lipstick on you, mate?"

I laugh. "It sure is."

36

Weatherly

"WHERE WILL YOU GO?" Stascia stops with a box of tampons in her hands and looks up from the floor where she sits.

I pull a drawer from my bathroom cabinet and dump it into a large box. "Anywhere but to my parents' home. I can't forgive them for what they've done. My father actually thought he could hold a job over my head when it was never in my best interest, but his. I will never let him, Lloyd, or anyone control me again."

She nods in agreement. "You can stay at my house."

"Thanks, friend, but that hits awfully close to where they live."

"I know. I just wish I could help."

I sit on the floor next to her and open another cabinet. "You are. You're helping me pack and clear my stuff out of here." I pull a tray out and set it in the box. "At this rate, I'll be out by tomorrow."

"We'll work until it's done."

We move steadily through the bedroom over the next

few hours, leaving the closet for last. Two hours after that, we've almost packed the kitchen.

"You've never talked about what happened at the party," she says.

"You know what happened."

"I'm talking about with Lloyd . . . when he hit you."

My hands still with a can open, but then I squeeze the cold metal, remembering more than I want to. "He . . . I'd left Dare out front. I should have never left him . . ."

The paper crinkles as she wraps it around the stem of a wine glass, so she stops. "Sorry."

"It's okay. It just happened so fast I haven't really allowed myself to process it." My cheek heats from where he slapped me. "I went in, and he pulled me into my dad's office, trapping me. Threw me against the bookcase and told me I owed him what I'd given my boyfriend."

"Oh Weatherly, I'm so sorry."

"He hit me when I told him if he raped me he'd still never have my heart. That only belonged to Dare. He squeezed my cheeks so hard I thought he'd bust my teeth. Kissed me roughly."

"How'd you get free?"

"There are books at the top of the bookcase. We must have loosened them because one fell and hit him. He grabbed me when I tried to reach the door, so I scratched the hell out of him and escaped."

"That's horrifying." She comes to me and hugs me so tenderly, warm, and comforting. "I'm so sorry."

"I'm okay. As soon as I figure out to help Dare and the band, I'm pressing charges against him."

"If you need my help in any way, just tell me."

"Thank you."

We're exhausted by ten p.m. With a bottle of water in her

hand, she stares at a bottle of champagne we left on the counter. "April chose Lloyd over us."

"Good. We no longer had enough of a bond to keep us together as friends."

"Will you miss her?"

I know the answer. I can say it, but I don't. I hold it in and mull it over, looking for the wounds she inflicted instead. This time when I answer, it's the truth instead of what I'm supposed to say. "No. I imagine she feels lighter like I do. One less thing to concern herself with."

"We've been friends since we were little."

"Our parents were friends. It was circumstantial. Now we get to choose who we let into our lives." Leaning on the bar, I say, "I choose you."

She grins. "I choose you, too."

Still leaning forward, I say, "I heard from April. One nasty voicemail the day after the party."

"Are you kidding me?" Disgust is heard in her words.

I pull out my phone and find it. Pushing play, we both listen. "You are not special, Weatherly Beck. You may think you are, but you're not. Are you really going to destroy years of friendship over some guy from the east side? Trust me, he's not worth it. I'll give you twenty-four hours to make your choice. The loser or me, your lifelong best friend."

I look at Stascia, who says, "Wow. She's delusional. Does she not remember what she said to you? What she did to you? I take it you never called her back?"

"I called."

Wide eyes reveal her surprise. "You did?"

"I told her I'm choosing the guy from the east side because he has more class than she does."

After a gasp, she laughs. "What did she say?"

"That Lloyd never wanted me. He only wanted to secure a partnership at the law firm."

"She's cold-hearted."

"Her so-called insult doesn't hurt. I'd have to care for it to affect me."

A soft smile works its way onto her face, giving her the slightest crinkles around her eyes. I like her best like this. Real in every way. Genuine. "You're stronger than I am."

"No. I just opened my eyes. You have too. I can tell." I take the rubber band from my wrist and twist my hair up off my neck. "Now you can be who you want instead of trying to fit the mold she wanted to keep you in."

"Very true." She leans forward and whispers, "I don't miss her."

I grab the champagne and remove the foil. "You know what? We should celebrate."

"What are we celebrating?"

"Our rebirth."

I toss the second bottle of champagne in the recycling bin and then take another bite of my pizza. "The Four Seasons has decent room service."

"I prefer the W," Stascia replies, lying on the couch. "You'll be out tomorrow. Where will you go?" She snort-laughs. "Maybe you should move to the east side."

The bubbles must have gone to my head because I'm not laughing. "Maybe I should." I look around the apartment that holds nothing personal of mine anymore. "I don't fit in this world, and I don't know what I'm going to do with my life. But I do know that my heart lives on that side of the highway."

"Home is where the heart is."

Truer words have never been spoken. Dare is my home,

and I have a revelation. "I have an idea. I know where I'm going to live."

"Where?"

Dare

I didn't know what to expect when it came to Weatherly. I can't contact her, and we can't see each other until this order is dismissed. But what I didn't expect was to wake up the next morning to the sound of an RV beeping as it backs up to make its home on the street in front of our neighbor's house.

Looking out the window, the thing is a beast. I wander through the living room into the kitchen where English is making breakfast. "What's with the rig out front?"

"Weatherly."

"What do you mean?"

He pulls the milk from the fridge and sets it on the counter. "I mean, it's Weatherly's RV."

"I don't get it. She can't be here."

He smells the milk. "She says she has it all figured out, but I can just add that you two move fast."

"We can't move at all because of the order."

"Go tell Miss-I-can-do-it-myself because she's making a home whether you're living in it or not. And let's talk about that. Shall we? I thought for sure you guys were just full of the lust for each other—"

"The lust?"

"Yeah, but now you're going to jail for her and she's breaking restraining order laws or rules, or whatever they're called here in America. You get the drift. If this is how love works, I'm going to be looking over my shoulder to avoid it at all costs. For Christ's sake, I've had this milk longer than you've known her and look at the mess you're in." Holding the carton up, he says, "Well, fuck. This expired two days ago."

"See? We've outlasted it. Proof that this is more than the lusts. Like so much more that I'm willing to say we'll last longer than . . ." Twisting my lips to the side, I delve into deep thought, and then say, "Pasta."

"Pasta? Does that even expire?"

"Nope."

"Damn, dude. You have it bad."

"I do, but guess what?" I point at the door. "She does, too."

That makes him laugh. "Good luck, mate. You're going to need it."

"I don't need luck. I'm in love."

He makes a gagging noise while he walks back to his room. "That was so bad, Marquis."

I'm still laughing when I head out front. Standing on the porch, I try to get her attention. She shifts the big brown beast into park and slides the door open. "Good morning." She waves.

Making sure there are no cops or spies around, I lean on the railing. "What are you doing, Pepper?"

"Fifty feet. That's the order. So fifty feet and one inch is the safe zone." Her arms go wide. "Voila."

"Didn't you have to break the order to measure the distance?"

"No. English helped me."

I grin and mutter, "Sappy fuck."

She jumps to the curb and twirls in the grass. "I actually have room to play because I parked in front of the neighbors. I'm fifty-five feet away," she calls loud enough for the neighbors to hear and quite pleased with herself.

"The neighbors will complain. They complain about everything."

"The neighbors approved."

"How much did you pay them, Beck?"

"Enough to pay off one year of their mortgage."

Chuckling, I say, "Damn." I pull a rickety chair from the corner over to the railing and rest my arms on it. "So how long are you staying?"

"Until the order is lifted."

"That could be months."

"I waited fourteen years to find you again. I can wait a few months."

And just like that, we were in a long-distance relationship . . . across my front yard. Neither of us is breaking the law or order, but toeing the line to be together.

Weatherly moved a mountain to be with me. *Just as she promised.*

37

Weatherly

"I'm going to make you come so hard that you'll forget your name," Dare whispers in my ear. "How does that sound?"

"God, so good." With my eyes closed, I press the phone tighter to my ear and add, "I can't wait. I want your tongue all over my body."

"Ew!"

Startled, my eyes fly open to find Stascia hightailing toward the exit of the RV.

"Oh, my God! Stascia is here. Let me call you back."

"Bummer. It was just getting good, babe." He exhales loudly. "Call me back."

"I will." I jump out of bed and tuck my phone in my pocket. I'm still a little shaken when I get outside and surprised she's here. "Stascia?" I call when I don't see her.

"Up here."

I look up as I walk to the back of the RV. I can't see her, but I know she's climbed to the top. We've sunbathed there a few times over the last week. "Hey, what are you doing? I wasn't expecting you."

"Obviously," she mumbles. "I wish I could un-hear what I just heard."

"I was on a private phone call." I climb up the ladder.

"You were having phone sex."

"Actually, we didn't get that far. It was more . . ." I see her sitting in a lawn chair with her gaze to the stars. "It was phone foreplay, technically."

When she sees me, she starts laughing. "Is that what the kids are calling it?"

"Why yes, yes we are." I step on the top deck and work my way carefully to the beach chair next to hers, sit down, and look up. "It's a clear night."

"It is." We both glance at each other.

"We're violating the terms of the order by having contact of any kind, but since I didn't file it, I'm willing to go down for it."

"I won't tell. And sorry for walking in without knocking. I'm sort of mortified."

"Not as much as I am." That makes us both laugh.

The laughter tapers off, and she leans closer with curious eyes to whisper, "Will Dare really lick your entire body?"

"Oh." *My God.* Speaking of mortified . . . "Yeah, I guess that did sound really bad."

"It sounded good to me. No one has ever . . ." Her voice gets even quieter. "Gone downtown, if you know what I mean."

"What? How is that possible? You and April have always been so, you know, experienced. Like light-years ahead of me."

Shame fills her pretty features—green eyes saddened,

lips turned down, heavy heart weighted on her shoulders. "I lied."

"You lied?"

"I've had sex, but I'm just not that experienced." She whispers, "I've never had an orgasm. Not like April. I wanted to fit in."

I sigh. "And leave her to ridicule me." I could be mad, but I'm tired of being upset. "It would make me a hypocrite to call you out on that. Sex should have never been used as a weapon. I won't use it against you now." I reach over and rub her arm. "Anyway, I like that we're finally on an even playing field."

"I think you're in the end zone while I'm still at the fifty-yard line. So as for even . . . I think you're light-years ahead of me," she says, laughing.

"Thank you for being honest with me." I'm sure there will be a few more revelations between us, but eventually, we'll all be clean of our past sins and have memories built on honesty.

"That's what friends do."

"It sure is," she says, looking back at the stars. Stascia usually overshares, so her visit tonight has thrown me. "Any particular reason you stopped by?"

Her momentary silence speaks volumes. "I was leaving the house and saw your light on. You should really lock your door."

"Lennox was here a little while ago. He brought me flowers."

Sitting up abruptly, she's shocked. "What? Why?"

"I mean," I start but stop because I'm laughing. "From Dare. He stayed for a few minutes and we talked, but the flowers are from Dare."

"You've really taken to these guys."

"I have. When you hang out with them individually, they have something so unique about each of them, but then together, their loyalty is limitless. But you know what I love the most? Their hearts. Pure gold. They've done nothing less than fully support Dare and me. They don't blame me or complain about the charges. There's something special about each of them, and their support of each other is envious."

"I've seen it." This time, she reaches over and clasps my hand. "I love you."

"I love you, too."

"Remember how you asked me what I wanted to do with my life? And we talked about my degree?"

"Yeah."

"I think you're the first person who ever cared to ask me that."

"No one ever asked me before Dare, so I get it. I care about you and want you to find what makes you happy."

Mischievousness widens in her eyes. "Don't make fun of me, okay?"

"You don't have to say that. I'm not April."

Nodding, she whispers, "I want to be a mom."

My hands fly to my chest. "Aw, I love that. That's so sweet. I'm just sad I never knew before." I rib her just a little. "What about Romeo?"

"Oh God, Weatherly. I don't know. I like him, but I'm not sure we're ready to take it to the next level."

"I thought you had."

"Nope." Leaning in conspiratorially, she says, "This is going to sound so weird, but we talk. We talk about everything and nothing, and time just flies by."

I understand this more than she realizes and grin. We have endless conversations across the front lawn when we're not talking on the phone or by video. "It's amazing how spending time with someone you like . . . or more, is contentment on a new level. With Dare, we don't go out much. We spend time in, and I don't know, it's hard to explain, but I fell in love with him before I knew I'd fallen."

"That's way ahead of where we are. He treats me different, not like a groupie. He's . . . ugh. Ignore me. I'm making no sense."

"Dare was the same. He may have seemed like a playboy, but he was hiding his heart. I like to think he was saving it." And I'm thankful every day that he held on to it for me.

Pulling lip-gloss from her pocket, she holds it to her lips but doesn't apply. "He's nurturing." The distraction is in play as she covers her lips with the gloss.

"Nurturing is not what I expected, but it makes me happy to hear."

"He's just so damn caring. He makes you feel like the only woman alive."

"There's a lot to be said about that."

"There is. I'm just not ready to say it."

"So where do you go from here?"

She stands. "Home. It's been fun to hang out, but I think I need to sleep in my own bed tonight and figure out my next move."

We start to climb down. "Keep me posted, and you know where to find me."

"Yes, with your doors unlocked while having phone sex."

"I wasn't having phone sex."

"Yet. Whatever. I'm not judging."

We hug. "Because real friends don't."

"Exactly." She looks at me once more as though she's seeing me for the first time. Maybe she's never met the real me before. I wore the face I thought they wanted for so long that even I forgot who I was. Dare reminded me.

"How's the research going?"

"With the power my dad and the Sanders hold, I can't figure out an angle. I'm starting to worry they might win."

She steps up to the sidewalk. "I hope you nail those assholes. Lloyd is horrible, but he learned it from his father. I've called him Mr. Handsers for years. He once grabbed my boob, a full-on hand grab, and then claimed it was an accident when I called him out. Later, when no one was around, he went on to tell me how soft it was and not fake like his wife's."

"He once grabbed my ass and told me how'd I'd grown so luscious. Luscious. I wanted to puke. He got a feel in at the party too."

She's shaking her head just as disgusted as I am. "Like I said, take them down, Weatherly. For all of us." She walks a few feet, and then adds, "I'll stop by tomorrow to hang out."

"Okay. Night."

As soon as I climb back in the RV, I lock the door and double-check it. I pull my phone from my pocket and flop back on the bed as I dial. Dare answers, "Hi, beautiful."

"Now where were we?"

I'VE RACKED my brain over this protection order for the past five days, the charges against not only Dare but also the whole band. I keep coming up empty of options. My father and Bob Sanders are two of the most powerful lawyers in the country, and by far in Austin. I have nowhere to turn for answers.

So I rely on myself.

I'm smart.

Capable.

Determined.

And in love. Nothing and no one can stop me.

"You've been so quiet," Dare says. He's been playing guitar, and it's easy for me to get lost in my thoughts to the melody. This is how we spend time together each night. Unlike last night's sexy time, tonight we're more low-key. I've been studying with his video company while he plays. I look up at the screen to see Dare's handsome face smiling back at me. "Hi. Remember me?"

"I do. Very well." I smile, but it's short-lived. "Sometimes I still think you're right here, close enough to kiss."

"I am." He kisses the camera, so I do as well.

"I love that, but I love you more. I'm frustrated that I can't figure out a way to fix this."

"Don't be frustrated. It's not your mess to clean up. It's ours."

"Because of me."

"No, because of them. Focus on studying for the bar exam instead. Things will work out how they're supposed to on my end. As for you, I want you to dream big, or small, if you prefer, but just know they're your dreams to own. No one else's. No one controls you. Not your father, not Lloyd, and not me. Own your destiny, babe. It's time to let all your hard work shine through."

Tears well in my eyes from the sweetest sentiment I've ever heard. I've never felt such love and support than I have from him. "I wasn't expecting such an incredible pep talk when we logged on. You're amazing, Dare. Inspiring in so many ways. I've never met anyone like you and feel so blessed to have you in my life. Thank you for being born." I start laughing because I know that's cheesy, but I'm so touched by his words that I'm struggling to say something deeper.

He chuckles. "I can't really take credit for that, but I'm happy I was too." He sips water, and I watch as he settles on the bed I wish we were still sharing. He sticks to one side, leaving the other open for me as if I'm about to climb in right next to him. He asks, "You still want to practice law, right?"

I angle my laptop away and rest my head in my hand. "The practice of law was never the problem. Lloyd, Bob, and my father are. Those ties have been severed. For two of them, it's forever. Maybe my dad and I will see eye to eye one day, but that's not something I want right now. A lot of damage has to be fixed—your situation and pulling the apartment out from under me like they did." I close my eyes and take a breath. When I reopen them, I can see the intensity built in his, the struggle he fights not to run to me. I recognize it because it's an hourly battle I fight as well.

"I'm going to be very upfront, but know it's because I care about you. I also worry about you and your money situation. You don't have a job and you can't live in an RV at the curb forever. Do you need help?"

"I appreciate it, but I'm fine. I have money separate from my parents, but they haven't cut me off yet, so I'll live on their dime for now."

"I'm surprised they haven't cut you off yet."

"I think it's my mom tempering the fires between us. I'm not going to question it, though."

He chuckles. "I wouldn't either, but promise me you'll let me know if you need anything."

"As soon as I pass the exam, I'll find a job to support myself, and I'll come into my inheritance from my grandparents for backup. So you don't need to worry about me."

"That's my girl. It's late. You need to study, and I should go to bed. Love you, babe."

"I love you, too."

After we disconnect, I get up to find a snack in the cabinet. A bag of chips and some tea will do. I need caffeine because there's still a lot I want to cover before bed. I just can't seem to get my head in the game. So many things are on my mind that I can't even prioritize them anymore.

Except for one.

Something Stascia said last night. That's when I realize I've had the answer in front of me all along. I've been so busy trying to play fair, not realizing I'll never beat them at their own game. If they want to play dirty, it's time to sink to their level. And I have a plan.

38

Weatherly

I THOUGHT it would take a week or so to gather the evidence to back my case, but I was wrong. It took all of twenty-four hours to find five women willing to come forward and put a statement on the record. So I called a meeting.

Nine days after the protection order took effect against Dare, I stood opposite my father with his large ornately carved desk between us. The desk feels like a fitting symbol representing our division. A large divide that feels impossible for us to bridge. Guess we'll see how this meeting goes.

Broderick Beck is surprising me, though. He's not impatient, which is something he considers an attribute. He's . . . I'm not sure what he is. Intrigued to see what I have up my sleeve seems to be the only words that fit.

Bob and my father built an empire with six locations worldwide. There's an arrogance that comes with their level of success, and it's present today, coming off Bob in waves. Oh, and Lloyd's here.

I didn't share my plan with Dare. I thought it best not to

involve him, but his words of encouragement are giving me the strength I need, even if they were shouted from fifty-five feet away. "*Knock 'em dead, Pepper. Own your dreams and make them pay.*" He also used the walkie-talkie feature on our watches, a gift I thought he'd enjoy using, which he has. Walkie-talkie sex anyone? "*It doesn't matter the outcome as long as you've made yourself proud, then we win.*"

Even with the threat still looming over his head, he was only thinking of me and worried about my well-being. My heart squeezes with giddiness. I don't ask how I'm this lucky or why I'm deserving of this great man anymore. We were written in the stars long before we reunited. But he's right. If I make myself proud, I'll make him proud. And that is a win.

"I don't want to waste anyone's time, so I'll get to the point. There's a sealed envelope in front of each of you." Lloyd starts opening it without hearing me out like I knew he would, so I keep going, "What's contained inside can stay that way or I can have a press conference instead."

My father's expression morphs to the legal shark he is. His narrowed eyes locked on the prey—me. "What is this, Weatherly?"

The tone that used to make me cower, I now use as motivation. "It's six accounts of sexual harassment against Bob Sanders. One sexual assault case against Lloyd Sanders."

Lloyd drops the file like there's poison inside.

"Impossible!" Bob stands, picking up and slamming the envelope on the table for dramatic effect.

"Impossible?" I ask, doe-eyed. "That's the defense you're going with?"

"I don't have to defend myself to you or anyone else. I know my rights. And I'm innocent until proven guilty."

Ignoring his unoriginal rant, I turn to my father. "*My*

statement is one of the six and the only one stated for the record against Lloyd."

"What do you mean your statement?"

The adrenaline drains from my body, and suddenly, I'm the little girl he used to scare into telling the truth. Only this time, my truth could be his downfall. I'm not looking for revenge against him, and my emotions aren't clouding my judgment. I've done my research and know my rights, so I won't cave under pressure. But his disappointment permeates the room. *Ignore. Do not feed into it.*

I want to right the wrong against Dare, his band, and every woman who was brave enough to speak to me so candidly. I speak clearly so everyone can hear. "Bob Sanders has been touching me inappropriately since I was a child. Maybe an ass grab or pat on the butt doesn't mean anything to him, but it's not something I was okay with. And despite being a minor on many occasions, I found my voice to tell him more than a few times. He's crossed lines, so when he gets his defense team to say he did no harm, he's dead wrong. I endured him because I was too scared of you to speak up most of the time."

Lloyd snips, "Apparently not. You're doing it now because you're jealous that I've moved on." Lloyd adds, "Revenge is such a bitter bitch, but I thought you were above it. You've proven that we were right in not bringing you into the firm. You're unstable, Weatherly, and need serious help."

What did I ever see in that manipulative bastard?

"Enough!" my dad yells. "You will *not* call my daughter a bitch." Lloyd has the decency to look affronted, but I know he's not.

But then I really look at my father's face. When he looks up, I see the first sign of weakness I consider strength—tears mixed with anger—real emotion. No poker face for the jury or heartless negotiation. Raw and real emotions.

Standing up, he comes around the desk, taking the envelope with him. He looks at Bob, who is watching my father with a scowl. I'm surprised he hasn't continued Lloyd's vitriol. Turning to Lloyd, my dad says, "You're fired. Get the fuck out of my house."

Bob stands. "You can't fire him!"

"I just did."

Lloyd looks at his dad. "He can't do that, right?"

"Shut up, Lloyd. I'll handle this."

Whining, Lloyd says, "This is so lame."

My dad huffs. "As for you, Bob, I'll see you in court."

"What? We're partners, Broderick. Business always comes first."

"Not this time." My dad hasn't looked at me in a minute, but it feels like an hour as I stand there smaller in stature than all three of these men, confident in my convictions, but alone.

When he does move, he walks to the door . . . wait, huh? He doesn't leave as I thought he would. Instead, he comes to me. Next to me, he turns to face them. "I stand with my daughter."

"She's a liar, Broderick!" Bob shouts, his tone is panicked, as sweat beads on his forehead. "She's causing trouble where there is none. Are you going to throw a three-hundred-million-dollar firm away on the accusation of a girl who can't handle a friendly gesture?"

My dad growls, "I'm not, but you just did. Get out!"

Bob storms to the doors. They fly open, and he yells, "This is bullshit! You'll see me in court all right. And you can forget the tee time on Sunday."

We walk into the foyer to see my mom standing with the

front door wide open and a big grin. As they walk down the steps, Lloyd starts sniveling, "Dad, what are we going to do?"

"Shut up, Lloyd!"

The door is slammed shut, and she dusts her hands.

Looking at the envelope in his hand once more, my dad says, "The protection order isn't real, Weatherly."

I do a double take, not understanding what he just said. "What do you mean it's not real?"

"Lloyd was considered an asset to the firm in his willingness to go the extra mile." He turns back to me. "Legally or illegally. He enacted the order on behalf of all three of us by drawing up a fake document and having it served, not through an officer, but a guy he paid on the side. Although I found out after the fact, I knowingly let it stick."

"But how? Dare has court next week. This would have come to light. Why would you do anything to hurt me, much less something illegal? Do you hate me that much?"

"I love you that much. I thought a little time would help you get over this tryst, that the fallout was too great for you two to further the relationship. I was wrong."

"Wrong?" I'm rubbing my forehead in disbelief. I don't even know what to say right now. Yes, I do. "I'm sorry, but your name is attached to a bogus document. If this goes public, you will all lose your licenses."

"Don't be sorry. Never apologize to the opposing team for beating them at their own game." My father's words echo my sentiment about playing dirty. I just never thought they would go this low.

"I'm not sorry for exposing you. I'm sorry it came to this at all."

"I am too, but I've never been more proud of the woman you've become than I am now."

"What?"

Words of kindness should be shared loudly so the receiving party hears them clearly, but his words sneak up on me and dive deep into my heart, trying to seal the cracks. My eyes don't well up this time. I just hold my emotions close to my chest and proceed.

He replies, "You've always made me proud. I've just never been good at showing my emotions."

My mom comes into the office. "That's what made you a good lawyer."

"It's what made me a bad father."

I'm rendered speechless. This has taken a turn I could have never predicted. My mom comes around and hugs me. "I hadn't realized how much distance had grown between us, Weatherly. I heard what April said at the party, and I was horrified. Your father told me what Lloyd did to you"—she sniffs in genuine pain—"and I . . . I'm just so sorry." She steps back. "You know how he found out?"

I shake my head, and she continues, "Your boyfriend told your father, and then he watched the security footage. It didn't show that he attempted to . . . it showed that he tried."

"I don't want to think about it." I'll process later when and how Dare spoke to my father, but as I look at his face, the anger and pain mixed, I can see that my dad is just as upset as Mom.

She gathers her composure, something she's always been able to do flawlessly. "Despite our flaws, we love you so very much. I think we both got caught up in expectations and keeping up with the Joneses that we lost who we were along the way."

I embrace her, closing my eyes and leaning on her shoulder. "I understand that all too well."

When I open my eyes, my dad is watching us with raw emotion in his eyes. I want to go to him, for him to make it all better, but it's bad because of him. Although I can feel the change in the air and in his demeanor, I'm not ready to give him my trust or forgiveness. But I won't hold my care for him hostage.

I go to him. "You have to make this right."

"I will."

Nodding, I add, "Then we can move on."

"I hope so."

As much as I want to run to see Dare, I don't rush from the room. I love my parents, but things have to change before we start again. "I'm going, but I hope to hear from you very soon."

"You will," he replies. "I need a few days to tie up some loose ends."

Frayed seems more apropos, but I have to give him time to fix things. Nothing is fast when it comes to the legal system—bogus or not. "Bye."

"Weatherly?" From the front door, I look back. He says, "I love you."

"I know you do. It's time to show it, though."

We all need tough love sometimes, and his time has come. His actions have far-reaching repercussions, but it's not too late to mend these fences.

39

Weatherly

I THINK I break every speed limit there is to be right here banging on their door. Lennox looks surprised when he sees me on the porch. "You're here?"

"Where's Dare?"

"In the garden. What about the restraining order?"

The back door is already closing behind me. I run to the side of the house and stop when I see him. There among the blooming bushes of light and deep pink roses, stands Dare with Romeo. Dare says, "I think she'll like that one—"

"Dare?"

He turns around with a big bouquet, and I about die from the sight of this gorgeous man. "What are you doing, Weatherly? You can't be here. I'll get arrested."

The words rush from my mouth, "It was fake. The order. It's not real."

"What?" The confusion on his face distorts his brow. "What do you mean? How do you know?"

"I beat them at their own game. I did it. They confessed.

My father told me it was fake. That's why an officer didn't serve you, but some guy."

Realization dawns in his expression. "That's why he said he was paid well for the job. Fuck. He would have been paid the same if it were real."

"Exactly."

"You trust your father?"

"After what just happened, I do."

"What happened?"

"Long story for later, but they can't keep us apart any longer."

He maneuvers through the prickly flowers and wraps his arms around me. He kisses my head a thousand times, and whispers, "Tell me you're not kidding."

"I would never joke about this."

"You did it, Pepper." He leans down and lifts me into his arms. With his head tucked to the crook of my neck, he whispers, "Thank you. Thank you, babe."

It's funny how I feel like I should be the one thanking him for my life, my future, and helping me resolve my past. He's given me blue skies when I had been living under rain clouds. "I love you," seems to be the only way to share how I feel instead, grateful that my destiny collided with this man.

Inside Dare's bedroom, I'm dropped on the bed. His shirt is already off, and he's working on his jeans. "We're going to make so much love together."

"You don't want to fuck?" I raise an eyebrow while teasing.

"Fuck, no. This is about love, babe." He takes me by the ankles and kisses each one. There are no ribbons just tiny buckles above the ankle attached to black patent leather heels. "I'm leaving these on because damn you look fine."

I pull my shirt off, but he tosses my skirt to the floor

before settling between my legs. "Do you know how much I've missed the taste of you?"

"Show me." This man knows how to show he cares and has every day we've been lucky enough to have together. But I help move this along because I miss him being inside me.

I press gently on the back of his head, and oh, holy Sunday, he shows me several times over.

Later, we break to recover for a bit. The sun is setting, and we're sitting on the front porch together. Together. That's my absolute favorite way to be.

A black Mercedes pulls to the curb, and I know who it is before I see him. "My father is here." I look down at the Dare's boxer shorts and tee on me but don't stress. I'm not a little girl anymore. I'm the woman who moved a mountain for my man. Bold and brave.

We stand and move to the railing. Dare says, "Shit. You look a mess."

"Why thanks," I say, rolling my eyes.

"I mean that you look gorgeously made love to and fucked. There's no hiding we've reunited."

Bumping him on the side, I say, "I wouldn't hide it anyway."

My father walks along the driveway and then stops at the base of the steps. "I thought I should personally tell you the news."

"What's that?" I ask.

"There was only one way I could deal with him for what he did to you that wouldn't land me prison serving a death sentence."

"What's that?"

"I turned the envelope over to the police."

I stare in amazement. "You did?"

He looks down, and it's the first time I've seen him

nervous. I'm glad. He should be. He says, "I couldn't let him get away with how he's hurt you. By turning a blind eye, I endangered my employees, but most of all, you."

I let him share what so obviously weighs on his mind. "I didn't protect you as I should have. I have to live with that, but worse is the damage I've done as well. I've clearly aligned myself with the wrong people. For money. I got what I wanted but at your expense." He looks to the side, and I can actually see remorse in his expression. "What Lloyd did to you, said to you . . . I'm sorry, Weatherly." My dad has never apologized for anything in his life. *Until now.*

I'd love to revel in that apology, but it doesn't fix things. It just muddies the water. How do I forgive him when Dare still has charges over his head?

"I resigned as well today. I'm not the leader I wanted to believe I was and shouldn't be sitting in the office like I am. I'll face the consequences of the order." He looks at Dare. "All charges have been officially dropped as of an hour ago."

Dare eagerly asks, "For real?"

"For real."

"What about the weapons charge for Romeo?" I ask.

"They reviewed the footage released online. They realized it's his drumsticks from jumping up so fast, not that he was using them as a weapon, and dropped that charge as well."

I'm tempted to run into his arms and hug this man, my father, but I tighten my hold on the railing, knowing we need to take this slowly. "Thank you."

"No thanks needed." He looks back at the RV. "How are the new digs?"

"Not as nice as my old ones."

I laugh, and it's as if that gives him permission to join in. I like hearing his laughter. It's so opposite of what he had become. Maybe through all of this he can find who he is too. He says, "You can move into the cottage if you want to."

On their property? *Not if my life depended . . .* wait. "Gram's?"

"It's just sitting there empty. It's an option if you want it."

I feel Dare's hand rub my back. I make my boldest move yet. "Actually, Dad, I think I'm going to move in with Dare." I take his hand and hold it in front of me.

My dad looks at the house and then at me. "It's probably too soon for you, but you're both welcome to live there. No rent. No rules. On your own terms. I blinked, and you became an adult. It seems this might be my last chance to get to know you."

"I don't know what to say, Dad."

"You don't have to say anything. Maybe just call or drop by sometime?"

I nod. He turns to leave and is almost to his car before I dash down the steps and stop him in the driveway. "I love you."

"I don't deserve it." *He's offering an olive branch, and I know we'll be okay.*

"I love you anyway."

"You take after your mother. She loves me despite my many flaws." This time, he comes to me, and we hug. "I love you, Weatherly."

When he's gone, I return to the porch and sit in a chair next to Dare. "Is this how we'll be when we're old and gray?"

"Sexy as all get-out? Absolutely."

Giggling, I ask, "Sitting together on our porch watching the day slip away."

He reaches for my hand to hold it. "Yes."

Just that easy.

Despite my father making amends, he's not the hero of

this story. Dare is, but maybe he'd say I was. You never know with us being equals, partners in crime, and partners in life.

Pepper and Rob.

Weatherly and Dare.

Boyfriend and girlfriend.

Babe and hero.

Us forever.

I've had a crush on him since the day I laid eyes on Robert Dare Marquis. The universe just finally decided to catch up to our destiny.

40

Weatherly

"THEY'RE SKULLS," English says, knocking on the side of his head. "You swing like this if you need to take someone down, bird." He's been trying to teach me to fight as he calls "properly" since he liked my moxie a few months ago when I tried to punch Lloyd. I finally indulged him. He crosses his arms and winks at me. "Although I never thought of you as the scrappy kind, it was an impressive attempt to take that dickhead down."

"If Dare hadn't caught my fist of fury," I say, laughing through my words.

"You would have broken your hand, and that wasn't going to happen on my watch." Dare wraps his arm around me and kisses my head. "Don't fuck with her," he teases, adding to the conversation. "She's savage." But my hand is brought to his mouth with such gentleness and kissed delicately. "I never got to tell you I'm sorry for ruining your party. I know this isn't as big as the one your parents threw for you, but I thought you might like a dinner to make up for it and for passing the bar exam."

"You didn't ruin that party. Other people did." Turning into his arms, I rest my head on his chest as he holds me. "You didn't have to go to this trouble."

"Helen helped me." I look through the glass patio door at my best friend sitting at a picnic table with Romeo and Lennox. English tells us to get a room and heads for the cooler of beers outside. Helen's in the kitchen busy refilling a platter of veggies.

I squeeze him to me and close my eyes. His scent—that vacation I know we'll take one day, and the escape I thought I needed—is all wrapped up in his arms like I am. I've never been happier than with this motley crew I now call family.

Seeing Helen grab the roast out from the oven, I hurry to help her.

The kitchen is nothing like the one I grew up with in my family's home. This one is better. Decorated with ceramic roosters and mismatched coffee mugs hanging from hooks under the counter, there's no marble to be found.

Four pots crowd the stove as she looks for a place to set the hot dish down. She says, "Can you grab a dishtowel and toss it down on the counter for me?"

Dozens of magnets cover the front and sides of the refrigerator with artwork, quotes printed out, and photos catch my eyes when I grab a towel from the handle of the fridge and set it out for her. "Thank you for hosting this dinner."

"It's not every day that I know someone who passes the bar exam. I'm thrilled Robert suggested it and more than happy to host."

"Thank you. It means a lot to me." I return to the front of

the white fridge again, amazed by the crazy colors, shapes, and designs covering it. "You have so many—"

"It's a mess, but I love them all."

What most would call clutter, each seems to have meaning to her, like Dare's tattoos—each one chosen to be displayed. While I look at the art that is signed Rob age seven, I smile. Helen comes up beside me and smiles too. "He loved to create—art, music, adventures. This was one of my favorites. It's hung on each fridge I've had over the years. Like Lennox's. Everything on here holds a memory."

"All happy?"

"All happy. I went through some terrible things for years. There's no room to let anything that doesn't make me happy take up more time or space than I've already given."

"I'm sorry you had to go through that."

"Me too. More sorry that Lennox did, but we're here. We're healthy and happy. This good life is worth celebrating."

"Yes, it is. Which is your favorite?"

She taps her chin and purses her lips scanning the front and sides of the fridge. "I have many, but if I had to choose one for each of us, I'd say this one for my son." She takes a magnet from above the ice machine. "Lennox made this in kindergarten for Mother's Day. It may look like a blue blob. It's a flower. The petals have broken off over the years, but it's still beautiful."

"That's sweet."

I lean on the counter and watch as she replaces that one and takes a magnet that says San Antonio on it. "Robert gave me this one five years ago, so it doesn't have the same history, but when he came back from that trip, he was different, finally starting to heal. Hope had returned to his eyes after his mother's death. The band saved him in so many ways. I'd hate to think what would have happened if he hadn't found these guys. He had a way of expressing his feelings, releasing the anger, and finding what fed his soul again. They work hard, and I truly believe their gifts will make their dreams come true." While staring at the magnet in her hand, a warm hand graces my back. "You're a lovely complement to his life."

"He is to mine."

"Oh! You must see these photos. They're my absolute favorite. I really need to get them framed one day." She leans around to the other side of the fridge and pulls three photos down. "This one is a quote that Laura—"

"Used to say." My heart skips a beat just seeing it. I look at the turquoise cinder block wall with the quote spray-painted on it. "Dare said this the first time we met."

"I got a little of that story from Rob, but you know he has a way of making a short story shorter. Men." She laughs, rolling her eyes. "But you met Laura when you were little?"

"I did. Just by chance."

"Nothing is by chance. It was meant to be."

I've had that thought so many times. Out of all the people in the world, in Austin, the houses, and the years, they were at mine exactly when I needed them. Just as the band saved him, he saved me. I'm already living a life that makes me happy because I was reunited with someone who believed in me.

There's strength in our union, an understanding that whatever we are, wherever we're from, and no matter where we're heading, Dare and I are meant to be. My soul knew the moment I met him.

"I believe in destiny." Glancing at the man on the back patio playing his guitar, I add, "I believe in Dare."

That gets me brought into a warm side embrace. "It's too

soon to talk marriage, but like I said, you make a lovely couple."

Is it too soon? I feel like we spent so many years trying to find each other that I'm not sure I want to waste anymore time. My life is better with him in it, and that is worth celebrating.

She hands me the next picture, and this time my heart stops as I stare at it. "Where'd you get this?"

"From Rob. He never confirmed it, but I think he did that graffiti after his mom died. There was this house she loved. I never saw it. It was something just for them. Over on the—"

"West side. Off Red Bud Trail."

Angling her head, curiosity enters her tone when she says, "That's right."

"My house."

She looks down at the photo again with a furrowed brow. "If that's your house . . ." Holding up the last photo, she asks, "Is this you?"

Just when my heart had recovered, kismet strikes again and throws another curve ball. I remember that so well, and here I am faced with not only my past but also my future all in one fell swoop.

I remember wearing that outfit all the time when I was nine.

Red heart-shaped sunglasses situated on my head.

Yellow ribbons dangling from my pigtails.

Blue eyes thrilled to have someone to play with.

Smile full of hope a lot like she described Dare's.

"That is me."

"Well," she starts, but stops with her hand covering her heart. "That is just incredible." Turning it over, she reads, "Pepper."

"That's what he called me because I asked so many questions."

"A lawyer even then."

A giggle escapes her, and she turns to me with tears in her eyes. "Laura had this printed and told me how she'd met the cutest little girl that day. Bold and beautiful. Inquisitive and clever. But what she loved most was that you still believed in fairy tales and saw the good in everyone. You were exactly who she wished for her son one day."

I used to cry from frustration and sadness. These days, I don't deal with either of those emotions. It's happiness. My heart swells, and the tears start flowing. And when Dare enters the kitchen, he pauses, his gaze volleying back and forth between the two of us. "What's wrong?"

"Nothing," Helen replies.

I say, "Everything is perfect."

PROPPED by my elbows on the bar behind me, I watch my man on stage singing songs that I feel deep inside were written for me long before we met, before we were reunited. A girl next to me calls Jake, the bartender. I overhear her order, "A beer for the lead singer."

I could step in and mark my territory, but I'm not jealous. Jealousy comes from an insecurity I don't possess when it comes to him. I don't have to be. I feel his love every day. I laugh when Jake says, "I'll add it to his tab."

The song ends, and Dare finds me again, always seeking me out in the crowd. "This is for my girlfriend," he announces for the world, or at least Shep's on Sixth Street. "Without her, I'm nothing."

With him, I'm everything.

A guy next to me says, "I'm told you're the singer's girlfriend?"

I turn away from the band. By the man's polite demeanor, I don't think he's hitting on me. "Yeah. That's my hero up there."

He hands me a card. "I can't seem to get the band to return my call. I was wondering if you might give me some insight."

Flipping the card over in my hand, I read Outlaw Records. "Is this for a record deal?"

"It's for a meeting. Most bands jump at the chance for a meeting."

"They've been really busy the past few months." I leave out the arrest, charges, Dare and me moving into together, my exam, the band finishing their album, and just life.

His eyes watch The Heroes play. "I get that, but I'm trying to get a feel for what their big goals are." Turning to me, he asks, "Any idea?"

"I think that's something you'd have to speak to them about."

"Do they have a manager or a rep I can talk to? I couldn't find anything on their website."

Dare to be bold. "I'm their attorney and handle their contracts and negotiations."

"They have an attorney but no manager?"

"It's a unique situation."

"Seems so." Eyeing the card in my hands, he says, "I'll leave that card with you then, but I'd like to set up a meeting with the band soon to discuss an opportunity."

"I'll talk to them."

"Thank you. Do you have a card?"

"No." We shake hands and introduce ourselves.

He looks back at the stage. "They're good. Damn good.

Raw. Rough. Captivating energy. We only sign bands we believe in."

"And you want to sign The Heroes?"

"I think it would be stupid to let them go."

I watch Dare hold the microphone to his mouth, my whole body clenching in memory of how he holds me—possessive, passionate, appreciating every last inch of my body. "Did you hear about them from Dick James?"

"Who?"

"The DJ?" From the blank expression, I get my answer. "Never mind. I'll let them know you came by tonight." A DJ holding an invisible future over their head for so long makes me angry. Dick James didn't make them, and he sure as hell won't break them. I tuck the card in my back pocket.

"Thanks. I hope to hear from you soon."

"We'll be in touch."

The last person to say that was Lloyd. What a loser. He came around begging me to get my father to put in a good word for him. I told him I'll have him arrested for trespassing if he ever comes around again. Then I slammed the door in his face. He was lucky Dare wasn't home at the time.

Sadly to report, he landed on his feet as an entry-level clerk down at a small attorney's office just northeast of the city . . . for a short time. But karma got her revenge and like his father, Lloyd's license has been revoked, and they must face the charges against them. Times are tough for the Sanders these days.

Good.

Just as he leaves, Stascia returns from the bathroom. "That line is ridiculous. I missed half the show."

"I told you not to break the seal. Once you do, you're stuck back in that line every thirty minutes."

She laughs. "Yes, my mistake. But I've drunk five gallons

of water today from the move. Why did I decide to move in August? It was miserably hot today."

"What did you move exactly? If my memory serves me correctly, it was Romeo moving your clothes into Dare's old room."

"I still can't believe I agreed to live with these guys."

"When opportunity arises, you have to jump on it. They needed someone to help with rent, and you wanted a change of scenery."

Jake sets a bottle of beer from Dare's tab in front of her. She says, "Mission accomplished. My parents are still freaking out. I can only imagine the gossip during bridge this week."

We both laugh. "More importantly, how is the west side girl adapting to being an Eastsider?"

"It's been all of five hours, so I'll have to report back on that. Great so far."

The set ends, and Dare hands his guitar to English before jumping off the stage to head my way. The crowd moves for him like he's Moses parting the sea. Cupping my face, he kisses me, marking his territory. *I'm weak in the knees with this man.*

With his forehead against mine, we catch our breaths, and then as if air isn't enough, he takes a deep breath and inhales mine. When his warm eyes meet mine, he asks, "You ready to go home?"

Home.

Wrapped in his arms.

When he's deep inside me.

Our little bubble of two. One day becoming three.

Together.

That's home to me.

But tonight, the little one-bedroom cottage at the back of

my parents' property will do. We have been given all the privacy we could ever want or need, and the free rent isn't bad as we start our future together. This new beginning has not just been about Dare and me, but also my family.

But with Dare? I had no clue that you could fall more in love with someone daily. Dare pushes me, challenges me, catches me when I fall. So when I think back on what Helen said a few weeks ago about too soon for marriage, I don't believe that when it comes to Dare. Our past, our present, and our future . . . he's the man who I'll always love, no matter where life takes us.

He says, "I can't wait to make love to you."

And he can't get enough of me.

"Let's go home."

EPILOGUE ONE

Weatherly

"How much longer?"

"Not long. Be still, babe."

"I can't be any stiller than I already am." Lying flat on my stomach, I shift my head and rest my cheek on the other hand, trying not to let my impatience leak out more than it has. "It hurts."

"Breathe through it and take it out on my hand."

"I'll take it out on you all right." *In the bedroom.* My inside joke makes me laugh.

Dare scowls, "C'mon babe. Don't move. We don't want to screw this up. One shot is all we've got."

"I can't believe I agreed to this. How much more until you're done?"

When he leans back in the chair, he's smug, proud of his work. "Your ass is incredible. The tattoo isn't bad either."

The tattoo on the side of my wrist has healed. *Dare to be Bold* reminds me to live this life I've been given without regret and to never let anyone hold me back from owning my dreams. I love it so much that I came back for another. Dare thinks this one on the upper part of my ass is for him, but like his tattoos, mine mean something special to me. "Very funny. For real, though, how does it look?"

Dare takes a photo and shows me. "What do you think?"

Smiling, I stare at the little rose-colored heart-shaped glasses I used to wear everywhere when I was a kid. I don't have them now, but this tattoo will always be a reminder that nothing is impossible. "I love it."

"Me too. It suits you, Pepper."

I'm cleaned up and the tattoo area prepped for healing. My dress falls loosely around me when I stand. Dare's arm comes around me so naturally that I don't think he even realizes we haven't always been one. He then asks the artist, "You ready for me?"

Soon, he's in the chair adding another tattoo to his collection. This one is just for me. The artist has known Dare for years, so like many others, he asks, "You sure you want to commit to this so soon?"

"Never more sure about anything in my life," Dare replies. "I was committed to Weatherly the minute I met her."

The needle punctures his skin, and over the next hour, we watch as the yellow ribbon is combined with his favorite tattoo—the abstract heart inked on his chest. *Two becoming one.*

Once upon a time, a boy full of hardships and bravery found a girl with ribbons in her hair who still believed in fairy tales. The words he spoke that day were locked away until she found him again.

Through true and unconditional love, he opened her heart to their destiny. Because what he said was true: *Beauty attracts the eye, but the soul captures the heart.*

EPILOGUE TWO

Dare

I used to have highs and lows, days that seemed to mimic my mood with no in between. That has changed over the past four months. Life is good, steady, and opportunities are ahead for Weatherly, the band, and me.

Helen is right. It's too soon to get married, but it doesn't stop me from wanting to lock this relationship down permanently. I look back over my shoulder toward the car where my girl is waiting for me. She gives a little wave.

Turning back to the plaque under the abstract heart sculpture, I rub my finger over it. "Why do I feel like you had a hand in this, Mom?" I think it's easy to credit fate that Weatherly and I were always meant to be, but I think my guardian angel had a hand in our destiny. Without her, I don't know that we would have ever met. "Thank you." I stand and shove my hands in my pockets. "Wish me luck."

The wind whispers in the breeze that comes from nowhere, causing me to pause. "You're right, Mom. I just have to own my dreams." I walk back to my girl and kiss her.

"You ready to hit the road?" she asks.

"If my Pepper wants to swim, let's swim."

She reads over the emails from Outlaw Records and the contract on our drive to the swimming hole. While hiking to the secret spot, she says, "I've gone through the entire contract. It's a good deal, Dare. It's Johnny Outlaw and The Resistance. They're musical legends. They launched The Crow Brothers and Faris Wheel. This is the break you've been wanting."

"The call last week went well, but we were waiting to hear the details. Securing a deal is why The Heroes made an album. Trust me, the guys want a deal, but they want the right deal, or we'll stay indie until it is right. If you say this is good for us, we'll take the meeting in LA."

"It's a solid offer. Life-changing, and from the research I've done, it's more fair than any other major label will give you."

We reach the emerald pool just beneath the rapids and short waterfalls of the rock cliffs. "I've never been to LA." Stripping off my shirt and shoes, I walk around and jump in. "The guys told me if you think it's a good contract, then we'll sign. So I guess we're signing our first record deal."

She tugs her clothes off, revealing that hot bikini-clad body. Standing at the top of the rocks, she scans for the best place to jump in. My arms . . . I wave at her. Her trust was given to me the night we met. She never fails to make me feel incredible. Landing in my arms—her trust, her love, her heart and soul—I kiss her the moment she surfaces from under the water.

"Congratulations, hero. You just got yourself a deal."

"I already have the best deal in town." I kiss that soft spot behind her ear and watch as her body covers with bumps. "That's you, babe." Working for a small law firm keeps her busy, but with a long holiday weekend, she's all mine again. And I intend to take full advantage of every minute I get to spend with her.

"My boyfriend is a sexy fiend." With a smile, she dips back, relaxing in my arms. "I love it here." When she lifts back up, the water reflects in her clear blue eyes, and her pink lips are ripe for kissing.

I struggle to breathe as her beauty overwhelms me. I say it, not because I'm nervous to commit and want to get it over and done with, but because she's the air my lungs need, the missing puzzle piece to my soul. "What about your fiancé?"

She laughs, but when I don't, she asks, "Are you being serious right now?"

"Yes." With her body wrapped around mine under water, I hold on to her. "We're young and still new, but I know I want to spend my life with you." I shrug. "I don't care what anyone says. I only care about what I feel, and God, I fucking love you."

Pushing off, she says, "Are you asking me to marry you?"

My heart is thundering in my chest, and the more I look at her and see that future I want so badly in her eyes too, I reply, "I think I am."

"You think?"

"I am. I love you and want to marry you, Pepper." Although her face is frozen in shock, she's treading water like a pro. Reaching underwater, I take her hand and pull her back to me. "Will you marry me?"

She hugs me and with her lips to my ear, she whispers, "I love you so much, Robert." She grins. "*Rob* Dare Marquis. Of course, I will."

I lean back and capture her lips. "You just made me the happiest man." I kiss her, moving through the water with her in my arms.

We swim apart, and she dives under. When she pops up, she's a sun goddess in an emerald sea.

I say, "Now that we're engaged, when's the wedding?"

"My mom will go insane with the planning. How do you feel about a long engagement?"

I swim to where I can stand on the rocky bed. "If it ends in marriage with you, I'll wait as long as I have to."

"We could get married here."

"It's a great place."

"It's the most peaceful place on earth," she says. I sit on the shore watching her float on the surface of the water. "It's our place."

Looking around, there's not another soul for what feels like miles. She's right. "This is our place."

Swimming toward me, she adds, "It's really our place."

"Yeah. Our secret place."

She reaches me and sits on my lap with her arms around my neck. "And on paper." I'm kissed on the head and then on the temple as I process what she said.

"What do you mean?"

"I bought it."

Angling her way, I ask, "You bought what?"

Her arms tighten around me. "Don't freak out. I got it for a steal."

"You bought this swimming hole?"

"And the land. All one hundred and thirty-seven acres," she replies, nodding. "Anyway, my dad told me that property is always a good investment." I have a million questions yet can't seem to form one. Speechless, I still stare at her. So she continues, "I figure it's the beginning of our portfolio."

I'm still not sure what to say. "Weatherly." *It's a start.*

Standing, she sloughs water from her stomach. "Are you mad?"

Distracted by her hot body? Absolutely. *Mad?* "No. I'm just . . . why'd you buy it?"

"So we'd always have it. We can build a house out here to escape to whenever we want. If you're worried about money, you don't have to be. It barely ate into my trust fund—"

"I'm not worried about money. You said *we'd* always have it."

"We will. Especially since we're engaged and will eventually be married."

I dive in because I want to be with her. Grabbing her, I pull her back to my lap as she breaks into a fit of giggles, echoing around us. God, I hope to have a life full of this happiness, a life full of her. "I want a redo."

"For what?"

"Asking you. I had a plan and then blew it. But I want you to know how much I love you."

"I do, Dare."

"I didn't ask your dad."

"You don't need to."

"I wouldn't have anyway. I'm not down on one knee. I don't have the ring, but I have you in my arms instead and looking into your gorgeous blue eyes, telling you that I want to spend my life with you. Never a night apart or a day without you in it. I promise to be the man who will always make you feel as beautiful as you are and love you more than your soul can hold. You asked me how I feel about a long engagement. Terrible. I want to be married to you soon."

Her smile feels like my own, one full of the possibilities of our future together. Leaning her cheek against mine, she whispers, "I've loved you my whole life."

We don't need music. We just need each other. On the

shores of our own piece of paradise, we begin to dance. "Say you'll always dance with me in this life and the next. Will you marry me, Weatherly?"

Stroking my wet hair back, she kisses my forehead and starts to cry. Tears of joy, not sadness. From this day forward, they're the only tears I hope will ever be in her eyes. "Yes, I'll marry you soon and happily dance with you forever."

We'll own our dreams together. "I love you in spades."

She smiles, and it's brighter than the sun above. "I love you in spades always."

Doesn't matter that we've only dated for months, our destiny was always entwined. It was just a matter of time until our souls met again because we aren't just forever. We're for eternity.

I hope you loved Dare as much as I loved writing this book. I would be honored if you left a review on the platform where you purchased this book.

If you would like to meet my *New York Times* bestselling rock star, Johnny Outlaw, make sure to check out *The Resistance*.

The Crow Brothers are mentioned in DARE. They are MUST read rock stars. Check out their series of standalones starting with Spark today. ***TURN THE PAGE TO MEET Jet Crow NOW.***

SPARK

One break is all The Crow Brothers need and we're about to get it.

Johnny Outlaw, rock legend and lead singer of The Resistance, is here to watch us play. But he's not the only familiar face in the crowd—killer little body, heart-shaped face, and drop-dead gorgeous.

Hannah Nichols sitting at the bar makes it hard to concentrate, sparks already reigniting. The beauty was never a groupie and tonight she's not here to catch our show. She came to drop a bomb. "You have a son."

She underestimated me. I'll prove to my son, and her, that I can be the dad he needs.

What is it about musicians? Why are they so damn sexy?

My heart was Jet Crow's the moment he opened his sexy mouth and sang that first song. One stolen night with that man would never be enough, but I'm not here to fall into his bed. Again. I'm here to fight for custody of a son he's never known.

There's just one problem. Those sparks between us have become flames. If we're not careful we're both going to get burned.

PROLOGUE

Jet Crow

Subtle scents of cinnamon mix with the taste of whiskey on her skin. I lick her from collarbone to the back of her ear, her moans enticing me to take more than a gentle share of what I want.

I'm well past hooking up with groupies, but something drew me to the beautiful brunette. Under the bright spotlight of that stage, my eyes found hers as I sang about finding the missing piece of me. Maybe it was the way she pretended not to care—catching my eyes and then turning away as if she was too shy to come speak to me, but too good to be bothered. It didn't matter. I was already caught up in her as much as she was caught up in me.

The set ended, and I made my way over to the mystery woman, the one who hid in the dark of the bar just as two shots were served. I took the shot of Fireball and then took her home shortly after.

Fuck. She feels good.

Hard little body, but soft in all the right places. Tits that fill my large hands and legs that spread enough for me to squeeze between her thighs. I bet she wouldn't reach my shoulders in heels. Speaking of, "Keep them on."

I like the feel of the leather against my lower back, the hard heel scraping across my skin when she tries to power play me by tightening around my waist and pulling me closer. I didn't ask her to my bedroom. I didn't have a chance. What started out as laughing while we shared a two a.m. snack of Cheetos, hummus, and whiskey turned into me eating her as a snack on top of my kitchen counter. I don't ever do that with a one-nighter, but damn if she didn't make me want to break more rules with her.

She kisses me like a woman in need of water, taking as much as she wants while pressing her heels into my ass. The heat between us emanates until I'm dragging my shirt off to try to cool down.

I knew she was different the moment she opened her mouth back at the bar. "You sing rock with so much soul. Who hurt you?"

"No one gets close enough to do me any harm."

"That's a pity."

"It's a pity I've never been hurt?"

"No, it's a pity you've never loved anyone enough to get hurt."

My heart started beating for what felt like the first time as I looked into her sultry eyes. I could blame the booze, but I can't lie to myself. She had me thinking twice about things I never considered once before.

Who was this woman?

Even with our stomachs full, we weren't satisfied. She dragged me by the belt down the hall to my bedroom. Her clothes were off and mine quickly followed before we tumbled into bed.

Fast. I want to fuck her fast and hard, but every time our eyes connect, there's such sadness found in her grays that I slow down. Wanting her to hold the contact, I cup her cheek. "Hannah?"

Her eyes slowly open, the long lashes framing the lust I find between them. "What?" she asks between heavy breaths.

"Are you okay?"

"I'm good."

"Just making sure."

She runs her hands up my neck and into the hair on the back of my head. "I'm sure." Pulling me down to her, our mouths are just a few inches apart when she whispers, "I want you. I want to do this."

Shy isn't something I'd call her, considering we were in my bed two hours after meeting. I like a woman who knows what she wants, and Hannah knows. And fuck if it isn't a turn-on that she wants me.

I nod before kissing her, getting lost in the soft caresses of her tongue mingling with mine and the feel of her nails lightly scraping my scalp as she holds me close.

We don't know each other, but I already know when I slip my fingers under the lace and into her wetness, she purrs for me. When I kiss behind her left ear, her back arches. When I press my erection against her to seek relief, her kisses become more frenzied.

When I slide my bare chest down hers, leaving a wet trail of kisses and taking the lace that divides us down as I go lower, her breath audibly catches. My body reacts—hardening for her, craving her.

Reaching over, she takes the glass of whiskey on the nightstand and sips, her eyes staying on mine as I slip the thong from her ankles and spread her legs wider. And somehow, desire replaces her sadness. In the dim light, her gray eyes appear bluer. I close my eyes and breathe her in—cinnamon.

She hands me the glass, and I take it. Finishing the amber liquid, I let it coat my mouth and burn on the way down. The ice clatters in the glass, so I fish it out and let it roll around my tongue while she watches. Placing it between my lips, I run it between hers. Her fingers tighten in my hair, tugging, urging me for more. "You like that, baby?"

"So much."

I crush the ice and swallow, ready to swallow her instead. I take her sweet pussy with my mouth, kissing and sucking until she's squirming under me. I flick my gaze up and visually trace her breasts and then go higher to see the underside of her jaw as she presses her head into the pillow beneath her.

Playing her body with my tongue like my fingers play my guitar, I set her on fire, feeling the burn deep inside. "I want to be buried inside you."

"I want that, Jet. I want you," she says, her body sinking into the mattress as she comes back to me from the high.

I grab a condom from where I tossed a few on the nightstand when we came crashing in here on a high of alcohol to continue what was started in the kitchen. Sticking the packet between my teeth, I rip it open and sit up.

Hannah lifts on her elbows, eyeing my body unashamedly. "Three crows," she says, eyeing my tattoos. "For three brothers."

"We all have them."

"They're sexy on your bicep." A wry grin appears. "How are you so fit if you drink every night?"

Chuckling, I continue to cover my cock and reply, "I do a lot of damn sit-ups."

"Every last damn one you do is worth it."

"What's your trick for staying in shape?" I ask, bending over and biting her hip just enough to tease her into thinking I'll break the skin. I won't, but I like the indentation from my teeth on her body.

"I like to fuck."

Shit. "You've got a dirty mouth."

"Maybe Jet Crow's just the one to help me clean it up."

Positioning myself above her, I angle my hips until I'm pressing against her entrance. "I have no intention of keeping this clean when it's so much more fun to play dirty."

Lying back, her chest rises and falls heavy with each breath. Her words starting to stick to her throat when she speaks. "With that handsome face, I have no doubt you use your looks to get what you want."

"I know how to use more than my looks," I start, pushing in just enough to feel her heat wash through me, "to get what I want." I push the rest of the way when her thighs butterfly for me. Seated deep inside her body, I close my eyes, the warm sensations taking over. On instinct, I move, and she moans.

I pick up my pace, but when I rise up on my elbows, I pause. *Fuck.* I shake my head.

"What is it, Jet? What's wrong?"

"Nothing," I'm quick to reply, hoping she doesn't see how much she's affecting me. What the fuck? I just met her, but when I close my eyes, it's not just the high of good sex taking over my mind. Normally, I don't pay a lot of attention to the body beneath me. Why should I? They only want me for one thing. But with Hannah? The girl with the haunted eyes? I want to erase the sadness. I want to replace her melancholy with other emotions.

What. The. Fuck?

Just fucking move.

We have chemistry, but I want more than just a physical connection with this woman. I want to know why she was alone tonight. Why she was drinking shots at the bar? Why she ordered me one before she knew me? I just want to know her.

Fucking move, Crow.

I do. Finally. But it's tainted with thoughts of tomorrow and hoping she stays tonight. Fuck.

This is just sex. Sex. Just a good time. *Focus.*

God, she feels amazing. *Too good.* "So good."

A warm hand caresses my cheek, and I open my eyes to find hers on me already. She smiles. "So good." Lifting up, she kisses me, dragging me out of my head and into her world. Her mystery is an aphrodisiac, and I want to learn all her secrets. Will she let me into her mind? It's a place I could lose myself forever in if I'm not careful.

Hannah isn't just another pretty face. She won me over the first time I saw her with that come-hither stare and devilish tilt of her lips.

We exhaust ourselves, pouring my soul into hers while hers fills me. As I hold her in the aftermath of ecstasy, I whisper into her hair, "Stay."

Turning her head, there's just enough light to see a flicker of happiness flaming in her eyes. "Ask me tomorrow," she replies with a small teasing smile as she closes her eyes and snuggles her back to my chest.

"I will."

I did. When her eyes open the next morning, I toss my

cigarette out the window, lean forward, and ask her to stay. While she gets dressed, I tell her I want to know her mind as well as I know her body. I confess too much too soon, more than I have to anyone in years.

She listened with a sly smile peeking through, her eyes brighter in the daylight, her worries seem to have lifted. When she kneels before me, she says, "You were the best time I ever had."

I'm tempted to tell her she's my worst. I hate feeling this way—reliant. Somehow, I've kept my emotions in check, a lock without a key for years.

Then she shows up with the right bow and shoulder, her cuts and tip fitting inside, the anatomy of a key made to unlock the deepest parts of me.

My chance starts slipping away as she does. I offer her coffee, to make her breakfast, and then I offer her a ride back to her car downtown where she parked behind the small bar where we met. I offer her anything to keep her from leaving. I don't offer my heart and I don't beg, but I offer her what I can.

The blue electric car surprises me. I mistakenly took her for a sports car or something less reliable and more rebellious. Her sexually carefree demeanor juxtaposed against her mysterious side fascinates me. Hearing the alarm click off and watching her open the car door, I know she's different. I felt it last night; not just in the way we connected, but in the way she makes me feel. "Maybe I'll see you around?"

"Maybe. I just moved here."

"I can show you around."

"I don't have a lot of free time right now, so I don't get out much."

Her jeans hug the curves of her hips, and I like the way she'd knotted my band's shirt, causing it to hug her upper body and exposing the skin of her stomach. Those boots that rubbed against my ass last night look just as sexy on her today. "Well, if you do, maybe you can come see the band play again."

Just before she slides into the driver's seat, she stops and looks back at me. Resting my elbow out the open window, I watch the sway of her hips as she comes back to me. *Come back to me.*

She lifts up on her toes and kisses me, our tongues meeting slick against each other's. Leaning back, she says, "I had a good time with you, Jet." Lowering back on her heels, she looks disappointed, that sadness making her eyes gray again. I miss the fire of the blue.

"I had a good time, too."

"My life is complicated. It's really not even my own these days."

I'm pathetic for saying anything to get more time with her, but it's worth a shot to explore our connection from last night. "Maybe I can help uncomplicate things."

"I wish you could. My cousin is sick, and I'm here to help her out. She needs me, but she also has a young son. His mom's illness has taken a toll. I need to be there for him."

"Sorry to hear that."

When she touches me, I savor the feel of her nails trailing through my hair. For a foolish split second, I think she's changed her mind, my chest feeling fuller as hope expands. Then the bubble bursts as she says, "If I get some free time, you'll be the first person I look up."

"We could make it easy and exchange numbers."

"That comes with expectations, and I don't want to hurt or disappoint you. If last night is all we get, it was pretty damn good."

"Yeah," I reply, already disappointed I won't know how

to contact her. I sit back, take her hand, and bring it to my lips. I kiss it once and then again, pressing the tip of my tongue to her skin. "Take care of yourself."

Maybe I don't hide my feelings as well as I thought. Lifting up once more, she kisses my temple, then whispers, "The weather is too nice for such a sorrowful goodbye."

"Then let's not say it at all."

Nodding, she pushes away gently and returns to her car, opens the door, and slips in. With one foot still firmly on the ground, she looks back. "Take care of yourself, Jet."

Continue Reading Spark today. ***Now Live!***

ACKNOWLEDGMENTS

My husband and boy are my world. I'm so fortunate to have their endless love, support, and hugs. I love you so much, guys. XOXO

I'm so blessed to be around so many brilliant, loving, and kind women. From my friends, family, editors, readers, designers, and every other facet of this process is developed through their beautiful minds.

Dear Adriana Locke, Andrea Johnston, Candi Kane, Jenny Sims, Kerri Q., Kim Cermak, Kirsten B., Kristen Johnson, Lynsey Johnson, Letitia Hasser, Marion Archer, and Marla Esposito, I adore you and could not have done this without you. You are truly the best!

I love you, Mama, Sis, and Niece <3

ALSO BY S.L. SCOTT

To keep up to date with her writing and more, visit her website: www.slscottauthor.com

To receive the Scott Scoop about all of her publishing adventures, free books, giveaways, steals and more, sign up here: http://bit.ly/2TheScoop

Join S.L.'s Facebook group here: S.L. Scott Books

Audiobooks on Audible - CLICK HERE

Hard to Resist Series (Stand-Alones)

The Resistance

The Reckoning

The Redemption

The Revolution

The Rebellion

The Crow Brothers (Stand-Alones)

Spark

Tulsa

Rivers

Ridge

The Crow Brothers Box Set

The Everest Brothers (Stand-Alones)

Everest - Ethan Everest

Bad Reputation - Hutton Everest

Force of Nature - Bennett Everest

The Everest Brothers Box Set

The Kingwood Series

SAVAGE

SAVIOR

SACRED

SOLACE - Stand-Alone

The Kingwood Series Box Set

Playboy in Paradise Series

Falling for the Playboy

Redeeming the Playboy

Loving the Playboy

Playboy in Paradise Box Set

Talk to Me Duet (Stand-Alones)

Sweet Talk

Dirty Talk

Stand-Alone Books

Missing Grace

Until I Met You

Drunk on Love

Naturally, Charlie

A Prior Engagement

Lost in Translation

Sleeping with Mr. Sexy

Morning Glory

From the Inside Out

Made in the USA
San Bernardino, CA
21 August 2019